Old Jack

by

William Henry Giles Kingston

Double 9
BOOKS

Old Jack

by William Henry Giles Kingston

Copyright © 2024

ISBN: 978-93-64280-78-5

Published by

DOUBLE 9 BOOKS

2/13-B, Ansari Road
Daryaganj, New Delhi – 110002
info@double9books.com
www.double9books.com
Tel. 011-40042856

ABOUT THE AUTHOR

William Henry Giles Kingston (1814-1880) was a highly regarded British author known for his numerous adventure novels and books aimed primarily at young readers. His works often centered around maritime themes and the exploration of distant lands, reflecting his own experiences and interests. Here's more about the author William Henry Giles Kingston, focusing on his background, literary career, and legacy: Kingston was born on February 28, 1814, in London, England. He came from a literary family, with his father and grandfather being writers as well. Genre and Themes: Kingston specialized in adventure fiction, particularly stories set in nautical settings. His novels often featured themes of exploration, survival, and courage. Kingston's writing style was characterized by its straightforward narrative, vivid descriptions of maritime life, and emphasis on moral values such as honesty, perseverance, and loyalty. Apart from "Old Jack," his notable works include "Peter the Whaler," "The Three Midshipmen," "The Young Rajah," and "The African Wanderers. Kingston's contributions to literature lie in his ability to engage and educate young audiences through thrilling tales of adventure. His books provided readers with insights into the challenges and rewards of life at sea and exploration. Later Years, He continued writing prolifically until his death on August 5, 1880, leaving behind a legacy of adventure literature that remains influential in the genre.

William Henry Giles Kingston's "Old Jack" exemplifies his skill in crafting adventurous narratives that capture the spirit of maritime exploration and the resilience of characters facing adversity. His works continue to inspire readers with their timeless themes and captivating storytelling.

CONTENTS

Chapter One
Donnybrook Fair

Jack began his story thus:

Of course you've heard of Donnybrook Fair, close to the city of Dublin. What a strange scene it was, to be sure, of uproar and wild confusion—of quarrelling and fighting from beginning to end—of broken heads, of black eyes, and bruised shins—of shouting, of shrieking and swearing—of blasphemy and drunkenness in all its forms of brutality. Ay, and as I've heard say, of many a deed of darkness, not omitting murder, and other crimes not less foul and hateful to Him who made this beautiful world, and gave to man a religion of love and purity. There the rollicking, roaring, bullying, fighting, harum-scarum Irishman of olden days had full swing for all the propensities and vile passions which have ruined him at home, and gained him a name and a fame not to be envied throughout the world. Often have I wondered whether, had a North American Indian, or a South-Sea Islander, visited the place, he could have been persuaded that he had come to a land of Christian men. Certainly an angel from heaven would have looked upon the assemblage as a multitude of Satan's imps let loose upon the world. They tell me that the fair and its bedevilments have pretty well been knocked on the head. I am glad of it, though I have never again been to the spot from the day of which I am about to speak.

I remember very little of my childish life. Indeed, my memory is nearly a blank up to the time to which I allude. That time was one of the first days of that same Donnybrook Fair; but I remember *that* and good reason I have so to do. I was, however, but a small chap then, young in years, and little as to size.

My father's name was Amos Williams. He came from England and settled in Dublin, where he married my mother, who was an Irishwoman. Her name I never heard. If she had relations, they did not, at all events, own her. I suspect, from some remarks she once let drop which I did not then understand, that they had discarded her because she had become a Protestant when she married my father. She was gentle and pious, and did her utmost, during the short time she remained on earth, to teach me the truths of that glorious gospel to which, in many a trial, she held fast, as a ship to the sheet-anchor with a gale blowing on a lee-shore. She died young, carried off by a malignant fever. Her last prayers were for my welfare here and hereafter. Had I always remembered her precepts I should, I believe, have been in a very different position to what I now am in my old age. My poor father took her death very much to heart. For days after her funeral he sat on his chair in our little cottage with his hands before him, scarcely lifting up his head from his breast, forgetting entirely that he ought to go out and seek for work, as without it he had no means of finding food for himself and me. I should have starved had not a kind woman, a neighbour, brought me in some potatoes and buttermilk. Little enough I suspect she had to spare after feeding her own children.

At length my father roused himself to action. Early one morning, seizing his hat and bidding me stay quiet till his return, he rushed out of the house. He was a stonemason. He got work, I believe, but the tempter came in his way. A fellow-workman induced him to enter a whisky shop. Spirits had, in his early days, been his bane. My mother's influence had kept him sober. He now tried to forget his sorrow in liquor. "Surely I have a right to cure my grief as best I can," said he. Unhappily he did not wait for a reply from conscience. Little food could he buy from the remnant of his day's wages. Thus he went on from day to day, working hard when sober, drinking while he had money to pay for liquor.

Still his affection for me did not diminish. While in his right mind he could not bear to have me out of his sight. Every morning we might have been seen leaving our cottage, I holding his hand as he went to his work; yet nearly as certainly as the evening came round I had to creep supperless to bed. All day he would keep me playing about in his sight, except when any of his fellow-workmen, or people living near where we happened to be, wanted a lad to run on an errand. Then I was always glad of the job. Whenever, by happy chance, he came home sober in an evening, he would take me between his knees, and, parting my hair, look into my face and weep till his heart seemed ready to burst. But these occasions grew less and less frequent. What I have said will show that I have reason to love the memory of both my parents, in spite of the faults my unhappy father undoubtedly possessed.

Several months had thus passed away after my mother's death, when one afternoon my father entered our cottage where he had left me since the morning.

"Jack, my boy," said he, taking my hand, "come along, and I will show you what *life is*." Oh, had he said, "what *death is*," he would have spoken the truth.

I accompanied him willingly, though I saw at a glance that he had already been drinking. Crowds of people were going in the direction we took. For some days past I had heard the neighbours talking of the fair. I now knew that we were bound there. My mother had never allowed me to go to the place, so I had no notion what it was like. I expected to see something very grand and very beautiful—I could not tell what. I pushed on into the crowd with my father as eagerly as any one, thinking that we should arrive at the fair at last. I did not know that we were already in the middle of it. I remember, however, having a confused sight of booths, and canvas theatres, and actors in fine clothes strutting about and spouting and trumpeting and drumming; of rope-dancers and tumblers with painted faces; and doctors in gilded chariots selling all sorts of wonderful remedies for every possible complaint; and the horsemanship, with men leaping through hoops and striding over six steeds or more at full gallop; and the gingerbread stalls, and toy shops, and similar wonders; but what was bought and sold at the fair of use to any one I never heard.

My father had taken me round to several of the shows I have spoken of: when he entered a drinking-booth, and set himself down with me on his knee, among a number of men who seemed to be drinking hard. Their example stimulated him to drink harder than ever, and in a short time his senses completely left him. As, however, even though the worse liquor, he was peaceable in his disposition, instead of sallying forth as many did in search of adventures, he laid himself down on the ground with his head against the canvas of the tent, and told me to call him when it was morning. Some one at the same time handed me a piece of gingerbread, so I set myself down by his side to do as he bid me.

Those were the days of faction fights; and if people happened to have no cause for a quarrel, they very soon found one. The tent we were in was patronised by Orangemen, and of course was a mark for the attacks of the opposite party. My poor father had slept an hour or so, with three or four men near him in a similar condition, when a half-drunken body of men came by, shillelah in hand, looking out for a row. Unhappily the shapes of the heads of most of the sleepers were clearly developed through the canvas. The temptation was not to be resisted—whack—whack—whack! Down came the heavy stick of a sturdy Irishman upon that of my father. "Get up out of that, and defend yourselves!" sung out their assailants. Most of his companions rushed out to avenge the insult offered them, but my father made no answer. Numbers joined from all directions—shillelahs were flourished rapidly, and the scrimmage became general. I ran to the front of the tent and clapped my hands, and shouted with sympathy. Now the mass of fighting, shrieking men swayed to one side, now to the other; now they advanced, now they retreated, till by degrees the fight had reached a considerable distance from the tent.

I then went back to my place by my father's side, wondering that he did not get up to join the fray. I listened, he breathed, but he did not speak. Still I thought he must be awake. "Father, father," said I, "get up, do. It's time to go home, sure now." I shook him gently, but he made no reply. At length I could hear no sound proceeding from his lips. I cried out in alarm. The keeper of the booth saw that something was wrong, and came and looked curiously into his face. He lifted up my father's hand. It fell like lead by his side.

"Why won't father speak to me?" I asked, dreading the answer.

"He'll never speak again! Your father's dead, lad," answered the man in a tone of commiseration.

With what oppressive heaviness did those words strike on my young heart, though at that time I did not fully comprehend the extent of my loss,—that I should never again hear the tone of his voice—that we were for ever parted in this world—that I was an orphan, without a human being to care for me. But though bewildered and confused at that awful moment, the words he had uttered as we left home rung strangely in my ears—"Lad, I'll show you what life is." Too truly did he show me what death was. Often and often have I since seen the same promise fulfilled in a similar fearful way. What men call *life* is a certain road to *death*; death of the body, death of the soul. Of course I did not understand this truth in those days; not indeed till long, long afterwards, when I had gone through much pain and suffering, and had been well-nigh worn-out. I was then very ignorant and very simple, and I should probably have been vicious also had not my mother watchfully kept me out of the way of bad example; and even after she was taken from me, I was prevented from associating with bad companions.

When I found that my poor father was really dead, I stood wringing my hands and crying bitterly. The sounds of my grief attracted many of the passers-by; some stopped to inquire its cause, and when they had satisfied their curiosity they went their way. At last several seamen, with an independent air, came rolling up near the tent. The leader of the party was one of the tallest men I ever saw. Though he stooped slightly as he walked, his head towered above all the rest of the crowd.

"What's the matter with the young squeaker there, mate?" he asked in a bantering tone, thinking probably that I had broken a toy, or lost a lump of gingerbread from my pocket.

"His daddy's dead, and he's no one to look after him!" shouted an urchin from the crowd of bystanders.

"He's in a bad case then," replied the seaman, coming up to me. "What, lad! is it true that you have no friends?" he asked, stooping down and taking me by the hand.

"No one but father, and he lies there!" I answered, giving way to a fresh burst of grief as I pointed to my parent's corpse.

"He speaks the truth," observed the man of the booth; "he has no mother, nor kith nor kin that I know of, and must starve if no one takes charge of him, I suspect."

The tall sailor looked at me with an expression of countenance which at once gained my confidence. "What say you, lad, will you come with us?" he asked, pointing to his companions; "we'll take you to sea, and make a man of you!"

"We may get him entered aboard the *Rainbow*, I think, mates," he added, addressing them. "He'll do as well as the monkey we lost overboard during the last gale; and though he may be as mischievous now, he will learn better manners, which Jocko hadn't the sense to do."

"Oh ay! Bear him along with us," replied the other sea men; "he'll be better afloat, whichever way the wind blows, than starving on shore."

"Come along, youngster, then," said the tall seaman; and, without waiting for my reply, he seized me by the arm, and began to move off with me through the crowd.

"But what will be done with poor father? Sure I cannot leave him now!" I exclaimed, looking back with anguish at my father's corpse.

"Oh, we'll see all about that," answered my new friend; "he shall be waked in proper style, and have a decent funeral; so you may leave home with a clear conscience. Never fear!"

I need not dwell longer on the events of that sad day. Aided by some of the men who knew my father, and who returned to the tent after the fray was over, the kind-hearted seamen bore the corpse to our cottage. The promise of a supply of whisky easily induced some of the neighbours to come and howl during the livelong night. This they did with right good will, although my father was a Protestant and a foreigner; and I cried and howled in sympathy. I would fain, however, have forgotten my grief in sleep. The seamen had taken their departure, promising to return to look after me.

As there was no chance of a man with a fractured skull coming to life again, the funeral speedily took place. The small quantity of furniture remaining in the cottage was sold; but the proceeds were barely sufficient to pay the expenses.

Thus I was left, with the exception of a suit of somewhat ragged clothes on my back, as naked and poor as when I came into the world about twelve years before, with a much more expensive appetite than I then had to supply. Some boys at that age are well able to take care of themselves, but, as I have said, I was small for my years, and I had been kept by my poor mother so much by myself, that I knew nothing of the world and its ways.

Alter the funeral a compassionate neighbour, with a dozen or more children of her own to feed, took me to her house till it was settled what was to become of me. She and her husband laughed at the idea of the tall sailor coming to take me away.

"I know what sailors are," said the husband; "they'll just chuck a handful of silver to the first beggar who asks them for it, and then they'll go away and forget all about it! Maybe your friend was only after joking with you, and is off to sea long ago!"

"Oh no! he meant what he said," I replied; "I know that by the look of his face. He's a kind man, I'm certain!"

"It may be better for us all if he comes, but it's not very likely," was the answer. Still I trusted that my new friend would not deceive me.

I was standing in front of the cottage which was next to that my father and I had inhabited, when my heart beat quick at seeing a tall figure turn a corner at the other end of the street. I was certain it was my sailor friend. "It's him! It's him! I knew he'd come!" I shouted, and ran forward to meet him.

He smiled as he saw my eagerness. "You've not forgotten me, I see, lad," said he; "well, come along. It's all arranged; and if you're in the same mind, you've only to say so, and we'll enter you aboard the *Rainbow*!"

I told the tall sailor that I was ready to go wherever he liked to take me. This seemed to please him. After I had wished the neighbours, who had been so kind to me, good-bye, he took me by the hand, and led me rapidly along in the direction of the docks. Before reaching them, we entered a house where some old gentlemen were sitting at a table. One of them asked me if I wished to go to sea and become an admiral. I replied, "Yes, surely," though I did not know what being an admiral meant; and on this the other old gentlemen laughed, and the first wrote something on a paper, which he handed across the table.

On this a sunburnt fine-looking man stepped forward and wrote on the paper, and I was then told that I was bound apprentice to Captain Helfrich, of the *Rainbow* brig. The fine-looking man was, I found, Captain Helfrich. "Well, that matter is squared now!" exclaimed the tall sailor; "so, youngster, we'll aboard at once, before either you or I get into mischief."

On our way to the brig, we stopped at a slop clothes-shop. "Here, Mr Levi! I want an outfit for this youngster," said my friend, taking me in. "Let his duds be big enough, that he may have room to grow in them. Good food and sea air will soon make him sprout like a young cabbage."

The order was literally fulfilled, and I speedily found myself the possessor of a new suit of sailors' clothes, of two spare shirts, and sundry other articles of dress. My friend made me put them on at once.

"Now, do the old ones up in that handkerchief," said he; "we'll find a use for them before long."

The spare new things he did up into a bundle, and carried it himself.

"I did not want the Jew to get your old clothes, for which he would have allowed nothing," said he, as we left the shop. "We shall soon fall in with a little ragged fellow, to whom they'll be a rich prize."

As we went along, two or three boys begged of us, and pointed to their rags as a plea for their begging. "They'll not do," said he; "the better clothes would ruin them."

At last, passing along the quays, we saw a little fellow sitting on the stock of an anchor, and looking very miserable. He had no shoes on his feet; his trousers were almost legless, and fastened up over one shoulder by a piece of string, while his arms were thrust into the sleeves of an old coat, much too large for him, and patched and torn again in all directions. He did not beg, but just looked up into my tall friend's face, as if he saw something pleasing there.

"What do you want?" said the sailor.

"Nothing," answered the boy, not understanding him.

"You're well off then, lad," said the tall sailor, smiling at him. "But I think that you would be the better for some few things in this world—for a suit of clothes, for instance."

"The very things I do want!" exclaimed the lad. "You've hit it, your honour. I'd a dacent suit as ever you'd wish to see, and they were run away with, just as I'd got the office of an errand-boy with a gentleman, and was in a fair way to make my fortune."

"Well, then, here's a suit for you, my lad," said the sailor; "just get your mother to give them a darning up, and they'll serve your purpose, I daresay. Give him your bundle."

"Sure your honour isn't joking with me!" exclaimed the lad, his countenance beaming with pleasure as he undid the bundle of clothes, which were certainly very far better than those he had on. "I'm a made man—that I am! Blessings on your honour, and the young master there!"

"You're welcome, lad, with all my heart," answered my friend.

"Oh, it's Terence McSwiney will have to thank you to the end of his days, and ever after!" exclaimed the boy, as we were walking on.

"Well, Terence, I hope you'll get the post, and do your duty in it," said the tall sailor, moving off to avoid listening to the expressions of gratitude which the lad poured forth.

The incident made a deep impression on me. I learned by it that others might be worse off than I was, and also that a gift at the right time might be of the greatest service. Of this I had the proof many years afterwards. If the rich and the well-to-do did but know of what use their own or their children's cast-off clothes would be to many not only among the labouring classes, but to people of education and refinement, struggling with poverty, they would not carelessly throw them away, or let them get into the hands of Jews, sold by their servants for a sixth of their value. I must observe that, in the course of my narrative I shall often make remarks on various ideas which, at the time I speak of, could not possibly have occurred to me.

The tall sailor and I walked along the quay. All of a sudden it occurred to me that I did not know his name. I looked up in his face and asked him.

"I'm called Peter Poplar," he answered, with one of his kind smiles. "The name suits me, and I suit the name; so I do not quarrel with it. You'll have to learn the names, pretty quickly too, of all the people on board. There are a good many of us, and each and every one of them will consider himself your master, and you'll have to look out to please them all."

"I'll do my best to please them, Mr Poplar," said I.

"That's right! But I say, lad, don't address me so. Call me plain Peter, or Peter Poplar; we don't deal in misters aboard the *Rainbow*. It is all very well for shore-going people to call each other mister; or when you speak to an officer, just to show that he is an officer; but sharp's the word with us forward—we haven't time for compliments."

"But I thought you were an officer, Peter," said I. "You look like one."

"Do I?" he answered, with his pleasant smile. "Well, Jack, perhaps I ought to have been one, and it's my own fault that I am not. But the truth is, I haven't got the learning necessary for it. I never have learned to read, and so I haven't been able to master navigation. Without it, you know, a man cannot be an officer, however good a seaman he may be; and in that point I'll yield to no man."

Peter, as he spoke, drew himself up to his full height, and I thought he looked fit to be a very great officer indeed; even to be an admiral, such as the old gentleman in the office had spoken of.

"I am very bad at my books too," said I. "I can just read a little though, and if I can get the chance of falling in with a book, I'll like to read to you, Peter."

My friend thanked me, but said books were not often seen aboard the *Rainbow*; nor were they found in many other merchant-craft, for that matter, in those days.

We found the brig just ready to haul out into the outer basin, preparatory to putting to sea. She was a fine large craft, and had been built for a privateer in the war-time. Her heavy guns had been landed, but she still carried some eight six-pounders; and as she had a strong crew of fully twenty men, she was well able to defend herself from any piratical craft, or other gentry of that description.

When Peter first took me on board, some of the seamen would scarcely believe I was the same little boy they had seen at the fair, I looked so much stouter and stronger in my seaman's dress. I did not much like the look of the forepeak, into which Peter introduced me, telling me that it was to be my house and home for the next few years of my life. I had been accustomed to the dingy obscurity of an Irish cabin, but never had I been, I thought, in a more dark and gloomy habitation than this.

"Never fear, Jack, you'll soon find yourself at home here," said Peter, divining my thoughts. While he was speaking, a seaman lighted a lantern which hung from a beam, and its glare showed me that the place was more roomy than I had supposed, and that every part of it was perfectly clean. I found, indeed, afterwards, that it was very superior to the places merchant-seamen are compelled often to live in. Some of the crew slept in standing bed-places ranged round the sides of the vessel, or rather inside her bows, while for others hammocks were slung from the beams which supported the deck. The chests were arranged to serve as seats, while there was a rack for the plates and mugs belonging to their mess.

The greater part of the crew was still on shore. "Now, Jack, that you know the sort of place we have to live in, I'll show you the accommodation prepared for the captain and his passengers. It must not make you envious any more than it does me, for I think that those who have learning and education should enjoy advantages in proportion. I feel that it is my own fault that I do not live in as fine a cabin as the captain does."

Even though Peter had thus prepared me to see something very fine, the richness of the cabin fittings and furniture surpassed anything I had in my simplicity imagined to exist. Perhaps those accustomed to such things might not have thought it so very great. I know that there were damask curtains, and coverings to the sofas, and mirrors, and pictures in gold frames, and mahogany tables and chairs, and cut-glass decanters, and china in racks, and a number of pistols and muskets and cutlasses, all burnished and shining, fixed against a bulkhead.

"Why, this is a place fit for a king," I exclaimed; "sure he can't have anything grander."

Peter laughed. "The captain prides himself on being very natty, and having everything in good order," said he; "but kings, I fancy, live in finer places than this. However, my reason for bringing you here was to show you the place, that you may know how to behave yourself should you be sent for to attend on the captain. You must obey him quickly, try and understand his wishes, and keep things clean and in their places. If you do this, you are certain to please him."

Thus it was that my friend kindly tried to prepare me for my new career. "Now, Jack," said he at last, "I've done my best to set you on your legs. You must try to walk alone. I don't want to make a nursing baby of you, remember." From that day forward Peter left me very much to take care of myself. Still I felt that his eye was watching over me, and this feeling gave me a considerable amount of confidence which I should not otherwise have possessed.

By the next day at noon, the rest of the crew had assembled; the captain and several passengers, mostly merchants and planters, came on board. There was a fair wind blowing down the Liffey. "Open the dock-gates, Mr Thompson, and let her go. She'll find her own way to Jamaica and back again by herself, without a hand at the helm, she knows it so well," the captain, as he stood on the poop, sung out to the dock-master. I found that this was a standing joke of his.

The *Rainbow* was a regular West India trader, and had had many successful voyages there. Captain Helfrich was chief owner as well as master, and was a great favourite with the merchants and planters at the different islands at which he was in the habit of touching, and consequently had always plenty of passengers, and never had to wait long for freight. He was very proud of his brig, and of everything connected with her. He himself also was a person not a little worthy of note. He was, as I have said, a tall, fine man, robust and upright in figure, with large, handsome features, and teeth of pearly whiteness. He was probably at this time rather more than forty years old, but not a particle of his crisp, curly, brown hair had a silvery tint. He had a fine beaming smile, though he was very firm and determined, and could look very fierce when angry. I had an unbounded respect for him. Thus commanded, and with as good a crew as ever manned a ship, the *Rainbow* dropped down the Liffey, and made sail to the southward; and under these propitious circumstances I found myself fairly launched in my career as a sailor.

Chapter Two
The Bitters and Sweets of a Sea-Life

"And so, Jack, you like a sea-life, do you?" said Peter Poplar to me one day after we had been about two weeks from port. We had had very fine weather all the time, with a north or easterly wind, and I expected to find the ocean always as smooth and pleasant as it then was. One good result was, that I had been able to pick up a good many of the details of my duty, which I should not have done had I been sea-sick, and knocked about in a gale.

"Yes, thanks to you, Peter, I like it much better than running errands on shore," I answered. "I don't wish for a pleasanter life."

Peter laughed. "You've had only the sweets as yet, boy; the bitters are to come," he observed. "Still, if you get a fair share of the first, you'll have no reason to complain."

I did not quite understand him. I then only thought of the sweets, as he called them. The truth was, I had generally been very kindly treated on board. To be sure, I got a kick, or the taste of a rope's end, now and then, from some of the men if they happened to be out of humour; but those were trifles, as I never was much hurt, and Peter told me I was fortunate to get nothing worse. There was one ill-conditioned fellow, Barney Bogle by name, who lost no opportunity of giving me a cuff for the merest trifle, if he could do so without being seen by Peter, of whom he was mortally afraid. In his presence, the bully always kept his hands off me. Of course it would not have been wise in me to complain of Barney to Peter, as it might have caused a quarrel; so I contented myself with doing my best to keep out of my enemy's way, just as a cat does out of the way of a dog which has taken a fancy to worry her. Captain Helfrich had hitherto taken no notice whatever of me, and he seemed to me so awful a person, that I never expected to be spoken to by him. Now and then the mates ordered me to do some little job or other, to fetch a swab or a marlinespike, or to hold a paint-pot, but they in no other way noticed me.

I remember how blue the sky was, and how sparkling the sea, and how hot the sun at noon shone down on our heads, and how brightly the moon floated above us at night, and formed a long, long stream of silvery light across the waters; and I used to fancy, as I stood looking at it, that I could hear voices calling to me from far, far-off, and telling me of my sweet, calm-eyed mother, still remembered fondly, and of my poor father, snatched from me so suddenly. I won't talk much about that sort of thing. It seems now like a long-forgotten dream—I believe that, even then, I was dreaming.

Well, as I said, the fine weather continued for a long time, till I was awoken one morning by a loud, roaring, dashing, creaking sound, or rather, I might say, of a mixture of such sounds; and as I began to rub my eyes, I thought that I should have been hove out of the narrow crib in which I was stowed away in the very bows of the vessel. Sometimes I felt the head of the brig lifted up, and then down it came like a sledge-hammer into the water; now I felt myself rolled on one side, now on the other. I fully thought that the vessel must be on the rocks. Not a gleam of light reached me, nor could I hear the sound of a human voice. I wanted to be out of the place; but when I tried to get up, I felt so sick and wretched, that I lay down again with an idea that it would be more comfortable to die where I was. At last, however, Barney Bogle came below and discovered me.

"Turn out, you young skulker; turn out!" he exclaimed, belabouring me with a rope's end. "Didn't you hear all hands called to shorten sail an hour ago?"

I had no help for it, so on deck I crawled, where the grey light of morning was streaming from beneath a dark mass of clouds which hung overhead, and a gale was blowing which sent the foam flying from the tops of the seas, deluging us fore and aft. Now the brig was lifted up to the summit of a wave, and now down she sank into the trough of the sea, with a liquid wall on one side which, as it came curling on, looked as if it must inevitably overwhelm her. She was under close-reefed topsails and storm-jib, and two of the best hands were at the helm. Peter was one of them. I managed to climb up to windward, and to hold on by the weather-fore-rigging, where the rest of the crew were collected.

I shall never forget the dark, dreary, and terrific scene which the ocean presented to my unaccustomed sight. At first, too, I felt very sick and miserable, and I thought that I would far rather have been starving on shore than going to be drowned, as I fancied, and being tossed about by the rough ocean. Barney, who was on deck before me, abused me as I crawled up near him, and contrived to give me a kick, which, had I let go my hold, as it was calculated to make me do, would probably have been the cause of my immediate destruction. At that moment a huge sea came rolling up towards the brig, topping high above our deck. I saw Peter Poplar and the other man at the helm looking out anxiously at it. They grasped tighter hold of the spokes of the wheel, and planted their feet firmer on the deck. Captain Helfrich and his mates were standing by the main-rigging.

"Hold on, hold on for your lives, my men!" he sung out. The crew did not neglect to obey him, and I clung to a rope like a monkey. Most of the passengers were below, sick in their berths. Down came the huge sea upon us like the wall of a city overwhelming its inhabitants. Over our deck it rushed with terrific force. I thought to a certainty that we were sinking. What a horrible noise there was!—wrenching and tearing, and the roar and dashing sound of the waves, and the howling of the wind! All contributed to confuse my senses, so that I forgot altogether where I was. I had an idea, I believe, that the end of the world was come. Still my shipmates did not shriek out, and I was very much surprised to find the brig rise again out of the water, and to see them standing where they were before, employed in shaking the wet off their jackets. The deck of the brig, however, presented a scene of no little confusion and havoc. Part of her weather-bulwarks forward had been stove in, the long-boat on the booms had been almost knocked to pieces, and a considerable portion of the after-part of the lee-bulwarks had been washed away, showing the course the sea had taken over us.

"We must not allow that trick to be played us again," said the captain to the mates. I had crept as far aft as I dared go, for I did not like the look of the sea through the broken bulwark, so I could hear him. "Stand by to heave the ship to!" he shouted, and his voice was easily heard above the sounds of the tempest. "Down with the helm!—In with the jib!—Hand the maintopsail!" The officers and men, who were at their stations, flew to obey their orders. I trembled as I saw the third mate, with several other men, taking in the jib. Having let go the halliards, and eased off the sheets, hauling away on the down-hauler; and having got it down on the bowsprit-cap, though nearly blown out of the bolt-ropes, stowing it away in the foretopmast staysail-netting. As the bows of the brig now rose and now plunged into the trough of the sea, I thought they must have been, to a certainty, washed away. The maintopsail was, in the meantime, taken in, and I felt that I was very glad I was not obliged to lay-out on the yard with the other men. It seemed a wonder how they were not shaken off into the sea, or carried away by the bulging sail. The great thing in taking in a sail in a gale, as I now learned from Peter, is not to allow the sail to shake, or it is very likely to split to pieces. Keep it steadily full, and it will bear a great strain. Accordingly, the clew-lines, down-haul-tackle, and weather-brace being manned, the halliards were let go, the weather-brace hauled in, the weather-sheet started and clewed up; then the bowline and lee-sheets being let go, the sail caught aback, and the men springing on the yard, grasped it in their arms as they hung over it. Folding it in inch by inch, they at length mastered the seeming resistless monster, and passing the gaskets round it, secured it to the yard. Those who for the first time see a topsail furled in a heavy gale may well deem it a terrific operation, and perilous in the extreme to those employed in it. I know that I breathed more freely when all the men came down safely from the yard, Barney Bogle among the number; and the helm being lashed a-lee, the brig rode like a duck over the seas.

There was no time, however, to be idle, and all hands set to work to repair damages. I now saw that the captain, who appeared so fine a gentleman in harbour, or when there was nothing to do, could work as well, if not rather better, than any one. With his coat off, and saw, axe, or hammer in hand, he worked away with the carpenter in fitting a new rail, and planking up the bulwarks; and the steward had twice to call him to breakfast before he obeyed the summons. His example inspired the rest; and in a very short time the bulwarks were made sufficiently secure to serve till the return of fine weather.

"I told you, Jack, that you would have a taste of the bitters of a sea-life before long," said Peter, as soon as he had time to have a word with me. "Let me tell you, however, that this is just nothing, and that we shall be very fortunate if we do not fall in with something much worse before long."

I knew that Peter would not unnecessarily alarm me, and so I looked up at the dark clouds driving across the sky, and saw the hissing, foaming waves dancing up wildly around us, looking as if every moment they were ready to swallow up the brig, I asked myself what worse could occur, without our going to the bottom. I had never then been in a regular hurricane or a typhoon, or on a lee-shore on a dark night, surrounded by rocks, or among rapid currents, hurrying the ship within their power to destruction; nor had I been on board a craft when all hands at the pumps could scarcely keep her afloat; nor had I seen a fire raging. Indeed, I happily knew nothing of the numberless dangers and hardships to which a seaman in his career is exposed. I must not say that I was in any way frightened. I resolved to keep a bold heart in my body. "Never mind," I answered to Peter's remark; "while I've got you and the captain on board, I don't fear anything."

Peter laughed. "We may be very well in our way," said he; "but, Jack, my advice is: Trust in God, and hold on by the weather-rigging. Should the ship go down, look out for spar or a plank if there's no boat afloat; and if you can find nothing, swim as long as you can; but whatever you do, trust in God."

I have never forgotten Peter's advice. Never have I found that trust deceive me; and often and often have I been mercifully preserved when I had every reason to believe that my last hour had come. I should remark also that, badly off as I have often fancied myself, I have soon had reason to be thankful that I was not in the condition of others around me.

While Peter was speaking, one of the crew sung out, "a sail on the weather-bow!" Sure enough, as we rose on the summit of a sea, a ship could be seen with all her topsails set running before the wind. Peter remarked that she was standing directly for us. "She is a large ship, by the squareness of her yards; probably either from the West Indies or South America, or maybe China, or from some port in the Pacific, and she has come round the Horn."

We watched her for some time. "She has a signal of distress flying, sir," said the first mate, who had been looking at her through a glass.

"She is in a bad way, then," remarked the captain. "I fear that unless the sea goes down, and she in the meantime can heave-to near us, we can render her no assistance."

On came the ship right for us. I thought that she would run us down; so, indeed, I found did others on board. The mates, indeed, went to the wheel to put the helm up to let the brig fall off, that we might get out of her way; but as she approached, she altered her course a little, so that she might pass clear under our stem. Never shall I forget the look of that strange ship; for, as she came near us, rolling in the trough of the sea, we could see clearly everything going forward on her decks.

She was a Spaniard, so Peter told me, as he knew from the ensign which flew out, hoisted half-way to her peak. She was a high-pooped ship, with a deep waist and a lofty forecastle, her upper works narrowing as they rose, with large lanterns, and much rich carved work all gilt and painted. Such a craft is never seen now-a-days.

She was crowded with people. Some were soldiers, worn-out men, with their wives and families returning home from the colonies; others were cabin passengers. There were rich Hidalgos, attended on by their slaves—old men, who had spent their lives abroad in the pursuit of wealth; and there were fair girls, too, probably their daughters, some young and lovely; and there were young men, with life before them, and thinking that life was to be very sweet; and there were children, and infants in arms, and their fond mothers or nurses anxious to shelter them from harm. Then there were the officers of the ship and the crew; fierce, dark-bearded men—a mongrel set of various ranks and many nations. She was evidently a rich galleon, returning to old Spain from one of her ill-governed dependencies in South America. But it was the way in which all these people were employed that made so deep an impression on me. Then the scene looked only like a strange picture. It was not till long afterwards, when I reasoned on what I had observed, that I understood what I now describe.

The greater number of the men were at the pumps, labouring in a way which showed that they fancied their lives depended on their exertions; but the clear streams of water which came out of the scuppers, and the heavy way in which the ship plunged into the trough of the sea, showed that their labour would too probably be in vain. Others seemed paralysed or pitied, and sat down with their heads on their breasts waiting their fate. Many, as they passed us, came to the side of their ship, and held out their hands imploringly towards us, as if we could help them. But what seemed most dreadful—some of the sailors and soldiers had got hold of a quantity of wine and spirits, and were reeling about the decks, offering liquor to every one they encountered, and holding out bottles and cans of wine mockingly at us, or as if inviting us to join them. Several, although they must have given up all hope of assistance from man, might have looked for it from Heaven, for they were on their knees imploring help—was it from Him who alone can give it, or was it from their various saints? I don't know.

Two groups of figures on the poop especially struck me. In the centre of one stood a tall man in rich vestments of gold, and white, and purple. He had a shorn crown. He was a priest. He was holding aloft a golden crucifix, which I thought the wind would have blown out of his hand, but he must have been a powerful man, and he grasped it fast. Assisting to support him and it were two monks in dark dresses, kneeling on the deck on either side of him. Around them knelt and clung, holding on to each other, a number of men and women, and among them were some little children, holding up their tiny hands in supplication towards the crucifix. Of course, no sound could reach us, but there seemed to be much wailing, and crying, and groaning. Some were stretching out their arms, others were beating their breasts and tearing their hair. The priest stood unmoved, with head erect, uttering prayers, or pronouncing absolution. At some distance from them were a couple, not to be overlooked either. One was a fine handsome young man, in the uniform of a military officer; the other a young and beautiful girl, who lay nearly fainting in his arms. He looked towards us eagerly, hopefully, as if he fancied that he would plunge with his precious charge into the water. I thought that at that moment he was going to make the daring leap. Some of the officers of the ship were gathered round the wheel. Just then the helm was put down, and we saw some of them with blows and threats urging the drunken crew to take in the headsails, leaving the maintopsail only to steady the ship. In the operation, however, carelessly performed, the sails were blown to ribbons, and the ship drifted away to leeward of us. She had before this evidently suffered severely. Her boats were gone; her bulwarks in many places stove in; and her bowsprit and foretopmast had been carried away, while, of course, still more serious damage had been sustained in her hull.

"Shall we be able to do anything for all those poor people?" I asked of Peter, who stood near me.

"No, Jack, we shall not," he answered; "man can't help them. This ship, by the look of her, will not keep above water another half-hour; and then Heaven have mercy on their souls! I doubt if the captain will venture to lower a boat in this sea to attempt to save them, or if a boat could lift if he did."

"It's very dreadful," said I.

"Yes, Jack; but it's the lot all sailors must be prepared for," answered Peter. "Remember, it may be my fate or yours one of these days. We should not be afraid; but I repeat it, Jack, we should be prepared." I did not quite understand Peter then.

"Then, Peter, you would not go in the boat if one was lowered?" I observed.

"Wait till the captain says what he wants done," he answered calmly. "If he thinks a boat can live, and wants volunteers, it's my duty to go, you know. Remember, Jack, obey first, and calculate risk afterwards."

Peter's predictions as to the fate of the Spanish ship were fulfilled sooner even than he had expected. That moment, while we were looking at her, she settled lower and lower in the water; she rolled still more heavily; her bow looked as if about to rise, but instead her stem lifted high—up it went. There seemed a chasm yawning for her. Into it she plunged, and down, down she went—the waves wildly rushing over her decks, and scattering the shrieking multitude assembled on them far and wide over the foaming ocean; mothers, children, husbands, wives, lovers, and friends, the priests and their disciples, were rudely torn asunder, and sent hither and thither. Numbers went down in the vortex of the huge ship—the men at the pumps, the drunken seamen, some who had clung madly to the rigging. Others supported themselves on anything which could float; and brave swimmers struck out for dear life.

"I can't stand this," cried our captain, unconscious that he was speaking aloud; "we must try at all risks to save the poor wretches."

"I'll go," cried the second mate, Harry Gale, a fine, quiet, gentleman-reared young man as ever I met.

"I'm one with you, Mr Gale," cried Peter Poplar, springing aft to the falls of the lee-quarter-boat, the only one which could be lowered. "Bear a hand here, mates; there'll no time to be lost!"

"Hold fast!" shouted the captain. "No hurry, my men; those who go clear the boat. The mates will stand by the falls with Jackson and Farr. All ready now!—Lower away!"

The captain gave the word, so that the boat touched the water just at the best time. Peter Poplar stood in the bows, boat-hook in hand, and moved off; Mr Gale steered; the three other men were the strongest of the ship's company; and truly it required all the care and seamanship mortal man could possess to keep a boat alive in such a boiling caldron as the wide Atlantic then was. I was very anxious for Peter's safety, for he was indeed my friend. I feared also for the rest. I was fully alive to the danger of the expedition they were on.

The boat, keeping under the lee of the brig, dropped down towards the scene of the catastrophe. So fiercely boiling, however, were the waves, that with awful rapidity the greater number of those who had lately peopled the deck of that big ship were now engulfed beneath them. Some, however, still struggled for existence.

Had the sea been less violent many might have been saved; for as we stood on the deck we could see the poor wretches struggling among the foam, but by the time the boat reached the spot they had sunk for ever.

The captain had gone into the main-rigging, and with his outstretched arm was indicating to the second mate the direction in which to steer; but of course she could venture to go very little out of one particular direction without a certainty of being swamped. It was very dreadful to watch one human being after another engulfed in the hungry ocean. We have just to picture to ourselves how we should be feeling if we were in their places, to make us eager to save those under like circumstances.

The most conspicuous object was the tall priest, and towards him the boat was accordingly making her way. Two other figures were at the same time seen. One floated only a short distance to leeward of the brig; it was that, I felt certain, of the beautiful girl I had seen supported by the young officer. She was unconscious of all around, and I believe that even then life had left her frame. She was supported by a piece of plank, to which probably she had been secured with the last fond effort of affection by him who had thus been unable to provide any means of escape for himself. He, however, must have struggled bravely for existence, for I made him out at a short distance beyond, now rising on the crest of a wave, now sinking into the trough of the sea, but still swimming on with his eye gazing steadily in the direction of that floating form.

Meantime the boat was making towards the priest. "Give way, lads!" shouted several of our people in their eagerness, forgetting that they could not possibly be heard. No time was to be lost, for already the priest's rich dress was saturated with water, and he was sinking lower and lower, and what at first had supported him was now dragging him down. Still he did not give in, but, cross in hand, waved the boat on. The distance he was from the boat must have been greater than we supposed. Suddenly he threw up his arms, and a white-crested top of a sea breaking over him, he disappeared for ever amidst a mass of foam.

Mr Gale saw what had occurred, and instantly turned the boat's head towards the young officer, who was still swimming on with wonderful strength. In this instance the men were more successful; the boat's head dropped down close to him, and Peter, stretching out his arm, grasped the young man by the shoulder, and hauled him in over the bows, and passed him on into the stern-sheets. Though faint at first, the Spaniard instantly recovered himself, and stood upright in the boat, gazing eagerly around. As the boat rose on a sea, he caught sight of the object of his search. He pointed towards the floating form of the young lady. Even when first seen, the line by which she had been hurriedly and imperfectly secured to the plank I observed was loosened. The wash of the sea now parted her from it entirely. The young man saw what had occurred. With a cry of anguish, before our people could seize him, he sprang from the gunwale towards the object of his love, as her dress carried her down beneath the foaming waters. I think he reached her. They disappeared at the same moment, and never rose again!

Still a few people kept above water, holding on to planks, or swimming, chiefly seamen or soldiers; but most of them had been carried to too great a distance from the brig for a boat to save them. It was only by keeping under our lee, our hull preventing the sea from breaking so much, that the boat avoided being swamped. Thus we could expect that only a very few of those who floated to the last could be saved. No one could have ventured further than did our brave mate and his crew;—they would in all probability have thrown away their own lives had not Captain Helfrich recalled them. He signalled with his hand, but Mr Gale did not observe him. "Fire a gun there," he shouted; "quick, for your lives!" A gun had been ready loaded for the purpose. Its report served as the funeral knell of many a despairing wretch.

The boat put about. The returning alongside was as perilous an operation almost as the lowering the boat had been. All hands not required at the falls stood ready with ropes to heave to our shipmates should she be swamped alongside; but the oars being thrown in, Mr Gale and Peter seizing the fall-tackles at the right moment, hooked on, and the rest of the people handing themselves up by the ropes hanging ready for them, the boat was hoisted up before the sea again rose under her bottom. It was sad to think: that all their gallant efforts had been unavailing. In two or three minutes more not a human being of all the Spaniard's crew was to be seen alive; and except a few planks and spars, and here and there a bale or a chest, mere dots in the ocean, we might have fancied, as we looked out on those foaming waters, that all that had passed was some hideous dream. Often, indeed, have I since had the same dreadful drama acted over before my eyes while I slept; so deep was the impression made on me by the reality. Very many things which long after that time occurred have entirely faded from my memory.

Had it been possible, (as Peter told me he thought it would have been, had all the crew done their duty), to keep the galleon afloat a few hours longer, in all probability we should have been the means of saving the people. In the course of the day the wind fell, and the sea went down sufficiently to have allowed our boats to have passed between the two vessels without any great risk. Captain Helfrich was certainly not a man to have deserted her while a chance remained of saving a human being. While she floated he would have stuck to her. "Remember, Jack," said Peter, "the first duty of a ship's company is to stick by each other—to keep sober, and to obey their officers. Without a head, men can do nothing. They are like a flock of sheep running here and there, and never getting on. What is a man's duty is best; and you see here, for instance, that the lives of all depend on their doing their duty."

Sail was again made on the brig, and she was able to lay her course. At night, however, it came on to blow again, and by next morning we were once more hove-to with more sea, and the wind chopping about and making it break in a far more dangerous way than it had done on the previous day. I found, when I came on deck after my watch below, all hands looking out at an object which had just been discovered a little abaft the lee-bow. Some said it was a dead whale; one or two declared that it was a rock; but the officers, after examining it with their glasses, pronounced it to be a vessel bottom uppermost! The question was, whether the wreck was deserted, or whether any people still clung to it. Hove-to as we were, we made of course considerable lee-way; and keeping in the direction we were then driving, we should before long get near enough to examine her condition. Had not the brig already received some damage, Captain Helfrich would, I believe, have run down at once to the wreck; but this, a right care for the safety of his own vessel would not allow him to do. Every instant, too, the gale was increasing, till it blew a perfect hurricane; and not for a moment could a boat have lived had one been lowered. The wreck drove before the wind, but of course we moved much faster; it was some hours, however, before we got near enough to the wreck to discover if anyone was upon it.

"There are three or four people at least upon it," exclaimed Mr Gale. "Poor fellows! can we do nothing for them, sir?"

"I cannot allow you to throw away your life, as you would if you had your own way," answered the captain, to whom he spoke. "All we can do is to hope that the wind will go down before we drift out of sight of each other."

Unhappily our course took us some way from the wreck, though near enough to see clearly the poor fellows on it. How intense must have been their feelings of anxiety as they saw us approaching them! and how bitter their disappointment when they discovered how impossible it was for us to render them any assistance till the weather moderated!

The wreck appeared to be that of a schooner, or brig of a hundred and fifty tons or so. The people were holding on to her keel. There were three white men and two blacks. They waved their handkerchiefs and caps, and held out their hands imploringly towards us. Some were sitting astride on the keel; one was lying down, held on by his shipmates; and another lay right over it looking almost dead. We made out this through the glasses. Peter got me a look through a telescope which one of the men had. It brought the countenances of the poor fellows fearfully near—their expressions of horror and despair could be seen. We longed more than ever for the gale to abate that we might help them. Still it blew on as fiercely as ever all day. The wreck remained during this time in sight, but of course we were increasing our distance from her.

"What would have happened," said I to Peter, "if it had been night instead of day; and if, instead of passing by the wreck, we had struck against her?"

"Why, we should have given her a finishing-stroke, and very likely have stove in our bottom and followed her," he answered. "I like to hear you ask such questions; they show that you think. The event you have spoken of occurs very frequently, I suspect. Numbers of vessels leave port, and are never again heard of. They are either run down, or they run their bows against a wreck, or the butt-end of a tree or log of timber; some are burned; some run against icebergs, or fields of ice; and some are ill put together, or rotten, and spring leaks, and so go down: but to my mind the greater number are lost from the first cause I have spoken of. You'll find out in time, Jack, all the perils to which a seaman is exposed, as well as the hardships I once before spoke to you about." I did not think at the time how true Peter's words would come.

We were nearly a mile from the wreck, I suppose, when night came on; but the captain took her bearings by the compass, that he might know in what direction to look for her should he be able to make sail before the morning. I had got pretty well accustomed to the tumbling about by this time, but I could scarcely sleep for thinking of the poor fellows on the wreck. The night passed away without any change in the weather. When morning came all hands were looking out for the wreck; but we all looked in vain. There was the leaden sky, the dark-green foaming sea, but not a spot on it to be observed far as the eye could reach. Before noon the wind once more moderated, and making all sail we stood over the place where, by our captain's calculations, the wreck would be found. Not a sign of her was to be seen. It was too certain that she must have gone down during the night.

Every day seemed to have its event. We were again on our proper course, though the sea was still running high, when towards evening an object was seen floating ahead of us, just on the lee-bow. We were at no great distance, little more than half a mile or so, when first seen, so that we were not left long in doubt as to what it was. "A raft!" said one; "A piece of a wreck," said another; "Some casks," said a third.

"Whatever it is, there is a man upon it," exclaimed Peter; "and, messmates, he's alive! Steady you," he added, looking at the man at the wheel. "Keep her away a little," he said, addressing Mr Gale, who had charge of the deck.

The news of what was seen at once spread below, and all hands were soon on deck on the look-out. The man was alive, and saw us coming, for he waved a handkerchief to attract our notice, lest he might not have been observed. We waved to him in return, to keep up his spirits. As we approached, we saw that the man was dressed as a sailor. He was seated on a grating, made more buoyant by several pieces of spars and planks. He was leaning against another plank, which he had secured in an upright position by means of stays on the grating. Had not the sea been still very high, we could have run alongside his raft and picked him off without difficulty; but as it was impossible to steer with the necessary nicety, there was a risk of running him down by so doing. We therefore hove-to to windward of him; and Mr Gale, with the boat's crew who had before volunteered, being lowered, they pulled carefully towards him. The man stood up as he saw them approach; and scarcely had the bow of the boat touched the grating, than he sprung on board, and without help stepped over the shoulders of the men into the stern-sheets. When there, however, his strength seemed to give way, and he sank down into the bottom of the boat in what appeared to be a fainting fit. A few drops from a flask, which Mr Gale had thoughtfully carried in his pocket, partially revived the man, though he was unable to help himself up the side. He was therefore slung on deck, and the boat being hoisted in without damage, we again made sail.

The man, who was placed on deck with his back against the companion-hatch, remained some time in an almost unconscious state; but at length, after much care had been bestowed on him, he recovered sufficiently to speak. He was a fine, good-looking young man; and his well-browned countenance and hands showed that he had been long in a tropical climate. A little food, taken slowly, still further revived him; and he was soon able to lift himself up and look about him.

"How was it you came to be where we found you?" asked Captain Helfrich, who was seated near him on the companion-hatch, while I was employed in polishing up the brass rail of the companion-ladder.

"Why, I belonged to a ship, the *Oak Tree*, bound from Honduras to Bristol with mahogany and logwood," answered the stranger. "We had made a fair run of it, three days ago, when we were caught in a heavy squall, which carried away our maintop-mast, and did us much damage. Fortunately, I was at supper when all hands were called to shorten sail; and not thinking what I was about, I clapped a whole handful of biscuit and junk into my pocket before I sprang on deck. A few hours after dark, a heavy sea struck the ship, and carried away our boats and bulwarks, washing me with one or two other poor fellows overboard. I was without my shoes, and had only a thin cotton jacket on; so, being a good swimmer, I was able to regain the surface, and to look about me. Away flew the ship before the wind, without a prospect of my being able to regain her; so I did not trouble myself upon that point. The other men who had been washed overboard with me had sunk: I could do them no good. I therefore had only to look after myself. I first cast my eyes about me, to see what I could get hold of to keep me afloat. The wreck of the bulwarks and boats, with the spars which had been washed overboard, had sent me some materials; and I got a couple of pieces under my arms to support me while I looked for more. In the heavy sea that was running, I could not have made much of a raft, when fortunately my eye caught a grating; which I managed, after much exertion, to reach. By degrees I fished up other pieces of plank and broken spars, till I had formed the raft you found me on. Fortunately, I had started on my cruise just after supper, so that I was able to hold out for some time without eating. But when morning came, and there was not a sail in sight, I began to feel somewhat down-hearted. However, I soon plucked up again. Said I to myself, 'Though the ocean is wide, there are a good many craft afloat, and it will be hard if someone doesn't make me out before very long.' I tried to think of all the wonderful escapes people had made who had been in a similar condition; and I prayed that God would deliver me in the same way. One thing weighed on my mind, and still weighs there: I left a wife and a small child at home, near Bristol; and when the ship arrives there, the poor girl will hear that I was was washed overboard, and will believe me dead. When you got near me, I saw that you were outward-bound; and the thought that she might have to go many a month and not hear of me, served more than anything else to upset me. My strength gave way, and I went off in a faint, as you saw, in the bottom of the boat." He then told the captain that his name was Walter Stenning. The captain, who was a kind-hearted man, did his best to raise his spirits; and promised him that if we fell in with a homeward-bound ship he would endeavour to put him on board.

As it happened, we did not speak any vessel till we reached the West Indies; so we had to carry Walter Stenning with us.

Chapter Three
The West Indies

"Land! land on the starboard-bow!" was shouted from the foretopmast cross-trees, where several of our men had been, in spite of a pretty hot scorching sun, since dawn, on the look-out for it.

"Who saw it first?" asked the captain, who was always more anxious when nearing the coast than at any other time.

"Tom Tillson," was the answer from aloft.

"A glass of grog for you, Tom, if it proves to be the land, and you have kept your eyes open to good purpose!" said the captain, preparing himself to go to the mast-head, where the mates followed him.

They were satisfied that Tom had fairly won his glass of grog, I suppose; for, after some time, when I went aloft, I saw a high blue-pointed mountain rising out of the sparkling sea with ranges of lower hills beneath it.

As we drew in with the shore, we could distinguish the fields of sugarcane surrounded by lime-trees, and the white houses of the planters, and the huts of the negroes; and I thought that I should very much like to take a run among the lofty palmetto and the wild cotton-trees and the fig-trees, and to chase the frolicsome monkeys I had heard spoken of among their branches. A light silvery mist hung over the whole scene, and made it look doubly beautiful. I asked Peter what land it was, for I thought that we had arrived at America itself. He laughed, and said that it was only a little island called Saint Christopher's; and that he'd heard say that it was first discovered by the great admiral who had found out America, and that he had called it after his own name. Peter, though he could not read, had a great store of information, which he had picked up from various people. He was not always quite correct; and that was from not being able to read, as he was less able to judge of the truth of what people told him; but altogether, I learned a great deal from his conversation.

We came to an anchor before the town of Basseterre, the capital of the island. It was a clean handsome-looking place, and a number of ships lay before it; while behind it, rising from the wide valley, richly cultivated and beautiful in the extreme, rose the lofty and precipitous crags of Mount Misery, 3700 feet high. It may well be so-called, for it would be pain and misery to have to climb up it, and still greater not to be able to come down again!

After the events I have before described, we had come south till we fell in with the trade-winds, which had brought us on a due westerly course to this place. I did not go on shore; but I heard the captain say that the merchants and planters were very civil and polite to him. They had, however, suffered very much in the late war with France. It was in the year 1782 that a French general, the Marquis de Bouille, having eight thousand men with him, besides a fleet of twenty-nine sail of the line, commanded by the Admiral Count de Grasse, captured the island from the English. It was, however, restored to Great Britain when the war ended the following year.

We had a quantity of fruit brought off to us, which did most of us a great deal of good, after living so long on salt provisions. I remember how delicious I thought the shaddock—which is a fruit something like a very large orange. Its outer coat is pale, like a lemon, but very thick. It is divided into quarters by a thin skin, like an orange; and the taste—which is very refreshing—is between a sweet and an acid. The colour of the inside of some is a pale red—these are the best; others are white inside. Peter told me that he had heard that the tree was brought from the coast of Guinea by a Captain Shaddock, and that the fruit has ever since borne his name.

We spent three or four days at anchor before this beautiful place; and then, having landed two or three of our passengers, and put Walter Stenning on board a vessel returning to England, once more made sail for our destination. The trade-wind still favoured us, though it was much lighter than it had been before we entered the Caribbean Sea.

"Jack," said Peter to me the afternoon we left Basseterre, "I've good news for you. The captain wants a lad in the place of Sam Dermot, whom he has left on board a homeward-bound ship, for he found that he was not fit for a sea-life, and Mr Gale has been speaking a word in your favour. I don't say it's likely to prove as pleasant a life as you lead forward, but if you do your duty and please him, the captain has the power to advance your interests—and I think he is the man to do it."

This was good news, I thought; and soon afterwards Mr Gale told me to go into the cabin. The captain, who was looking over some papers, scarcely raised his head as I entered. "Oh, Jack Williams—is that your name, boy?"

said he. "You are to help Roach, the steward. Go to him; he'll show you what you are to do." The steward soon gave me plenty of work cleaning up things; for the captain was a very particular man, and would always have everything in the best possible order.

The next morning at daybreak, Mr Gale—whose watch it was at the time—roused me up, and sent me to tell the captain that there was a strange sail on the starboard-bow, which seemed inclined to cross our fore-foot. The captain was soon on deck and examining the stranger with his glass.

"Well, what do you make of her, Mr Gale?" he asked. She was a low, little vessel, with considerable beam, and a large lateen mainsail, and a jib on a little cock-up bowsprit—something like a 'Mudian rig.

"She's a suspicious-looking craft; and if it were not that we are well-armed, and could sink her with a broadside, I should not much like her neighbourhood, sir," answered the second mate. As he spoke, a gun was fired by the stranger, but not at us.

"He wants to speak us, at all events," observed Captain Helfrich. "If he had intended us mischief he would have fired at us, I should think."

"Not quite so certain of that, sir," answered Mr Jones, the first mate. "Those pirating fellows are up to all sorts of tricks; and if he's honest he belies himself, for a more roguish craft I never saw. He doesn't show any colours, at all events."

"We'll not be taken by surprise, then," answered the captain. "Arm the people, and see the guns all ready to run out. Boy, get my pistols and cutlass from the steward. Tell him to show himself on deck; and let the gentlemen in the cabin know that if they get up, they may find something to amuse them."

I dived speedily below to deliver my message. While the steward was getting ready the captain's arms, I ran round to the berths of the passengers. One had heard me ask for the pistols; thus the report at once went round among them that there was fighting in prospect. In a few minutes, therefore, several gentlemen in straw-hats, with yellow nankeen trousers and gay dressing-gowns, appeared on deck.

"What!—is that little hooker the craft we are going to fight, captain?" exclaimed one of them. "We shouldn't have much difficulty in trouncing her, I should think."

"Not the slightest, sir, if we have the chance," he answered. "But her crew would have no difficulty either in cutting all our throats, if we once let them get on board! The chances are that she has a hundred desperadoes or more under hatches, and as she can sail round us like a witch, they may choose their own time for coming alongside. I tell you, gentlemen, I would rather she were a hundred miles away than where she is!"

These remarks of the captain very much altered the manner of some of the gentlemen. They were all ready enough to fight, but they put on much more serious countenances than they had at first worn, and kept eyeing the stranger curiously through their telescopes. Still the stranger kept bowling away before us on our starboard-bow, yawing about so as not greatly to increase his distance from us. If he could thus outsail us before the wind, he would be very certain to beat us hollow on a wind. We had, therefore, not the slightest prospect of being able to get away from him so long as he chose to keep us company. Suddenly he luffed up with his head to the northward.

"He thinks that he had better not play us any tricks; he has found out that we are too strong for him," observed Mr Jones. Scarcely had the mate spoken, when a dozen men or so appeared on the deck of the felucca, and launched a boat from it into the water. As soon as she was afloat, two people stepped into her. One seized the oars, and the other seated himself in the stern-sheets.

"Well, that is a rum-looking little figure!" I heard one of our passengers exclaim, bursting into a fit of laughter. "I wonder if he is skipper of that craft?"

"She's not a craft that will stand much joking," observed the first mate. "See, sir; she has begun to show that she is not lightly armed."

He pointed to the deck of the felucca, on which there now appeared at least full thirty men. They looked like a fierce set of desperadoes. They were of all colours, from the fair skin of the Saxon to the ebony hue of some of the people of Africa. The captain saw, I suppose, that there was no use in trying to prevent the boat from coming alongside; for had he done so, the felucca would very quickly have been after us again, and might not another time have treated us so civilly. He therefore, as soon as the boat shoved off from the side of the felucca, ordered the sails to be clewed up, to allow her more easily to approach.

As she pulled towards us, we were able to examine the people in her. He who sat in the stern-sheets was a little old man, with a little three-cornered hat on his head, and a blue long-skirted coat and waistcoat, richly laced. He had on also, I afterwards saw, knee-breeches, and huge silver buckles to his shoes. His countenance seemed wizened and dried up like a piece of parchment. Some of the younger passengers especially seemed to think him, by their remarks, a fair subject for their ridicule. The person who pulled was a huge negro. He must have been as tall as Peter Poplar, but considerably stouter and stronger of limb. He was clothed in a striped cotton dress and straw-hat. It would have been difficult to find two people associated together more unlike each other. The old man took the helm, and by the way he managed the boat it was clear that he was no novice in nautical affairs. "What can he want with us!" exclaimed the captain. "We'll treat him with politeness, at all events!" Side-ropes and a ladder were therefore prepared; but scarcely had the bowman's boat-hook struck the side, than the old gentleman had handed himself up by the main-chains on deck with the agility of a monkey, followed by the big negro. I then saw that he had a brace of silver-mounted pistols stuck in his belt, and that he wore a short sword by his side; but the latter was apparently more for ornament than use. The negro also had a large brace of pistols and a cutlass. In the boat were two iron-clamped chests, one of them being very large, the other small.

The old gentleman singled out the captain as soon as he reached the deck, and walked up to him. "Ah, Captain Helfrich, I am glad to have fallen in with you!" he exclaimed, in a singularly firm and full voice, with nothing of the tremulousness of age in it. "I've come to ask you for a passage to Jamaica, as I prefer entering Port-Royal harbour in a respectable steady-going craft like yours, rather than in such a small cockle-shell as is my little pet there!" As he spoke he pointed with a smile—and such a smile! how wrinkled and crinkled did his face become—to the wicked-looking little felucca.

"Impossible, sir," answered the captain; "my cabins are already so crowded that I could not accommodate another person!"

"Oh! how are the places of Mr Wilmot and Mr Noel occupied then?" asked the stranger with a peculiar look. They were the gentlemen who landed at Saint Kitt's!

The captain started, and looked at his visitor with a scrutinising glance; but he remained unabashed.

"How did you learn that?" asked the captain quickly.

"Oh, there are very few things which happen in these parts the which I don't know," answered the stranger quietly. "However, captain, even if all your cabins are full, that excuse will not serve you. I can stow myself away anywhere. I've been accustomed to rough it, and Cudjoe here won't object to prick for a soft plank!" The black, hearing his name pronounced, grinned from ear to ear, though he said nothing.

Still the captain, who evidently could not make out who his visitor was, and much mistrusted him, was about to refuse the request, when the old gentleman took him by the button of his coat, as a man does a familiar friend, and led him aside. What was said I do not know, nor could I judge from his countenance how the captain took the communication made to him—I saw him start, and examine the old man attentively from head to foot. The result, I know, was that the boat and the chests were hoisted on board—the sails were let fall and sheeted home. The stranger went to the taffrail and waved his hat. On his doing this, the felucca hauled her wind and stood to the northward.

Just under the companion-stair was a small cabin, which had been filled with stores. This was cleared out, and our strange passenger took possession of it with his chests, while Cudjoe slept at the door. He at once made himself at home, and entered into conversation with every one. No one seemed, however, inclined to quiz him. When he was on deck, I heard the gentlemen in the cabin wondering who he was, for none of them had the slightest notion about the matter; and if the captain knew, he certainly would not tell them. The negro never spoke to any of the passengers or crew. Some said he was dumb; but I knew that was not the case, for I often heard him and the old gentleman talking, but in a language I could not understand. His only care appeared to be to watch over the old gentleman's chests, which had been placed in his cabin, and to keep an eye on the little skiff which had brought them on board.

Those of the passengers who had lived in the West Indies could do nothing for themselves, and were constantly wanting me to perform some little job or other for them. I was thus oftener in the cabin than out of it. While I was attending on them, my great amusement was listening to the yarns which the old gentleman used to spin. They took in all he said for fact; but there used to be often a twinkle in his eye which made me doubt the truth of all he said.

"A man who can look back the larger part of a century, as I have done, must have heard a number of strange things, and seen a number of strange people and strange sights, unless he has gone through the world with his eyes and ears closed, which I have not," he remarked one day when several of the passengers were collected in the cabin. "Gentlemen, I have served both on shore and afloat, and have seen as many shots fired as most people. I cannot quite recollect Admiral Benbow's action in these seas, but I was afloat when that pretty man Edward Teach was the terror of all quiet-going merchantmen. His parents lived at Spanish Town, Jamaica, and were very respectable people. Some of his brothers turned out very well; and one of them was in the king's service, in command of a company of artillery. He, however, at an early age showed himself to be of a somewhat wildish disposition, and rather than submit to control, ran away to sea. For many years he knocked about, among not the best of characters perhaps, in different parts of the world, till he became as daring a fellow as ever stepped a plank. In a short time, while still very young, he got together a band of youths much of his own way of thinking; and they commenced, after the old fashion, the life of gentlemen rovers. Their mode of proceeding was to run alongside any merchantman they fell in with, which they thought would prove a prize worth having. Having taken possession of everything they wanted, they then made every landsman walk the plank, as they did likewise every seaman who would not join them. Those only who would take their oaths, and sign their articles, were allowed to live. Mr Teach used to dress himself out in a wild fashion, and as he wore a great black beard, he certainly did look very ferocious. From this circumstance he got the name of Blackbeard. I don't fancy that he committed all the acts imputed to him, but he did enough to gain himself a very bad name. The governors of the West India Islands, in those days, and the American settlements, were rather fonder of their ease than anything else, so they allowed him to range those seas with impunity. At last, however, a naval officer, feeling indignant that one man should hold a whole community in awe, undertook to destroy the pirate. He got a ship fitted out, well-armed and well-manned, and larger than any Teach was likely to have with him. After a long search, he fell in with the pirate. Teach had never given quarter, and it was not expected that he would take it. More than half drunk, the pirates went to their quarters, and fought more like demons than men. The crew of the king's ship had to fight desperately also. For a long time it was doubtful which would come off the conqueror. At length, however, a large number of the pirates being killed or wounded. Teach was about to blow up his ship. Before, however, he could get below, his ship was boarded by his enemies, and he had to defend himself from the attack of the gallant English officer. For a long time he fought most desperately, but at last he was brought on his knees; and as he would not surrender, he was cut down, and died on the spot. Scarcely a third of his men were taken alive, and they were mostly wounded. His head was cut off and carried to Virginia, where it was stuck on a pole; and where the greater number of the pirates taken were hung in chains, to show to others what very likely would be their fate if they should design to follow the same course."

"Why, you seem to know so much about the matter, I suppose you were there, sir," said one of the passengers, intending his remark to be jocose.

"That is possible, young 'un," answered the old gentleman, fixing his eyes on the speaker. "Perhaps I formed part of the pirate crew; but you don't fancy I was hung, do you?"

The young man did not venture a reply.

"I'll tell you where I saw some service," continued the old gentleman. "The Spaniards had for a long time ruled it insultingly over the English in these seas, fancying that, because we didn't bark, we could not bite. At last a fleet was fitted out in England, and despatched to the West Indies, under the command of Admiral Vernon, in 1739. He first touched at Jamaica, where he refreshed his men, and took on board a body of troops and some pilots, as well as provisions; and, on the 5th of November, sailed for the Spanish town of Porto Bello, which lies on the north side of the Isthmus of Darien. Its harbour and strong forts afforded protection to the Guarda Costas, or Spanish cruisers, which attempted to put a stop to the commerce of other nations in these seas; and it was, likewise, the great rendezvous of the Spanish merchants from various quarters. The town consisted of five or six hundred houses, and some public buildings. The inhabitants depended almost entirely on the fair, which was held there every two or three years, and which lasted about six weeks. The fair took place according to the time when the galleons arrived from Carthagena, where they first touched to dispose of part of their goods. At Porto Bello they were met by the merchants from Lima and Panama, who came, with millions of dollars, to purchase their merchandise. So crowded was the place during the fair, that there was scarcely room to stow the chests of money! The entrance of the harbour is narrow, but widens within; and at the bottom lies the town, in the form of a half moon. At the east end of the town is a huge stable for the mules employed in the traffic between it and Panama. It is very unhealthy, as on the east side there is a swamp; and in the harbour, at low tide, a wide extent of black slimy mud is exposed, exhaling noisome vapours. The town was defended by three forts. The Iron Fort was on the north side of the harbour's mouth, and had a hundred guns. The Gloria Castle was a mile from the first, on the south side of the harbour, and had a hundred and twenty guns. And lastly, there was the fort called Hieronymo, with twenty guns. The Spaniards having been warned of the approach of the English squadron by a fast-sailing vessel which escaped from them, were prepared to receive them, and hoped to send them to the bottom at once. The fleet consisted only of the *Burford*, commanded by the Admiral; the *Hampton Court*, Commodore Brown; the *Norwich*, Captain Herbert; the *Worcester*, Captain Main; the *Princess Louisa*, Captain Waterhouse; and the *Stafford*, Captain Trevor. On the 21st they came up with the harbour. The *Hampton Court* first entered, and came to action not a cable's length from the Iron Fort; and in twenty-five minutes' time fired away about four hundred shot; so that nothing was to be seen but fire and smoke. The *Norwich* came next, the *Worcester* next, and then the Admiral, who anchored within half a cable's length of the castle: and though he was warmly received, the Spaniards were soon driven from their guns. Then, although no breach was made, the troops were landed, and the boats' crews, climbing up through the embrasures, struck the Spanish flag and hoisted the English colours! The other two forts capitulated next day, and all three were completely demolished; the Spanish troops being allowed to march out with their arms. The work was done by four ships, for the other two had not come up; and its history serves to show what men can do, if they are not afraid of the consequences. The same spirit, in a juster cause, animated Vernon which had animated Morgan and the Buccaneers of old, and enabled them to succeed in their desperate enterprises. If a thing must be done, or should be done, never calculate consequences. If a thing is not urgent, then balance the probable consequences against the value of the desired result. That has been my way through life, gentlemen. I have never undertaken anything unless I wished to succeed and had secured the necessary means; and then I have guarded as best I could against unforeseen circumstances."

This was the sort of way the old gentleman talked. He told the gentlemen one day that he was not born when the earthquake occurred during which Port-Royal was swallowed up; but that he had often heard people speak of it who had witnessed it. It began about noon on the 7th of June 1692. Nine-tenths of the city and all the wharves sunk at once; and in two minutes from the commencement of the earthquake several fathoms of water lay over the spot where the streets had just stood. Two thousand persons perished. Some, it was said, who were swallowed up in one place, rose again in another still alive; but that I do not think possible. Very likely they were washed from one place to another, clinging to beams or rafters; and not knowing, in their horror and confusion, where they had been, were picked up and saved. A mountain toppled over into a river, and, by blocking up the course, a vast number of fish were taken, which afforded food to many of the nearly starving inhabitants. Nearly all the vessels in the harbour were lost; but one ship of war, the *Swan* frigate, was driven over the tops of the houses without capsizing. She received but slight damage, and was the means of saving many lives. Scarcely had the earthquake ceased than a fever broke out, which carried off numbers of people. What with hurricanes, plagues, insurrections of the blacks, and attacks from foreign foes, Jamaica had an uneasy time of it; and it proves her unbounded resources that, in spite of all drawbacks, she has continued wealthy and flourishing.

The old gentleman said a great deal more about Jamaica, but this was the substance, I know, of his remarks. That there was something mysterious about the old man was very evident. The captain, I thought, stood somewhat in awe of him, and in his absence never even alluded to him. The rest of the passengers, however, indulged in all sorts of suspicions about him, though they never expressed them, except among themselves. They spoke freely enough before me, for they fancied, I believe, that I did not understand them. I was one day beginning to tell Peter what I had been hearing. "Jack," said he, "I have a piece of advice to give you, which you'll find useful through life. Never go and repeat what you hear about anybody. It's done by people through idleness sometimes, and often through ill-nature, or with a downright evil intention; but whatever is the cause, it's a contemptible propensity, and is certain to lead to harm." I promised that I would follow this advice, and I did so.

Though we had light winds, the strong current which set in from east to west across the Caribbean Sea helped us along, and enabled us to reach Jamaica about seven days after we left Saint Kitt's. After coasting along some way, we cast anchor in Port-Royal Harbour, about five miles from Kingston. There were from two to three hundred sail of craft of all sizes brought up in the harbour.

Scarcely had we dropped our anchor, when the wind, which had before been very light, fell completely. I saw the old gentleman come on deck, and look round earnestly on every side, and then up at the sky. He then went to the captain, and took him aside.

"I tell you it will be down upon us before very long," I heard him say. "House your topmasts, and range your cables, and have every anchor you've got ready for letting go."

The captain seemed to expostulate: "Not another craft seems to be expecting danger."

"Never mind what other crafts are doing," was the answer. "Take the warning of a man who has known these seas from his earliest days, and do you be prepared. If they are lost, it is no reason that you should be lost with them."

The captain at last yielded to the advice of the old gentleman. The topmasts were struck and every particle of top hamper was got down on deck. The cables were all ranged, and two other anchors were carried out ahead, while full scope was given to the best bower which we had down. The old gentleman went about the deck seeing that everything was done properly. Had we not, indeed, been well-manned the work could not have been accomplished at all. Oh, how hot and sultry it was! I had never before felt anything like it. The pitch bubbled and boiled out of the seams on the deck, and the very birds sought shelter far away in some secluded spot.

"Why has the ship been gut into this condition?" I asked of Peter.

"Because they think a hurricane is coming, Jack. If there is, we have just got into harbour in time. I don't see any signs of it myself, except the wind dropping so suddenly; but I suppose the officers know best."

I told him that the old gentleman had persuaded the captain to prepare for whatever was coming.

"Ah! he knows, depend on't, Jack," said Peter. "I can't tell what it is, but there is something curious about that old man. He knows a great deal about these parts." Such was the opinion all forward had formed of the stranger.

When the wind fell the sea became like a sheet of glass. A feather could not have moved over it. It became hotter and closer than ever, and we were glad to get anywhere out of the sun, stifling even as the heat was below. Even the old hands, who were inclined to laugh at the newcomers' complaints of the heat, confessed that they would rather have it cooler. The rest of the vessels in the harbour, with few exceptions, had not hitherto been prepared to meet any unusual tempest but lay as if their crews were totally regardless of any signs of a change. A few, however, had followed our example by striking their topmasts and getting out fresh anchors.

Some of the passengers, meantime, were very anxious to go on shore; but the stranger urged them to remain on board, and assured them that before they could be half-way there the hurricane would be upon them. Two of them, however, were incredulous. The boat of a merchantman lying not far from us, was just then passing with her master in her.

"Ah! I know Captain Williams well. If he is bound for Kingston, he will give us a passage!" exclaimed one of the gentlemen; and he hailed the boat. She came alongside, and refusing all warning, they, taking their portmanteaus, got into her.

"We'll take any message for anyone," they sung out jokingly as they shoved off. "The storm you are afraid of will blow over, depend on it."

"Fools are wise in their own conceit," muttered the old gentleman, as he turned on his heel. I remember, even now, the sound of their laughter as they pulled away up the harbour.

The heat continued to increase, though a thick reddish haze overspread the sky; but as yet not a vapour floated in it. Suddenly, as if by magic, from all quarters came hurrying up dark lowering clouds, covering the whole concave of heaven, a lurid light only gleaming out from near the horizon. Then, amidst the most terrific roars of thunder, the brightest flashes of lightning, and the rushing, rattling, crashing sound of the tempest, there burst upon us a wind, which made the ship reel like a drunken man, and sent the white foam, torn off the surface of the harbour, flying over the deck in sheets, which drenched us through and through. In an instant, the surrounding waters were lashed into the wildest foaming billows. The vessels pitched fearfully into the seas, and began, one after the other, to drag their anchors. Some broke adrift altogether, and were hurled along till they were cast helplessly on the shore; and fortunate were any of the crew who could scramble clear of the hungry waves which rolled after them up the beach. Some of the smaller craft pitched heavily a few times, and then apparently the sea rushed over them, and down they went to rise no more. I was holding on all the time to the fore-rigging with hands and feet, fearing lest I should be blown away, and expecting every moment to see our turn come next to be driven on shore. We were, however, exposed to a danger on which I had not calculated: the vessels breaking adrift, or dragging their anchors, might be driven against us, when we and they would probably have been cast on shore or sunk together. On land, wherever we could see, a terrific scene of confusion and destruction was taking place; tall trees bent and broke like willow wands, some were torn up by their roots, and huge boughs were lifted high in the air and carried along like autumn leaves; houses as well as huts were cast down, and their roofs were carried bodily off through the air. I doubted whether I would rather be afloat or on shore, unless I could have got into a deep cave, out of the way of the falling walls, and trees, and roofs. All this time every one was on deck,—the officers and crew at their stations, ready to try and avert any danger which might threaten us. With a steady gale we might have cut or slipped and run out to sea; but in a hurricane the wind might have shifted round before we were clear of the land, and sent the ship bodily on shore.

While all hands were thus on the look-out, a boat, bottom uppermost, was seen drifting down near us amidst the foaming waters. One man was clinging to the keel. He looked imploringly towards us, and seemed to be shrieking for aid. No assistance could we give him. I could distinguish his countenance: it was that of one of the passengers who had just before persisted in leaving the ship! His companion, and the master and crew, where were they? He, poor wretch, was borne by us, and must have perished among the breakers at the mouth of the harbour. We had not much time to think of him, for we soon had to look to our own safety. A large ship, some way inside of us, was seen to break adrift, and soon after came driving down towards us. Being twice our size, she might speedily have sunk us. Mr Gale and Peter were at the helm to try and sheer the brig clear of her as she approached us. This, however, was not easily effected when there was but a slight current. Down came the ship! "Stand by with your axes, my lads, to cut her clear if she touches us!" shouted the captain. The ship was still some way off, and before she reached us, a schooner broke from her anchorage just ahead of us and drove towards us.

The poor fellows on board stood ready to leap on our deck had she touched us; but she just grazed by, her main-rigging for an instant catching in ours. A few strokes of an axe cut her clear, and before any of her crew could reach us she was driven onward. In another instant the wind catching her side, she turned completely over. There was a wild shriek of despair from her hapless crew. For a few moments they struggled desperately for life; but the wind and the waves quickly drove those off who had clung to the driving hulk, and soon not a trace of them or her could we perceive.

While this was occurring the old man stood unmoved near the helm, watching the approaching ship. "Arm your people with axes, Captain Helfrich, you'll want them," said he quietly. His advice was followed. The ship came driving down on us on the starboard bow. It appeared that if she struck us she must sink us at the moment. Our helm was put to starboard, and by sheering a little to the other side, we escaped the dreaded blow. At that instant she turned round, and her main-yard got foul of our after-rigging. This brought our sides together, and she hung dragging on us. Instantly all hands flew to cut her adrift, for already we had begun to drag our anchors. If we escaped sinking at once, there was certain prospect of both of us being cast on shore. Some of her crew endeavoured to get on board the *Rainbow*; but at the moment they were making the attempt, down came our mainmast, crushing several of our people beneath it. I saw the captain fall, and I thought he was killed. The first mate was much hurt. Still the ship hung to us, grinding away at our side and quarter, and destroying our bulwark and boats. The foremast, it was evident, would soon follow the mainmast, when the stranger wielding a glittering axe, sprung, with the agility of a young man, towards the stays and other ropes which held them, and one after the other severed them. His example was followed by Mr Gale and the crew, and in a shorter time than it has taken to describe the scene, we were freed from our huge destroyer. She went away to leeward, and very soon met her fate.

Still the hurricane raged on. We were not safe, for other vessels might drive against us. However, our next work was to clear the wreck. No one was more active in this than the stranger. At first we thought that the captain was dead; but the news spread that, though much injured, he was still alive. Almost blinded by the spray and rain and vivid lightning, the crew worked on. At length the storm ceased almost as suddenly as it had begun;

but words cannot describe the scenes of destruction which were presented to our eyes on every side, wrecks strewed the shore, and the plantations inland seemed but masses of ruin. Night at last came, and the ship was made snug. When I went on deck early in the morning, I looked about for the stranger. Neither he nor his black attendant, nor his chests and boat were to be found. Yet it was declared that no one had seen them leave the ship! This unaccountable disappearance made all hands wonder still more who the mysterious stranger could be. Such was my first introduction to the West Indies.

Chapter Four
The Return Home

"Hurrah! hurrah! Erin-go-bragh!" Such were the cries which the Irish part of our crew uttered, and in which I through sympathy joined, as once more the capstan was manned, and the anchor being hove up, and the topsails sheeted home, we made sail for Dublin. We had been longer than usual at Kingston; for the damage the brig had received in the hurricane, and the illness of the captain, which impeded the collection of freight, had much delayed us. In reality our return home brought very little satisfaction to me. I had no friends to see, no one to care for me. I therefore remained on board to assist the ship-keeper; and the whole time we were in the Dublin dock I scarcely ever set my foot on shore.

The same thing occurred after my second voyage. I did not attempt to form a friendship with anyone. Not that I was of a sulky disposition; but I was not inclined to make advances, and no one offered me his friendship. The ship-keeper, old Pat Hagan, had seen a great deal of the world, and picked up a good deal of information in his time, and I was never tired of listening to his yarns; and thus, though I had no books, I learned more of things in general than if I had bad; for I was but a bad reader at any time. Pat trusted to a good memory, for he had never looked into a book in his life. Thus, with a pretty fair second-hand knowledge of the world, I sailed on my third voyage to the West Indies in the *Rainbow*. We had the same officers, and several of the crew had rejoined her, who were in her when I first went to sea. I had now become strong and active, and though still little and young-looking, I had all my wits wide-awake, and knew well what I was about. The captain had taken another boy in the cabin instead of me, and I was sent forward to learn seamanship; which was, in reality, an advantage to me, though I had thus a rougher life of it than aft. Still I believe that I never lost the captain's good-will, though he was not a man to talk to me about it.

Once more, then, the stout old brig was following her accustomed track across the Atlantic. Peter Poplar was also on board. We had been about a fortnight at sea, when, the ship lying almost becalmed with a blue sky overhead, a large white cloud was seen slowly approaching us. The lower part hung down and grew darker and darker, till it formed almost a point. Below the point was a wild bubbling and boiling of the water, although the surrounding sea was as smooth as glass.

"What can that be?" said I to Peter. "Are there any fish there?"

"No—fish! certainly not; but you'll soon see," he answered. "I wish it were further off; I don't like it so near."

"Why, what harm can it do?" I asked.

"Send as stout a ship as we are to the bottom with scant warning!" he answered. "That's a water-spout. I've seen one rise directly ahead of a ship, and before there was time to attempt to escape it, down it came bodily on her deck like a heavy sea falling over a vessel. She never rose again, but went down like a shot."

"I hope that won't be our fate," said I.

At that moment the captain came on deck. "Get ready a gun there, forward!" he sung out. "Quick now!" While I had been talking to Peter, a pillar of water had risen out of the sea, so it seemed; and, having joined the point hanging from the cloud, came whirling towards us. Had there been sufficient wind to send the ship through the water, we might have avoided it; but there was scarcely steerage-way on her. I thought of what Peter had just told me, and I thought if it does break over us, it will certainly send us to the bottom. The captain ordered the slow match to be brought to him, and went forward to the gun, which had been loaded and run out. On came the water-spout. I could not conceive what he was going to do. He stooped down, and, running his eye along the gun, fired a shot right through the watery pillar. Down came the liquid mass with a thundering sound into the sea, but clear of the ship, though even our deck got a little sprinkling; and when I looked up at the sky, not a sign of a cloud was there. Peter told me that we ought to be thankful that we had escaped the danger so well, for that he had never been in greater risk from a water-spout in his life.

We used frequently to catch dolphins during the passage, by striking them with a small harpoon as they played under the bow of the brig. They are not at all like the creatures I remember carved in stone at the entrance of some gentleman's park near Dublin. They measure about four feet in length; are thick in the middle, with a green back and a yellow belly, and have a sinking between the tip of the snout and the top of the head; indeed, they are something like a large salmon. We used to eat them, and they were considered like a fat turbot.

Frequently flying-fish fell on our deck in attempting to escape from their two enemies—the dolphin and the bonito: but they fell, if not from the frying-pan into the fire, from the water into the frying-pan; for we used to eat them also. Indeed nothing comes amiss to a sailor's mess. The flying-fish, which is about the size of a herring, has two long fins which serve it as wings; but it can only keep in the air so long as its fins remain wet. These fish, like herrings, also swim together in large shoals, which, as their pursuers come among them, scatter themselves far and wide. Nothing very particular occurred on the passage, till once more we made the land.

I went aloft when I heard the ever-welcome cry from the foretopmast-head: "Land! land on the starboard bow!" Then I saw it rising in a succession of faint blue hills out of the sparkling sea. Peter told me that it was the large island of Hispaniola, or Saint Domingo, and that it belonged partly to Spain and partly to France; but that there were a great number of blacks and coloured people there, many of whom were free and possessed considerable wealth. Not long after this, in the year 1791, these coloured people rose on the whites, who had long tyrannised over them, and having murdered vast numbers, declared their island an independent kingdom.

We were entering, I found, the Caribbean Sea by the Porto Rico passage; and were to coast along the southern shore on our course to Jamaica. Now and then we were sufficiently close in with the land to make out objects distinctly; but, in general, we kept well out at sea, as it is not a coast seamen are fond of hugging. The silvery mist of the early morning still lay over the land, when, right ahead of us, the white canvas of a vessel appeared shining brightly in the rays of the rising sun. The officer of the watch called the attention of the captain to her. Peter and I were also looking out forward. "Why, Jack!" he exclaimed, "she's the very craft which put that old gentleman aboard the time we came away from Saint Kitt's, you remember?"

"Of course I do," said I. "She is like her, at all events; and as for that old gentleman, I shall not forget him and his ways in a hurry."

"He was a strange man, certainly," observed Peter. "The captain seems to have a suspicion about the craft out there. See, he and the mates are talking together. They don't like her looks."

Still we stood on with all sails set. Much the same scene occurred which had happened before, when we saw the felucca off Saint Kitt's. Ammunition was got up—the guns were all ready to run out—the small-arms were served out—and the passengers brought out their pistols and fowling-pieces. Everybody, indeed, became very warlike and heroic. Still the little craft which called forth these demonstrations, as she lay dipping her bows into the swell, with her canvas of whiteness so snowy, the emblem of purity, looked so innocent and pretty, that a landsman would scarcely have expected any harm to come out of her. Yet those accustomed to the West Indies had cause to dread that style of craft, capable of carrying a numerous crew, of pulling a large number of oars, and of running up a narrow river, or shallow lagoon, to escape pursuit.

At last we came up with the felucca. She lay hove-to with her head towards us. There was, certainly, a very suspicious look about her, from the very apathy with which the few people on deck regarded us. However, as we looked down on her deck, we saw six guns lashed along her bulwarks, and amidship there was something covered with a tarpaulin, which might be a heavier gun than the rest. We stood on till her broadside was brought to bear on our counter. At that moment, up sprung from each hatchway some sixty as ugly-looking cut-throats as I ever wish to see; and they were busily engaged in rapidly casting loose their guns; and we were on the point of firing, when, who should we see on their deck, but the old man who had been our passenger! He instantly recognised Captain Helfrich, who was standing near the taffrail, and making a sign to the crew of the felucca, they dived below as quickly as they had appeared. He took off his three-cornered hat and waved it to our captain, who waved his in return; and then he made a sign that he would come on board us.

Instantly the captain ordered the sails to be clewed up. Had the old gentleman been an admiral, he could not have been obeyed more promptly. A boat shoved off from the felucca with four hands in her, and he came on board us. The big negro was not with him, nor did I see him on the deck of the felucca. The captain and the stranger were closeted together for a quarter of an hour or more; and the latter then coming on deck, bowed, with somewhat mock politeness to the passengers, who were assembled staring at him, and stepped into his boat.

No sooner had he gone, than we again made sail. The felucca lay hove-to some little time. She then wore round, and stood after us. So rapidly did she come up with us, that it was very clear we had not the slightest chance of getting away from her, however much we might wish to do so. She kept us company all the day, and at night, in the first watch, I could see her shadowy form gliding over the sea astern of us.

Peter and I talked the matter over together in a whisper. "I'll tell you what I think is something like the truth," said he. "To my mind it's this:— When the captain was a young man out in these parts, he fell in with that old gentleman,—who isn't so old though as he pretends to be. Well, the captain went and did something to put himself in his power; and that's the reason the captain is so afraid of him. And then, from what I see, I suspect that the captain saved him from drowning, or maybe from hanging; or in some way or other preserved his life; and that makes him grateful, and ready to do the captain a good turn; or, at all events, prevents him from doing him a bad one. If it was not for that, we should have had all our throats cut by those gentry, if we hadn't managed to beat them off; and that would have been no easy job. I may be wrong altogether, but this is what I think," continued Peter. "There's one thing, particularly, I want to say to you, Jack: never go and do anything wrong, and fancy that it will end with the thing done. There's many a man who has done a wrong thing in his youth, and has gone through life as if he had a rope round his neck, and he has found it turning up here and there, and staring him in the face when he has least expected it. When once a bad thing is done, you can't get rid of it—you can't undo it—you can't get away from it, any more than you can call the dead to life. You may try to forget it; but something or other will always remind you of it, as long as you live. Then, remember there is another life we've got to look to, when every single thing we've done on earth must be remembered— must be acknowledged—must be made known. You and I, and every sailor, should know that any moment we may be sent into another world to begin that new life, and to stand before God's judgment-seat. I think of this myself sometimes; but I wish that I could think of it always; and that I ever had remembered it. Had I always thought of that awful truth, there are many things I could not possibly have ventured to do which I have done; and many things which I have left undone, which I should have done. Jack, my boy, I say I have done you some little good, but there's no good I could ever possibly do you greater than teaching you to remember that truth always. But I must not knock off this matter without warning you, that I may be thinking unjustly of the captain: and I certainly would not speak to anyone else aboard as I have done to you."

I thanked Peter for the advice he had given me, and promised that I would not repeat what he had said.

"Can you see the felucca, Tillson?" I heard Mr Gale say to Tom, who was reputed to have the sharpest eyes aboard.

"No, sir; she's nowhere where she was," he answered, after peering for some time into the darkness astern.

We all kept looking out for some time, but she did not reappear. The mate seemed to breathe more freely, and I must say that I was glad to be rid of the near neighbourhood of the mysterious stranger. When morning broke, she was nowhere to be seen. Whenever, during that and the following days, a sail appeared anywhere abaft the beam, till her rig was ascertained, it was instantly surmised that she was the felucca coming back to overhaul us. Even the mates did not seem quite comfortable about the matter; and the captain was a changed man. His usual buoyant spirits had deserted him, and he was silent and thoughtful. I could not help thinking that Peter's surmises were correct.

At last we brought up once more in Port-Royal Harbour. Having landed our passengers, and discharged our cargo, we sailed again for Morant Bay, Saint Thomas's, and other places along the coast, to take in a freight of sugar, which was sent down in hogsheads from the plantations in the neighbourhood.

We were rather earlier than usual, and we had some time to wait till the casks were ready for us. On one of these occasions the captain was invited by a planter, Mr Johnstone by name, to pay him a visit at his farm, which was some way up the country. In that climate every gentleman has a servant to attend on him; and all the planters, and others who live there, always have negroes to help them to wash and dress in the morning, to put on their stockings, and all that sort of thing. As the captain had no black fellow to wait on him, he told me that he should want me to accompany him, and I was too glad to have a chance of seeing something of the country. Meantime, to collect our freight faster, he had chartered a schooner which was lying idle in the harbour, and sent her round to the various smaller ports to pick it up, and to bring it to the brig. He had put her under charge of Mr Gale, who had with him Peter Poplar and several other of our men, and also a few blacks, who were hired as seamen.

I thought it very good fun when I found myself once more on a horse; I had not got on the back of one since I was a little boy in Dublin, and then, of course, there was no saddle nor stirrups, and only an old rope for a bridle. They are generally razor-backed beasts, with one or two raws, and blind, at least, of one eye. The captain was mounted on a strong Spanish horse well able to bear him, and I followed on a frisky little animal with his valise and carpet-bags.

I wish that I could describe the wonderful trees we passed. I remember the wild plantains, with huge leaves split into slips, and their red seed-pods hanging down at the end of twisted ropes; the tall palms, with their feathery tops; the monster aloes, with their long flashy thorny leaves; and the ferns as large as trees, and yet as beautifully cut as those in our own country, which clothed every hillside where a fountain flowed forth; and then the countless variety of creepers, whose beautiful tracery crowned every rock, and hung down in graceful festoons from the lofty trees. Now and then, as passing through a valley and mounting a hill, we stopped and looked back, we caught sight of the blue sparkling sea, with the brig and other vessels in the harbour; a few white sails glancing in the sun, between it and the horizon; and nearer to us, valleys with rich fields and streams of water, and orchards of oranges, limes, and shaddocks; and planters' houses with gardens full of beautiful flowers, and negro huts under the shade of the plantain-trees. Then there were those forest-giants, the silk-cotton-trees, and various kinds of fig-trees and pines, such as in the old world are never seen. But the creepers I have spoken of make the woods still more curious, and unlike anything at home. First, a creeper drops down from a branch 150 feet high, and then another falls close to it, and the wind blows and twists them together; others grow round it till it takes root, and form a lofty pillar which supports the immense mass of twisting and twining stems above. As we rode along, I saw from many a lofty branch the net-like nests of the corn-bird hanging at the end of long creepers. Those mischievous rascals, the monkeys, are fond of eggs, and will take great pains to get them; so the corn-bird, to outwit them, thus secures her nest. It has an entrance at the bottom, and is shaped like a net-bag full of balls. There the wise bird sits free from danger, swinging backwards and forwards in the breeze.

We slept that night at the house of a friend of the captain's, who had come out with him in the brig. It was a low building of one storey, with steps leading up to it, and built chiefly of wood. A veranda ran all the way round it. The rooms were very large, but not so handsomely furnished, I thought, as the captain's cabin. People do eat curious food in the West Indies. Among other things, there was a monkey on the table; but if it had not been for the name of the thing, I cannot say there was any harm in it. I got a bit of it after it was taken from the table, and it was very like chicken. There were lizards and snakes, which were very delicate. There was a cabbage cut from the very top of a lofty tree, the palmetto; but that tree is too valuable to be cut down often for the purpose. Then there were all sorts of sweetmeats and dishes made with them. I recollect a mass of guava-jelly swimming in a bowl full of cream, and wine, and sugar, and citron. There were plenty of substantials also; and wines and liquids of all sorts. I know that I thought I should very much like to live on shore, and turn planter. I had reason afterwards to think that they had bitters as well as sweets to taste, so I remained contented, as I have ever been, with my lot.

At night, the captain had a sofa given him to sleep on in the dining-room, and I had a rug in another corner. It was many a long night since I had slept on shore, and I was constantly startled by the strange noises I heard. Often it was only the wind rustling in the palm-trees; but when I opened my eyes, I saw one whole side of the room sparkling with flashes of light; then it would burst forth on the other side; and then here and there single bright stars would gleam and vanish; and lastly, the entire roof would be lighted up. I dared not wake the captain to ask what was the matter, and it was not till afterwards that I discovered that the light was produced by fireflies, which are far more brilliant than the glow-worms of more northern climes. I had gone to sleep, when, just before daybreak, I was again awoke by a most terrific yelling, and screeching, and laughing, and roaring. I thought that the savages were down upon us, or that all the wild beasts in the country were coming to devour us. I could stand it no longer, but shrieked out, "O captain, captain! what's going to happen us?" The captain started up, and listened, and then burst into a fit of laughter. "Why, you young jackanapes, they are only some of your brothers, the monkeys, holding a morning concert," said he. "Go to sleep again; don't rouse me up for such nonsense as that."

I found afterwards that the noise did proceed only from monkeys, though I did not suppose that such small animals could have made such hideous sounds. To go to sleep again, however, I found was impossible, as I had already enjoyed much more than I usually got on a stretch. The captain, on the contrary, went off again directly; but his sleep was much disturbed, for he tumbled about and spoke so loudly, that at times I thought he was awake and calling me. "You'll make me, will you?" I heard him say. "I don't fear you, Captain Ralph. I—a pirate—so I might have been called—I was but a lad—I consented to no deed of blood—It cannot be brought against me— Well, I know—I know—I acknowledge my debt to you.—You exact it to the uttermost—I'll obey you—The merchants deem me an honest trader—What would they say if they heard me called pirate?—Ha, ha, ha?" He laughed long and bitterly.

I was very glad that no one else was in the room to hear what the captain was saying. A stranger would certainly have thought much worse of him than he deserved. I had now been so long with him that I was confident, whatever he might have done in his youth, that he was now an honest and well-intentioned man. At the same time I could no longer have any doubts that Peter's surmises about him were correct, "That old gentleman aboard the felucca is Captain Ralph, then," I thought to myself, "If I ever fall in with him, I shall know how to address him, at all events." At length the captain awoke; and after an early breakfast, the owner took him round the plantation, and I was allowed to follow them.

The sugar-cane grows about six feet high, and has several stalks on one root. It is full of joints, three or four inches apart. The leaves are light green; the stalk yellow when ripe. The mode of cultivation is interesting. A trench is dug from one end of the field to the other, and in it longways are laid two rows of cane. From each joint of these canes spring a root and several sprouts. They come up soon after they are planted, and in twelve weeks are two feet high. If they come up irregularly, the field is set on fire from the outside, which drives the rats, the great destroyers of the cane, to the centre, where they are killed. The ashes of the stalks and weeds serve to manure the field, which often produces a better crop than before. The canes are cut with a billhook, one at a time; and being fastened together in faggots, are sent off to the crushing-mill on mules' backs or in carts. Windmills are much in use. The canes are crushed by rollers and as the juice is pressed out, it runs into a cistern near the boiling-house. There it remains a day, and is then drawn off into a succession of boilers, where all the refuse is skimmed off. To turn it into grains, lime-water is poured into it; and when this makes it ferment, a small piece of tallow, the size of a nut, is thrown in. It is next drawn into pots to cool, with holes in the bottom through which the molasses drain off. Rum is made from the molasses, which being mixed with about five times as much water, is put into a still.

There are three sorts of *cotton-trees*. One creeps on the earth like a vine; another is a bushy dwarf tree; and the third is as high as an oak. The second-named, after it has produced very beautiful flowers about the size of a rose, is loaded with a fruit as large as a walnut, the outward coat of which is black. This fruit, when it is fully ripe, opens, and a down is discovered of extreme whiteness, which is the cotton. The seeds are separated from it by a mill.

The stem of the cacao-tree is about four inches in diameter. In height it is about twelve feet from the ground. The cacao grows in pods shaped like cucumbers. Each pod contains from three to five nuts, the size of small chestnuts, which are separated from each other by a white substance like the pulp of a roasted apple. The pods are found only on the larger boughs, and at the same time the tree bears blossoms and young fruit. The pods are cut down when ripe, and allowed to remain three or four days in a heap to ferment. The nuts are then cut out, and put into a trough covered with plantain-leaves, where they remain nearly twenty days; and, lastly, dried three or four weeks in: the sun. Indigo is made from an herb not unlike hemp. This is cut, and put into pits with water; and being continually stirred up, forms a sort of mud, which, when dry, is broken into bits for exportation.

I will mention one plant more of general use—coffee. It is a shrub, with leaves of a dark-green colour. The berries grow in large clusters. The bean is enclosed in a scarlet pulp, often eaten, but very luscious. One bush produces several pounds. When the fruit is ripe, it turns black, and is then gathered; and the berries, being separated from the husk, are exposed to the sun till quite dry, when they are fit for the market.

However, I might go on all day describing the curious plants, and trees, and animals, and birds I saw. I must speak of the ginger. The blade is not unlike that of wheat. The roots, which are used, are dug up and scraped free from the outward skin by the negroes. This is the best way of preparing it, and it is then soft and white; but often, from want of hands, it is boiled, when the root becomes hard and tough, and is of much less value.

I shall never forget the beautiful humming-birds, with magnificent plumage gleaming in the sun, and tongues fine as needles, yet hollow, with which they suck the juices from flowers.

We did not, on account of the heat, recommence our journey till the afternoon. The planter accompanied us. I heard him and the captain talking about the outbreaks of the fugitive negroes in former days. "They are a little inclined to be saucy just now," I heard him remark. "But we taught them a lesson which they will not easily forget. Those we caught we punished in every way we could think of. Hanging was too mild for them. Some we burned before slow fires; others were tied up by the heels; and others were lashed to stakes, their bodies covered over with molasses to attract the flies, and then allowed to starve to death. Oh, we know how to punish rebels in this country."

I listened to what the planter was saying. I could scarcely believe the testimony of my ears. Was it really a man professing to be a Christian thus talking, thus boasting of the most horrible cruelties which even the fiercest savages could not surpass?

The captain replied, that he supposed they deserved what they got, though, for his part, he thought if a man was deserving of death, he should be hung or shot outright, but that he did not approve of killing people by inches.

From what I heard I was not surprised to find that there were large numbers of these revolted negroes, under the name of Maroons, living among the mountain-fastnesses in the interior of the island, where they could not be reached; that their numbers were continually augmented by runaway slaves; and that they declined to submit to the clemency of the whites. It was quite dark before we reached the house of the planter, where the captain proposed to spend a few days. It stood on the side of a hill covered with trees, and had a considerable slope below it. It was a rough wooden edifice, of one storey, though of considerable size, and had a veranda running round it. Besides the owner, there were the overseer, and two or three white assistants; and an attorney, a gentleman who manages the law business of an estate; and two English friends. Altogether, there was a large party in the house. During dinner the company began to talk about pirates, and I saw the captain's colour change. The attorney said that several piracies had been committed lately in the very neighbourhood of

Jamaica; and that unarmed vessels, in different parts of the West Indies, were constantly attacked and plundered. They remarked that it was difficult to find out these piratical craft. Sometimes the pirates appeared in one guise and sometimes in another; at one time in a schooner, at others in a felucca, or in a brig; and often even in open boats. "Yes," observed the attorney, "they seem to have excellent information of all that goes on in Kingston. I suspect that they have confederates on shore, who tell them all they want to know." I thought the captain would have fallen off his chair, but he quickly recovered himself, and no one appeared to have remarked his agitation. They did carry on, to be sure! What quantities of wine and rum-punch they drank! How their heads could stand it I don't know. Two or three of them did roll under the table, when their black slaves came and dragged them off to bed; which must have raised them in the negroes' opinion. Even the captain, who was generally a very sober man, got up and sang songs and made speeches for half an hour when no one was listening. At last the slaves cleared the dining-room, and beds were made up there for several of the party. I was afraid that the captain might begin to talk again in his sleep of his early days, and accuse himself of being a pirate; and I was anxious to warn him, lest anyone might be listening; but then, I thought to myself, they are all so drunk no one will understand him, and he won't like to be reminded by me of such things as that.

The night seemed to be passing quietly away. As I lay on a rug in the corner of the room, I could hear the sound of some night-birds, or frogs, or crickets, and the rustling of the wind among the plantain-leaves, till I fell asleep. Before long, however, I started up, and thought that the monkeys had begun their concert at an earlier hour than usual. There were the most unearthly cries and shrieks imaginable, which seemed to come from all sides of the house, both from a distance and close at hand. For a moment all was silent, and then they were repeated louder than before. Had not the company been heavy with drink, they must have been awoke at once. As it was, the second discharge of shrieks and cries roused them up, and in another minute people came rushing into the dining-hall from different parts of the house, their pale countenances showing the terror they felt. "What's the matter? what's all this?" they exclaimed.

"That the negroes have come down from the hills, and that we shall all be murdered!" exclaimed the master of the house, who had just hurried in with a rifle in his hand. "Gentlemen, we may defend ourselves, and sell our lives dearly, but that is all I can hope for."

"Let us see what can be done," said Captain Helfrich coolly. "This house may not stand a long siege, perhaps, though we'll do our best to prepare it. We'll block up the windows and all outlets as fast as we can. See, get all the rice and coffee bags to be found, and fill them with earth; we may soon build up a tolerably strong fortification."

The captain's confidence and coolness encouraged others, and every one set to work with a will to make the proposed preparations. All the household slaves, and several blacks residing in the neighbouring huts had come into the house to share their master's fortunes but the greater number had run away and hid themselves. There was no lack of muskets and ammunition; indeed, there were among us weapons sufficient to arm twice as many men as were assembled. The white gentlemen were generally full of fight, and began to talk hopefully of quickly driving back the Maroons: but the blacks were in a great state of excitement, and ran about the house chattering like so many monkeys, tumbling over each other, and rather impeding than forwarding the work to be done.

Though matters were serious enough, I, with a youngster's thoughtlessness, enjoyed a fit of laughter while we were in the middle and hottest hurry of our preparations. It happened that two stout blackies rushed into the hall from different quarters, one bearing on his back a sack of earth, the other a bundle of canes or battens. Tilt they went with heads stooping down right against each other. Their skulls met with a clap like thunder, and both went sprawling over on their backs, with their legs up in the air. The sack burst, and out tumbled the earth; and the bundle of canes separating, lay in a confused heap.

"For what you do dat, Jupiter?" exclaimed he of the canes, as he jumped up ready to make another butt at his opponent.

"Oh, ki! you stupid Caesar, you 'spose I got eyes all round," replied Jupiter, leaping on his legs with the empty sack hanging round his nook, and stooping down his head ready to receive the expected assault.

The black knights were on the point of meeting, and would probably each have had another fall, when one of the overseers passing bestowed a few kicks upon Caesar. Off ran the hero, and Jupiter expecting the same treatment, took himself off to bring in a fresh bag of earth.

Ten minutes or a quarter of an hour passed away, but still the rebels did not commence their attack. The overseer said that they had uttered the shrieks to frighten us, and also to get the slaves to desert us, that they might murder us alone. I should have supposed that, like other savages, they would have crept silently on us, so as to have taken us unawares; but negroes, I have remarked, seldom act like other races of people.

During the short time which had passed since the alarm was given, we had made very tolerable preparations to receive the rebels. I had been running about, trying to make myself as useful as I could, when the captain called me up to him.

"I'm glad to see you wide-awake, Jack," said he. "Remember, when the fight begins, as it will before long, stick close to me. I may want to send you here and there for something or other; and if the worst comes, and we are overpowered, we must try to cut our way out through the rascals. Now set to work, and load those muskets; you know how, I think. Ay, that will do; keep loading them as fast as I discharge them. We may teach the Niggers a lesson they don't expect."

I was very proud of being thus spoken to by the captain, for it was the first time that he had ever condescended to address me in so familiar a way. It was generally—"Boy, bring me my shoes;" "Jump forward there, and call the carpenter." I resolved to do my best not to disappoint him.

I placed the powder-flask and bullets on one side of me, and the muskets on the other, so that I could load one after the other without altering my position. It never occurred to me all the time that there was the slightest degree of danger. I thought that we had only to blaze away at the Niggers, and that they would run off as fast as their legs could carry them.

Never was I more mistaken. Soon after the captain had spoken to me we were startled by another thunder-clap of shouts, and shrieks, and unearthly cries, followed by several shot, the ringing taps which succeeded each showing that the bullets had struck the house. Presently a negro, who had been sent to keep a look-out on the roof, came tumbling through a skylight, exclaiming, "Dey is coming, dey is coming, oh ki!" Directly after this announcement, the shrieks and cries were heard like a chorus of demons, and it was evident that our enemies were closely surrounding us. Whichever way we turned, looking up the hill or down the valley, the terrific noises seemed to come loudest and most continuous from that quarter.

Captain Helfrich, as if by the direct appointment of all, took the command. "Now, my lads, be steady," he exclaimed; "don't throw your shots away. You'll want all you've got, and a bullet is worth the life of a foe."

Each man on this grasped his musket; but the negroes held theirs as if they were very much more afraid of the weapons doing them harm than of hurting their enemies. The greater number of the lights in the house had been put out, a few lanterns only remaining here and there, carefully shaded, to show us our way about. Not a word or a sound was uttered by any of us, and thus in darkness and silence we awaited the onslaught of our enemies.

Chapter Five
The Planter's House Besieged

The Maroons did not leave us long in suspense. Once more uttering the most fearful and bewildering shrieks, they advanced from every quarter, completely surrounding, as we judged, the house. For a minute they halted, and must have fired every musket they had among them. Loopholes had been left in all the windows, and every now and then I peeped through one of them, to try and discover what was taking place. There was just sufficient light to enable me to see the dusky forms of the rebels breaking through the fences and shrubberies which surrounded the house. As they arrived, they formed in front, dancing, and shrieking, and firing off their muskets and blunderbusses in the most irregular fashion, expending a great deal of gunpowder, but doing us no harm.

Captain Helfrich was watching them. When some hundreds had been thus collected, he suddenly exclaimed, "Now, my lads, give it them! Don't throw your shots away on the bushes!"

Obedient to the order, every man in the house fired, and continued firing as fast as he could load his musket. I dropped on my knee alongside the arms the captain had appropriated, and as I handed a loaded musket to him he gave me back the one he had fired, which I reloaded as rapidly as I could.

This continued for some minutes, the constant shrieks and groans of our black assailants showing us that the shot frequently took effect. I believe, indeed, that very few of the captain's missed. Though he fired rapidly, it was always with coolness and steadiness, and it appeared to me that he had singled out his victim before he turned round to take the musket from me.

As yet none of our people had been killed, though some of the enemy's shot had found their way through the loopholes in the windows and doors. Growing, however, more desperate at the loss of their companions, and burning for revenge, they rushed up closer to the house, pouring in their fire, which searched out every hole and cranny. Some of the slaves who incautiously exposed themselves were the first to suffer. A poor fellow was standing at the window next to me. A bullet struck him on the breast. It was fired from a tree, I suspect. Down he fell, crying out piteously, and writhing in his agony. It was very dreadful. Then the blood rushed out of his mouth in torrents, and he was quiet. I sprang forward, intending to help him. The pale light of the lantern fell on his countenance. He looked perfectly calm. I thought he was resting, and would get up soon and fire away again. My glance was but momentary, for the captain called me back to my post.

The fire on this became hotter and hotter. Two more negroes were struck. They did not fall, but cried out most piteously. One of the English gentlemen was next shot. He fell without a groan. The captain told me to run and see where he was hurt. I tried to lift him up, but his limbs fell down motionless. There was a deep hole in his forehead, through which blood was bubbling. I suspected the truth that he was dead. I told the captain that he was hit on the head. "Leave him, then, Jack," said he; "you can do him no good."

On my return, I looked at the negro who had been first hit. He, too, was motionless. I tried to place him in a sitting posture, but he fell back again.

"Let him alone, Jack," cried the captain; "his work is done; he's no longer a slave."

I thus found that the negro also was dead. It seemed very dreadful to me; I burst into tears.

I cried heartily as I knelt loading the muskets, forgetting that in a short time the captain, and I, and every one in the house, might be in the same state. Had not the whites shown great determination, all must before this have fallen victims to the rage of the Maroons. Numbers of our enemies were shot, but still they rushed on, resolved to destroy the house and all in it.

While the uproar they made was at its height, a loud battering was heard at one of the doors. The enemy had cut down the trunk of a young tree, and were endeavouring to break in the door with it. The captain and the other gentlemen shot down several who were thus engaged, but still they persevered; and, as some fell, fresh assailants rushing up, seized the battering-ram, and continued the work. The door was stout, but we saw that it was giving way. It began to crack in every direction. Pieces of furniture and sand-bags were piled up against it, but with little avail. Each blow shattered a part of it, and soon, with a loud crash, it was driven in, and the fierce, excited faces of our dark foes were seen above the barricade formed by the bags, and furniture, and broken door. Several who attempted to pass over it were shot down, but our people being now much more than ever exposed to the fire of the enemy, proportionably suffered. The shot came in thick among us, and one after the other was wounded.

While the captain and others were defending the breach, the battering-ram was withdrawn; why, we were not long left in doubt. To our great horror, the battering, cracking sound was heard in the rear of the house. Still we were not at once to be defeated, and some of our party hurried to defend the spot. The attack on the front-door had cost the negroes so many lives that they were more cautious in approaching the second; and, when our party began to fire, they retreated under shelter, leaving the trunk of the tree on the ground. At the same time, they began apparently to weary of their ill success in front of the house; for of course they could not be aware that they had killed any of its defenders. We were thus hoping that they would at length withdraw, when the whole country in front of us seemed to burst into flame.

"They have set the fields on fire!" exclaimed the planter.

"No, no," said Captain Helfrich; "worse than that—see there? Our watch is out, depend on that. Not one of us will see another sun arise. So, my men, let us sally out, and sell our lives dearly."

I looked through one of the loopholes to see what he meant. Emerging from among the trees came hundreds of dusky forms, each man bearing in his hand a torch which he flourished wildly above his head, dancing and shrieking furiously.

I thought the captain's advice would be followed, but it was not. The rest of the party were either too badly wounded or wanted nerve for the exploit, and the slaves could not be depended on. All we did was to guard the battered-in door, and to fire away as before.

On came the Maroons with their frantic gestures, and, to our horror, as soon as they reached the door, they began to throw their torches in among us. At first we tried to trample out the fire under foot, but they soon outmastered our powers, and the furniture which composed our barricade ignited, so did the walls of the house, and the negroes shrieking and cheering, encouraged each other in throwing in fresh torches to overwhelm us. Still, induced to fight on by my gallant captain, we continued our exertions, when the attack on the back-door was renewed. It gave way! Loud shouts burst from the Maroons. Their revenge was about to be satiated.

"Now, my lads, follow me," shouted the captain; "we'll cut our way through them. Stick to me, Jack, whatever you do!"

As he said this, he seized a cutlass which lay on the ground, and, before the negroes had time to bring the torches round to that side, he rushed through the back-door which they had just battered down. I clung to his skirts as he told me, springing along so as not to impede him; and so heartily did he lay about him with his weapon, cutting off by a blow a head of one and an arm of another, that he speedily cleared himself a wide passage. Several of our party endeavoured to follow him with such weapons as they could seize, but, unable to make the progress he did, they were either knocked down and captured or killed on the spot. On we went towards the wood behind the house, but we had still numberless enemies on every side of us,—enemies who seemed resolved not to allow any of their intended victims to escape them. I did not think it possible that any man could keep so many foes at bay as did the captain. Just as I thought we should escape, his foot caught in a snake-like creeping root which ran along the ground. Over he went almost flat on his face; but he did not lose a grasp of his sword. He tried to rise, and I endeavoured to pull him up. He was almost once more on his feet, when another creeper caught his foot. Again he fell, and this time our enemies were too quick for him. Rushing on him by hundreds, they threw themselves on his body, almost suffocating him as they held him down by main force. I was treated much in the same way, when a huge negro caught me up by the back of the neck, and made as if he was about to cut off my head. He did not do so, but held me tightly by the collar while the rest secured the captain.

Flames were now bursting forth from every part of the planter's house, and lighted up the surrounding landscape,—the tall plantains and cotton and fig-trees, the tangled mass of creepers and their delicate tracery as they hung from their lofty boughs, the fields of sugar-cane, the cactus-bushes, and numberless other shrubs, and the grey sombre mountain-tops beyond. From the way the blacks were running here and there in dense masses, and the excited shouts I heard, I discovered that they were in pursuit of some of the late defenders of the house, who, when too late, were endeavouring to make their escape. Had they closely followed the captain, they might all, perhaps, have cut their way through the enemy.

The blacks seemed to consider the captain a perfect Samson, for they lashed his arms and legs in every way they could think of; and then making a sort of litter, they put him on it, and carried him along towards the mountains. They treated me with less ceremony. My first captors handed me over to four of them, who contented themselves with merely binding my arms, and driving me before them at the points of their weapons. Now and then one of them, more vicious than the rest, would dig the point of his spear into me, to expedite my movement. I could not help turning round each time with a face expressive, I daresay, of no little anger or pain, at which his companions all laughed, as if it were a very good joke. They seemed to do this to recompense themselves for the loss of the booty they might have supposed the rest were collecting from the burning house.

We had not proceeded far before we were joined by a large band, carrying along, bound hand and foot, the survivors among the defenders of the house. The planter himself, and four or five of his guests, were there, and seven or eight slaves. From the disappearance of the rest of the Maroons, I concluded that they had gone off to attack some other residences.

On we went hour after hour, and when the sun rose, exposed to its broiling heat, without stopping. The negroes ate as they went along, but gave us nothing. It would have been a painful journey, at all events; but when we expected to be tortured and put to death at the end of it, I found it doubly grievous to be endured. I longed for a dagger, and that I might find my arms free, to fight my way out from among them. At last I thought that it would be the best way to appear totally unconcerned when they hurt me, so that I became no longer a subject for their merriment.

At length, about noon, we stopped to rest; and most of our guards, after eating their meal of plantains, went to sleep. I thought that it would be a good opportunity to try and get near the captain, to learn if he thought that there was any chance of our escaping. Some few of the Maroons, with arms in their hands, sat up watching us narrowly; I therefore put on as unconcerned a manner as possible, and lay down on the ground, pretending to go to sleep likewise. I in return watched our guards, and one by one I saw sleep exerting its influence over them. Their eyes rolled round in their heads like those of owls; their heads nodded; then they looked up, trying to appear prodigiously wise; but it would not do, and at length the whole camp was asleep. I considered that now or never was my time for communicating with the captain. Though I saw that no one near was likely to observe me, I thought that some one at a distance might, and therefore that it would be necessary to be cautious. Instead of getting up and walking, I rolled myself gently over and over till I got close up to him.

"Captain," said I, very softly — "Captain Helfrich, sir. I am here. What can I do?"

He was drowsy, and at first did not hear me; but soon rousing himself, he turned his eyes towards me, for he could not move his head. "Ah, Jack! is that you?" said he; "we are in a bad plight, lad."

"Do you think the savages are going to kill us, sir?" said I.

"No doubt about it, Jack, if we are not rescued, or don't manage to escape," he answered. "I see little prospect of either event."

"But what can I do, sir?" I asked.

"Little enough, I am afraid, lad," he replied, in a subdued, calm tone. "But stay, if you can manage to get your hands near my teeth, I will try and bite the bands off them, and then you can loosen the lashings round my limbs. We must wait for the night before we try to escape. We should now be seen, and pursued immediately."

I did as he bid me, and by means of his strong teeth he was soon able to free my hands from the ropes which had confined them. I also at length, with much more difficulty, so far slackened all his bands and the lashings which secured him to the litter, that he might with ease slip his limbs completely out of them. Having accomplished this important undertaking, I crawled back to the spot I had before occupied. Scarcely had I got there, when a black lifted up his head and looked around. I thought he had fixed his malignant eyes on me, and had probably been a witness of what I had done. I lay trembling, expecting every moment to have the wretch pounce upon me and bind my hands tighter than before. However, after a little, he lay down again, and grunted away as before.

Soon after this another Maroon sat up and looked round, and then another, and another; so that I was very glad I had not lost the opportunity of which I had taken advantage. In another quarter of an hour, the whole force was on the move. I looked anxiously to ascertain whether they had discovered that the captain's bands had been loosened; but without examining him, they lifted up the litter, and bore him on as before. In consequence of this I walked on much more cheerily than I had previously done, though I still got an occasional prick to hasten my steps.

As we advanced, we got into still more hilly and wild country. All signs of cultivation had ceased, and vegetation revelled in the most extravagant profusion. Our chief difficulty was to avoid the prickly pears, and the cacti, and the noose-forming creepers, which extended across our path. We were in the advance party; the rest of the white men followed at a distance from us, so that we had no prospect of communicating with them.

The encouragement the captain had given me helped to raise my spirits, and I endeavoured further to keep them up by whistling and singing occasionally, but it was with a heavy heart that I did so. My great consolation was all the time that my friend Peter Poplar was not in the same predicament. He would have felt it more than any of us. He had long been prepared for any misfortune which could happen to him at sea, but he had not made up his mind to undergo hardships on shore as well.

At last I began to grow very weary of walking so far over such rough and uneven ground, and I was glad to find that the blacks were approaching their encampment or village. It consisted of a number of rude huts, built on the summit of a high rock, with steep precipices on every side. A narrow causeway led to it from another rock, which jutted out from the side of the hill. It was a very strong place, for it extended too far into the valley to be reached by musketry from the hill; and the hill itself was too rugged to allow cannon to be dragged up it. The rock appeared to have rude palisades and embankments, to serve as fortifications, over a large portion of its upper surface. As I examined it, I saw that our chance of escape from such a place, by any method I could imagine, was small indeed. I do not know what the captain thought about the matter, but he was not a man to be defeated by difficulties, or to abandon hope while a spark of life remained.

As we went along the causeway, a number of women, and children, and dogs came out to meet us, our welcome consisting in a most horrible screaming, and crying, and barking, which, I suspect, as far as the prisoners were concerned, was far from complimentary. Among them were some dreadful old crones, who came stretching out their withered, black, parchment arms, shrieking terrifically, and abusing the white men as the cause of all the misery and hardships it had been their lot to endure. Their accusations were, I believe, in most respects, too just. Certainly white men had torn them or their ancestors from their native land—white men had brought them across the sea in the crowded slave-ship—white men had made them slaves, treated them with severity and cruelty, and driven them to seek for freedom from tyranny among the wild rocks and fastnesses where they were now collected. The other prisoners seemed to feel, by their downcast, miserable looks, that they were in the power of enemies whom they had justly made relentless, and that they had no hope of escape. The old crones went up to them, pointed their long bony fingers in their eyes, and hissed and shrieked in their ears. What was said I could not understand, but they were evidently using every insulting epithet they could imagine to exasperate or terrify their victims.

I have often thought of that dreadful scene since. How must the acts of those white men have risen up before them in their true colours—the wrong they had inflicted on young and innocent girls—the lashes bestowed on men of free and independent natures—the abuse showered on their heads—the total neglect of the cultivation of all their moral attributes! Oh, you Christian gentlemen, did it ever occur to you that those slaves of yours were men of like passions as yourselves; that they had minds capable of cultivation in a high degree, if not as high as your own; that they had souls like your souls to be saved—souls which must be summoned before the judgment-seat of Heaven, to be judged with yours; and that you and they must there stand together before an all-righteous and pure and just God, to receive the reward of the things you have done in this life? Did it occur to you that, had you made those people true Christians; that, had you taught them the holy religion you profess—a religion of love and forgiveness—that they would not now be taking pleasure in tormenting you, in exhibiting the bitter vengeance which rankled in their souls!

I could not help thinking that some such accusing thoughts as these rose to the consciences of the planter and his companions. I know that I would not for worlds have changed places with him, though he was the owner of rich fields and wealth long hoarded up, which he was on the point of returning to England to enjoy.

Either on account of my youth, or because, as they saw, I was a sailor, the rebels must have known that I could not have treated them cruelly, and I was allowed to remain quiet. After the whole population had given vent to their feelings by abusing the prisoners in every possible way, they were thrust into a hut together, and a guard placed over them. The captain and I were then put into another hut, and ordered not to stir on pain of being shot.

"Not bery good chance of dat!" observed one of our captors, a grey-headed old negro with a facetious countenance, looking at the numerous lashings which confined our limbs.

"Better chance than you suppose, old fellow!" thought I to myself; but I kept as melancholy and unconcerned a look as I could assume.

I concluded, that as the other prisoners were guarded so were we, and that we should have very little chance of effecting our escape, unless our guards fell asleep. The difficulties were, at all events, very great. We should, in the first place, have either to scramble down the sides of the rock, or to cross the narrow causeway, where one man as a guard could instantly stop us. There was every probability that the Maroons would place one there.

For some hours there was a great deal of noise in the village. The blacks were rejoicing over their victory, and there was no chance of our guards outside the hut being asleep. I waited, therefore, without moving, till the sounds of revelry subsided, the tom-toms were no longer beaten, the trumpets ceased braying, and the cymbals clashing. Then I could hear the guards talking to each other outside. The few words I could comprehend out of this jargon were not very consolatory. I made out clearly that they proposed to shoot all their prisoners the next day, and that, besides those already in camp, they expected a number more from other estates which were to be attacked. There appeared only a possibility that our lives might be prolonged another day, till all their forces out on various expeditions were assembled. Little did those at home, looking at the map of Jamaica, fancy that, in the very centre of that beautiful island, there existed so numerous a band of savages in open revolt against the authority of the king.

At first our guards were animated enough in their conversation; then their voices grew thicker and thicker, and their tones more drowsy and droning, till they could scarcely have understood what each other said. At last one began to snore, then another, and the last speaker found himself without auditors. I longed for him to hold his tongue, and to go to sleep, but talk on he would, though he had no listeners. This, I thought, was a good opportunity to allow me to speak to the captain, so I crawled up to him. He was awake, waiting for me.

"What's to be done now, captain?" said I.

"We must wait the course of events, Jack," he answered. "I have been turning over every plan in my mind which affords a chance of escape. If we were to start off now, we should certainly be caught by some of these black gentlemen; and if brought back, we should be put under stricter watch and ward than hitherto. Something may occur during the night, or perhaps to-morrow. At all events, I do not intend to die without a fight for it. Try and go to sleep now, and get some rest; you'll want it for what you may have to go through. Go, lie down, lad; my advice is good. Don't fear."

I followed the captain's advice, though it was difficult to go to sleep, and still more so not to fear. I did go to sleep, however, and never slept more soundly in my life. I was awoke by feeling a hand placed on my shoulder. It was that of the captain.

"Jack," he whispered, "be prepared to follow me if I summon you, but not otherwise. If we can manage to get down the rock, or to cross the causeway without being seen, we will go; but if not, we must wait another opportunity. I do not feel as if either of us had come to the end of the cable yet, but how we are to get free I don't know."

Saying this the captain gently lifted up some of the leaves which formed the side of the hut, and crept out. His words and tone gave me great encouragement. I wished that I could have gone with him, but I knew that I must obey him.

O how anxiously I waited his return! Minute after minute passed away, and still he did not come back. I began to fear that some harm had happened to him—that he might have fallen over the precipice in the dark, or have been captured. It never for a moment occurred to me that he would desert me. An hour or more must have passed. Still he did not appear. I began to consider whether I could not creep out to search for him. I could have loosened from off me the ropes which bound my arms in an instant; but I did not want to do so unless I was prepared to run away altogether. I have heard of people's hair turning grey in a night; mine would, I think, have done so with anxiety had I been older.

At last the side of the hut was lifted up, and the captain crawled in, and placed himself on the litter on which he had been brought to the place. "Quick, Jack," he whispered, "put the ropes round me as they were before! Those blacks are more wide-awake rascals than I fancied. I have been most of the time lying down not twenty yards from the hut, afraid to move. I was creeping along when I saw a black fellow, with musket on shoulder, emerge from behind a hut. He stood for some time looking directly at me, as if he had seen me. He had not though; but directly afterwards he began pacing up and down with the steadiness of an old soldier. I crept on when his back was turned, but never could move far enough before he was about again, and scrutinising all the ground before him. The only direction in which I could move without the certainty of being seen was towards this spot, so back again I have come, with the hope still strong that we might find some other way of escaping. Once or twice I thought of springing up and killing the man; but in so doing I should very likely have roused others, and we should have lost any future chance of escaping."

This result of the captain's expedition put me into low spirits again, for I fully expected that the blacks would kill us all in the morning, and my only surprise was that they had not so done already. I did not say so to the captain, but he, having with his teeth secured the bands round my arms again, I went and sat down where the blacks had first placed me. I did not sleep soundly again, nor did he. I sat silent, anxiously waiting for the morning.

I think I must have gone off into a doze, when, before daybreak, I was roused up by a chorus of loud cries and shouts, which was soon answered by every man, woman, and child in the village, who came rushing out of their huts. It was to welcome, I found, a party of their comrades from an attack on one of the neighbouring estates, in which they had come off the victors, with numerous prisoners and much spoil. There began, as before, a horrible din of tom-toms and other musical instruments, mixed with the very far from musical voices of the old women who had been tormenting us. This continued till the sun rose, and then there was a comparative silence for an hour or so. I suppose the savages were breakfasting. An this time we were left in suspense as to what was to be our fate. We did not talk much, and, of course, did not allude to any plan for escaping, lest we should be overheard.

At last several stout negroes entered the hut, and while some of them lifted up the captain and carried him out, two seized me by the collar, and dragged me after him. I thought that they were about to throw us over the cliffs, or to hang us or shoot us forthwith. I could only think of one way by which we had the slightest prospect of escaping. It was that the government authorities might have heard of the outbreak, and sent troops to attack the rebels. I did not know in those days that those sort of gentlemen considered the art of tying up packages neatly with red tape to be the most important of their official duties, and that they were not apt to do anything in a hurry of so trifling importance as attempting to save the lives of a few people!

We very soon reached a large concourse of people in an open space. On one side of the ground there was a steep bank, on the top of which a chair or throne was placed, whereon sat a tall fine-looking negro, dressed somewhat in military style, while a number of other men sat round him. On the level ground, on one side, was a group of some twenty white men, among whom I recognised our companions in the defence of the house. They had their hands bound, and were strongly guarded by armed negroes. We were carried up and placed among them. Two or three other prisoners arrived after us, and served to increase our unhappy group.

A sort of trial was then commenced, and several Maroons stepped forward, accusing the whites of unheard-of cruelties, and especially of being taken with arms in our hands against the authority of the true and proper chief of the island. It is impossible to describe the absurd language used, and the ceremonies gone through. It would have been a complete burlesque had not the matter been somewhat too serious. As it was, when one of the counsellors kicked another for interrupting him, and the judge threw a calabash at their heads to call them to order, I could not help bursting into a fit of laughter, which was soon quelled when one of my guards gave me a progue with the tip of his spear, to remind me where I was. I very nearly broke out again when the one who was hit looked up and exclaimed, "What dat for, Pompey, you scoundrel you?—What you tink me made of, hey?"

The judge took no notice of this address, but coolly went on summing up the evidence placed before him. It was, I must own, clearly condemnatory of most of the prisoners. On the oaths of the negro witnesses, they were proved to have committed the most atrocious acts. Some had hung blacks for no sufficient cause, or had shot them, or had beaten them to death, or even burned them, or had tortured them with every refinement of cruelty. Scarcely one present who had not given way to passion, and barbarously ill-treated their slaves, or caused them to submit to the greatest indignity. At length the judge rose from his seat. He was a remarkably fine, tall man, and as he stretched out one arm towards the prisoners, I could not help acknowledging that there was much grace and dignity in his whole air and manner. To what had been adduced by others, he added the weight of his own testimony.

"Me prince not long ago in me own country,—me would be king now,—me carried off—beaten—kicked—wife torn away—me piccaninnis killed—me made to work with whip—beat, beat, beat on shoulders—me run away—nearly starve and die. Dose men do all dat, and much worse! Day deserve to die! Shoot dem all—quick! De earth hate dem—no stay on it longer!" I cannot pretend to say that these were the exact words used by the chief, but they had a similar signification.

Immediately we were all seized, each prisoner being held by four blacks, and marched along to an open space near the edge of the precipice. A firing-party of twenty blacks, which had been told off, followed us, their horrible grins showing the intense satisfaction they felt at being our executioners. The judge or chief and all the rest of the people accompanied us as spectators. The captain was carried along on his litter, for the negroes had conceived a very just idea of his prowess, and kept him, as they fancied, more strongly secured than was necessary with regard to the rest. I stood near him waiting the result.

Things were now, indeed, looking very serious, and I could not see by what possible means we should escape. Still, there was so much buoyancy in my disposition, that, even then, I did not give up all hope. I am afraid that I cannot say I was sustained by any higher principle. The thought of what death was, did, however, come over me; and I tried to pray, to prepare myself for the world into which I saw every probability that I was about to enter. Still, though I wanted to pray, and wished to go to heaven, I made but a very feeble attempt to do so. I had been so long unaccustomed to pray, that I could not now find the thoughts or the words required. My heart was not in a praying state. I had not sought reconciliation with God. I did not know in what to trust, through whom I could alone go into the presence of my Maker cleansed from my sins, relieved from the weight of the sinful nature in which I was born. Of all this I remained perfectly ignorant. I felt very wretched, like a drowning wretch without a spar or a plank of which I might catch hold.

I learned, however, an important lesson. Oh! do you, who read this notice of my life, learn it from me. Do not suppose that the time is *coming* when you may begin to prepare for another world. The time is *come now* with all of you. From the period you entered this world, from the moment the power of thought and speech was given you, the time had arrived for you prepare for the world to come—that eternal world of glory and joy unspeakable, or of misery, regret, and anguish. Remember this—note it well—don't ever let it be out of your thoughts. You were sent into this transient, fleeting world, for one sole object—that you might prepare yourselves in it for the everlasting future. Not that you might amuse yourselves—not that you might gain wealth, and honours, and reputation—not that you might study hard, and obtain prizes at school or college—that you might be the leader in all manly—exercises—that you might speak well, or sing well, or draw well, or attain excellence in science—or that you might become rich merchants, or judges, or generals, or admirals, or ambassadors, or, indeed, attain the head of any professions you may choose. These things are all lawful; it may be your duty thus to rise, but it should not be your aim, it should not alone be in your thoughts; you should have a far higher motive for labouring hard, for employing your talents: that motive should be to please God, to obey the laws and precepts of our Lord and Master. All should be done from love to him. If you have not got that love for him, pray for it, strive for it, look for guidance from above that you may obtain it.

But, as I was saying, in those days I could not have comprehended what I have now been speaking about. Finding my efforts to pray almost unavailing, I did pray for deliverance, though I waited my fate in sullen indifference, or rather, indeed, somewhat as if I was an unconcerned spectator of what was taking place.

The chief lifted his arm on high as a sign that the execution was to commence. The first person led forward was the planter whose house we had attempted to defend. Oh! what scorn, and loathing, and defiance there was depicted in his countenance! What triumph and hatred in that of his executioners! Should such feelings find room in the bosom of a dying Christian? I wot not. Again the fatal sign was given. The firing-party discharged their muskets, and the planter fell a lifeless corpse. I tried to turn my eyes away from the scene, but they were rivetted on the spot.

Chapter Six
A Terrible Execution, and a Narrow Escape

One after the other my white companions were led out for execution. Every moment I expected that my turn would come. Very few showed any great signs of fear, with the exception of the overseers, who had been often and often the actual instruments of cruelty towards those who now had them in their power. I am surprised that the ignorant savage blacks did not torture them as they had themselves been tortured, before putting an end to their existence. Perhaps they wished to set an example of leniency to the civilised whites. They went about the execution, however, with deliberation, sufficient to make it a very terrible affair.

They shot the planter dressed as he was taken. When he had fallen, numbers of the blacks rushed up, and having stripped him, they threw his body, after inflicting numberless wounds on it, over the precipice. As his clothes had been injured by the bullets, they proceeded to strip the next person of his garments, with the exception of his trousers and shoes, which they allowed him to retain—the latter, at all events, being of very little use to them. He was one of the overseers, a fierce, dark, stern man. He looked as if he was incapable of experiencing any of the softer sympathies of our nature. He was standing close to me while the planter was being shot, and not one of us knew who would next be selected for execution. When the men who had taken out the overseer seized hold of him, he turned deadly pale, and shrieked out for mercy.

"Don't kill me! don't kill me!" he exclaimed. "I am not fit to die. I cannot go as I am into another world. Oh, let me live! let me live! I will toil for you; I will build your cottages; I will till your fields. Kind Africans! hear me: if I have injured anyone, I will repay him an hundred-fold. I'll do anything you require of me; but don't, oh, don't kill me!"

The negro chief smiled at him scornfully, and the others who surrounded him grinned horribly in his face. "Hi! hi! you mark my back with hot iron," said one, gripping him by the shoulder; "you take out de mark?"

"You kill my piccaninni!" cried another in a hissing tone in his ear. "You gib him back, eh? You make him smile in me face 'gain, eh?"

"You take away me young wife!" exclaimed another, in a hoarse voice, looking him in the face. "Where she gone to now, eh? You give her back good and fond as she once was—no! You repay a hundred-fold!—you undo the harm you have done!"

"Wretched man! go meet the Judge whose laws you have outraged; go encounter the reproachful spirits of those who, in life, you have irretrievably injured! You are a blot on the world; you must be put out of it. You must stand before your Almighty Judge, your God. He is a God of mercy to those who have shown mercy. But have you shown it? No! Still you must die!"

The latter expressions were, of course, not uttered by the negroes, but something very similar was said; and amid the shouts and execrations of the multitude, the wretched man was dragged out, and being shot down, a hundred weapons were plunged in his yet warm and writhing body ere he was thrown over the cliff to be food for the fowls of the air, which, in spite of the firing, had already settled on the body of the planter, once his superior, now his wretched equal.

The same scene was enacted with several others. In vain they pleaded for life, in vain they offered rewards—large bribes, freedom to some, the means of returning to Africa to others who had been brought over. The negroes laughed all offers to scorn. No promises were believed: too often had they been made and broken; too exquisitely cruel and barbarous had been the punishments inflicted on prisoners taken in former outbreaks, to allow them to lose the gratification of their present revenge.

Often, as this scene has occurred to my mind, have I thought of what would be the fate of the planters, and overseers, and other white residents in the Slave States of the American Union, should the negroes ever find an opportunity of revolting. What sanguinary massacres would take place! what havoc and destruction would be the result! Few men have a better right to speak on the subject than I have. I was born before that great country called the United States was a nation. When I could walk, they were part and parcel of England. I have talked with men who were engaged in active life before the great Washington saw the light; who fought against the French on the heights of Abraham, under the hero Wolfe, and aided to win one of the brightest of her jewels for the British crown. I, therefore, cannot help looking on the Americans in the light of children—dear relatives; and when I address them, I speak to them with love and affection. I say to them, take warning from the scene I have been describing; do not submit to the incubus of slavery a moment longer than you can avoid it. No sensible man expects you to throw it off at once; but every right-feeling, right-thinking man, does expect you to take every means and make every preparation for its abolition, as soon as that important work can be accomplished. The only means you have of effecting this object with safety to yourselves, and with justice to those beings with immortal souls now intrusted by an inscrutable decree of Providence to your care, is by educating them, by making them Christians, by preparing them for liberty, by setting them an example which they may hereafter follow. Teach them to depend on their own exertions for support—to govern themselves—raise them in the scale of humanity: treat them as men should men, and not as Christians so-called treat the hapless sons of Africa. Remember that the British West India Islands were brought to the verge of ruin, and numberless families depending on them were ruined, not because the slaves were made free, but because they were not properly prepared for freedom. Whose fault was that? Not that of the British Government, not that of the nation; but of the planters themselves, of the white inhabitants of the island. They refused to the last to take any steps to Christianise, to educate, to raise the moral character of the negroes; and of course the negroes, when no longer under restraint, revelled in the barbarism in which they had been allowed to remain, with all the vices consequent on slavery superadded.

Should these remarks be read by any citizens of the American Slave States, I trust that they will remember what Old Jack says to them. He has reason to wish them well, to love them, for he has received much kindness at the hands of many of their fellow-countrymen; and he repeats that they have the power in their own hands to remove for ever from off them the stigma which now attaches to their name. He does not urge them to do it in consequence of any pressure from without—not at the beck and call of foreigners, but from their own sense of justice; because they are convinced that they are doing their duty to God and man; and lastly, that they will be much better served by educated, responsible freemen, than by slaves groaning in bondage, and working only from compulsion. (See Note.)

But avast! I cry. I have been driving a long way from the scene I was describing. The negroes I have been mentioning were men who had been slaves, and had made themselves free, and we see the way they treated the whites whom they had got into their power. They were, it must be granted, savages, barbarians, heathens. Their people, who had been captured as rebels, had been treated by their white Christian conquerors with every refinement of cruelty which the malice of man could invent: they had been slain with the most agonising tortures; and yet these savages, disdaining such an example, merely shot their prisoners, killing them without inflicting an unnecessary pang. I cannot say that at the time, however, I thought that they were otherwise than a most barbarous set.

One after the other my companions were led out and shot, and treated as their predecessors. One, a sturdy Englishman, who had not been long in the country, it seemed, broke loose, and knocked down several of his guards. He fought long and bravely with them. Had he been able to get hold of a weapon, he would, I believe, have cut his way out from among them. As it was, his fists served him in good stead; and he had already very nearly cleared himself a path, when a shot from pistol struck him on the knee, and brought him to the ground. Still he struggled bravely; but the negroes, throwing themselves on him, completely overpowered him, and he was at once dragged up to the place of execution. Before he had time to look around, or to offer up a prayer to Heaven, a dozen bullets had pierced his body, and he who was but lately so full of life and strength was a pallid corpse! I scarcely like to describe the dreadful scene. Even now I often shudder as I think of it. I have seen men shot down in battle—I have beheld numbers struggling in the raging sea, which was about to prove their grave; but I never saw men in full health and strength waiting for their coming death without the means of struggling for life—I have never seen men deprived of life in so cool and deliberate a way—I have never so surely expected to be deprived myself of life.

Our numbers had now been dreadfully thinned; the captain, and I, and three others only remained alive. One of those had become a raving maniac, his mind had given way under the horror of death; but now he feared nothing; he laughed the murderers to scorn; with shouts of derision on his lips he was shot down. The next man was seized: calmly he walked to the spot, and he likewise fell. Will it be the captain next, or I, or the only other remaining prisoner? The latter was seized: he looked up to the bright blue sky; to the green woods, waving with rich tropical luxuriance of foliage; to the dark faces of the surrounding multitude; and then at us two, his companions in misfortune; and I shall never forget the look of anguish and terror I saw there depicted. He saw no help, no chance of escape; in another instant he also was numbered with the dead. Then, indeed, my heart sank within me, for I expected to be like those who were to mortal eyes mere clods of earth. But instead of seizing me, they approached the captain. Before, however, they could lay their hands on him, his bonds seemed as if by superhuman strength to be torn asunder, and up he sprung to do battle for life! The negroes literally sprung back as they saw him with amazement, and on he bounded towards their chief. No one tried to stop him, and in another instant he had thrown his powerful well-knit limbs so completely around him, that the negro, tall and strong as he was, was entirely unable to help himself.

While this scene was enacting I remember seeing another tall negro with a few followers coming along the causeway. When I saw what the captain had done, remembering also that my bonds could be easily slackened, I cast them off, and sprang after him; and so sudden were my movements, that before any of the astonished blacks could stop me, I had clung to the legs of the black chief as tightly as I ever clung to a top-gallant-yard in a gale of wind. The chief and his followers were so much taken by surprise, that no one knew what to say or how to act. The awe with which the captain had inspired them, and the supernatural mode, as it seemed, by which he had freed himself from his bonds, and freed me also, made them afraid of approaching lest he should destroy them or the chief.

The captain saw his advantage, and was not a man to lose it. His life depended on his resolution. The horror he must have felt at the scene just enacted made him resolve not to throw a chance away. As he held the chief in his vice-like grasp, with his arms pinioned down, he looked him fully in the face and laughed long and loudly.

"You thought to kill me, did you?" he exclaimed—"you thought that you could deprive me of life as easily as you did those miserable men you have just destroyed—me, a man who never injured you or yours; who has never wronged one of the sons of Africa. Ay, I can say that with a clear conscience. Often have I benefited them, often have I saved them from injury; and perhaps even here there are some who know me, and know that I speak the truth."

"One is here who can prove all he says to be true," exclaimed a tall negro, stepping forward from among the crowd. He was the very man I had remarked approaching the spot along the causeway.

"My friends, hear me," he exclaimed. "We have already satisfied our just vengeance, and do not let us destroy the innocent with the guilty. Some years ago a ship from Africa, laden with the children of her fruitful soil torn cruelly from their homes, struck on a coral-reef. A heavy sea dashed over the devoted vessel. Land was in sight, but yet far-off, blue and indistinct. The white crew had many boats. They launched them and pulled away with heartless indifference, leaving three hundred human beings, men, women, and helpless children, to almost certain destruction. Night came on. Oh, what a night of horrors! Many died, some from terror; many were drowned, manacled as they lay in the noisome hold. When the morning broke a sail appeared in sight. She approached the spot. Some of the negroes who had broken loose made signs to notify that human beings were still alive on board. The storm had much abated; a boat was lowered and came close to the wreck. When they saw that no white men were on board, did they pull away and leave us to our fate? No; they hailed us as fellow-creatures, and told us to calm our alarms, and that they would do their best to save us. I was there—a slave—I who had been a chief in my own country! I asked how many the boat would hold, and as many, about a dozen, I allowed to enter her at a time. Another boat from the ship soon came to our assistance, and one remained uninjured on board the wreck. We launched her, and many of the Africans being able to paddle, helped to carry her people to the ship. Thus all who remained alive on board the wreck were saved. The ship sailed from the spot and approached the land. I asked the brave captain how he would dispose of us. Some of the people believed that he would carry us into a port, and there sell us as slaves. He looked at me hard. 'I am no slave-dealer,' he exclaimed. 'Men have called me what they deem worse, but that matters not. I should obtain a large price for you all, and steep my soul in as black a sin as ever stained our human nature. No; I will land you on yonder coast, far from the habitations of men. There fruit, and roots, and numberless productions of kind Nature will amply supply you with food. There you may be free. I cannot take you back to your own country. I have no other means of helping you.' The generous captain was as good as his word—we were landed in safety ere the sun set; and more than that, he supplied us with such food as he could spare to strengthen us for our journey inland to the spot he advised us to seek, where we might remain in safety. Yes, my friends; there is the man who did this noble deed—there is the man whom you were, in your blindness, about so cruelly to slay!"

While the stranger was speaking, I recognised in him the tall negro who had come on board the brig, on my first voyage, with the mysterious old man, whom I supposed to be Captain Ralph. As soon as he stepped forward I felt almost certain that our lives would be spared; but still I did not let go the chief's legs. He did not often get them so thoroughly pinched, I suspect.

"I have yet more to tell you," continued the tall negro. "The noble deed which that brave man had done was discovered by some of his white countrymen, and he was persecuted by them, and compelled to fly for his life, and for long to become a wanderer over the face of the ocean. They drove him to take to a course of life which they themselves condemned; and had they captured him, they would have made it plea for his destruction."

The harangue which the negro made was even longer than I have given, and the language was perhaps somewhat more suited to the comprehension of his hearers. The effect, at all events, was most satisfactory. Enthusiastic shouts of applause burst from every side; and the chief, in words and by looks not to be mistaken, assured the captain that both his and my life would be preserved, and only begged that he would have the goodness not to squeeze him so tightly.

On this the captain released him, and the negroes rushing forward, lifted him up on their shoulders, and bore him in triumph round their village. The boys, not to be outdone by their elders, got hold of me as soon as I had let go the chief's legs, and lifting me up in the same way, followed the captain. Tom-toms were beat, and horns sounded, and cymbals were clashed, and men, and women, and children shrieked and shouted at the top of their voices, and never was heard a wilder outcry and hubbub than that with which we were welcomed as we passed through the rebel village. It was far pleasanter than being shot, I thought. The truth is, that so great and sudden was the change in our position, that I could scarcely collect my ideas and convince myself of its reality. Everything seemed like a dream, both past and present. Still I felt that my life was spared. I tried to be serious, and to be thankful for the mercy shown me; but I am conscious that I succeeded very ill, and allowed my mind to be entirely occupied with the scene going forward before my eyes.

While we were being thus paraded about the village, the women were engaged in preparing a feast, of which we were invited to partake; and I know that, however excited had been my feelings, I had not lost my appetite.

"Captain," said I, holding the leg of a roasted monkey in my fist, while he was munching away at a stewed snake, or lizard, or some creeping thing or other, "this is pleasanter than feeding the crows down below there. I want, sir, to beg the chief's pardon for pinching his legs so tight. I hope that he was not offended." I spoke in a very different tone to that in which I had ever before addressed my captain. The truth was, I felt and acted almost as if I were tipsy.

The captain looked at me somewhat sternly. "Be more serious, Jack," he answered; "we should be thankful to Heaven that we are not as those unhappy men are. We have both been mercifully preserved. Restrain your feelings, lad; you'll have much to go through before you are out of the fire."

I do not remember much more about the feast. The negroes ate, and drank, and laughed, and then got up and danced and sang as merrily as if they had not just been the principal actors in a terrific tragedy. Before the feast was over, our old acquaintance the tall negro came up to the captain, and sat himself down by his side.

"Prepare to leave this at a moment's notice," said he in a low tone of voice. "These people's tempers may change again as rapidly against you as they have lately turned in your favour. They believed what I told them of your generosity; but as there is no one here to corroborate the account, they might as easily be taught to discredit it."

"Thanks, my friend," answered the captain, grasping the negro's hand. "Thanks, Michael; you have indeed repaid any debt you might have thought you owed me. I'll follow your advice, and shall be ready to start whenever you give the sign."

"Directly it is dark, then, we must away, you and your young follower there," answered the tall negro, whom the captain addressed as Michael. "I have another reason for wishing to be off. This work they have been about will certainly bring the military up here; and though they might hold the place against an army if they knew how, none of them can be depended on. Now, if you remain here, our friends would expect you to fight for them; and if you were captured by the white men, you would to a certainty be treated as a rebel."

"Your arguments are quite strong enough, Michael, to make me wish to be off," answered the captain, laughing. I did not hear the remainder of the conversation.

The young negroes who had carried me about on their shoulders continued to treat me very kindly, and brought me all sorts of things to eat, till really I could not stuff in a mouthful more. They were much amused by examining my hands, and face, and clothes, for many of them till that day had never seen a white boy. They had been born up in the mountainous district, where we then were, and where no white person had ever ventured to come.

At last the negro Michael called the captain and me, and in the hearing of the people, pointing to a hut, told us that it was to be our home. The whole population having had plenty of work for the last few days, retired to their huts, and left us in quiet. As may be supposed, neither the captain nor I ventured to sleep, though, for my part, I would very gladly have done so. We waited for some time with no little anxiety. It was at last relieved by the appearance of Michael.

"Come," he whispered, "follow me. I could only ask seamen to take the path by which I must lead you." He glided out, and we stepped after him.

There was no moon, but the stars shone forth brightly, and gave us sufficient light to see what was near at hand. Michael led the way close to the spot where our companions had been murdered in the morning. On a sudden he disappeared, and I thought that he had fallen over the precipice. A pang shot through me. But no, he had merely begun to descend by a narrow path cut in the rock. It was indeed both narrow and steep. Sometimes we had to drop down several feet to a ledge below. There were probably holes in the rock by which people might ascend, but it was too dark to see them. Often we had to press along with our breasts to the precipice, holding on to its rugged sides, and with our backs over a yawning gulf. I would rather, however, have been on the topsail-yard-arm in the heaviest gale that ever blew: with a good honest rope in my hand, than where I then was. But darkness prevented our seeing half its terrors. More than once I thought that I should have gone over; but the captain, whose steps I closely followed, supported me with his powerful arm, and brought me along in safety. He did not utter a word, and his breath often came fast, as if he was undergoing great physical exertion, and was well aware of our perilous position. I know that my knees trembled beneath me when Michael told us that we had reached the bottom.

"We have gained some miles by this path towards the sea," said he, "and escaped the risk of being observed. Few even of the people up there know the path, and fewer still would venture to descend by it. Now, let us on; we have many miles to go before morning."

I need not describe our night's journey. For several hours we walked, and often ran on, without stopping even a moment to rest. It is extraordinary what people can do when they are pressed by circumstances.

We had not accomplished many miles when the moon arose, and shed her light over the strangely wild and beautiful scene, her beams glancing through the tall trees and the numberless creepers which decked their branches. Suddenly Michael stopped, and then pressing us back without speaking, conducted us into a thicket composed of prickly pear, cacti, and other strangely-shaped shrubs. Scarcely had he done so when the tramp of men and the sound of horses' feet were heard coming through a rocky defile ahead of us, and soon afterwards a body of cavalry passed along, their helmets and shining arms playing in the moonbeams. They were immediately followed by a regiment of infantry, less showy but more useful in the style of warfare in which they were likely to engage. It would scarcely be believed, at the present day, that several troops of dragoons were stationed at that time at Kingston, to do what it would be difficult to say, as they were totally unfit for mountain warfare, and would scarcely have been of much use to repel invasion. We remained silent and concealed as they passed. I concluded that Michael or the captain had good reasons not to wish to encounter them. They were going, of course, to attack the rebels; but I understood afterwards that they obtained but a very slight success, and had to return without in any way contributing to put a stop to the outbreak. That was not done till some time afterwards, when, by a general amnesty, and a guarantee being given for their safety, the Maroons were induced to break up their confederacy, and return within the pale of civilisation.

When daylight came we concealed ourselves in a thick wood, where I could not help feeling terribly alarmed lest some snake or other noxious reptile should injure us while we slept; but Michael assured me that I need not fear, and that he would watch that no harm should happen to us. Thus for three nights and a portion of one day we travelled on, till once more the bright blue waters of the ocean gladdened our sight. From a hill we climbed we looked down into a sheltered bay, and there lay calmly at anchor a schooner, which we recognised as the one which had been sent away from the brig under command of Mr Gale.

We were not long in descending the hill, and hailing her from the shore. Here Michael parted from us, under the plea that he had business which would detain him longer in that part of the island. The schooner's boat took us off, and we were soon on board. Mr Gale had heard rumours of the attack on the planter's house, and that every one had been murdered, and he was truly glad to see his captain safe; while my kind friend Peter assured me that he was not a little pleased to find that I had not lost the number of my mess.

Note. The above was written before the late American Civil War, which emancipated the slaves of the Southern States.

Chapter Seven
A Pirate Stronghold

The little schooner very soon got her cargo on board, and we then put to sea, to return to the brig. We had to make a long reach off-shore to weather a headland, which ran out towards the north, and we were just about to tack when the wind, which had been very light, failed us altogether. There we lay, with our sides lazily lapping up the burnished water, and throwing it off again in showers of sparkling drops, as we rolled away helplessly in the swell. At the same time a strong current was running, which was setting us imperceptibly off-shore. However, after having been exposed to it for three or four hours, I found, on looking up, that we had very much increased our distance from the land. The day passed away and the night came, and there we lay like a log in the water, drifting further and further from the land.

It was truly a solemn night. Every star which floated in the vast expanse above us was reflected on the surface of the deep; and as I looked over the side, I fancied that I could see numberless bright orbs floating far, far down in the limpid water. Strange sounds reached my ears. Suppressed shrieks, and groans, and cries—loud hisses, and murmuring voices, and strange monsters came up from their rocky weed-covered homes, their fins sparkling, and their eyes flashing as they clove through the sea. Some would now and again spring into the air and fall back with a loud splash. Others, of huge bulk, I thought, would come and float silently, looking at the little schooner, an intruder on their domain, seemingly devising means how they might drive her from it. I ought to have been below resting, as the captain had ordered me, but I was hot and feverish, and could not remain in the close atmosphere of the forepeak. As I stood gazing at the sea, I thought I saw the forms of all the unhappy men murdered by the Maroons pass before me. Each countenance bore the agonised look which I had beheld before the fatal signal was given to the firing-party to perform the work of death. They stretched out their hands to me to help them, and moaned piteously, as I stood spell-bound, unable to move. One after the other they came gliding by, and then sank down into the water ahead of the schooner. I could stand the dreadful sight no longer, and shrieked out in an attempt to go and help them.

"What's the matter, lad?" said the voice of Peter Poplar close to my ear. "You are overtired—no wonder. Here—I have put a mattress and a blanket for you under shelter. Lie down and take a little rest. You'll want to use your strength perhaps before long. A sailor should always eat when he can, and take his sleep when he can. He is never certain when he may have to go without either food or rest."

I took Peter's advice, and very soon the feelings which oppressed me wore off, and I fell soundly asleep.

I did not awake till the bright sun was just rising out of the mirror-like sea. The calm was as perfect as before; and when I looked for the land, I could only just make out its blue and hazy mountains rising out of the ocean. Hot enough the weather was; but as the sun glided upwards in the sky, a thick mist was drawn over the whole face of nature. The captain and Mr Gale were on deck, and I saw them scanning the horizon anxiously on every side. They seemed far from satisfied with the look of the weather. Still for some time they could not make up their minds how to act.

"What's going to happen now?" said I to Peter some time after this.

"Do you remember the breeze we had in Kingston Harbour on your first voyage?" he asked.

"What? the hurricane do you mean? Indeed I do," I replied. "I hope we are not going to have such another in this little craft out here."

"I'm not so sure of that, Jack," he replied. "The captain begins to think so likewise. He'll be for making everything snug, if I mistake not."

Peter was right. The order was soon given to strike topmasts, to furl sails, to set up the rigging, to fasten down the hatches, to secure everything below, and to lash the boats and all spare spars on deck. Everything that could be accomplished was done to prepare the little craft for the expected tempest.

Still everything around us was so calm and quiet that it required no little faith in the judgment of our officers to believe that all this preparation was necessary. Much in the same way do men feel it difficult to believe in the importance of preparing for another world, when the tide of prosperity carries them along, without care or anxiety, over the sea of life. I have often thought that a gale of wind, a lee-shore on a dark night, and the risk of shipwreck, are of use to seamen, to make them prepare for the dangers which sooner or later must come upon them. So are all misfortunes—pain, sorrow, loss of friends, deprivation of worldly honours or position—sent to remind people that this world is not their abiding-place; that they are sent into it only that they may have the opportunity of preparing in it for another and a better world, which will last for eternity.

Hour after hour passed away. Still the calm continued. I suspect the officers themselves began to doubt whether the looked-for hurricane would ever come. I asked Peter what he thought about it.

"Come! ay, that it will," he replied. "More reason that it will come with all its strength and fury because it is delayed. Look out there! do you see that?"

He pointed towards the now distant land. A dark cloud seemed to be rushing out from that direction, and extending rapidly on either side, while below the cloud a long line of white foam came hissing and rolling on towards us. As it reached the spot where we lay, the little vessel heeled over till I thought she would never rise again, and then she was turned round and round as if she had been a piece of straw. Loudly roared and howled the fierce blast, and on she drove helplessly before it. Every instant the sea rose higher and higher, and the schooner began to pitch, and toss, and tumble about, till I thought she would have been shaken to pieces.

"Peter," said I, "we are in a bad way, I am afraid."

"We should have been in a very much worse way had the wind come from another quarter, and driven us towards the land," he replied, gravely. "Some of the people had begun to grumble because we had been drifted so far off-shore. We may now be thankful that we were not caught nearer to it, and have already made so much offing. We shall very likely have it round again, and then we shall require all the distance we have come to drive in, and none to spare."

"I was thinking of the chance we have of going to the bottom," said I, looking at the huge seas which kept tumbling tumultuously around us.

"Not much fear of that," he answered. "We are in a strongly-built and tight little craft; and as long as she keeps off-shore, she'll swim, I hope."

Peter's prognostications as to a shift of the wind were speedily fulfilled, and we found the vessel driving as rapidly towards the dreaded shore as she had before been carried from it. To struggle against it was hopeless; our only prospect of safety, should she be blown on it, was to find some creek or river into which we might run; but the probabilities of our finding such a shelter were so very remote, that all we could do was to pray that we might once more be driven away from the treacherous land. Happily such was our fate. Another eddy, as it were, of the whirlwind caught us, and once more we went flying away towards the coast of Cuba. That was, however, so far distant that there was but little fear but that the tempest would have spent its fury long before we could reach it. No sail could be set; but the vessel being in good trim, answered her helm, and kept before the wind.

Away! away we flew! surrounded with sheets of hissing foam, the wild waters dancing up madly on every side, threatening, should we stop but for a moment in our course, to sweep over our decks! Even careless as I then was, I could not help feeling grateful that we were not driving on towards a shore which must speedily stop us in our career; and I thought of the many poor fellows who would that day meet a watery grave, their vessels cast helplessly on the sea-beat rocks. As the wind took us along with it, we got more than our fair share of the hurricane; and the night came on while we were still scudding on, exposed to its fury.

If the scene was wild in the day-time, much more so was it when we were surrounded by darkness, and a thousand unseen horrors presented themselves to our imagination. Though I was not very easily overcome, I had suffered so much lately that I felt that I could not endure much longer the continuance of this sort of work. At last I fell into a sort of stupor, and I believe that I should have been washed overboard had not Peter secured me to the rigging, close to himself. I knew nothing more till I awoke and found myself lying on the deck, with the sun glancing brightly over the sparkling waters; the schooner, with all sail set, close-hauled, and a gentle breeze blowing. On one side was seen a range of blue hills rising out of the ocean. Peter was kneeling by my side.

"Get up, Jack," said he; "you've had a long snooze, but you wanted it, lad, I'm sure. There's some breakfast for you; it will do you good after all you have gone through."

I thanked my kind friend, and swallowed the cocoa and biscuit which he brought me with no little relish.

"What! have we so soon got back to Jamaica?" said I, looking over the side, and seeing the blue ranges of hills I have spoken of.

"Jamaica! no, lad—I wish it was," he replied. "That's the island of Cuba; and from what I know of it, I wish that we were further off than we are. Some ugly customers inhabit it! There has been a suspicious-looking craft for the last hour or so standing out from the land towards us, and as she has long sweeps, she is making good way. I suspect the captain don't admire her looks, for I have never seen him in such a way before from the moment he came on deck and caught sight of her. If we were in the brig we need not have been afraid of her, but in this little cockle-shell we cannot do much to help ourselves."

"We can fight, surely!" said I. "We have arms, have we not?"

"What can eight or ten men do against forty or fifty cut-throats, which probably that craft out there has on board?" answered Peter. "We'll do our best, however."

The approaching vessel was lateen-rigged, with two masts, and of great beam; and though low in the water, and at a distance looking small, capable of carrying a considerable number of men. Certainly she had a very dishonest appearance. I saw the captain often anxiously looking out on the weather-side, as if for a sign of more wind; but the gentle breeze just filled our sails, and gave the craft little more than steerage-way. All hands kept whistling away most energetically for a stronger wind, but it would not come. The felucca, however, sailed very fast. As we could not get out of her way, the captain hailed, and very politely asked her to get out of ours, or rather to steer clear of us. Instead of replying, or acting according to his request, some forty ugly fellows or more, of every hue, from jet-black to white, and in every style of costume, sprung up on her decks from below, and directly afterwards she ranged up alongside of us. The captain, on this, ordered her to sheer off; but instead of so doing, grappling-irons were thrown aboard us, and her fierce-looking crew made a rush to leap on our deck. They were met, however, by our captain, Mr Gale, Peter, and the rest of our people, who, with pistol and cutlass in hand, were prepared to dispute their passage.

The pirates, for such there could be no doubt our visitors were, had four or more guns mounted on their deck; but they seemed resolved to depend rather on their overwhelming numbers than on them for victory. They had not calculated, apparently, what a few determined men could do. "Stand back, ye scoundrels!" shouted our brave captain, in a voice which made the ruffians look up with amazement, though I do not think they understood his words. He gave them further force by a sweep of his cutlass, with which he cut off the head of the nearest of his assailants. Peter, whose arm was almost as powerful, treated another in the same way; and Mr Gale knocked a third over with his pistol before any of them had time to get hold of our rigging. This determined resistance caused them to draw back for an instant, which enabled Peter, with one of the other men, to cast loose the grappling-irons forward. At the same time two of the pirates, who were attempting to leap on board, were dealt such heavy blows on the head that they were knocked overboard before any of their companions could help them. "Well done, my lads!" cried the captain. "Keep up the game in this way, and we may yet beat off the villains!" Saying this he sprang aft to drive back a gang of the pirates, who were attempting to board on our quarter. Two of the first paid dearly for their temerity, and were cut down by either the captain or Mr Gale. I got a long pike, and kept poking away over the bulwarks at every fellow I could reach. Several pistols were fired at me, but missed their aim; but at last the pike was dragged out of my hands, and thrown overboard. Unfortunately there was so little wind that the pirates, by getting out a sweep on the opposite side of their vessel, brought her head aboard, and at the same time made a rush to get on our deck. Peter, with two of our men, hurried to repel them; but a bullet at that moment struck one of them on the breast, and knocked him over. Poor fellow! I tried to save him as he fell; but the heavy way in which he came to the deck showed me that his fighting days were over. I ran to help Peter and my other shipmates, but the pirates pressed us so hard that we had little hope of keeping them out. In the meantime also a stout active little Spaniard, followed by two or three blacks and another white man, made a spring at our bulwarks about midships; and though one of our men, Tom Hardy, most bravely threw himself before them, they gained the deck, and cut him down before any further opposition could be offered. Others followed them, and gaining the whole centre part of the vessel, our crew were completely divided. We had lost two men. Thus the captain, Mr Gale, and one man held the deck aft; while Peter, another man, and I still stood at our post forward. But what could we hope to do against the crowd of ruffians who swarmed on board? At the same moment they pressed towards us and the captain, and would have carried us overboard had we not sung out, and asked for quarter. The bravery which the captain and the rest had displayed seemed to have won their admiration and respect; for instead of cutting us down and throwing us into the sea, they instantly granted us the quarter we asked. Our arms were taken from us, and we were ordered to go on board the felucca, while the pirates proceeded to rifle the schooner. Except the hogsheads of sugar, which would not have been of much use to them, they found very little, I suspect, to repay them for the heavy cost of our capture. The vessel, however, would probably have been of some value to them, as she was a fine little craft.

The schooner having a crew put on board her, the two vessels stood away to the westward. Peter told me that he suspected we were bound to one of the numerous small islands—keys they are called—which are found in great numbers off the south coast of Cuba. We were allowed to walk about the deck without molestation; but our position was far from a pleasant one, for any moment our captors might take it into their heads to make us walk the plank, or to get rid of us by some other means. I had never seen a person made to walk the plank, but I had heard it described as a favourite method employed by pirates to get rid of their prisoners. A long plank is run out over the side, and the victim, blindfolded, is made to walk along it. When he gets to the outer end, the inner part is tilted up, and he is slid into the sea. I earnestly prayed that such might not be our fate, and yet I could not see what better we could expect. We had evidently fallen into the hands of desperate outlaws, not likely to be influenced by any of the dictates of humanity. At all events, we were likely to be kept prisoners, and probably made to work as slaves for these villains, without a chance of escaping. The captain seemed most cast down. He would, of course, most certainly be thought to be lost. His vessel would sail without him, and report his death at home. As he was a married man, with several children, the trial was indeed great to him.

I tried to make out who was the captain of the pirates, but they appeared at first to me to be all equal. A fat, sturdy mulatto, was, I after a time suspected, the chief mate, or one of the principal officers; and the Spaniard, who had first succeeded in boarding us, was another. Not one of them spoke a word of English, though from the first I suspected that two or more of the white men understood it, if they were not Englishmen or people from the American colonies. At all events, I followed Peter's advice—not to say anything about which it might be well not to have heard. I have often seen people get into great scrapes, and bring most disagreeable consequences on themselves, from disregarding that rule. Never say anything among foreigners, in your own or any other language, which you do not wish them to understand; or even give expression to your feelings in looks, which even savages, you should remember, can frequently comprehend.

Our two poor shipmates who had been wounded died, I hope, before we left the schooner. At all events, the pirates threw them overboard. Including Peter and me, there were thus only three foremast-men, besides the blacks, and a mulatto who had been shipped as pilot for the trip round the coast. We all kept together sitting on and about one of the guns; but very little conversation passed between us. The captain and Mr Gale walked the deck near us, but they said very little to each other. A negro brought us, towards the evening, a large dish of farina, with some sort of meat stewed in it. Though not over pleasant to the look, it was acceptable enough to hungry men, for we had had nothing to eat since the morning. A more palatable-looking dish was placed before the captain and Mr Gale. This care of us showed that they did not, at all events, intend to starve us to death, as they would scarcely have fed people whom they intended to kill.

I observed the Spaniard and the mulatto mate occasionally going down an after-hatchway, which I supposed led into the chief cabin, but for what reason they went I could not tell; and I observed that whenever the captain and Mr Gale approached the spot, a guard stationed there turned them back. When night came on, a sail was handed to us, which we spread over the gun, and crept under it; and I observed that a couple of mattresses were sent on deck, and that a sail was secured over the bulwarks, to make a somewhat better tent for our officers.

We passed the whole of the next day much as we had done the first. The black, and white, and coloured crew did not regard us with very friendly looks; but they did not molest us. A dark-skinned lad would, however, occasionally come up to me when neither of the mates were looking, and touching a formidable-looking knife he wore in his sheath, signify that he should enjoy running the point into me. Some relation of his had been among the men killed, and this made him feel bitter towards us. Peter, who saw the action, advised me to remain quiet, and to take no notice of it. "He only wants an excuse for a quarrel, and therefore, unless you wish to please him, do not give it," observed my friend. I followed his advice, not only at the present, but on many future occasions, and thus avoided many of the quarrels and disputes into which I saw others plunged. The men who brought us our food growled a little at us, as if they would much rather have been making us food for the fish; but as we made them no answer, they went away and left us to ourselves. As the wind was generally light, we did not make much progress. Thus another night passed away.

When the morning of the next day broke, I saw that we were running in among reefs, which I could tell by the ripple of the otherwise calm water breaking over them. Ahead was a low sandy shore, mangrove-bushes lining some portion of it, with palms and plantains, and a few other tropical trees, rising beyond them. As we sailed on, threading the glass-like channels, the sun rose higher and higher, and shone down with intense heat on our heads, drawing forth, at the same time, a thin gauze-like mist over the whole scene. "This is a regular trap," observed Peter. "If a man once gets in here, I defy him to find his way out again, unless he was born and bred on the spot." The captain and Mr Gale were watching the progress of the vessel, and tried to look as unconcerned as possible; but they were evidently considering if it were possible to take a vessel out by the way they had come in.

At length we entered the mouth of a narrow creek, lined with the mangrove-bushes I have spoken of on either side; some growing in the bright pure water, others with their branches just dipping into the clear liquid, and so distinctly reflected that I could not tell where the real bough ended and its phantom-likeness began. After running on for half a mile, and making frequent turns, we found ourselves in a wide lagoon, several other craft of different sizes and rigs being at anchor in it. On shore, there was a collection of large wooden sheds looking like stores, and some huts, and a few buildings of more pretensions, apparently dwelling-houses. There was nothing like order or regularity in the arrangement of the village; but each store or cottage seemed to have been placed as suited the fancy of the owner, the whole wearing a very nautical, shipwreck appearance. Many of the roofs were formed of the bottoms of boats; sails, with a coating of paint or tar, were nailed over others; and the planks and ribs of vessels had entered largely into the construction of all the edifices. I made these observations as we were shortening sail and coming to an anchor. It was very clearly a pirate stronghold, and had been probably so for some years. The pirates had allowed us to remain on deck and see the approach to it, evidently trusting to the difficulties of the navigation to prevent any of us finding our way out of it, or in again, should we obtain our liberty. Though art had done nothing, nature had done everything to make the place impregnable, unless a pilot could be found to show an enemy the way. Against such a result they had several safeguards: each man of this fraternity had bound himself by an oath not to betray any of their secrets. The Spanish authorities took very little cognisance of them, as their own vessels were not attacked; while at that time the governors of the West India Islands did not trouble themselves much about rooting out piracy; and it was only when some act of especial atrocity had been committed, that, if a man-of-war was in the way, she was sent in chase of the pirate.

As soon as we had dropped our anchor, several boats came off from the shore with people eager to learn the news we brought. They looked suspiciously at us, and seemed not very well satisfied at the result of their inquiries. It was far from pleasant to see a number of cut-throat-looking fellows parading up and down before us with their hands on the hilts of their long knives, with which they kept playing as if anxious to try their temper in our bodies. Captain Helfrich stood all the time with folded arms leaning against the bulwarks, and all we could do was to imitate his example. I was not sorry, however, when the mulatto mate intimated to us that we were to get into the boat and go on shore, as I thought that we should then probably be more out of the way of our irascible-looking friends. We were ordered into one boat with Mr Gale, while the captain was carried away in another. This seriously excited our apprehension, as we could not tell what evil might be intended him. He, however, though very grave, seemed to be under no apprehension, but stepped into the boat as if he was going on shore on his own business.

As soon as we landed, we were marched up to one of the store-like buildings; and a ladder being shown us, up which we went through a trap which closed behind us, we found ourselves in a large airy loft. The furniture consisted of some heaps of the straw or leaves of Indian corn. It looked clean, and was, therefore, more suited to our wants than would have been any number of pieces of the handsomest furniture—such as marble tables, mahogany sideboards, satin-wood wardrobes, or gold and china vases. As Peter observed, when he threw himself on one of the heaps: "Never mind, my lads, we're rich if we've got what we want. If our friends below would send us up a dish of turtle and rice, or some of their ollas, we, at any rate, shall have no reason to complain of our lot. We shall get out of this one of these days; so, in the meantime, let us make ourselves comfortable." Peter's good temper kept up the spirits of the rest of our party. I have often found the advantage of having a person like Peter among a number of people placed in circumstances like ours, either in prison, or cast away, or detained in some disagreeable place; and I have, therefore, always endeavoured to imitate him in that respect, as well as in others, by keeping up my own spirits, and by cheering my companions in misfortune. Mr Gale, under most circumstances, would have contributed to support us; but on the present occasion he was evidently too much weighed down with grave apprehensions as to what was likely to befall us all, to act as he would otherwise have done. Not having anything else to do, and being very tired, we all went to sleep.

After some hours, for the sun was low by that time, we were awoke. Hearing a bolt being withdrawn, and looking up, I saw the trap lifted, and a negro appeared. On his head he carried a large bowl, with some wooden spoons in it. He placed the bowl before us, and signified that we might eat its contents. Curiously enough, it contained the very thing Peter had been wishing for—a stew of turtle and rice, a thing not to be despised by hungry men. It was very good, I know. After eating it, we went to sleep again, and for my own part I did not awake till daylight. After some time, a bowl of a sort of porridge was brought us, and some plantains, which, with pork, forms the common food of the people of Cuba. Twice in the day food was brought us. It was both abundant and good, so that we had no reason to complain of the way the pirates treated us. The great puzzle was to discover why it was that they were so civil. Had they kept us on bread and water, and spared our lives, we should have had reason to be grateful; as the usual mode of proceeding of such gentry, we understood, always was to shoot all who would not take the oaths and join them.

We were not allowed to go out of the place, or to hold intercourse with anybody. The only light which was let into the place came from a hole in the roof above our heads. It was so placed that we could not manage to climb up to it. I managed, however, to find a chink in the floor, near the trap; and whenever I looked through it, I saw a man with a musket standing there as a guard.

Three or four days thus passed away. We could hear nothing of the captain, for the only person we saw was the negro, and when we asked him, he only shook his head, and intimated that he did not understand what we said. Mr Gale, after a time, aroused himself, and gave us instructions in various matters; and Peter and one of the other men told some capital stories, and we all took it by turns to sing songs. I was not a bad hand at that, by-the-by; I had learned several as a child, and had picked up others since then, and as my voice was a good one, my songs were generally favourites.

The time, however, began to hang rather heavily on our hands, when one evening a stranger made his appearance, and looking at me, said in English, "Youngster, you are wanted." I was startled at hearing the sound of an English voice; but I, of course, thought the captain wanted me, so I went, very willing to accompany him. The trap was bolted behind me. He took me to one of the largest cottages I had observed, and entering it, pointed to a door, and told me to go in. I did so, and there I saw seated at a table the identical old gentleman whom I believed to be called Captain Ralph. He did not look a day older than when he came on board the *Rainbow* off Saint Kitt's, and he wore the same old-fashioned three-cornered hat and laced-coat.

"You have seen me before, lad," said he, eyeing me closely.

"Yes, sir," said I, resolving to be frank with him; "on board the *Rainbow*."

"You are attached to your captain, and would wish to do him a service?" he added.

"Yes, sir," said I. "What do you want me to do?"

"Tell him that all his people have taken the oaths and joined the confederacy," he answered, looking at me hard.

"I don't know what oaths, or what else you mean, sir," I answered. "I cannot tell him anything that is not true."

"What? a ship-boy with a conscience?" he exclaimed, bursting into a fit of laughter. "I tell you, lad, you must do as you are bid."

"Yes, sir, I'll do what my captain tells me," I replied, simply. "But for the matter of saying anything to deceive him, I won't do it. I'll tell him the truth, and then he'll know how to act."

He looked at me very hard for a moment or so, and then rang a bell by his side. From what he had said, I hoped that the captain was safe and well. The same man who had brought me in appeared.

"Send Diego here to take care of this youngster, and bring in one of the other men, the tall one—I will try what I can make of him," he said; and the white man disappeared.

Directly afterwards, a sturdy black man came in. Captain Ralph pointed to me. He seized me by the collar, and held me a prisoner on one side of the room. In a short time Peter was brought in.

"You find life and liberty sweet, my man?" said the old gentleman, addressing him.

"I've no objection to either," answered Peter sturdily.

"You've been well-treated since you've been here?" said Captain Ralph.

"I've no reason to complain," was Peter's laconic reply.

"Very well; you may judge that I do not wish you ill," observed Captain Ralph. "Now, I won't conceal it from you, we have a body of people on this island who don't own any laws except those of our own making. A large number of them are Spaniards, and I want a few honest Englishmen, who will stick by one another, to join us. What do you say? Are you inclined to join us? Your captain will, I have no doubt, and so will this lad and the rest of your shipmates."

I shook my head. Captain Ralph did not see me, but the negro did, and gave me a cuff on the head in consequence. I had not fancied that the negro understood English, but from this circumstance I have no doubt he did.

Peter gave a hitch to his trousers when the question was put to him, and then vehemently scratched his head. "Look ye here, sir," he answered in a firm voice, which showed that he had made up his mind how to act, "I am much obliged for the treatment I and my shipmates have received since we came to this place, barring the being kept inside a sort of prison, so to speak; but you must just understand, sir, that I've been brought up to be an honest man, and an honest man I hope to remain to the end of my days; and so, as to taking any oath to turn pirate, or in any way to associate with those who do, I'll not do it. So now you've my answer."

The pirate chief—for so I may as well at once call him—seemed to be somewhat taken aback at this answer; but he laughed as I had before heard him. "You *Rainbow* lads have odd notions of your own about honesty! We'll see what the rest of you have to say on the subject."

Mr Gale was next sent for. He, as may be supposed, at once refused to join the pirates. The other men, fancying that we had joined them, promised to do so; but it struck me that Captain Ralph did not look particularly well satisfied at hearing their reply.

What his intentions were we could not tell, for he ordered us all at once to be taken back to our place of confinement, under a guard of five or six men, who stood outside ready for that purpose. What had become of the captain puzzled us most to discover. We said nothing, however, as we went along, for we were pretty certain that the people who had charge of us perfectly understood English, if they were not mostly Englishmen.

We remained two or three days longer shut up, in a state of great doubt and uncertainty. Sometimes we fancied that we should be taken out and shot; at others, that we might be set at liberty. However, I could not help hoping that Captain Ralph was well-disposed towards us. What the pirates were about all this time we could not tell; but we supposed that they could scarcely remain idle, and if we were to make our escape at all, we looked forward to the time when the greater portion were gone away on some expedition.

We very soon got tired of not being able to see what was going forward in the outer world. We accordingly hunted about the roof, to find a spot where we could remove the shingles, or split planks of wood which formed it, without leaving any marks which might be observed. This, after a little time, we succeeded in doing with our knives; and thus we formed a look-out hole on each side of the building. On one side, we could see all over the harbour; on another, we looked down towards the mouth; a third looked over a very uninviting country inland, with the mountains of Cuba seen in the far distance, blue and indistinct; while, by looking through the fourth, we discovered that we were separated from the open sea by a piece of land little more than a mile in width. We could not, of course, see what was going forward close under the buildings, but we could observe the movements of people on shore at a little distance off. Our ears, however, helped us when our eyesight failed. One of us was always on the look-out at each hole, while the fifth kept watch at the chink, to give timely notice of anybody's approach to the ladder.

For some days we had observed the people busily employed in fitting, rigging, and in shaping and altering spars. At length there was an unusual bustle, and boats were continually going backwards and forwards between the vessels, carrying stores of various sorts. It was clear that there was at length an expedition on foot. We naturally fancied that it would produce some change in our position, but whether for better or worse remained to be seen.

The next morning the harbour was covered with boats carrying people on board the vessels; and directly afterwards six of them got under way, and stood out towards the sea. Whether or not Captain Ralph went with them we could not discover. We could not perceive our own schooner in the harbour, but there was a vessel which we thought might be her lying out towards the mouth of the creek. There were still, we remarked, a good number of people left on the island. We saw them moving about in all directions for some hours after the fleet had sailed, and then they retired into the huts and sheds which served as their homes. Such was the state of things when we lay down to rest that night.

About midnight, we were startled by hearing the trap-door lifted. At the same time a man appeared with a lantern in his hand. I recognised him as the person who had conducted me to the presence of Captain Ralph.

"I have come here as a friend, my men," he said in a low voice, putting down the lantern. "You have shown that you can be faithful to your own captain, and mine, therefore, believes that he can trust you to do him a service. Is he right?"

"Yes," answered Mr Gale, speaking for the rest of us; "anything which, as honest men, we can do to help him we will gladly undertake."

"That's right," said the stranger. "You must know, then, that we have here men of various nations. Many of them are Spaniards. They and other foreigners have lately been growing more and more jealous of our captain. He has done two or three things lately to offend their prejudices, certainly. The consequence is, that they have hatched a conspiracy, which has just been discovered, to murder him and all the English in the place; you all will be among the first victims. In asking you to fight for us, I invite you to fight for your own lives. To show that I trust you, I have brought you some pistols and ammunition, and a bundle of swords done up in this sail. The villains have fixed on an hour before daybreak to begin the attack on us. Arm yourselves, and be ready to sally forth at a moment's notice. They will sound a trumpet as a signal to their party to begin the work of slaughter. I will try to be here before then. If I am not, make your way to Captain Ralph's quarters. He will have, before that, released your captain, who will put himself at your head. You will also be joined by four or five men, who, like me, will be glad to get away from this den, and regain our liberty at any cost. I must stay no longer, or I may be missed. Be prompt and firm, and we may come off conquerors. Remember, however, it is victory or death for all of us!"

These words came like a thunder-clap among us. We could scarcely believe our ears. Mr Gale, however, at once replied, that we would undertake exactly to follow the stranger's directions, as we clearly understood the dangerous predicament in which we all stood. The instant he received our reply, he hurried from the loft, and we could see his figure from our loophole proceeding to the upper part of the settlement.

Our first care was to examine the package, which we found contained the arms he had promised. We immediately loaded the pistols, and buckled on the cutlasses, and then stood ready to descend at the expected signal. To men long shut up as we had been, any excitement is acceptable; so that, far from feeling any alarm at what we had heard, scarcely anything could have contributed so much to raise our spirits. I truly believe that we valued the prospect of obtaining our liberty much more from the chance of having to fight for it. We were only eager for the fray to begin. We could not tell exactly how we were to find out our enemies; but Mr Gale charged us not to attack anyone till we were attacked, unless we received directions from Captain Helfrich, or the stranger who had just visited us.

The state of things which existed, it appeared, among this community of sea-robbers, showed me a truth which I have since found frequently confirmed, that oaths are of little or no value among men who are continually breaking God's laws. They are kept as a rule only as long as it is convenient or necessary to each individual to keep them; but the moment he thinks it to his advantage to break them, he does so without the slightest compunction. The terrific oaths which were supposed to bind together the ruffians of the Blackbeard school, were over and over again broken, and would never have been kept unless interest, or the lowest superstition, had held the ruffians faithful to them. The value of an oath, as a pledge taken in the sight of the Almighty God, they could not comprehend. Much the same was evidently the case in the present instance; and here there was every prospect of a long existing community of outlaws breaking up from internal dissensions. We could only earnestly hope that such might be their fate. "Depend on it, Jack, my boy," said Peter to me, when talking on the subject, "there's only one thing can bind men truly together, and that is honesty of purpose. Real friendship cannot exist among knaves." In my long life I have invariably found his remarks verified.

Hour after hour passed away while we waited for the signal. Of course we were very anxious, but our spirits rather rose than fell as we talked over the various plans which it might be necessary for us to adopt to effect our escape. We had an advantage the pirate who visited us did not suspect: we had surveyed the ground from our look-out, and knew that our own schooner, or one like her, was at the mouth of the harbour. We agreed, as soon as we had driven back the Spaniards and their party, to set fire to their stores; and while they were endeavouring to put them out, to make a rush for the boats, and thus to effect our escape down the lagoon.

The night had become very silent—not a sound was heard, either on shore or on the water. There was a gentle land-breeze blowing, which would be all in our favour if once we could get to the vessel. Suddenly the shrill blast of a trumpet was heard. Peter gave one glance through the loophole, and said he saw torches flaming in the upper part of the village; and presently loud shouts and cries burst forth from the same direction. We slid down the ladder as fast as one could follow the other, Mr Gale leading. If a guard had been there, he had run off at the first sound of the trumpet. We hurried on in the direction we had been desired to take. We had not gone far when we were met by the stranger. "No time to lose; on, my lads!" he exclaimed, leading the way. Before us torches were waving, and there were the flashes of fire-arms. Their reports were heard, as was the clash of steel. We advanced together rapidly. Suddenly flames burst out of one of the large stores. The building itself and its contents, probably being of inflammable materials, blazed up fiercely, and its light fell on the figures of a number of men fighting desperately. One person was conspicuous above those of all the others. It was that of our own captain. As we saw him we raised a cheer, which must have reached his ears. He answered it with a shout such as few but he could give. Again we cheered, and dashed on with redoubled speed. We were but just in time to help him. He stood with his back against a wall, almost surrounded with enemies, bestriding the body of Captain Ralph; while his right hand wielded a huge sword, such as few but he could use to advantage. "On, my lads! Charge the villains!" he shouted. We needed not the command, but rushed against the mass of Spaniards, mulattoes, and blacks, who were besetting him, with such hearty good-will, and our attack being, at the same time, so unexpected, that we drove them back, helter-skelter, some hundred yards, killing and wounding a number of them in the way. We should have gone further, but we were recalled by the captain's voice. We found him lifting Captain Ralph's body in his arms. "To the boats! to the boats!" shouted some of the Englishmen, each of whom bore, I perceived, a considerable bundle on his shoulders. We, supporting our captain, followed the way they led. Five or six boats, with their oars and sails in them, were in the water at a rough wooden quay. We jumped into them, and shoved off.

Several English had been killed, and some had been wounded, whom their comrades had assisted to the water-side. The scene was lighted up by the blaze of several wooden stores and other buildings. Among them was Captain Ralph's cottage. The lights from the flaming mass fell on a large body of Spaniards, who had rallied, and were advancing rapidly towards us. "It matters not," shouted some of our new companions, with a laugh of derision; "they'll find no boats to pursue us; and when they get back to their homes, they'll discover that not a few of their gold ingots are gone. Hurrah! hurrah! Give way, my lads, though! They'll bring their guns to bear upon us if we do not make good way down the creek." We had all jumped into the nearest boats at hand, without any respect to order, and the stoutest hands had seized the oars. I found myself in the boat with my captain and Captain Ralph. The old man lay in the stern-sheets supported in my captain's arms. He still lived, but he appeared to be badly wounded. Neither spoke for some time. The captain told me to take the yoke-lines, and to steer according to his directions. Peter pulled one of the oars, and our boat took the lead; but, to my surprise, my captain seemed to know all the turnings of the creek as well as any of the pirates.

We had got but a short distance when our opponents reached the side of the water, when, finding no boats, they began rapidly firing away at us. Though the light from the blazing buildings fell on us, it did not enable them to judge accurately of the distance we were from them, and most of their shot went over our heads. Though we had plenty of arms in the boat, we did not attempt to return their fire; but some of our lawless companions gave vent to their anger in shouts and execrations.

Wild as the scene had hitherto been, it was yet further heightened by a loud explosion, which sent fragments of burning embers falling even around the boats. At the sound, Captain Ralph raised his head and looked towards the village. "They have lost their expected prize, and many of them have received what they little expected!" he exclaimed, with that peculiar low laugh in which I had before heard him indulge. He had for the moment forgotten his condition. He was, I saw clearly, desperately wounded. The exertion of moving and speaking was greater than he could bear, and he sunk back into the captain's arms.

The bullets were all this time flying thickly about the boats, though we were rapidly increasing our distance from the shore. Several of them had whistled by my ear. Then I heard one strike close to me with a peculiar dead sound. At the same moment a sharp, unearthly cry rung in my ear. It was uttered by Captain Ralph. "Helfrich!" he exclaimed, "they have done for me. I thought that I had secured all I required, and might live henceforth in peace. I die with unnumbered sins on my conscience, without one good act performed, with every advantage neglected, with a thousand opportunities of reformation thrown away. I have lived a life of imposture, outraging all laws, human and divine, and I die miserably without hope—without hope—without hope! Oh, save me! save me! save me!" The last words the miserable man gasped out with difficulty. Scarcely had he spoken them, when his head fell down over his breast, a convulsive shudder passed through his frame, and the once dreaded pirate was dead!

Chapter Eight
Pirates in both Hemispheres

The balls from the pirates' muskets not a little increased the rapidity of our movements. Two or three men in the other boats were hit, and one was killed. When Captain Helfrich discovered what had occurred, he carefully closed the old pirate's eyes, and placed the body on the seat by his side. His men, however, evinced very little sorrow at his death. Who he was, and what he had done during his life, I was never able clearly to learn. He was a man of education, and a first-rate seaman, as I had had an opportunity of observing; and I should think that he would have succeeded in any line of life he might have chosen to adopt. He selected, unhappily, a very bad one, for I believe that his whole career had been lawless; but that, rather from the peculiarity of his temper than from any fear of committing evil, he had usually abstained, when he had the power in his own hands, from shedding blood.

The grey dawn broke as we were pulling down the creek, and just as the headmost boat touched the side of a schooner which lay at its mouth, the sun rose in a blaze of glory out of the smooth dark blue ocean. Peter, looking over his shoulder, recognised her as our little sugar vessel. We were soon alongside. Friends to our lawless companions were on board. The cable was hove short, the mainsail was set, and all was ready to weigh in a moment. As many boats as the schooner could stow on deck: were hoisted on board; the rest went ahead to tow her out. The plan of escape had been well arranged by Captain Ralph and his followers. When they found that their long-trusted leader was dead, their dismay was great. No time, however, was to be lost. A man who had gone to the mast-head, whence he could look over the mangrove-bushes into the lagoon, reported that some of the vessels there were making sail in pursuit. We, however, had a good start of them. Still, without a leader, there was some confusion, and the energies of the people were not applied to their full advantage.

Suddenly there arose a cry among them that a captain must be chosen. "The English captain! the English captain!—Captain Helfrich is our man!" was shouted by all the pirates; and it was very evident that, whether he would or not, they would compel him to take the post.

"My men, I am obliged to you for your good opinion of me," said Captain Helfrich, standing up among them; "still I cannot be your captain. I will be your pilot to take you out of this harbour, and to enable you to gain a place of safety, on one condition, that you disperse at the time I point out to you. I make this agreement for your own advantage. If you keep together, you are certain before long to get into trouble. Will you trust me?"

"We agree! we agree!" was replied on all sides. "We trust you, sir, for we know you mean us well."

"Then heave up the anchor, sheet home the headsails, up with the helm, and let her cast to starboard," cried the captain, almost in the same breath.

A man was stationed at the bowsprit-end, and another at the mast-head, to give notice of any rocks beneath the water which might lie in our course; but Captain Helfrich seemed scarcely to require such information. The little schooner threaded the narrow and intricate passage with unerring accuracy, every instant the rapidity of her progress being increased by the freshening wind. It was well, indeed, for our safety that we had a steady breeze, for while we were still within the labyrinth of reefs, several vessels were seen emerging from among the mangrove-bushes. As they advanced, they fired their guns at us; but we were still far beyond their range. Had it not been, indeed, for the many turns in the passage, we should have been so far away that they could not have hoped to reach us. We had only our heels to depend on, for, with so overpowering a force, the Spaniards must easily have overcome us. Our great danger consisted in the possibility of striking on a rock before we could get clear of the reefs. On this probability our enemies calculated when they came in pursuit.

We had several reaches to pass through, which in no way increased our distance from them through the air, and at last several of their shot came whistling over our mast-heads. One went through our mainsail. We could only stand still and look at our enemies, while our little vessel made the best of her way from them.

"Hurrah, my lads! we are in the last reach," shouted our captain; "in five minutes we shall be in clear water!"

The men shouted in return. Stronger blew the breeze, making the blue sea sparkle and leap outside. On either hand it broke in masses of foam, which leaped high into the air. On we flew! A narrow channel of smooth water was before us. We glided through it. "Hurrah—hurrah! we are free— we are free!"

I remember how fresh and pure I thought the sea air smelt. With what freedom I breathed, after being shut up so long in a hot loft! The breeze was easterly—a wind which would carry us on a bowline to Jamaica. Every sail the little schooner could carry was set on her. Our pursuers were not, however, yet willing to give up the chase. Once clear, with the open sea before us, we distanced them fast, and the sailing qualities of the little schooner being very fair, we had little fear of being overtaken.

From what I saw of our present companions, I certainly should not have liked to have associated much with them. While danger threatened, they were quiet enough; but as the prospect of being overtaken decreased, they grew more reckless and overbearing in their manner, and showed with how little provocation they would be ready to break into a quarrel with us, or among themselves. Thanks to Mr Gale's and Peter's example, we were not likely to give them cause for that. As they had been prepared for flight, they had not only put on a considerable quantity of additional clothing, but each man carried round his waist a belt filled with gold and silver coins, while his pockets were filled with jewels and such silver ornaments and other articles of value which he could manage to stow away in them. This much impeded their activity, though, of course, it was but natural that they should wish to carry away with them as much as they could of those spoils, to gain which they had hazarded the loss both of life and soul!

"It will be as well, for their own sakes, that none of those fellows fall overboard," observed Peter to me when none of them were near to listen; "they'll go down like a shot, and then what will be the use to them of all the dollars and the gold they have collected? What's the use of it to them now? just to spend in the grossest folly and debauchery; and for the sake of collecting it, they have been living a life of murder and rapine! All I can say is that I don't want to change places with them, though their pockets are full and mine are empty!" I agreed with Peter that neither would I, and we had good reason before long to think the same.

We were still not clear of danger from our pursuers. The breeze freshened so much that it was with difficulty we could stagger along under the press of canvas we carried; and as the Spaniards' vessels were much larger, had we been compelled to shorten sail, they might easily have come up with us. If they did, we well knew that we could expect no mercy from them. Still the chase was very exciting. However, I would rather be the pursuer than the pursued; and I suppose that a hare, or a fox, or a stag would, if it could express its opinion, agree with me in the latter remark. Fortunately for us the breeze kept very steady; and as, after a time, the Spaniards found that they lost ground rather than gained on us, they tacked and stood back towards the Cuban coast. This event was noticed with loud cheers by all our people, nor was I slack in joining them.

Our passage, till we sighted the coast of Jamaica, was very rapid. Captain Helfrich had made some arrangement with the pirates as to their future course. I do not know what it was. Some were to go away in their boats in different directions; some wished to land, and others to be put on board homeward-bound vessels. They wanted to take the schooner, but, of course, he could not willingly let them have her, as she was not his property. I suspect that they had formed a plan to take her; but their designs, if such existed, were defeated.

Among the cargo were some small casks of rum. A knowledge of this fact the captain wished to keep concealed from everybody on board. Unhappily, however, the pirates discovered them, and, in spite of Captain Helfrich's remonstrances and warnings, they very soon had them up and broached on deck. Every minute they became more and more riotous and inclined to quarrel among themselves. Again the captain warned them that they would betray themselves; but laughingly they answered that they knew him well, and that he would take care that they got into no mischief.

The wind heading us, we had to stand in-shore, so as to beat up towards Kingston. There was a little sea on, but not enough to prevent our observing objects some way below the surface. Peter and I were looking over the side— one of the other men being at the helm—when we noticed a dark pointed object floating alongside; another came up near it. Looking down, we with a shudder discovered the long tapering bodies of two sharks swimming just on our quarter. Nothing is so hateful to a sailor, even when he has a sound plank under his feet, as a sight of those tigers of the deep. Happening shortly after to go over to the other side, and glancing my eye over the bulwarks, with almost a thrill of horror I saw two others precisely in the same relative position. At first I thought they must be the same, but going back to the other side, there were those first seen just as they had been before.

"I don't like the look of those brutes," said Peter. "I am not superstitious, but I never have seen sharks swimming along as those are but what some mischief or other has happened—a man has fallen overboard, or something of that sort!"

I, as may be supposed, shared fully in Peter's feelings, and set to work wondering what the harm would be.

I had not long to wait. The schooner had tacked, and was laying pretty well along-shore, with her head off it, and about a mile distant. One of the pirates, with drunken gravity, had insisted that he was not going to be idle, and that he would tend the fore-sheet. The state of things on board had made the captain doubly anxious to get in before night, and we were, therefore, carrying on perhaps even more sail than the little craft could well bear. We were taking the water in well over our bows; but that seemed in no way to inconvenience the hardy pirates, as they sat on the deck at their levels. I will not attempt to paint the picture presented by the pirates. The horrid oaths and blasphemy, the obscene songs, the shouts of maniac laughter, may be better imagined than described.

Peter and I and the other men had gone aft, where was also the captain, while Mr Gale stood at the helm. The sun was perhaps an hour above the horizon. Frequently the captain had turned his eyes in the direction of Kingston Harbour. A sail was seen standing out of the harbour, steering towards us, for the purpose, evidently, of getting a good offing before nightfall. As her topsails appeared above the horizon, we could make out very clearly that she was a brig.

"Hand me up my glass, Jack," said the captain with animation. He took a long, steady look at her, and then handed the glass to Mr Gale, whose place Peter took at the helm.

While they were all looking eagerly at the approaching brig, I felt the schooner heel over even more than she had been doing. The captain likewise became sensible of the movement. He looked round—

"Let go the fore-sheet!" he shouted loudly. Mr Gale at the same moment sprang forward to execute the order; but the pirate who was tending it held it on tight with drunken stupidity. Mr Gale tried to drag him away from it; but the man, instead of letting go, gave a turn, and jammed the sheet. Down came the squall on us with redoubled strength. The little vessel heeled over till her gunwale was buried in the sea. The water rose higher and higher up her deck. It was too late to cut the sheet. No skill could save her.

Down, down went the vessel! Shrieks and cries arose, but they were no longer the sounds of revelry. They were those of horror and hopeless dismay, uttered by the pirates as they found the vessel sinking under their feet and they were thrown struggling into the water. So suddenly did she go over, and so rapidly did she fill, that even the most sober had no time to consider how they could save themselves, much less had those wretched drunken men. Overloaded as they were with clothes and booty, they could neither swim nor struggle towards the spars, and planks, and oars, and boats, which were floating about on every side.

When Mr Gale found that it was too late to save the schooner, he sprung back towards one of the boats which had been stowed right aft on the weather-side; the captain, Peter, and I, with our men, had been cutting the lashings which had secured it with our knives; and giving it a shove as the deck of the vessel touched the water, we were able to get clear just as she went down. The mate had not quite reached the boat, but Peter, leaning forward, hauled him in before he was drawn into the vortex made by the schooner as she sunk. To clear her, we had of necessity to shove astern, and this drove us still further from the spot where the rest of the people were still struggling in the waves. Some of the soberest had managed to disencumber themselves of their clothing, and to clutch hold of spars to support themselves; but they had another danger, from the seaman's remorseless enemy, to contend with. We now guessed why the sharks had been accompanying us; or could they have scented the dead body of the pirate chief, which we had still on board? Why the captain had not buried him I do not know.

Scarcely had we leaped into the boat, when the terrific shrieks of the struggling pirates reminded us of what we had seen. In an instant the monsters were at them, and one after the other, with fearful rapidity, they were dragged from the supports to which they clung, their bodies mangled, and limbs torn asunder. We got out our oars as quickly as possible, and pulled back, endeavouring to save some; but before we could reach the nearest man a shark had seized him, and we could see his arms helplessly stretched out, as he was dragged down through the clear waters. On we pulled towards another, but he likewise was carried off after he had already seized the boatswain's oar, and thought himself safe. A third cried out to us piteously to come and save him. We pulled towards him with all our might; but fast as we flew through the water, two huge sharks went faster, and before we could reach him he was their prey, literally torn in sunder between them. He was the last who yet floated; the others had gone down at once, or had been torn to pieces with all their wealth about them. While we were looking round, an object rose to the surface.

"What means that?" exclaimed our captain with an expression of horror and alarm such as I did not believe his countenance capable of wearing.

It was the body of the old pirate: his face was turned towards us, and one of his arms moved as if beckoning us to follow him!

"No, no—you do not want me! I have visited you once at your summons! I'll no longer obey you!" shouted our captain with a hoarse voice, staring wildly; then he sank down into the stern-sheets overcome with his emotions.

For a minute, fancying that the old pirate was alive, we pulled towards him; then we remembered that he had been placed in a rough coffin of thick light wood, the lid of which had not been secured. Some nails, probably, had caught the clothes and kept the body in. When the vessel sunk the coffin had floated through the hatchway, the lid being knocked off; and thus the old man was once more presented to our view.

The monsters who had so speedily disposed of his wretched followers now darted forward to attack the coffin. Round and round they turned it; one arm was seized, then another, and we saw the body dragged down with a dozen sharks surrounding it, tearing it limb from limb!

Our captain very quickly recovered himself, and passing his hand over his brow, as if to shut out some dreadful vision, ordered us in a calm tone to pull towards the approaching brig. As we pulled from the spot, the water appeared here and there tinged with a crimson tint; but scarcely a vestige of the unfortunate little schooner remained. The brig approached.

"She is the *Rainbow*, sir; there can be no doubt of it!" exclaimed Peter, who had been eyeing her narrowly over his right shoulder.

He was right. On her people seeing a boat she was hove-to, and we were very quickly on board. I need not describe the surprise of Mr Jones, the first mate, who had now command of her as captain, or of the officer who had been shipped instead of Mr Gale. Of course, we had all long been given over as lost.

Mr Jones very willingly gave up his command to Captain Helfrich, and re-occupied his post as first mate; but the new officer who had been shipped, in a most foolish way nourished a peculiar dislike not only for Mr Gale for superseding him, but towards all of us, and took every opportunity of showing it. The vessel had got a full cargo in, and was on her way back to Dublin. At first, however, he pretended that he wished to be very kind to me, in consequence of the hardships I had gone through, and the narrow escape I had of death from the Maroons. Of course, there was no reason for keeping that part of our adventures secret, so I gave him a full account of all that had occurred; but then he led me on to describe the hurricane, and our capture by the pirates; and from the interest he took in the questions he asked me, I felt that he had some sinister motive for his inquiries. This made me hold my tongue for the time; and when I told Peter all the mate had asked me, he told me that I was perfectly right not to give him any further information, as he was sure that he would make a bad use of it. We neither of us liked the expression of the man's countenance, or his manner to his superiors, or us his inferiors. Time was to show us that we were right in our conjectures.

When the extra mate found that he could get nothing out of Peter or me he attacked the other men; and from what they confessed to us they had told him, we feared that he had obtained from them all the information he required. He left the brig directly we entered port, and immediately returned to Jamaica.

Captain Helfrich was received in Dublin as one who had returned from the dead; for the account of his supposed death had preceded us, and his wife had actually assumed widow's mourning for him. His sudden appearance very nearly cost her her life.

We took the usual time to refit the brig, and then sailed once more for the same destination. We had the usual number of passengers, and all went well till we reached Kingston.

After we had lain a little time there, we saw from the captain's manner that all was not going well with him; and Peter told me that from what he heard on shore, that he was accused of having been leagued with pirates; and that all sorts of things were said about him. This, to a man of the captain's temperament, was very trying. Those who knew him best, must have been perfectly convinced that, for many years past, he could not possibly have been guilty of any act of piracy; although I could have little doubt that, in his early days, he must, in some way or other, have been connected with the person whom I knew alone by the name of Captain Ralph. It was a practical evidence of the truth of that saying of Holy Writ, that the sins of his youth rise up in judgment against a man in his old age.

We had little difficulty in tracing the reports to the malignity of the man who had acted as mate during the last passage home. In consequence of these reports, Captain Helfrich had considerable difficulty in obtaining a cargo for the brig; and so disgusted was he with all the annoyance he had received, that he resolved not to return again to the West Indies.

At last, however, we were ready to sail. The evening before we were to go to sea, a boat came alongside, pulled by black men, with one man only in the stern-sheets. He asked to see Captain Helfrich. I looked over the side, and recognised him as Michael, the tall negro who had been the means of rescuing us from the Maroons. Mr Gale sent me to let the captain know that a person wanted to see him, and of course I told him who he was. The captain accordingly directed me to invite him below at once. I did so, and remained in the cabin.

"I've come, captain," said he, "to ask a favour of you."

"Anything you ask I am bound to grant," answered the captain.

"All I have to beg is a passage to England," replied the negro. "I go to seek in your country that liberty which I can find nowhere else. For years have I been striving to instil into my unhappy countrymen a knowledge of their true position; but they are too ignorant, too gross-minded to understand me. I have had no wish to set them against their masters. In most instances, both parties have been born to the position they occupy, and cannot help themselves. All I want is, that the masters should do them justice, and should treat them as men—as human beings with souls, with like passions, with like thoughts as themselves—that they should do their best to improve their minds, to educate them, to prepare them for that liberty they must sooner or later obtain. The question is, how will it be obtained? By fair and gentle means, granted—not taken by force as a right, or by violence and bloodshed. I have tried all means. I have leagued with all classes of men to commence, in some way or other, the work. Thus, for a time, I associated with Captain Ralph; but he grossly deceived me, as he did everybody else. I joined the Maroon bands, in the idea that force might avail; but in that respect I found that I was totally wrong in my calculations. I have tried to influence the planters, to show them their true interests: that with a well-instructed peasantry they would get far more work done, and at a smaller cost, than they do now with their gangs of ignorant slaves; but they laugh my notions to scorn. They fancy, because they find the negro ignorant, brutal, and stupid, that he can never be anything else. They forget that they made him so when they made him or his ancestors slaves; and that it must take more than one generation of gentle, watchful, judicious education to raise him out of the wretched state in which he now grovels. No philanthropist would wish them to emancipate their slaves now without long previous training, to fit them for liberty. If they ever free them without that training, they will ruin their properties. I find fault with them for not commencing that training at once, for not teaching them the religion they themselves profess, for not in any way attempting to enlighten their ignorance. Perhaps I may induce people in England to advocate the negro's cause; but yet if Christian men here, on the scene of their sufferings, do not care for them, how can I expect people at a distance to listen to their cries, to labour that they may obtain justice?"

Michael said much more on the same subject. Our captain listened, but did not clearly understand him; nor did I at the time. He, however, willingly granted him a passage, and treated him with the attention he deserved at our hands during it.

Michael was a man far beyond his time. Not many blacks are like him; but I have met some with comprehensive minds equal to those of any white men. The vicious system to which the generality are subject, stunts or destroys all mental development; but had they the advantages of the whites, I believe as many buds in the one case as in the other would bear rich fruit. Michael left us in Dublin, and it was not till long afterwards that I heard his subsequent fate.

We had a prosperous passage to Dublin, and nothing occurred during it worthy of being mentioned. The captain very slowly recovered his usual spirits, but was completely himself again before we reached home.

The *Rainbow* remained longer in dock than usual, and during the time I had charge of her, Peter took the opportunity of visiting his friends, who lived some miles from Liverpool.

My life was almost like that of a hermit's though surrounded by multitudes. I scarcely spoke to anyone. I amused myself, however, in my own way. I cut out all sorts of things in wood and bone, and practised every variety of knot-and-splice. At last it occurred to me that I would try to make a model of the brig. I bought at a timber-yard a soft piece of white American pine, without a knot in it; and as I had charge of the carpenter's tools, I got some of the chisels and gouges sharpened up, and set to work. With rule and compass I drew two lines for her keel on one side, and then pencilled out the shape of her deck on the other. I first, by-the-by, made a scale of so many parts of an inch to a foot, and measured every part of the brig I could reach. Having got the shape of her deck exact, and her depth, I used to go ahead and astern and look at her shape, and then come aboard again, and chisel away at my model. I shaved off very little of the wood at a time, and my eye being correct, I made one side exactly equal to the other. Then fixing the wood in a vice, I scooped out the whole of the interior with an even thickness on every side. At length the hull was completed very much to my satisfaction. Then I got a piece of thin plank for her deck, and built on her bulwarks, with the windlass, the binnacle, caboose, and combings of her hatchway complete. Next I commenced rigging her. I formed all the blocks, and expended many a penny in purchasing whipcord and twine of different thickness, as well as linen for her sails. Having often carefully watched the sailmakers at work, and helped them when they would allow me, I was able not only to cut out the sails properly, but to fasten on the bolt-ropes, and to mark exactly the divisions of the cloths. I had also to bring the painter's art into play; and to fashion with a file various stancheons, and belaying-pins, and such like things, out of bits of iron and copper; indeed, I am vain to say that I made a very complete model. When she was perfectly completed, I walked round and round her with no little satisfaction, surveying her from every quarter, and placing her in every possible position—indeed, I was never tired of trimming sails. I had had a purpose in building her, for I wanted to present her to my kind captain for one of his little boys, whom I had seen occasionally on board.

Old Pat Hagan, though too advanced in years to be intrusted entirely with the charge of the ship, occasionally came down to enable me to take a run on shore. The first day, therefore, that he made his appearance, I started with my model on my head to the captain's residence.

"Who has sent you here, Jack, with that pretty little craft?" asked Captain Helfrich, as I was shown into his parlour, where he with his wife and children were sitting.

"Why, sir, as I hoped that you would not think me taking too much on myself in offering it to Master James, I made bold to bring it myself," I replied, looking down and feeling somewhat bashful at the praise my model was receiving.

"I cannot refuse your pretty gift, Jack, which, I am sure is given with a good heart. But where did you pick her up my man?" answered the captain. "But just let me look at her nearer. Why, she is the very model of the *Rainbow*!"

When I told him that I had built her myself, he still further praised me, as did his lady; and Master James was delighted with his present, and jumped about round her, and thanked me over and over again.

"I am very much pleased, my lad, with this little craft, and from the way you have built her, and, still more, from your general conduct, I tell you that you would be fitted to become an officer if you had but the necessary education. You must try and obtain that, and I will have my eye on you. The next time you come home, you shall go to school; and see if you cannot pick up some knowledge of reading during the voyage."

I constantly think of the saying, "Man proposes, but Heaven disposes." So I found it in this instance. My kind captain would have done all he intended, but his plans for my benefit were frustrated by circumstances then unforeseen by either of us.

A few days after this, we sailed for the Mediterranean. We had shipped a couple more guns, and four additional hands. In those days it was necessary for merchantmen frequenting that sea to be strongly armed, for it was sadly infested by pirates. There were Moorish pirates, Salee rovers, and others, who went to sea in large vessels as well as in boats, and robbed indiscriminately all vessels they could overpower; then there were Algerine pirates, who had still larger vessels, and were superior to them in numbers; and, lastly, there were Greek pirates, every island and rock in the Aegean Sea harbouring some of them. Long years of Turkish misrule and tyranny had thoroughly enslaved and debased the great mass of the people; and the more daring and adventurous spirits, finding all lawful exercise of their energies denied them on shore, sought instead for such excitement and profit as piracy could afford them afloat. Some of them darted out in small boats from the sheltered coves and bays when any unarmed merchantman was becalmed near them; while others, in well-formed and well-manned vessels of large size, cruised about in all directions in search of prizes. Sometimes their strongholds, when discovered by the Turks, were attacked and destroyed, but generally they carried on their system of rapine with perfect impunity; and though the people of other governments complained, they had no legal power to punish the subjects of a friendly nation. So the Greeks, rejoicing in impunity, grew more and more audacious, till they levied contributions on all the civilised nations of Europe whose traders ventured into the Levant. Such was the state of things when the *Rainbow* sailed on her first voyage to Smyrna. Captain Helfrich had been there before, and he knew the character of the people he had to deal with.

We met with bad weather soon after leaving the Channel, and had already been driven some way to the westward, when, as we were in about the latitude of Lisbon, it came on to blow harder than ever from the eastward. Had we been close in with the land, this would not have signified; but before we could beat up again, a continuance of northerly and easterly gales drove us to the southward of the Gut of Gibraltar. When there, they left us in a dead calm, with our sails idly flapping against the masts, and rolling bulwarks under in the heavy swell they had caused on Old Ocean's bosom.

The sun arose over the distant Morocco coast—not then in sight, however—and sent his rays down on our decks with an ardour which made the pitch bubble and hiss up out of the seams. Not a ripple disturbed the rounded smoothness of the heaving swells, while even the bubbles thrown off from our sides refused to float to any distance from us. We were not the only occupants of our own horizon. Some eight miles off, or so, there was another brig rolling away much in the same fashion that we were. All hands were anxious for a breeze, as we in no way liked the heat after the cold of a northern clime, though it mattered nothing to us whether we made a quick or a slow passage. We whistled, as sailors always whistle when they want a breeze; but the breeze did not come the faster for all our whistling. I never knew it do so, with all my experience. What folly, indeed, in man to suppose that He who rules the winds and waves should alter his laws in consequence of their puny efforts to make a wind with their mouths! In those days, of course, I did not think about the matter. I whistled because others whistled; but if any of us had been asked on what ground we founded our hope that the wind would come in consequence, I suspect that we should have been very much puzzled to return a satisfactory answer.

"What countryman do you make that craft out there to be, Mr Gale?" said the captain, handing the mate the glass through which he had been looking.

"Not an Englishman, certainly," was the reply, after the usual steady glance. "I should say, from the whiteness of her canvas, and her light upper-rigging, that she belongs to some of those turban-wearing people along the African coast in there, or up the Straits. They are seldom pleasant customers for an unarmed craft to come across."

"I had formed the same idea of her," observed Captain Helfrich. "We know pretty well, however, how to deal with such gentry: and if she come across us, she'll find that she has caught a Tartar."

I told Peter what I had heard; and he, I found, after looking through the telescope, formed much the same opinion of the stranger.

The day wore on, and still the calm continued, so that we in no way decreased our distance from her. Night also overtook us, while we lay rolling away helplessly as before. The swell, however, was going down gradually; as it did so, the brig became more steady in the water.

It was about the first hour of the morning-watch, which Peter and I were keeping, when he asked me suddenly if I did not hear oars. I listened: there could be no doubt about it. There was more than one boat, and the oars were pulled pretty rapidly too. The night was not dark, though there was no moon; but a mist floated on the surface of the water, and served to veil it from our sight, though right overhead the stars could still be seen glimmering faintly in the sky.

Peter instantly went and reported what he had heard to Mr Gale, who was officer of the watch. After listening for some time he could hear no sound, and seemed to doubt the correctness of our assertion. The boats had probably ceased pulling, for a purpose at which we could only then conjecture. At last the sound of the oars reached Mr Gale's ears also.

"There's something in this," he exclaimed. "Jack, go and call the captain."

Captain Helfrich was on deck in an instant.

"The crew of some vessel which has foundered, and taken to their boats," suggested the mate.

"From what quarter does the sound come?" asked the captain, listening attentively. "Visitors from the brig we saw last night," he cried out. "Depend on it, they come to us with no good intention."

His experience in the West Indies and elsewhere had taught him to be prepared for any such emergency as the present. He was not above being prepared, and he knew that the greatest folly is to despise an enemy.

"Turn the hands up, Mr Gale. Get the arm-chest open, and the guns loaded and run out. We must be ready. No noise, though: if anyone intends to surprise us, it is as well that we should surprise them instead."

The watch below were instantly on deck, and in a few minutes every preparation was made for the reception of an enemy. Still we could not see any boats, but the louder sound of oars in the rowlocks convinced us that they were approaching. Again the sound ceased.

"They are not quite certain of our position," observed Mr Gale. "If they were people escaping from a wreck, and not aware that a vessel is near, they would have pulled steadily on."

"You are right," said the captain. "Have a torch ready to heave in among them, that I may make certain who they are before I give the word to fire. It won't do to run the risk of hurting friends; but when once you hear the word, my men, blaze away with all your might. If they are enemies, they will not be such as will give us quarter, however loudly we may cry for it."

A murmur ran round among the people, to signify that we would obey the captain's orders. The atrocities committed of late years by the Algerines, and the subjects of the Emperor of Morocco, had made those people the dread of all sea-going people, and gained them a proportionate amount of hatred.

Once more the sound of oars was heard, and in a short time even their splash in the water could be distinguished. There are few things more trying to a man's nerves than to know that an enemy is approaching, and not to be able to discover his strength or form, or the quarter from whence he is coming. Our cutlasses were buckled on, our muskets were ready to be seized, and the slow matches were in our hands, but concealed, so that the enemy might not perceive them. Mr Gale stood with a torch ready to light at a moment's notice. Slowly the boats approached. Apparently they seemed to think some caution necessary, or perhaps they could not see how we lay, and wished to attack us according to some preconcerted plan. There was a pause. I know that my heart beat pretty quick to learn what would follow. Then there was a dash towards us, and we could hear the sound even from the rowers' chests as they strained at their oars. Dark forms were seen gliding out of the darkness. Suddenly the bright light of a torch burst forth on our deck. Mr Gale waved it above his head, and threw it towards the boats, its glare showing us swarthy features, and turbaned heads, and coloured vests, and jewelled arms. There could be no doubt as to the character of our midnight visitors.

"Fire!" shouted the captain; "fire! and aim low."

Our guns, loaded with langrage, sent forth a deadly shower among the pirate crew. Shrieks and groans arose in return. We followed it up with a discharge of musketry. The enemy were completely taken by surprise. Many, abandoning their oars, ceased pulling towards us. This gave us time to reload our guns and small-arms. Their leaders, it seemed, were attempting to rally them. Once more we could distinguish their dark forms amid the gloom of night.

"Fire!" again shouted our captain.

The shrieks and groans were redoubled, and the boats again disappeared in the darkness. We remained at our quarters expecting their return. They did not come. A light breeze from the southward and westward at length sprung up, and we were able to shape our course towards the Rock of Gibraltar, and when the morning broke no sail was in sight.

Chapter Nine
A Ship without a Crew

We touched at Gibraltar, that the captain might obtain information as to the ports he was to call at. Smyrna, we found, was to be our ultimate destination. He gave notice of the attack made on us by the pirate, and a brig of war was sent to look out for her. I shall have a good deal more to say about our turbaned friends by-and-by. Gibraltar I thought a wonderful place, with the face of its high rock, which stands out into the sea, cut full of galleries, and ports with heavy guns grinning from them in every direction. Of course, the seamen very often do not know at what port the ship is to touch, or whereabouts they are. Such was my case: I had never seen a chart of the Mediterranean. The first definite notion I got of it was from Peter, who afterwards drew one for me with a piece of chalk on the lid of his chest. I only knew that we were steering towards the east, and that we were likely to see several strange places and many strange people.

Some time after leaving Gibraltar, I had just come on deck one night to keep my watch, when out of the dark ocean, as it seemed, I saw a bright light burst forth and blaze up into the sky. I thought some ship must have blown up; but the light continued, and grew stronger and stronger, and reached higher and higher. The fire seemed to spout out, and then to fall in a shower on every side, something like the branches of a weeping ash, or some wide-spreading tree. The ship was standing towards it, and I thought we should certainly be burned.

"Oh, Peter, Peter," I exclaimed, "what is the matter? Surely the world has caught fire, and we shall all be destroyed!"

"No fear of that just yet, lad," he answered, laughing. "That's only a burning island, which is called Stromboli. There are some mountains in these parts, as I have heard say, which send out such a quantity of hot stones, and ashes, and boiling earth, that whole towns, and villages, and fields are overwhelmed and buried. In those countries you may buy for a penny as much fruit as you can carry, and get as much wine as you can drink for twopence, while all sorts of other good things are very cheap; and the weather is almost always like summer. But, for my part, I would rather live in Old England, with the foul weather and the fair we get there, and a piece of beef, often somewhat hard to come at, than in a country where your house may any moment be knocked down by an earthquake or covered up with hot ashes. To my mind, all countries have their advantages and their drawbacks; and the great thing is, to be grateful for the one, and to learn how to guard against the other."

We touched at several places on our passage. Malta was one of them. The English had not at that time taken possession of it.

At length we reached Smyrna, which is partly situated on level ground, the harbour backed by a lofty hill. There is more trade here than in any other place in the East. The climate, though hot, is very fine; but the place is often shaken by earthquakes, which have at times caused great destruction to lives and property. That dreadful scourge, also, the plague, is a frequent visitor. The former may truly be said to be beyond man's control; but the latter is, I am certain, brought about very much by the dirty habits of the people, and their ill-ventilated and ill-drained habitations.

In the neighbourhood of Smyrna grow great quantities of figs, which are dried and packed in boxes and baskets. They formed part of our cargo home. We had likewise raisins and other dried fruits, and preserves, and rich silks and embroideries. None of the seamen were allowed to go on shore, for Christians were very likely to get insulted, if not ill-treated, by the Turks. In those days they used to look upon all Christians as dogs, and to behave towards them as such. Besides Turks, there were a great number of Jews and Greeks, and people from every part of the East, living at Smyrna; but all had to submit to the caprices and ignorance of the first.

I was not sorry when we once more made sail, with the ship's head to the westward. We had a somewhat tedious passage down the Mediterranean, having frequent baffling or light winds. At times of the year gales, however, blow with great fury in that sea, though they seldom last long. Most to be dreaded are the sudden gales which, under the name of "white squalls," have sent many a vessel, caught unprepared, to the bottom.

At last we reached Gibraltar again. The Captain inquired if anything had been seen of the pirate which had attempted to surprise us with her boats; but the brig of war had returned without hearing anything of her. We remained but a day at the Rock. We took on board there the crew of a ship which had foundered at sea, and had been brought in by a Greek brig which had picked them up, and, for a wonder, had not murdered them. However, as they were nearly naked, and had promised the Greeks a reward if they arrived in safety, more was to be got by keeping them alive than by killing them. We were thus very strongly manned.

Foul winds and a heavy gale made us stand a good way to the westward on our passage home, after getting clear of the Gut. Soon after sunrise one morning a sail was reported away to windward, running down towards us, the wind being about on her quarter. As she approached with all sail set, she appeared to be sailing very wildly; that is to say, instead of keeping a steady, straight course, her head went now on one side, now on the other, as if a drunken man was at the helm. The captain and mates were looking at her through their glasses.

"She looks like an English craft, by the cut of her canvas," observed Mr Gale.

"I can make out the ensign at her peak, and there's no doubt she is English," answered the captain. "There is something wrong aboard her, however, depend on that. I suspect that they have had a fever among them, or the plague, and that all her people are sick, and they have not strength to shorten sail."

"Perhaps there is a mutiny aboard, or the people are all quarrelling among each other," observed Mr Gale. "I have known of such things: when the master and officers have ill-treated the men, the crew have risen against them, and either hove them overboard or confined them below, and carried the ship into an enemy's port."

I was surprised at the expression of the captain's countenance while the mate was speaking. The words seemed to remind him, I thought, of some occurrence of his youth.

"Depend on it, Gale, no good ever came of such a deed," he remarked. "Either the actors in such work have gone on all their lives afraid of detection, or have very speedily paid the penalty of it. Unless a man has become a hardened wretch, the recollection of such an act will throw a gloom over the whole of his after-life, and blight all his earthly prospects."

"Not if he feels that he is forgiven, surely, sir," said the mate, looking at him steadfastly. "Sincere repentance and firm trust in the merits of One who died for us will gain us that boon, I am certain. I am not learned in divinity, but this much I know and feel; and I believe that it is the sum and substance of what a Christian should know and feel."

I had never heard Mr Gale speak in that way before. I did not know even that he was what is called a religious man. I certainly never heard him swear or abuse any of the men, or accuse them wrongfully, as too many officers do; but I just thought him a quiet, brave, amiable young man, who was content to do his duty and let other people follow their own ways. I afterwards had reason to know that he was even more than that. He was eminently judicious, and he now felt that the time had arrived when he might speak a word in season to good effect. The captain listened, and after some time I saw him put out his hand and grasp that of Mr Gale; but he said nothing in reply. Meantime the brig was drawing near to us.

"Have a boat ready to board her," cried the captain, after he had again examined her through his glasses. "It is strange, indeed; I can see no one on her deck."

The *Rainbow* was now hove-to, and a boat was lowered. I went in her; so did Peter. Mr Gale had charge of her. We all were, by the captain's orders, strongly armed, and he directed the mate to approach cautiously, so as not to be taken by surprise. I never met a braver man than the captain, or one who, at the same time, was more cautious and careful of the lives of his people. During my apprenticeship with him, on several occasions, had it not been for this constant caution and care not to be taken by surprise, both he and all his people would have been destroyed.

While the boat pulled towards the stranger, the brig, with her guns run out, and the people at their quarters ready to fire, stood so as to cross her bows, and to punish her should any treachery be intended. We had to be careful in going alongside, lest she should run us down; for as her head now went in one direction, now in another, it was difficult to determine on which side she would come. She was a fine large brig, fully as large as the *Rainbow*, and it did look strange to see her sailing along over the wide Atlantic without apparently a human being to guide her course. Still, from what I had heard the captain say, I could not help fancying that there was some trick, and fully expected to see a number of men start up the moment we touched her side, and either send our boat to the bottom with a cold shot, or seize us and carry us as prisoners below. It was a satisfaction, however, to feel that, with the shipwrecked crew, we had plenty of men on board to carry the ship home, and to punish those who might injure us.

I must say that I felt rather curious as, giving way, we dashed alongside the stranger, and Peter with his boat-hook catching hold of the fore-chains, we, with our cutlasses in our mouths, scrambled on board. No one appeared. A perfect silence reigned over the deck. Our first business was to shorten sail, and round-to the ship. Mr Gale flew to the helm, and put it down, while we flattened in the topsail-braces, and clewed up top-gallant-sails, and brailed up the courses, throwing the foretop-sail aback. As this work occupied all our attention, we had no time to make any remarks as to the state of affairs on deck. As I was running forward, my foot slipped in a wet mass and I came to the deck. Jumping up again, I seized the rope at which I had been ordered to haul. When the work was done, and the ship hove-to, I looked at my hands. A cold shudder came over me: they were covered with *blood*!

I gave a cry of horror and disgust. It attracted the attention of my shipmates. We now looked along the deck. In several places were other dark clotted marks scarcely yet dry. Other signs there were which showed that plunder had been the object of the deadly attack, which, it was evident, had been made on the crew of the brig. Articles of dress were strewed about, and cases of provisions, nautical instruments, books and charts, and opened bales of merchandise; but there were no signs of a struggle—nothing to show that the hapless crew had even been enabled to fight for their lives.

"What has been the matter aboard?" shouted Captain Helfrich, as the *Rainbow* passed close to us.

"Murder, sir! foul murder!—there can be no doubt of it," answered Mr Gale, who was about to descend the companion-hatch. I with others followed him.

What a scene of havoc, confusion, and wanton destruction the cabin presented, as seen in the dim light which came down the companion-hatch, for the covering of the skylight was on. There had evidently been a fierce strife there. A mirror over the stove was broken to atoms—the chairs were overturned—china-plates and cut-glasses lay scattered about in fragments amid clothing, and books, and boxes; the cabin lamp and a cabin compass, and stores of every sort, of which the lockers had been rifled—chests and trunks lay open, despoiled of their contents, but no human form, either alive or dead, was to be seen.

Mr Gale ordered the hands on deck to lift off the skylight. As the bright sunshine came down into the cabin, the full horror of the scene was exhibited. Among a mass of articles, such as I have enumerated, which lay on the cabin table, were six human heads with ghastly grins, holding pieces of meat in their mouths! They were placed at each side of the table, and knives, and forks, and plates with food, were placed before them! They had evidently thus been arranged in savage mockery by their ruthless murderers, as they were about to leave the scene of their atrocity. We searched about: no bodies were found. On one side of the cabin there was a complete pool of blood, though part of it had been lapped up by the bedclothes, which had been dragged from one of the berths. The beds in the other state-rooms had been undisturbed.

Everything in the cabin showed us that the vessel was English; and this was confirmed by opening the books, which were all in English. So, as far as we could judge, were the countenances of the murdered people—I will not say men; for on examining one of the heads, our horror was increased by discovering that one of them was that of a woman—young and beautiful she had been. Oh, what a scene of horror must her eyes last have beheld; with what anguish must her heart last have beat! Even in death the features of the murdered men wore various expressions. Horror on one was clearly portrayed—desperate determination on that of another—fierce rage showed itself on the face of another. So I fancied; but, at all events, had I known any of the people, I think that I should have recognised them. There were the same Anglo-Saxon features common to all. The complexions of some were fair, and of others sunburnt. There was one with a weather-beaten countenance, and large bushy whiskers, whom we took to be one of the officers of the ship, while most of the others had the smooth complexions of shore-going people, and were probably those of passengers.

What we had already discovered plainly told the story of the catastrophe. The brig had been surprised in the evening by some piratical miscreants, while the captain and passengers, and some of the officers probably, were below at supper. The watch on deck must have instantly been overpowered before those below had time to come to their assistance. Some, probably hearing a scuffle, and coming on deck, were instantly slaughtered, or, it might have been, secured and carried off all prisoners. The people in the cabin could not even have been aware of what was going forward, and the first announcement of the misfortune which had befallen them, was the appearance of the pirates rushing into the cabin. Rising from the table, they had seized whatever weapons came nearest to hand to defend themselves. Desperately they might have fought, but all in vain. One clearly had been dragged from bed, holding fast to the clothes. Most likely the unfortunate lady had been so treated, and deprived of life on the body of her husband.

Mr Gale's opinion was, that the captain's head was not among those in the cabin; but that, on first hearing the scuffle, he had sprung on deck, as being nearest the door, to ascertain its cause. This opinion was afterwards confirmed by the discoveries we made. As soon as they had been overpowered, their heads must have been cut off, perhaps to make the rest show where any valuables they might possess were concealed. However performed, at all events the butchery was complete. Never, indeed, have my eyes beheld a scene of greater horror. Death alone, we know, may bring peace and joy; but death under such outrageous aspects as those I have described, affrights the soul.

While some of the men went forward to ascertain the state of matters in the forepeak, Mr Gale kept Peter and me to look after the ship's papers. We hunted about in a number of places for some time without avail. At last I went into what I concluded to be the master's cabin, and in a tin case, under his pillow, I found them. I took them to Mr Gale, who glanced over them.

"The *Dolphin*, the vessel is called," he observed. "Ah, and here's a name I think I remember,—Walter Stenning, master. Why, Poplar, is not that the name of the young man we picked up at sea a few voyages back to the West Indies?"

"Yes, sir; the very same," answered Peter. "I've had notice of him since then, and I heard say that he had become master and owner of a fine craft, and gone with his wife and family to live out in one of the colonies; I don't know which."

"Halifax, Nova Scotia, the brig hails from, I see. She was bound from Bristol to Demerara," continued Mr Gale, reading on from the papers. "I suppose, though, we shall have to send her to Halifax, where, as far as I can make out, her owners reside, as well as the merchants who have shipped most of her freight."

While the mate was still looking over the papers, Captain Helfrich, who had come on board in another boat, entered the cabin. He was more affected than any of us by the horrid sight which met his eyes.

"Who can have done this?" he exclaimed, casting his eyes round in every direction. "Ah, what is that I see in the corner there?" He pointed to what proved to be a Moorish turban; while near it lay a piece of a sabre, which, from its curved form, evidently belonged to the same people.

"This work was done, I doubt not, by the very villains who attempted to surprise us," he observed, as I handed him the articles to examine. "We may truly be thankful that they did not find us unprepared, as they did the unfortunate people of this vessel, or their lot might have been ours."

"Indeed we have cause of gratitude to God, who, in His mercy, preserved us," responded Mr Gale. "I wish that we could find the people who did this work, to stop their committing further mischief."

"The miscreants cannot be far-off," exclaimed the captain. "If we could fall in with them, we might punish them in a way they little expect."

"I suspect, sir, when the Moors let the brig go free, they must have hauled their wind, and kept away to the eastward," observed Mr Gale. "They are not fond, in general, of keeping so far away from their own shores."

"You are right, Gale," said the captain. "However, though I think we might find them, I should not be justified in going out of our course to look for them. We must, therefore, consider how we are to dispose of the brig. As far as I can judge, without thinking more of the matter, I am bound to send her to Halifax at once to her owners, from whom we shall obtain the proper salvage. Now, as I shall be glad to do what I think will be of service to you, I will give you the command of her, with a few hands whom I can spare; while with the seamen whom we have as passengers on board, the *Rainbow* will still be sufficiently manned to reach home in safety."

Mr Gale did not refuse the captain's offer, and I was far from sorry when I found that he had selected Peter Poplar and me among the people who were to accompany him. Besides us, as the shipwrecked seamen were all anxious to reach England, and would not volunteer, we had only three other men; so that, considering the size of the *Dolphin*, we were somewhat short-handed.

Before committing the heads to the deep, we examined their features, and it was the opinion of all on board, who had known Walter Stenning, that none of them bore any resemblance to him; so that if the young man, who had for so long been on board the *Rainbow*, was the same person who lately commanded this unfortunate vessel, his fate was still uncertain. Too probably, however, he had been murdered by the miscreants on deck. Scarcely less melancholy would be his lot if he still survived, for he would have been carried away to Morocco, and there sold as a slave, to labour in the fields or gardens.

One or two other bits of arms and ornaments were found about the deck; and the captain, on examining them, gave it as his opinion that the pirate was one of those craft which had long been known under the name of Salee Rovers. At one time the greater number of vessels fitted out by the Moors to plunder on the high seas hailed from that port. Before the captain left the vessel, every part of her was examined, but not a trace of a living being could be found. Still, too clearly to be mistaken did she tell her own dreadful tale. The log-book showed that, three days before, she had been in a dead calm since sunrise, and that a strange sail was in sight. Little did her crew dream of the woe that stranger was to work them!

We were allowed to go on board the *Rainbow* to get our chests, and to wish our shipmates good-bye; and then I bade farewell to my old captain, and the craft I had learned to love as a seaman only can,—the vessel within whose wide timbers I had spent many a happy day, and which had carried me in safety across many a wide sea.

We found nearly everything we required on board the *Dolphin*. It took some time, however, to get her to rights, to wash out the stains of blood, and to put the cabin in order, and to remove all remnants of the horrid deed which had been enacted there. It was some time, however, before Mr Gale could prevail on himself to take possession of the cabin. At last all the necessary arrangements on board the *Dolphin* were made, and Captain Helfrich ordering Mr Gale to proceed on his voyage, bore away to the northeast, while we kept to the westward of north. I felt very strange as I found myself on board a new vessel, and saw the old one, in which I had served for so many years, sailing away from us. I should have felt very forlorn and melancholy if Peter had not been with me. I was also very much attached to Mr Gale, and was very glad that he was now my captain.

The Irish, I have observed, generally possess a considerable amount of imagination, and I conclude that I inherited no small share of that quality from my poor mother. I remember that the first night I passed on board the *Dolphin*, I fancied in my sleep that I saw again the whole of the scene of horror which had so short a time before been enacted there. Several times I jumped up, thinking that the rovers were coming on board, and that I had to fight for my life. Then I fancied that I heard the cries and the groans of the poor fellows who had slept where I was sleeping, and had met their death close to where I lay; and I looked out and saw them writhing and struggling in the hands of their barbarous murderers.

Peter, instead of laughing at me when I told him of my dreams, answered me that the surest way to banish all such thoughts, was to say my prayers earnestly at night whenever I turned in, and to pray that I might be preserved from all dangers, and especially from the fate which had overtaken these poor men. I was very fortunate in falling in, at this time of my life, with two such men as Mr Gale and Peter Poplar. The latter was uneducated, certainly, but had learned his religion from the Bible, and therefore he possessed the true principles, the essentials of a saving faith; and he was the instrument of gradually opening my mind and heart to them.

Captain Gale, for so I shall now call him, had a very sharp look-out kept lest we should again fall in with the Salee Rover, or any of his consorts, which, it was very probable, might still be hovering about in that part of the ocean. The first day after parting company with the *Rainbow* passed by without a single sail heaving in sight. The breeze had got round to the southward, so that we had a fair wind; and as it was light, we were able to carry all the canvas we could set. At night, however, as we were somewhat short-handed, the captain ordered us to furl top-gallant-sails, and to take a reef in the topsails, that we might be better prepared should it come on to blow. The second night, however, passed away, and the same fine weather continued.

The next morning, soon after daybreak, Captain Gale came on deck, and ordered us to loose top-gallant-sails. On going aloft to obey the order, as I cast my eyes round the horizon, I saw, right away on our weather-beam, just rising out of the water, the top-gallant-sails of a brig, close-hauled, standing, I judged, across our course. I hailed the deck to say what I had observed; and after the reefs were shaken out of the topsails, the captain told me to keep aloft to watch the movements of the stranger. She stood steadily on till she rose her topsails out of the water, and then, as I judged, on seeing us, kept more away, so as to cut us off. On hearing this, the captain himself went aloft to have a look at the stranger. He remained some time, examining her narrowly through his glass. The breeze had freshened up a good deal, and it was not a time, I should have supposed, to have made more sail; but the moment he came down, he ordered us to set studden-sails and royals.

"We must make the craft put her best leg foremost," said he to Peter. "I do not altogether like the look of that ship out there. She is certainly not English; and by her movements she seems very much inclined to overhaul us. Just tell us what you think about the matter."

Peter took the glass, and went aloft. He also was some time there. When he came down, he handed the glass to the captain without speaking.

"Well, Peter, what do you think of her?" asked the latter. Peter took off his hat, and passed his hand over his brow. "Why, to say the truth, Captain Gale, I don't like her looks at all. If ever one craft was like another, she's like that strange brig which lay becalmed near us the time when we were attacked before going up the Mediterranean. It's difficult to tell one vessel from another, but I very much suspect that she's the very same piratical rascal we before fell in with, and that this brig is no stranger to her either."

The captain replied, that he was afraid his apprehensions were too well-founded.

The next question was, how we were to escape from the corsair, should the stranger really be her. A couple of hours passed away, and although we were going at a good rate through the water, there could be no doubt that she was coming up with us. It was now blowing a stiffish breeze, and I saw the captain and Peter often casting an anxious glance aloft, to see whether the masts and spars would bear the heavy strain put on them. Happily there was not much sea; and though the studden-sail-booms bent and cracked again, they held on bravely. Our great hope was, that we might be able to keep well ahead of the stranger till night came on; and then that, by hauling our wind, he might pass us in the dark. We had already got as much wind as the brig could stagger under, and thus one of the greatest dangers we had to apprehend was from carrying away any of our spars. Over and over again the captain looked up at the mast-head, and exclaimed, "Hold on, good sticks, hold on, and serve us a good turn!"

A stern chase is a long chase; and though this was not quite a stern chase, by-the-by, it was nearly one, and we hoped it might prove so long as to have no end. Still our pursuer kept after us. As he drew nearer, we had less and less doubt that he was the very Salee Rover we had before so much to do with. At the same time, our hopes of escaping him decreased. Peter had set himself down on the heel of the bowsprit to rest. I brought him his dinner there, for he had not left the deck for a moment since the morning. He did not look up for some time till I begged him to eat. Still he did not answer. At last I asked him what he was thinking about.

"Why, Jack, how we may manage to escape from the pirate," he answered after some time. "A very curious idea has struck me, and if the captain will listen to me, we'll put it into execution. It can do no harm, and if our pursuer comes up with us, I think it will make him haul his wind in a pretty considerable hurry."

I asked Peter to tell me his plan, wondering what it could possibly be.

"I take it, you see, that the brig out there is the very same which attacked this vessel, and her crew, of course, know that there was not a living soul left on board, but that there were six heads in the cabin," he answered, speaking very slow. "Now, in my wild young days, I was once for some time behind the scenes of a theatre, and if I had been a scholar I might have become a play-actor. When there, I saw what wonders a little paint, and canvas, and pasteboard could work. As there are six of us, I propose to put a false neck over each of our heads, and I'll manage to paint in a quarter less than no time, six as ugly faces as you ever saw, on as many balls of canvas, which I'll stuff with oakum. So each of us will have a head to hold in his hand. Unless some accident happens, we certainly can manage to keep ahead of the rover till nightfall. Then we'll just mix up a number of lumps of gunpowder and sulphur, and place them about the deck before each of us. As soon as the rover ranges up alongside, we'll fire them all at the same moment, and I shall be very much mistaken if the cut-throats don't think that there's a company on board they would rather not have anything to do with."

I could not help laughing at Peter's quaint notion—still, however little effect it might have on civilised people, I thought it was very likely to scare away the sort of men who composed the Moorish crew, and I advised him instantly to propose it to the captain. Peter, accordingly, bolting his dinner with a haste which showed that he was thinking more about his idea than it, went aft, and opened up the case. Captain Gale listened more attentively than I expected, and, after a little consideration, said that he thought it was very likely to succeed. The plan once adopted, all hands set energetically to work to make the required preparations.

There was, fortunately, an abundance of materials. I got out the paint-pots, and mixed the colours according to Peter's directions. He himself, with canvas and palm needles, fitted the necks, cutting holes for us to see through them; the other men were employed in making six prodigious round balls for heads, and covering one part with shakings, to serve as hair. He undertook to stand at the helm, and to have his head at the end of the boat-hook by his side, that he might lift it up at the proper moment. All the frying-pans and shallow pots which could be found were collected, and the captain made with damp gunpowder a number of what schoolboys call "Vesuviuses." These, however, were very much larger than the contents of a schoolboy's purse would allow him to make. He tried one of them, and found it sent forth a lurid glare, which even in the day-time showed what effect it would produce at night.

Before sunset all our preparations were completed; and when dressed up, a very curious and horrid crew we most certainly did look. Had there been more of us, the effect might perhaps have been increased. We now waited almost with boyish impatience for the coming up of the rover to put our trick into execution. Captain Gale was, however, too wise to trust to it till all other means of escape had failed. The wind had rather fallen than increased, and this was an advantage to us in two ways: it enabled us to shorten sail with less difficulty than we should otherwise have done; and we found that, with less wind, we went faster in proportion through the water than did our pursuer.

It was with feelings such as I had very seldom before experienced, that I saw the sun sinking towards the ocean, surrounded with a blaze of glory; its bright rays falling on the loftier sails of the rover, while they still reached our courses. Down it went beneath its watery home, and I questioned very much with myself whether I should ever again see it rise. I had no great confidence in Peter's trick, nor do I suppose that he had much himself, when he came seriously to think about the matter; but still, if overtaken, we had no other means of escaping—we could not fight, and still less could we have any hope from the mercy of our foes. I did not, however, mention my doubts to Peter, and far less would I have done so to any of the other men. Young as I was, I had seen enough of the world to have learned the value of discretion.

As the daylight disappeared, a grey canopy of clouds was spread over the sky, sufficiently thick to obscure the stars. Thus the night was more than usually dark. Still, as the atmosphere was free from mist, seamen's eyes could distinguish objects at a considerable distance off. With much anxiety we watched the rover, in the hope that the growing darkness would hide her from our view; but still we could see her following closely in our wake, and thus, of course, there was every probability that she could see us. We could not expect that the darkness would increase; consequently there would have been no use in altering our course, as it would have been perceived on board; so all we could do was to stand boldly on as before. At the rate she was overhauling us, as the captain calculated, she would be up with us by midnight. I should have liked to have shortened sail, and brought the matter to an issue, but Captain Gale was not a man to act thus unwisely. He knew that we might fall in with some friendly vessel, or that the pirate might give up the chase, or that some sudden change in the weather might enable us to escape at the last moment. Everything, however, was prepared; and thus standing at our posts, we waited the result.

Nearer and nearer drew the pirate. We were within range of her guns, still she did not fire. On she came. She was close upon our quarter.

"Wait till I give the word," said the captain, in a low voice. She was ranging up on our beam.

"Ready!" exclaimed the captain. "Now!"

In a moment a terrifically lurid glare was cast over our decks. Up went the helmsman's gory head at the end of a boarding-pike, though he steered as steadily as before, while we all shook ours in our hands, and at the same moment gave vent to the most unearthly shrieks, and groans, and cries, our headless helmsman shrieking and shouting louder than any of us. At this we all again shook our ghastly heads. Peter had given the necks the appearance of dropping blood, and again we shrieked and groaned louder than ever.

The effect on board the rover was instantaneous. The crew must have fully thought that they had got hold of some demon-craft as a punishment for their crimes. Down went their helm; the tacks and sheets seemed all to be flying away together; and the topsails came down on their caps. Ropes were let go, but no one thought of hauling on others, or belaying them; no one seemed to know what they were about; and many even shrieked and cried out with terror and dismay. Nothing could have been more complete than the success of our trick.

We were all eagerly watching its effect, when, just as the vessels were parting, a figure was seen to spring into the main-rigging of the rover. We all saw him, and all recognised the person as no other than Walter Stenning, the late master of the *Dolphin*. On we sailed. The dark outline of the rover grew less and less distinct, till it was totally lost in the gloom of night.

Chapter Ten
The Water-Logged Ship

For the remainder of the night we kept anxiously looking over the taffrail, lest our enemy should have again made sail in chase. More than once I thought I saw the rover's shadowy form stealing up towards us through the darkness; but just as I expected to make it out clearly, to my great relief it dissipated into mist. Voices, also, I thought, seemed to be shouting after us from out of the gloom; but neither did they ever assume any distinctness, and fancy, I found, had caused the creation of them both. Slowly the night passed away, and as soon as the first bright streaks of dawn appeared in the grey sky, the captain went himself aloft to take a survey of the horizon.

"There is not a sail in sight in any quarter," he exclaimed to Peter, as he returned on deck. "To your clever suggestion we owe our own lives and the safety of the ship; but clever as it was, I would not advise others to try a similar one. They might not meet with enemies so easily deceived."

"No, sir," answered Peter, "certainly not; and, for my part, I would much rather have beat off the scoundrels in a fair stand-up fight than with such a play-acting trick as that; but then, you see, air, it was Hobson's choice—neck or nothing with us!"

Peter's curious contrivances were kept, that they might be shown as an evidence of the way in which we had escaped from the rover. The appearance of Walter Stenning on board the rover was a subject of constant conversation among us. There could be no doubt, then, that he had been carried on board the rover, and that his life had been preserved. This would be a satisfaction to his friends, though a melancholy one, as his ultimate fate must still be uncertain.

We had still a long passage before us to Halifax, and might meet with many adventures. At all events, we could scarcely expect to escape some bad weather, though it was not likely we should encounter the rover, or any of her consorts, as gentry of that class were not fond of venturing into northern latitudes. For more than a couple of weeks the fine weather continued, and we met with no event worthy of note. We had, however, to learn somewhat more of the sufferings which people meet with on the wide ocean.

One morning the sky became overcast; the water was of that dull leaden hue, striped with white foam, which gives so gloomy an aspect to the ocean; and heavy squalls compelled us to shorten sail as fast as all hands could get through the task. For the greater part of the day the squalls continued; but in the afternoon, though it was hazy, the weather again improved.

I was looking out, when I saw through the mist what I took to be a sail. There was something strange about her rig—I could not make it out. Accordingly, I reported it to the captain, who came on deck. He called Peter to him.

"She looks to me like a vessel in distress, with most of her spars and upper-rigging carried away," he observed. She was about six miles off, on the lee-bow. Accordingly, the brig was kept away towards her.

Heavy squalls of rain occasionally blew over us, and for a time completely hid the wreck from view. When it cleared for an instant, we made out that she had an English ensign reversed secured to the main-rigging. Her mainmast alone was standing entire, her foremast had gone by the board, her mizzen-mast was carried away at the top, and part only of her bowsprit remained. Her maintop-mast-yard was still crossed; but the sail, torn to ribbons, now fluttered in the wind, and not another inch of canvas had she set.

"She looks dreadfully knocked about," observed the captain. "And from the way she rolls in the trough of the sea, there can be no doubt that she is water-logged. If it were not for the signal flying, I should scarcely expect to find anyone on board."

We had as much sail set as we could venture to carry, so that we could not make greater speed towards her; but the squalls increased in number, and night was coming on, so that we began to fear that we should be unable to get up to her before darkness hid her from our sight. Even when we had got up to her, unless she had her own boats, short-handed as we were, with a heavy sea running, we could scarcely hope to render her much assistance. Still Captain Gale was not the man to neglect making the attempt. Some, I am sorry to say, would have sailed on their way, and allowed any poor wretches who might have been on the wreck to perish miserably. As we approached the wreck, we could just distinguish through the driving mists and thickening gloom of night, several human beings leaning against the stumps of her masts, or sitting on her deck eagerly waving to us. The captain on seeing them exclaimed—

"Peter, we must do something to save those poor fellows."

"I should think: so, sir," was the answer. "If you let me have a boat, with Jack there, and one hand besides, I'll undertake to get on board and bring them off. I know that it would leave you terribly short-handed if we were lost; but I don't think that there's any chance of that, and I'm sure that we shall be protected in doing what's right."

"You shall have your way, Peter; I cannot refuse you," exclaimed the captain, warmly. "We'll heave the brig to to leeward of the wreck, so that if you can manage to get the poor fellows into the boat, you can with less difficulty drop aboard of us again."

According to this plan, we ran under the stern of the ship and rounded to. I never saw a more complete wreck yet floating on the surface. Her entire bulwarks, her boats, caboose, booms—indeed everything on deck—had been completely carried away, and the sea even now occasionally washed entirely over her. It was not an easy matter to lower our boat, but it was done without an accident; and Peter, Andrew Blair, a fine young fellow, and I, pulled away in her for the wreck. The unfortunate wretches on board waved us on. Several more made their appearance, as we approached, from behind a sail which had been triced up round the mainmast, which appeared to be the only shelter they had from the inclemency of the weather. They were all holding on to ropes secured to the masts or rigging, for without them they would certainly at once have been washed off the deck into the sea.

On getting nearer, we saw one or two heads looking at us from above the companion-hatch, which had escaped, and seemed to have afforded some shelter to others. We pulled as close to her as we could venture to go.

"Remember if we come alongside only four of you at a time must get into the boat, or we shall all lose our lives together!" shouted Peter. "Do you hear me there?"

They signified that they did hear; but Peter's caution was very unnecessary, for few of them could do more than crawl, and none of them, without assistance, could have got into the boat.

"I see what must be done," said Peter to us. "You two remain in the boat. There's a rope towing overboard from the main-rigging; I'll get hold of it, and haul myself on her deck, and then, as best I can, I'll drop the poor fellows into the boat!"

To propose was with him to act. As the boat with the send of the sea approached the wreck, while we fended her off he seized the rope, which he found secure, and though the water, as it came pouring down to leeward, washed over him, he hauled himself up in a moment on her deck, and stood among the miserable wretches who peopled it. They crawled round him, and grasped his legs, to show their gratitude to him as their deliverer. I saw by his action that he was telling them that there was not a moment to be lost.

Beckoning to us to approach, he seized one of them up in his arms as if he had been an infant, and grasping the rope with one hand, swung himself off from the side of the ship, and deposited his burden in the boat, or rather in our arms, as we stood ready to receive him. In a moment he was on the deck, and lifting up another human being, sprung as before into the boat.

"How many of you are there?" he asked of one who seemed to be the strongest of the crew, and looked by his dress like an officer. Once he had evidently been a stout, broad-shouldered, muscular young man, now he was a mere skeleton like the rest.

"Twelve or fourteen there were this morning, but I know not how many may since have died," was the answer, given in a hollow tone scarcely audible.

"Then we'll take four at a time to the brig, and we shall have to make three trips," answered Peter. "We must not venture with more, though as to weight the boat would carry the whole of you. Now, my lad," he continued, addressing the mate, for so the man who had spoken proved to be, "just do you come with us this trip. I'll lend you a hand into the boat."

"No, no!" answered the fine fellow; "take some of the others who are worse off than I am. There were a couple of women. They will be found aft under the companion-hatch."

As no persuasion would make the mate alter his determination, Peter hurried aft, and diving under the hatch, returned with what looked like a long bundle of clothes in his arms. "Gently, now," he sung out; "she has life in her, but very little of it."

The clothes enveloped a female form, but so emaciated that she seemed to be of no weight whatever. Before placing her in the boat, Peter poured a few drops of liquid down her throat from a flask the captain had given him.

"There's no use to bring the other poor thing; her sufferings are over," he observed, as he lifted in another man. "And now, my lads, we'll put these on board."

We soon dropped down to the brig, and with less difficulty got the poor wretches up the side. The captain proposed sending the two other hands instead of Blair and me, but we begged that we might be allowed to return to the wreck.

Once more we pulled away from the brig, the boat, it must be remembered, tumbling and tossing about, now sunk in the trough of the sea, now rising to the top of a foam-crested wave; the sky overhead threatening and cloudy; a dense mist driving in our faces; and darkness rapidly coming on. We had the lives of fellow-creatures to save, and we persevered. Again the undaunted Peter sprung on board the wreck.

"Take care of that man!" exclaimed the mate, as an extraordinary-looking figure, in a long dressing-gown, with strips of canvas fastened about his head, ran up from behind the woman; "he is not altogether right in his mind, I fear."

"Avaunt, ye pirates! ye plunderers! ye marauders!" shrieked out the person spoken of. "How dare ye venture on board my noble ship? Away with ye! away! away!" and flourishing a piece of timber which he had wrenched, it seemed, from the side of the ship, he advanced towards Peter.

My shipmate would have been struck down by the maniac's blow, had he not sprung nimbly aside, and then, rushing in, he closed with the wretched being, and wrenched the weapon out of his grasp. The madman's strength was exhausted.

"I yield! I yield me!" he cried; and though he was a tall man, Peter lifted him up as he had done the others, and handed him to us. He lay quiet enough in the bottom of the boat, regarding the wreck he was leaving with a stare of wonder.

Three other men were lifted in, but still the mate refused to leave while any remained alive on board. As we were leaving the wreck a second time, a man lifted himself up from the deck, and stood for a moment gazing at us.

"What! again deserted!" he exclaimed, shrieking frantically. "Oh, take me! take me!" and staggering forward, before the mate could prevent him he cast himself headlong into the sea. We endeavoured to put back, but he floated scarcely a moment, and then the foaming waters closed over his head. It was another of the numberless instances I have witnessed of the crime and folly of not waiting with calmness and resignation for what the Almighty has in his providence prepared for us. I trust that the poor man's mind had given way in this instance; but even that result is often produced by a want of reliance on God's mercy.

We put our hapless freight on board the brig, and a third time returned to the wreck. Besides the brave mate, Peter found only two more people alive on board. Several were dead. At the earnest solicitation of the mate, Peter helped him to commit them to the deep. It was a melancholy and loathsome task, for some had been long dead.

The delay also was of serious consequence. More than once I summoned Peter, for another thick squall of rain had come on, and when I glanced round for an instant to look for the brig, she was nowhere to be seen! A pang of dread ran through my heart, and all sorts of horrid ideas rushed into my head. I thought that the squall might have struck her, and that she might have capsized, or that she might have drifted so far to leeward that we might not be able to find her. I said nothing, however, but helped Peter to take the mate and the other two survivors off the wreck. Then, indeed, the question pressed on us, What has become of the brig?

"Cheer up, my lads!" cried Peter; "hold on yet a while; we'll see her presently."

We waited with intense anxiety, and the darkness seemed every instant increasing. It was, however, only the result of the tail of the squall passing by. Suddenly a bright light burst forth, which we knew must proceed from the deck of the brig.

"The captain has not forgotten the trick we played the pirates!" exclaimed Peter. "Shove off, my lads!"

With lightened hearts we pulled away to leeward, and were soon once more on the deck of the brig, with our boat hoisted up and secured. Every care and attention which we could possibly bestow was paid to the poor starving wretches. Captain Gale was enlightened as well as brave and generous, so that he knew well how to treat them. First he gave them only a little liquid—tea and cocoa; and then after a time a little simple arrowroot; afterwards he gave them some with broth; and, lastly, he mixed a few drops of wine with the arrowroot.

Scarcely, however, had we got them down below, than the gale which had been threatening came on; and while the captain went to the helm, all hands had to spring aloft to shorten sail. Happily the gale was in our favour, so that we were able to run before it, and keep our course. There can be little doubt that had we not providentially appeared that very night, everybody on board the wreck would have perished. We had hard work enough to do the duty of the ship and to attend to our passengers, who could for some days do nothing to help themselves. They were all too weak to speak without fatigue, so we forbore to question them as to the particulars of the events which had brought them into the condition in which we had found them.

For some days all we knew was, that the ship was the *Eagle*, from Quebec, laden with timber, and that she had been six weeks very nearly in the condition we found her—water-logged, with spars and sails carried away. The captain had died, and the lady we had rescued was his wife. Poor thing! at first she was almost insensible to everything; but when she recovered her health and strength, it was pitiable to see her grief.

The tall, gaunt man, whom we found deranged, had been a merchant's clerk, and had gone out to Canada in the vain hope of finding employment. Disappointed in his expectations, he was returning home. At first he appeared to recover strength, but a relapse took place, and he rapidly seemed to grow weaker and weaker. I was sent to watch him. Suddenly he sat up in his berth, and glared wildly around.

"Where am I?—where am I going?—what has occurred?" he exclaimed. "Tell me, young man. I have had a horrid dream. For worlds I would not dream it again!" Then his voice lowered, and, rubbing his hand across his brow, he added, in a low, calm tone—

"I know all about it. I am going to a land where I have only one account to render; but my Judge will be great and just; and there is One in whom I trust who has taken all my sins on Himself. Young man, thank all those who have been kind to me. I am grateful. Good-night!" He fell back on his pillow, and was dead.

Among those saved was one other passenger. The rest consisted of the first mate, and the crew of the ship. With one of the crew, a young Canadian, who was making his second trip to sea, I formed a strong friendship; Adam De Lisle was his name. From him I learned the particulars of the disaster.

"You must know," he observed, "that the timber which is sent from Canada to England is cut down from forests many hundreds of miles up the country. Numerous large and rapid rivers run into the great river Saint Lawrence. At the fall of the year gangs of woodcutters, under regular leaders, proceed up these rivers in canoes, with a supply of food, and every requisite, to enable them to spend the winter far from the haunts, of civilisation. Arrived at the forest they have selected for their operations, they build their habitations, and then set to work to cut down the trees they require. These, when shaped into square logs, as soon as snow has fallen, and ice covers the water, are dragged to the nearest stream. When spring returns, they are bound together in small rafts, and floated down towards the main river. Sometimes, when rapids occur, they are separated, and a few trees are allowed to glide down together. Slides have, of late years, been formed by the sides of the rapids, through which the timber descends without injury. At the foot of the rapids the rafts are re-formed, and ultimately, when they reach the Saint Lawrence, they are made so large that huts are built on them, in which their conductors live till they reach

Quebec. This they frequently do not do till the end of the summer, when all the ships have sailed. The timber, therefore, remains in shallow docks at the mouth of the Charles River, which runs into the Saint Lawrence on one side of Quebec, till the following spring. The timber is often shipped through a large port in the bow of a ship, but a quantity is also piled upon deck, and lashed there to ring-bolts, making a ship with so great a weight above board very uneasy in a sea. Thus, I think, more accidents happen to the spars and rigging of timber-ships than to any other, though they have an advantage in floating longer than other craft.

"The *Eagle* was one of the first ships which left Quebec this year, with a crew of eighteen, all told fore-and-aft, with the captain's wife and several passengers. Scarcely had we got clear of the Gulf when we fell in with bad weather; and about ten days afterwards, a heavy gale sprung up from the westward. It was night. The sea soon ran very high, and the ship being deep, and steering ill, before she could be got before the wind, it made a clear breach over her. There she lay helplessly in the trough of the sea, most of her bulwarks carried away, and the water pouring down her companion-hatch, and deluging the cabin. It soon found its way forward, and every instant we thought she would capsize. The captain ordered the main and mizzen topsail-sheets to be cut away, for there was no time to let them go, or clew-up the sails; but still the ship lay helpless and unable to answer her helm. Two men went to the helm, while others rigged relieving-tackles, and at length all the after-sail being taken off her, the headsail filled, and once more she ran before the wind. This was a great relief, but still the water was gaining on us. The seas continued rolling up after us high above the poop, and at length one broke on board, carrying the taffrail clean away, and sweeping the after-part of the deck. Had we not had safety-lines passed across the deck, the greater number of us would at once have been washed overboard. Our sufferings had now become intense, both from cold and hunger. All the provisions we could get at were spoiled with salt water, and the few clothes we had on were drenched also with water, and the wind pierced through them to our very bones. We still managed to keep a close-reefed foretop-sail on the ship, with a mainstay-sail and trysail, or we could not have avoided being constantly pooped. The gale, in a short time, increased in fury as the sea did in height. Again it made a clean breach over the ship. All the bulwarks were carried away; and the ring-bolts being torn from the decks, the deck timber, which consisted of large logs, was washed overboard, as were all our boats. At the same moment the foresail blew clean out of the bolt-ropes; and all those we could muster fit for duty had not strength sufficient to go aloft to set another. We knew well that our safety much depended on our being able to keep sail on the ship; but each man felt that his death would be the consequence if he attempted to go aloft, with that raging sea tumbling the ship about in every direction, the wind howling round him, and the torn sail flapping fiercely in his face. Still we managed to keep the ship before the wind, and thus, by easing the strain on her, she was prevented from going to pieces, which she would otherwise inevitably have done.

"Our first mate, James Carr, was a fine fellow. To look at him, you would not have supposed that he had so much endurance in his body. His spirit kept him up. When very few besides he and I could bear up, he went about the decks as if nothing unusual had occurred. He was a slight, fair man, and far from strongly-built; but he was a thoughtful, reading, and more than that, a religious man. Those who had led the wildest and most careless lives, and had no faith or hope to sustain them, were the first to succumb. I held out—first, because I believed that God would sustain me; and because I had a good constitution, which I had never injured by vice and debauchery, as too many of the rest had done. The captain was a good, kind man, and he did his best for us as long as his strength lasted. The little food we could get at was carefully husbanded, and all hands were put on short allowance. Many days thus passed away, the ship running before the wind, and still keeping together. At length the wind lulled, and we began to look forward with hope to the future. The caboose had hitherto stood, and the cook managed to light a fire in it, and to dress several meals, which we ate with comparative comfort. As long as there was a moderate breeze the ship ran steadily before it, but what many people would have thought an advantage, proved our greatest bane. Too much wind had injured us—too little almost destroyed us. It fell a dead calm; and this, far from bettering our condition, made the ship roll still more than ever, and soon reduced us to the condition in which you found us. The greater part of the bowsprit had already gone, the foremast was next rolled out of her, and then the mizzen-mast went—the mainmast must have been an unusually good stick, or that would have gone likewise. We had scarcely strength left to cut away the wreck. Hitherto, though all hands were growing daily weaker, no deaths had occurred, nor had anyone any particular sickness. However, anxiety of mind now helped to make our poor captain ill, and he took to his cot. The daily provision for each of us consisted also of but three ounces of bread, and half a pint of water. We agreed to this, because we felt that it was enough to sustain life for some time, and that it was better to have a little each day than have to go many days without any food at all. The officers proposed, however, before long, to diminish even this small allowance—though, by mixing a little spirits with the water, our food sustained us more than it would otherwise have done. Starvation, after a time, began to tell sadly on our tempers; and we, who had generally lived in good-fellowship with each other, spent the day in wrangling and peevishness. A breeze, however, had again sprung up, which seemed to steady the ship, though we could not keep her on her proper course. Such was the state of things, when one morning Mr Carr going on deck, as was his custom, to take a look-out, and to hoist our signal of distress, he shouted out, 'Sail, ho!'

"How did our hearts leap with joy as we heard those words! We all crawled up as best we could to take a look at the stranger, which we hoped would save us. She saw us, and drew nearer. The captain got the mate and me to help him up on deck, and then, as he saw the approaching vessel, his heart bursting forth with gratitude, he called on us all to return thanks to God for the deliverance he hoped was at hand. His poor wife, who had held out bravely, and scarcely ever left his side, wept with joy at the thought that his life might yet be spared.

"'Now, my lads, let's see if we cannot get the ship somewhat clear of water,' exclaimed Mr Carr, going to the pumps; 'It will never do to have it said that we did nothing to help ourselves.'

"I believe he did this to employ the men's minds till assistance could reach us. He set the example, which we all followed; and, weak as we were, we pumped away with such good-will that she rose perceptibly in the water, showing us that there was no leak to injure her.

"At last the stranger, a large brig, reached us, and heaving-to just to leeward, Mr Carr gave him an account of all that had happened to us.

"The master of the brig said that he was himself somewhat short of provisions, but would send us what he could venture to give in his own boat. We thanked him with grateful hearts. Still the boat did not come. There was some consultation on board; we could not tell what. A breeze from the westward again sprung up. It was a fair wind for the stranger.

"'What's he about now?' exclaimed several voices, trembling with agitation.

"He put up his helm and filled his headsails.

"'He'll go about directly, and heave-to on the other tack,' said Mr Carr.

"Still the stranger stood on.

"'Where can he be going to?' again exclaimed several of us.

"On, on he stood, steadily, with all sail set! Oh, how bitter were the words which followed him! Could that heartless stranger have heard them, would he have ventured to brave the fate to which he had left so many of his fellow-creatures? How completely had he forgotten that golden rule,

'Do unto others as you would wish others to do unto you!' What will be his thoughts some day when he is suffering from all the miseries to which we were exposed, when he remembers the wreck he deserted on the wild ocean! Hour after hour we watched him anxiously, scarcely believing, till his topsails dipped beneath the horizon, that so heartless a wretch existed in the creation."

"Ay, it's another proof of the depth of man's vileness, and wickedness, and contempt of the laws of a God of mercy," observed Peter Poplar. "I have known many such instances almost as bad; so I am not surprised."

"When we found that we really were deserted, the spirits of all of us and the minds of some gave way. Several of the crew broke into the spirit-room, which they could now reach, and, broaching a cask of liquor, endeavoured to forget their miseries by getting drunk. The mate and I, and most of the passengers, abstained from the temptation. Those who indulged in it were the first to pay the penalty by a miserable death.

"Still discipline had been maintained. Mr Carr called on me to accompany him round the ship in search of anything which might serve as food to stay the cravings of hunger. We discovered a few pounds of candles, some bits of old leather, leather shoes, a rug, a couple of hides; but our greatest prize was about a gallon of lamp-oil, and some oil intended to mix with paint. These we brought into the cabin, to be kept in safety. While we were there, Mr Carr's eyes fell on old Trojan, the captain's favourite Newfoundland dog, as he lay almost dying under his master's cot. The captain very naturally had not brought himself to order its death.

"'I am sorry, sir,' said Mr Carr, 'to propose what I do; but that dog may be the means of preserving the lives of all of us. We must kill him.'

"'You'll be proposing to kill and eat each other before long,' exclaimed the poor master, in a querulous tone.

"'Heaven forbid!' answered the mate. 'But to take the life of a brute beast is a different matter. I don't see how we can spare him. Even if we do, he will not live long, and now his blood alone will be of great importance.'

"At last the captain consented to the death of his favourite, and poor Trojan was led up on deck to be put to death. Before he was killed, we all of us took an anxious look round the horizon, to ascertain that no sail was near. We would gladly, even then, have saved the poor dog's life. The cravings of hunger soon, however, drove all feelings of remorse from our bosoms. The faithful brute looked up into our faces, and his eyes said as clearly as if he had spoken the words, 'I know that it is necessary—be quick about it.' How carefully we husbanded every drop of the blood! The mate got a teaspoon, and served it out with that measure full to each of us at a time, while the flesh was reserved for another day.

"I cannot describe how those wretched days passed away. Except the mate and three others of us, no one could even stand. The captain lay in his cot growing worse and worse. I was on deck one afternoon with Mr Carr, steering and keeping the ship's head to the eastward, when we were startled by a faint shriek from the cabin. Presently afterwards the captain rushed on deck.

"'Mutiny! mutiny!' he exclaimed, frantically flourishing his arms about. 'But I'll take care that no one takes the ship from me. I'll shoot the first man who approaches me, be he whom he may. See here here!'

"He drew a brace of pistols from his bosom, and presented them at us. Happily, one missed fire; the ball from the other passed close to Mr Carr's head.

"'That's right, sir,' said Mr Carr, quite coolly. 'Now you've quelled the mutiny, let's go below.'

"He signed to one of the other men, who crawled aft to help me to steer, while he took the captain below. This outbreak was the last flaring up of the poor man's almost exhausted strength. His wife watched him as the flame of life sank lower and lower in the socket; and two days after that, when I went into the cabin, I found her fainting beside him, and he was dead. She entreated that the body might be allowed to remain in the cabin another day; but the next she allowed the mate and me to remove it, and to commit it to the sea.

"Oh, how sad and melancholy were those long, dreary nights, as we stood at the helm, the gale howling over our heads, the ship groaning and creaking, and the seas roaring up astern and threatening every moment to wash us from our uncertain support—darkness above us, darkness on every side!

"At last not a particle of food remained. Mr Carr made another search into every cranny of the ship. Some grease was found; it served to keep life in us another day. Then the dreadful information spread among us that there was nothing else. Relief must come, or we must die.

"'Others have lived under like circumstances,' said one, looking up under his scowling brow.

"'Ay, if it's necessary, it must be done,' hissed another.

"'There is no need why we should all die,' growled a third.

"They clearly understood what each other meant. I was listening, but could not believe the horrid truth. Those who were but able to move crawled aft to Mr Carr, to tell him of their determination. For long he would not listen to them, but drove them forward, calling them cannibals, and telling them to wait God's providence. For my own part, I felt that I would rather have died than have agreed to their proposals. What they wanted was that lots should be drawn, and that he who drew the shortest should be put to death, and the one next should be the executioner. The captain's wife was to be free. At last their importunity became so great that Mr Carr agreed that, should no sail appear at the end of another twenty-four hours, he would no longer oppose their wishes. Before that time, two of those who were most eager for the dreadful mode of sustaining life, or most fearful of death, were summoned away. The crime was prevented; no one had to become a murderer. I will not describe how my wretched shipmates sustained life. Mr Carr abstained from the dreadful repast. So did I and one or two others; and though we lost in strength, our sufferings were much less acute, and our minds more tranquil, and our judgment far clearer than was the case with those who thus indulged their appetites. What we might have done I know not, had not God in his mercy sent your brig to our aid, with men on board with hearts to feel for us, and courage, in spite of all dangers, to rescue us. Some time before this the ship had become completely water-logged; and we, being driven from all shelter below, were reduced to the state in which you found us."

The account De Lisle gave of Mr Carr raised him very much in my opinion, and I thought at the time that he was just the man I should like to sail with. We more than once spoke on the subject of the condition to which the crew of the *Eagle* had been reduced.

"To my mind," observed De Lisle, "I cannot believe that people are justified in taking away the life of a fellow-creature even to preserve their own. I thought so at the time, and I think so now, that our duty is to resign ourselves implicitly to God's will—to do our very utmost to preserve our lives, and to leave the rest in his hands."

Peter agreed with him. He told him that he wondered Mr Carr did not mix up the grease on which they had fed with very fine saw-dust, as it would have made it go much further. De Lisle replied, that had they even supposed such a thing would have been beneficial, they had no means of making fine saw-dust, as they could get at no saw, and every particle of wood, as well as everything else, was soaked with wet.

After all the dangers and adventures we had gone through, it was with no little satisfaction that, as I was stationed on the look-out aloft, I espied land on the starboard-bow, which Captain Gale pronounced to be that of Nova Scotia, a little to the westward of Cape Spry. We were in sight of Sambro Head just at nightfall, but had to lay off till the morning before we could run in among the numerous islets which exist between that point and Devil's Island.

Thus another night had to be passed on board by our weary shipwrecked visitors. Dark and dreary it proved. The wind came off cold and cheerless, in fitful gusts, from the shore, and moaned and howled through the rigging; the rain beat on our decks; and broken cross-seas tumbled and danced round us like imps of evil, eager to prevent our escaping from their malign influence. Thus wore on the night.

Chapter Eleven
Adventures in Morocco—Search for the Lost Captain

As the morning sun arose, lighting up Sambro Head in the distance, the clouds of night dispersed from off the sky, and with a fair breeze we ran in under the forts which guard McNab's Island, at the entrance of the fine harbour of Halifax. The capital of Nova Scotia stands on the side of a hill facing the east, which rises gradually from the water's edge. Its streets are wide, well laid out, and handsome, mostly crossing each other at right angles, and extending along the shores of the harbour for a distance of two miles, and running inland about half a mile. Fine wharfs, at which ships of any burden can discharge their cargoes, extend along the water's edge; above them are the warehouses and merchants' stores; and then come the public buildings; and, lastly, the houses of the more wealthy inhabitants. The harbour is very fine, and would hold as large a fleet as ever put to sea. The naval dockyard is also a handsome establishment, and it is the chief naval station in British North America. As it is completely open to the influence of the sea air, its anchorage is very seldom blocked up by ice. It is altogether an important place, and would become still more important in war-time.

As soon as we had dropped our anchor, Captain Gale, taking me with him to carry his papers and other articles, went on shore to find out the owners of the *Dolphin*. Davidson and Stenning were their names, the latter being the brother of the master, who was also part owner. He was dreadfully overcome when Captain Gale announced his errand.

"What do you mean, sir? My brave brother Walter dead! murdered by rascally pirates!" he exclaimed. "Oh, impossible!—it's too horrid! What will his poor wife do?"

"I have my hopes that he may still be numbered among the living," replied Captain Gale. And he then recounted all that had occurred connected with the Salee rover.

Both the gentlemen complimented the captain on the way he had behaved, and then begged him to wait to see Mrs Walter Stenning, who was residing there. After some time, during which her brother-in-law was preparing her for the captain's communication, we were called in to see the lady. She begged that I might come too, that she might question me about having seen her husband in the rigging of the rover. She was not very young, but she was handsome, and very modest-looking; and as she was dressed in mourning, she appeared very interesting, and I for one thought that I should be ready to do anything to please her. She listened attentively to all the captain had to say; and after talking to him some time, cross-questioned me very narrowly as to how I knew that he was the man I had seen on board the rover.

"It was him—it was him, I am certain!" she exclaimed. "My good and noble husband cannot be killed. His life has been spared. I feel it—I know it. I'll go and find him out. I'll search for him everywhere. I'll rescue him even if he is in the very heart of Morocco."

"I fear, madam, that's more than you or any other woman can accomplish," answered Captain Gale. "But if any human being is able to rescue your husband, even though the risk may be very great, I for one shall be more than glad to engage in the work. If he's above the water and above the earth, we'll find him."

There spoke the warm-hearted impetuous sailor. He did not stop to consider difficulties, but at once undertook to do what his heart prompted. It was not quite at the spur of the moment either, because he had, from the moment he thought Stenning dead, been feeling a sentiment of pity for his widow; and now he saw her sweet, amiable face, he was still more anxious to relieve her grief.

Mrs Stenning, as may be supposed, could scarcely find words to thank Captain Gale for his offer; and when he repeated it the following day, the owners replied that they would most thankfully accept it, and would put him in charge of the *Dolphin*, that he might go out in her to commence his search.

In the meantime, the people we had picked up at sea were landed, and taken care of by the inhabitants of the place. Mrs Stenning insisted on taking charge of poor Mrs Ellis, the widow of the captain of the *Eagle*; and Mr Carr volunteered to join the *Dolphin*, to go in search of Walter Stenning, with whom, curiously enough, he was well acquainted. Captain Gale at once offered to take me instead of sending me home, as had been arranged he should do; and, of course, I was delighted to join him. Peter Poplar at once volunteered to accompany him; as indeed did all the crew of the brig, and some of the seamen we saved from the wreck: the greater number were, however, too ill to serve again at sea.

The articles, as it happened, which composed the cargo, being much in demand at the time, sold well; and the owners were the better able, therefore, to fit out the brig in as liberal a way as could be desired. She was, accordingly, strongly armed, and well able to contend with any rover or other vessel we might meet on the African coast. After the lessons we had received, also, we were not likely to be taken by surprise,—the mode in which the pirates of those days usually attempted to capture their prey.

Mrs Stenning used frequently to come on board, to superintend the outfit of the ship, and to hasten the workmen; and thus everybody working with a will, and with an important object in view, she was soon ready for sea. Often and often, on the contrary, have I seen work which might and should have been rapidly performed, most vexatiously delayed through the laziness, or ignorance, or carelessness of those employed on it. One man has not taken a correct measure; another has forgotten to give a simple order; a third has put off a small piece of work to do something else which was not so much required; a fourth has ill-fitted a portion of the machine, or has broken what he calls some trifle which he has not replaced; and so forth. How much better would it be if they, and all whose eyes read my story, would but remember that saying of Holy Writ—"Whatsoever thy hand findeth to do, do it with thy might."

Yes, in that Book, if men would but search earnestly, they would find with an overflowing abundance all that they can require to guide them aright, both in everything in regard to this life, as well as to make them wise unto salvation. But, then, they must not hope to be guided partly by the rules and maxims of the world, and partly by those of the Bible. They must study the Bible by the light which the Bible affords—not by man's light or man's wisdom. They must not suppose that a mere cursory or occasional reading will suffice. They must read it diligently with all their heart, with an earnest prayer for enlightenment, and with an honest wish to comprehend it fully, and a resolution to be guided by its precepts. Let the worldly-minded understand that those who do so succeed best, and are at the same time the happiest men in the world in the long-run. However, Old Jack does not want to preach just now. If his readers will not believe him, deeply does he mourn the inevitable consequences to them.

The brig, as I said, was soon ready for sea. It might have appeared that the shortest way to proceed about our expedition would have been to sail at once for Morocco; but as the productions of Nova Scotia are chiefly food and timber, and such articles were in no request in that part of Africa, it was necessary to go first to England with a cargo, and then to take in what was required, such as cotton and woollen manufactures, hardware, arms, and ammunition. Accordingly, we took on board some quintals of dry fish, and barrels of flour, and beef, and pork, and pickled fish, and staves, and shingles, and lath-wood, and hoops, and such like productions of the forest. At that time, however, the country did not produce any large quantity of those articles for exportation.

The owners directed us first to proceed to Bristol, where we were to discharge our cargo, and to take on board another suited to the Morocco markets. Our departure excited great interest in Halifax, where Walter Stenning and his family were well-known; and his poor wife was one of the last people to leave the brig before she sailed.

Once more, then, we were at sea. Several occurrences took place during the voyage which would be worth narrating, had not I other subjects of more interest to describe. People talk a great deal of the monotony of this or that existence, and especially of a long sea voyage. For my part, I have learned to believe that no day is altogether barren of incident, if people would but learn to look inwardly as well as outwardly. Something of interest is always taking place in nature, but men must keep their senses awake to observe it; so some process is always going forward in a man's moral being, but his conscience must be alive to take note of it.

We reached Bristol in six weeks—not a bad passage in those days, when navigation had not made the strides it since has. We brought the first account of all the events I have described, and as the passengers and most of the crew of the *Dolphin* had belonged to Bristol, several families of the place were plunged in deep grief, and a universal desire prevailed to recover any of those who might have been carried into captivity, and to ascertain further particulars of the tragedy. No time, therefore, was lost in shipping a fresh cargo, and in furnishing us with such supplies as might be required.

Our directions were to proceed first to the port of Alarache, where resided a merchant who corresponded occasionally with our Bristol consignees. From him we were to obtain an interpreter, and to proceed to such other ports as might be judged advantageous according to the information he might furnish. We had a fair run to Cape Spartel, the north-western point of Africa. It then fell calm for a day or so. After this we had very light and baffling winds, and we sighted more than one suspicious-looking craft; but they did not, apparently, like our appearance, and made sail away from us. At length we came off Alarache. A bar runs across the mouth of the harbour, which even at spring-tides prevents large ships from entering, though there were sufficient water on it to allow us to get over. No pilot came out, so Captain Gale resolved to make a bold stroke, and to carry the brig in by himself.

It was nearly high-water, and the breeze was favourable as we stood towards the land. The sky and sea were blue and bright, with a line of foam where the water ran over the shallower part of the bar. Dark rocks and yellow sands were before us, with white-washed, flat-roofed houses, and here and there a minaret or cupola of a mosque, and tall, slender, wide-spreading topped date-trees scattered over the landscape; while lower down, protecting the town, was a frowning castle or fort, with a few vessels at anchor before it. A boat-load of officials, with very brown faces, white dresses, and red caps, came off to inquire our business, and get bucksheesh, as the Turks call such gratuities as they can collect from travellers and voyagers. The captain could only reply by showing a document in Moorish with which he had been furnished, and repeating the name of Mynheer Von Donk, the Dutch merchant at the place, to whom we were consigned. This, in the course of a couple of hours, produced Mynheer Von Donk himself, to ascertain what was required of him. I cannot pretend to say that all Dutch merchants are like him, for if so, they must be a very funny set of people. He was very short and very fat, with queer little sparkling eyes, and a biggish snub-nose, and thick lips, and hair so long and stiff that his three-cornered hat could scarcely keep it from starting out all round his bullet-shaped head. He had on very very wide brown breeches; and very very large silver buckles to his shoes; and a waistcoat of yellow silk, embroidered all over with strange designs, and so ample that it almost superseded the necessity of breeches; and his brown coat looked as if made with a due preparation for the still further enlargement of its respectable owner. Mynheer informed the captain that he could speak every language under the sun like a native; but, as Peter remarked, then it must have been like a native who had lived away from home all his life, and forgotten his mother-tongue. We, however, made out that it was very necessary to be cautious in our dealings with the Moors, as they were the greatest thieves and rogues in the world, and that they would only desire an opportunity of seizing the brig, and making slaves of us all; but that while we remained in Alarache, we should be safe under his protection.

When Captain Gale explained to him the real object of the voyage, he brightened up considerably, as he saw that he might have an opportunity of making even more out of the ship than he at first expected. I do not say that Mynheer Von Donk was destitute of human sympathies; but he had gone out to that far from agreeable place to make money, and money he was resolved to make by every means in his power. He was ready enough even to promise to assist in finding poor Captain Stenning, provided he could be paid for it—he preferred labouring in a laudable object with pay, to labouring in an object which was not laudable, if no more money was to be made in one way than in another; but he had no desire to labour in anything without pay.

We saw very little of the shore in this place, for he asked that we should not be allowed to land, except in company with one of our officers and his interpreter. We had, however, a pretty brisk traffic for the goods we had brought, we taking chiefly hard dollars in return; however, the captain did not refuse some articles, such as bees-wax, hides, copper; dates, and almonds, and other fruits not likely to spoil by keeping. It was, at the same time, important that we should not fill up entirely with merchandise, that we might have an excuse for visiting other ports. As far as we could judge, the dangers we had heard of had been very much exaggerated, and arose chiefly from the careless and often violent conduct of those who visited the country. Captain Gale, aided by Mr Carr, kept the strictest discipline on board; and we must have gained the character of being very quiet well-disposed traders, without a thought beyond disposing of our merchandise. Our guns merely showed that we were able to defend what had been placed under our care.

Meantime Mynheer Von Donk was making every inquiry in his power for Captain Stenning, or any of the survivors from the massacre on board the *Dolphin*. He ascertained that no such vessel as we described had come into Alarache, but that one exactly answering her description belonged to the port of Salee, some leagues to the southward, and that she had been on a long cruise, and had returned about the time the captain calculated she might, with some booty and some captives on board. What had become of them he could not learn, but concluded that, as they had not been sent to the northward, they were still in the neighbourhood.

One day, the interpreter having come on board, we got under way, and without let or hindrance stood over the bar. We lay up well along-shore, which is in some places very mountainous and rocky, and the following day we were off Salee. This is also a bar harbour, but, waiting for high-tide, we ran over it, and came to an anchor opposite the town, and near an old fort, the guns of which did not look very formidable. As we ran up the harbour we looked anxiously around to ascertain if our friend the rover was there; but no vessel exactly like her could we see, though there were several suspicious-looking craft, which, no doubt, were engaged in the same calling. Salee itself is composed chiefly of mean houses, with very narrow dirty steep streets; but some of the dwellings in the higher part of the town are of greater pretensions as to size and architectural beauty.

Our consignee in this place was an Armenian merchant, who presented a great contrast in outward appearance to Mynheer Von Donk. Keon y Kyat was tall, and thin, and sallow and grave, dressed in long dark robes, and a high-pointed cap of Astrakan fur,—he looked more like a learned monk than a merchant; but in one point he was exactly like his respected correspondent,—he came to the country to make money, and money he was resolved to make, at all events! This circumstance, however, was an advantage to our enterprise, as he was willing for money to afford us that assistance which he would, probably, otherwise have refused.

Our interpreter, Sidy Yeusiff, was a character in his way, though certainly not one to be imitated. His mother was a Christian slave, an Irish Roman Catholic, married to a Mohammedan Moor. She had brought him up in her own faith, in which he continued till her death, when, to obtain his liberty, he professed that of his stepfather. He had all the vices consequent on slavery. He was cringing, cowardly, false, and utterly destitute of all principle; but, at the same time, so plausible, that it was difficult not to believe that he was speaking the truth. He was a young, pleasant-looking man; and as he used to come forward and talk freely with the seamen, he became a favourite on board. Poor fellow! had he been brought up under more favourable circumstances, how different might have been his character! His professed object was, of course, to interpret for the captain in all matters connected with the sale of the cargo; but he used to take every opportunity of going on shore to try and gain information about Captain Stenning or any of his companions.

I had few opportunities of making remarks about the people of this place, but Sidy corrected some of the notions I had first formed. The boys all go bare-headed; the men wear red caps. They have their hair shaved off their heads, with the exception of a tuft on the top, by which they expect Mohammed will draw them up to paradise. I have seen it remarked that Mohammed, who had very erroneous notions on scientific subjects, fixed the articles for the religious belief of his followers according to them, thereby entirely disproving their divine origin; whereas the writers of the Bible, guided by inspiration, made numerous statements which, with the knowledge then possessed by mankind, would have been impossible for them to understand clearly unless explained to them by the Holy Spirit, but which subsequent discoveries in science have shown to be beautifully and exactly correct.

Mohammed thought that the world was flat, and so placed his paradise in an atmosphere above it.

To return to the dress of the Moors. They wear long beards and large whiskers, but shave their upper lip and directly under the chin. A gentleman of the upper class wears a long shirt without a collar, and over it a sort of spencer or waistcoat, joined before and behind. Again, over this he puts a very large coat, ornamented with numberless buttons, and with sleeves reaching only to his elbows. His coat, which he folds round him, is secured by a thick coloured sash or girdle, into which he sticks a very long knife or dagger, and where he carries his money, supposing he has any. He wears only a pair of linen drawers reaching to the ankle. His shoes are of goat-skin, very well-dressed, the sole being but of one thickness. He wears over his dress a fine white blanket, with which he can completely shroud himself, leaving only his right arm exposed. It is called a haik. Some of these haiks are very fine and transparent, while others are thicker and more fit for general use. In cold weather he puts on a bournous or capote, with a hood such as the Greek fishermen and sailors wear. A labouring man does not wear a shirt, and his drawers come only as far as his knee, leaving the rest of his leg exposed.

The women's clothes are cut something like those of the men. Round the head they wear a coloured sash, which hangs down to the waist; their hair is plaited; and they have the usual gold and silver ornaments in their ears and on their fingers, and red shoes. The poorer classes wear necklaces, and silver or copper rings on their fingers and thumbs. Their shirts are beautifully ornamented in front, to look like lace. When they leave the house they put on drawers of great length, which they turn up into numerous folds over their legs, giving them a very awkward appearance. Besides the haik, which is like that of a man's, a lady wears a linen cloth over her face, to conceal it from the profane vulgar when abroad. Such were the people we saw moving about on shore.

Day after day passed by, and no account could we gain of poor Captain Stenning. It was very clear, also, that if we did, we should not be able to obtain his liberation by force. At last one day the captain sent for me.

"Williams," said he, "I have had news of one of the *Dolphin's* people, if not of Captain Stenning himself. I must myself go and see him, and I want a companion in whom I have perfect confidence. As you are a steady, sensible man, with good nerve, I shall be glad to take you with me, if you are willing to accompany me. I should probably have taken Poplar, but his figure is so conspicuous that he would have been remarked."

I was much pleased with the way in which he spoke of me, and I told him that I was ready to follow wherever he chose to lead the way.

"That is the spirit I expected to find in you," he replied.

"It is, however, right that you should understand that there is considerable danger in the expedition; for if our errand was to be discovered, we should certainly be sacrificed to the fury of the Moors."

"I've no fear about that, sir," said I. "A man cannot expect to be always able to do what is right without running some risk and taking some trouble."

Sidy that evening brought us off some Moorish clothes, in which the captain and I rigged ourselves out. We certainly did look two funny figures, I thought, as we turned ourselves round and round in them. Sidy had not forgotten a couple of long knives, to which the captain added a brace of pistols a piece. I was very glad it was dusk when we left the ship, for I should not have liked my shipmates to have seen me with my bare legs and slippers, and a dirty blanket over my head just like an old Irishwoman.

A shore-boat was alongside—a sort of canoe turned up at both ends, and flat-bottomed. An old Moor sat in her. Sidy had bribed him to put us on shore, and to ask no questions. He told him that we were Moors, who had had business on board the brig, and that we desired to land without notice. He accordingly pulled to an unfrequented part of the harbour, and we stepped on shore, as we believed, unnoticed. The captain and Sidy led the way, I following in the character of a servant. Of course, if spoken to, I was to be dumb. We passed along a narrow sandy road, with low stone walls on either side skirting the town, till we arrived at the entrance of a house of somewhat larger dimensions than those of the neighbouring edifices. This, I found, was the residence of a German renegade and a merchant, who had, by Sidy's means, been bribed to assist us.

We were ushered into his presence as Moorish guests come to visit him. He was seated cross-legged on a cushion at one end of a room, with a large pipe by his side. The apartment was not very finely furnished, seeing that it had little else in it besides a few other cushions like the one he sat on. Certainly he looked exactly like an old Moor, and I could not persuade myself that he was not one. He invited us to sit down; which the captain and Sidy did near him, while I tucked my legs under me at a distance. After he had bowed and talked a little through the interpreter, he clapped his hands, and some slaves brought each of us a pipe—not an unpleasant thing just then to my taste. Again he clapped his hands, and the slaves brought in some low, odd, little tables, one of which was placed before each of us. There was a bowl of porridge, and some plates with little lumps of fried meat, and rice, and dates, but not a drop of grog or liquor of any sort.

Afterwards, however, coffee was brought to us in cups scarcely bigger than thimbles; but it did little more than just warm up my tongue. As soon as the slaves had withdrawn, I was not a little surprised to hear the seeming Moor address the captain in tolerable English.

"So you want to find one of your captured countrymen?" said he. "Well, to-morrow morning I start on a journey to visit a friend who has one as a slave. His description answers that of him whom you seek. I will obtain for you a short conversation with him. You must contrive the means of rescuing him. I can do no more."

After some further talk on the subject our host got up, and, having carefully examined all the outlets to the room to ascertain that no one was looking in, produced a stout black bottle from a chest, and some glasses. I found that the bottle contained most veritable Schiedam.

"Now, as I don't think this good stuff was known to Master Mohammed when he played his pranks on earth, he cannot object to any of his faithful followers tasting a drop of it now and then."

Thereon he poured out a glass for each of us, and winked at Sidy, as much as to say, "We understand each other—we are both of us rogues." The captain took but little; so did I: but Muly Hassan the merchant, and the interpreter, did not stop their potations till they had finished the bottle, and both were very drunk. The merchant had sense enough left to hide his bottle, and then his slaves came and made him up a couch in one corner of the room. They also prepared beds for us in the other corners.

The next morning we were up before break of day, and mounted on some small horses, almost hid by their gaily-coloured saddle-cloths and trappings. And such saddles! Rising up in peaks ahead and astern, a drunken tailor could not have tumbled off one of them had he tried. I do not remember much about the appearance of the country. A large portion was lying waste; but there were fields of various sorts of corn, and even vineyards, though the grapes produced from them were not, I suppose, used for the manufacture of wine: indeed, I know that they are eaten both fresh and dried. Date-trees were, however, in great abundance, the fruit being one of the principal articles of food among the people. The roads were very bad; and altogether there was an air of misery and neglect which will always be seen where the ruler is a tyrant and the people are slaves. We rested in some sheds put up for the accommodation of passengers during the heat of the day, and in the afternoon proceeded on to our destination.

"Now, my friends, look out for your countryman," said the renegade. "You will probably see him tending cattle or labouring in the fields among other slaves. He is probably in his own dress, and you will easily recognise him."

Curiously enough, we had not ridden on for ten minutes further, when, not far from the road, we saw a man seated on a bank a short distance from the road, and looking very sorrowful and dispirited. His dress was that of a seaman. I looked round, and seeing no one near except our own party, I slipped off my horse, and ran up to him. Of course, he thought I was a Moor, and he looked as if he would have fainted with surprise when he heard me hail him in English.

"Who are you? What do you come here for?" he exclaimed, panting for breath.

"I belong to the *Dolphin* brig, and I came here to try and find Captain Stenning and any of his companions."

"Heaven be praised, then?" he exclaimed, bursting into tears. "He and I are the only survivors of that demon-possessed craft which he commanded. But how came your vessel to be called by the name of one which proved so unfortunate?"

"I cannot tell you all about that just now," I answered, seeing that much time would be lost if I entered into particulars. I therefore merely explained the steps we had taken to discover them, and asked him what had become of Captain Stenning.

"The captain! He has been in this very place till within the last three or four weeks, when the Moors carried him away to serve on board one of their ships—the very ship which captured us. They found out that he was the captain and understood navigation, so they took him to navigate one of their piratical craft. I was sick and unfit for work, or they would have taken me likewise; but they saw that I was only a man before the mast, and guessed that I did not understand navigation. What has since become of the captain I don't know. There is no one here I can talk to. They set me to work by signs, which, if I do not understand, they sharpen my wits with a lash; and they take care that I shall not run away, by securing me at night with a chain round my leg. There are several other slaves employed by the same master, but not one of them understands a word of English."

The young man's name was Jacob Lyal, he told me; and he said that he was just out of his apprenticeship when he joined the *Dolphin*.

"I have a father and mother, and brothers and sisters, at home, in Somersetshire, and it would make their hearts sorrowful if they heard that I was left a slave in this barbarous country; so you'll do all you can to help me," he exclaimed, as I was about to leave him, for I was afraid of remaining longer lest we should be observed.

Just as I was going, however, I told him to try and arrange some plan by which we might have a talk with him, and let him know how things stood before we left the place, should we be unable to take him with us. He also described very accurately the sort of place in which he was locked up at night; and I promised, if I could, to go and have some more conversation with him. As we did not lose time in talking of anything except the matter in hand, I was speedily able to rejoin the captain and his companions. The captain approved of the arrangements I had made, though he was very sorry that there was no immediate prospect of meeting with Captain Stenning.

We were received with all the usual marks of respect by the old Moor who owned the property. He had been a pirate in his youth, and cut-throats and robbed without compunction; but he was now a dignified old gentleman, who looked as if he had been engaged in rural affairs all his life. I came in for almost as much of the attention and good fare as the captain; for in that country a beggar may eat off the same table, or rather the same floor, and sit under the same roof as a prince. The excuse for the visit was to sell to the old Moor some of the goods aboard the *Dolphin*, specimens of which the captain had brought with him.

As soon after our arrival as we had shaken the dust out of our clothes, and washed our faces and our hands and feet, we were ushered by slaves into a hall, at one end of which sat the old Moor, and the captain and the renegade and the interpreter were placed on each side of him, and I sat a little further off, tucking up my legs as I had done before; and then some black slaves in white dresses brought in a little table for each of us, with all sorts of curious things to eat, which I need not describe, for in that country one feast is very much like another. The renegade had also brought a case; but that it contained something besides merchandise he proved by producing, one after the other, several of his favourite bottles of Schiedam, which apparently were no less acceptable to the old Moor than to him. I am not, however, fond of describing such scenes, or of picturing such gross hypocrites as the renegade and the old Moor.

I gained an advantage, however, from their drunken habits; for as soon as it was dark I stole out of the house, and tried to find my way to the shed where Lyal told me he was chained at night. I had taken good note of the bearings of the place as we rode along. I knew that if I was found prying about, I should run a great chance of being killed; but still I was resolved to run every risk to try and rescue the poor fellow from captivity. Of course, as the captain afterwards told me, we might have gone home to England, and laid the state of the case before the Government; and after a year or so spent in diplomatising, the poor fellow, if he was still alive, might have been released, or the Emperor of Morocco might have declared that he could not find him, or that he was dead; and thus he would have remained on, like many others, in captivity.

There was a little light from the moon, which enabled me to mark the outlines of the house I was leaving, as well as to find my way. Two servants were stationed in the entrance passage, but they had wrapped themselves up in their haiks and gone soundly to sleep, so I stepped over their bodies without waking them. Every person about the house, indeed, seemed to have gone to sleep, but the dogs were more faithful than the human beings, and some of them barked furiously as I walked along. They were either chained or locked up, and finding my footsteps going from them, they were soon silent. At length I reached the shed I was in search of. It was near a cottage, with several other similar sheds in the neighbourhood. As I came to the entrance, a voice said—

"Come in; but speak low."

At first I could see no one, but on going further in, I discovered the object of my search sitting in a corner on a heap of straw. He was chained there, and could not move.

"It gives me new life to see a countryman here, and one who wants to help me," said the poor fellow. "I thought all the world had deserted me, and that I should be left to die in this strange land, among worse than heathens, who treat me as a dog; or that I should be tempted to give up my faith and turn Mohammedan, as others have done."

I cannot repeat all our conversation. At last an idea struck me.

"I'll tell you what," said I; "just do you pretend to be mad, and play all sorts of strange pranks, and do all the mischief you can; and then the captain will propose to buy you, and perhaps the old Moor will sell you a bargain, and be glad to be rid of you."

"A very good idea," he answered. "But here am I chained up like a dog, and how am I to get free?"

"No fear," said I, producing a knife which Peter had given me, containing all sorts of implements, and among them a file. "You shall soon be at liberty, at all events."

Accordingly I set to work, and in less than an hour I had filed the chain from off his legs. While we were filing away, we arranged what he was to do. He was to make a huge cap, with a high peak of straw, and he was to cut his jacket into shreds, and a red handkerchief I had into strips, and to fasten them about him in long streamers, and he was to take a thick pole in his hand, covered much in the same way, and then he was to rush into the house, shrieking and crying out as if a pack of hounds were after him.

"They will not wonder at seeing me mad, for I have done already many strange things, and very little work, since I came here," he remarked. "But what it to become of the chain?"

"You had better carry that with you, and clank it in their faces," said I. "Make as if you had bitten it through. That will astonish them, and they will, at all events, be afraid to come near your teeth."

To make a long story short, we worked away with a will, and in half an hour or so he was rigged out in a sufficiently strange fashion. I have no doubt, had Peter been with us, he would have improved on our arrangement. I then, advising Lyal to follow me in a short time, stole back, and took my place unobserved in the old Moor's dining-hall. The captain guessed what I had been doing, but the rest of the party had been too much engaged in their potations to miss me. After a little time I stole over to the captain and told him the arrangements I had made, that he might be ready to act accordingly.

In a short time the silence which had hitherto prevailed was broken by a terrible uproar of dogs barking, and men hallooing and crying out at the top of their voices; while, above all, arose as unearthly shrieks as I had ever heard. Presently in rushed a crowd of black and brown servants, followed by a figure which I recognised as that of Lyal, though he had much improved his appearance by fastening a haik over his shoulders and another round his waist, while he waved above his head a torch, at the risk of setting his high straw-cap on fire. The people all separated before him, as he dashed on, right up to the old Moor, who, with a drunken gaze of terror and astonishment, stared at him without speaking.

"Ho! ho!" shouted the sailor, seizing him by the nose; "old fellow, I have you now!"

Thereon he kicked over the jar of Schiedam, the contents of which he set on fire with his torch; and keeping fast hold of the old Moor's nose, who in his fright knew not how to resist, dragged him round and round the room, shouting and shrieking all the time like a very demoniac.

The place would have been meantime set on fire had not the captain and I quenched the flames, while the renegade and the interpreter, in their drunken humours, could only lean back on their cushions, and laugh as if they would split their sides at the extraordinary predicament of our host.

"I say, countrymen, if you had but your horses ready, we might gallop away before all these people knew where they are," shouted Lyal. "Who'll just take a spell at the old fellow's nose, for I am tired of holding on?"

On this Captain Gale thought that it was time to interfere, and he and I going up to the old Moor, pretended to use great exertion in dragging away the sailor from him. The captain then led him back to his seat, while I held Lyal.

"Here, Sidy," said the captain to the interpreter; "tell the old man that if he will give me fifty dollars, I will take that madman off his hands."

When the old Moor had somewhat recovered his composure, Sidy explained the offer. "He says that he can kill him, and so get him out of his way!" was the answer. "He dare not do that," put in the renegade; "all the people here will own him as inspired. Abate your price, and stick to it."

Finally, the captain consented to carry away the madman on having twenty dollars added to the price he was to receive for his goods.

"Take him! take him!" exclaimed the old Moor. "The man who can eat through iron, drive all my slaves before him, set fire to my house, and pull me by the nose, is better away from me than near! Take care, though, that he does not come back again!"

The captain promised that he would take very good care of that; and the next day, with joyful hearts at our unexpected success, we set forward on our return-journey to Salee. As the renegade and Sidy were both to be rewarded according to our success, they were well content; and by their aid, the same night we got on board the brig with our recovered countryman without being observed. We had now to turn the whole of our attention to the recovery of Captain Stenning; and every excuse which Captain Gale could think of was made for our stay in the harbour. Still, we had very little of our cargo left, and every day saw it decrease. The spring-tides were also coming on, when there was the greatest depth of water on the bar, and we could the most easily make our escape without a pilot.

Chapter Twelve
The Salee Rover and the British Corvette

As we lay at our anchors off Salee, we had a view from the mast-head of the open sea, over a point of land which ran out below the town. Snug as we were, it was one day blowing a heavy gale outside from the northward. Dark clouds chased each other across the sky, and the ocean—black and gloomy—was sprinkled over with white-topped seas. I was engaged aloft about the rigging, when I observed a sail to the north-west staggering along with as much canvas as she could carry. So rapidly did she make her way through the water, that I soon perceived that she was a brig, and that she was standing towards the harbour. The reason of her carrying so much sail, with so heavy a gale blowing, was soon explained. Two or three miles astern of her came a large ship, with all her topsails set, evidently in chase. The latter, better able from her size to bear a heavy press of sail, was coming up with her rapidly. On seeing this I hailed the deck, and the captain, and Mr Carr, and Peter, and others, soon came aloft to watch the progress of the chase.

"I make it all out clearly," exclaimed the captain, after watching the state of affairs through his glass. "That craft is the very rover which plundered this vessel, or exactly like her; and the ship is a British man-of-war corvette, which is in chase of her. I can make out the English ensign clearly. The rover hopes to get into port before the guns of the corvette can be brought to bear on her; and that's just what I hope the rascal won't be able to do."

"But that's the very craft Stenning is said to be on board," observed Mr Carr. "Poor fellow, it will go hard with him when the corvette's guns begin to play on the brig."

"I wish that we could run out and bring her to action, so as to give the corvette time to come up and take possession," said I to Peter, who was near me.

"If the weather were moderate we might do it; but, with this gale blowing, I doubt if even our captain would run the risk," he answered.

"Besides you see, Jack, all the people we have had anything to do with here would get into a great scrape if we played such a trick to one of their vessels. Yet I tell you, lad, I would like the fun amazingly. The villains don't deserve any mercy at our hands."

While Peter and I were discussing the subject, so were the captain and Mr Carr. They gave up the idea of running out to meet the rover, as thereby they would have but little chance of saving the life of Walter Stenning, if he was still on board. By this time, both the brig and ship had drawn close inshore, and every movement could clearly be observed with the naked eye. Poor Jacob Lyal had come aloft; and as soon as he recognised the brig, he was nearly falling on deck, overpowered with all the dreadful recollections her appearance conjured up.

No vessel, unless one well acquainted with the coast, could have ventured to stand in as close as the brig had done. She was now about a mile from the entrance of the harbour; and the corvette, outside of her, had just begun to fire a bow-gun now and then, to try its range. At last a shot went through one of the brig's topsails. She, in return, fired, endeavouring to cripple her pursuer, thus to have time to run under the shelter which was so near. Never have I witnessed a more exciting scene. Our mast-heads were soon crowded with spectators. Even the sluggish Moors rushed out of their houses, and went to the neighbouring heights to watch what was going forward. Their interest was, however, on the other side of the question. Many of them must have had relatives and friends on board the rover, and they were as anxious for her escape as we were to see her captured. The action now became warm—both corvette and brig were firing away as fast as they could load.

"Hurrah! the pirate seems to be getting the worst of it," said I to Peter. "The rovers will meet with their deserts before long, I hope."

"So do I," he answered. "But do you know, Jack, I'm more anxious about the corvette. If she were to receive any damage, and not be able to haul off-shore, she is, do you see, on an enemy's coast, and all her people would be made prisoners, if not murdered; while the brig has a port under her lee, and can run in even if she gets a good deal of knocking about."

While we were thus talking, the corvette had drawn still nearer to the brig, and her shot began to tell with considerable effect. Down came the brig's maintop-gallant-mast, the spars hanging by the rigging. We next saw several hands going aloft to clear it away, when another shot struck the maintop-mast. The Moors attempted in haste to slide down the stays and shrouds, but scarcely had they begun their descent when the mast bent over to leeward, and down it came with a crash, jerking off many of them into the sea. There in vain they struggled for life; the combatants flew on, leaving them to their fate. Still the brig had her mainsail set, and with the gale there was blowing, that was sufficient after-canvas for her to carry with advantage. She ceased firing. "Hurrah! she is going to strike," we exclaimed; but the wreck of the maintop-mast was quickly cleared away, and she commenced again with greater briskness than ever. In return, the corvette plied her fast and furiously with shot, which must have told pretty severely among her people on deck, though, of course, we could not see the damage which was done. The brig was within a quarter of a mile of the mouth of the harbour. It was high-tide, but we well knew that there was not water sufficient on the bar to allow the corvette to enter. Still, on she boldly came in hot chase.

"She cannot surely fancy that she can venture in," exclaimed Captain Gale. "She'll be lost to a certainty if she does. Poor fellows! not one will escape with their lives should she strike. Carr, we must run out, and try and pick some of them up, at all hazards. The wind is sufficiently to the northward to carry us clear, and the people on shore are so engaged in watching the chase, that they will not observe us getting under way till we are clear from the guns of the castle."

"Ay, ay, sir, with all my heart," answered the mate. "I'm not quite certain that the brig will get scot-free either."

As he spoke, I saw a thick smoke ascending from the deck of the rover.

"She's on fire! she's on fire!" shouted several of us. But then we thought of poor Stenning, and what would become of him.

"All hands make sail," cried the captain, descending on deck. "We must slip, Mr Carr. There's no time for heaving up the anchor."

The crew could scarcely refrain from giving vent to their feelings of excitement in a shout.

"Silence, my lads; we must not let the Moors know what we are about."

Never did a crew let fall the topsails with greater good-will than we did. We had kept two reefs in them for an emergency. I now saw the wisdom of the captain's forethought when he gave the order, as some time before we had loosed sails.

We were riding with the ship's head towards the mouth of the river, the tide still running in. Thus, being strongly manned with willing hearts, we were soon under way. No one from the shore observed us, or, at all events, came off to stop us. Sidy, the interpreter, was fortunately on shore, so that we had no trouble about him, and the captain knew that he could easily pay him through the consignee of the ship. Captain Gale's intention was, I learned, to run down to the mouth of the harbour, and to anchor if necessary. We got a cable ranged accordingly, with an anchor ready to let go. The brig quickly felt the force of the wind, and, happily canting the right way, and her sails filling, away she flew, heeling over to the gale towards the open sea. The captain, or one of the mates, or Peter, had been constantly sailing about the harbour, as if to amuse themselves, or to catch fish, but in reality to sound the depth of the water, and to make themselves thoroughly acquainted with the harbour. We thus required no pilot to carry us out.

As we rounded the point I have described, the mouth of the river lay before us—a long line of surf, with heavy breakers rolling and roaring in from the sea, apparently barring our exit. Outside of it was the corvette, close-hauled with three reefs in her topsail, standing off-shore, and, as far as we could see, uninjured. But the pirate brig, where was she?

A dark mass of rocks lay at the northern part of the entrance to the harbour. Over them the sea broke furiously; and amid the masses of foam which flew high into the air was the black hull of a vessel, with shattered masts and spars heaving up amid the breakers; while from the centre of it, as if striving with the waves which should most speedily destroy it, bright flames were bursting forth and raging furiously. As we gazed with horror at the dreadful spectacle, feeling our compassion excited rather for our hapless countryman, whom we believed to be on board, than for the ruthless wretches who formed her crew, there was a loud explosion, and fragments of wreck, and what had once been human beings, were thrown up into the air; and by the time they had again fallen into the foaming water, no portion of the rover remained to show where she just had been.

We were now about a quarter of a mile from the bar, and not a moment was to be lost in deciding what was to be done, whether we were to bring-up or to attempt to cross. In the line of breakers which rolled over the bar, a spot was observed where the water was smoother, and which the captain knew to be the deepest channel.

"We may run out there without fear, light as we are; and if we remain, these Mohammedan fanatics will certainly revenge themselves on us for the destruction of their friends," he observed to Mr Carr, who agreed with him that the attempt should be made, though far from free of risk. And most people, indeed, would have agreed that the passage was hazardous in the extreme, but yet no one on board doubted that it was the right thing to do.

The second mate, who was at the helm with another steady hand, was ordered to steer towards the opening. The tide was still running in strong, which gave us greater command over the vessel than would have otherwise been the case. All hands were at their stations, and every one of us knew the position we were in. A shift of wind, the least carelessness, the carrying away a spar or rope, might bring upon us the same fate which had destroyed the rover. Scarcely had the determination I have mentioned been arrived at, when, as I was looking out ahead, I saw on the starboard-bow a spar floating in the water. I looked again; a man was holding on to it, and drifting up towards us. I was certain I saw him lift up his hand and wave it. I immediately reported the circumstance to the captain.

"Although he is probably one of those wretched Moors, he is a fellow-creature, and it is our duty to try and save him," he observed. "About-ship! helm a-lee!" he sung out.

The brig, under her topsails, worked like a top, and we had ample room to put her about and heave her to. Just as we had done so, the spar came drifting up close to us. Again the man clinging to it waved his hand. His unshorn head of light curling hair showed that he was no Moor.

"Here, mates, just pay out this line as I want it!" sung out Peter, passing the bight of a rope under his arms and leaping overboard. "I'll tackle him to, I warrant."

In an instant he was in the water, and a few strokes bringing him up to the spar as it floated by, he grasped hold of the person hanging to it, and then sung out, "Haul away, my lads; it's all right!"

The whole incident took place, it seemed, in a few seconds. Once more he was on the deck, and there could be no doubt of it, with no other than Walter Stenning in his arms! The poor fellow breathed, but the dangers he had gone through, and the sudden restoration to safety, had overcome him, and he lay almost unconscious on the deck.

"Now, sir, the sooner we fill and stand out of this the better," said Peter, turning to the captain, after he had placed Stenning on the deck. "I did not speak of it before, but just now I saw another of those piratical fellows getting under way just from opposite where we lay, doubtless to be after us."

Peter's remark was found to be true; and up the harbour another brig was seen making sail, of course with the hope of overtaking us. I, with another man, received orders to carry Captain Stenning below, which we did, placing him on a mattress on the floor of the cabin, and then hurried up again to attend to our duty.

Once more the brig was put about, and head up towards the passage. On we rushed, the foam flying over us as we approached the spot. She lifted to the first rolling sea, and then down she came, as if she must strike the sand below; but another roller came tumbling in, and mounting like a sea-bird on its summit, she descended on the other side amid clouds of spray, again to mount another huge wave, and then to rush on with impetuous force as she felt the blast which laid her over almost on her beam-ends towards the open ocean. Still, on either hand, wild foaming water broke in mountain masses around us; but on we sped. "Hold on! hold on for your lives!" shouted the captain, as yet another mountain sea came thundering on towards us, close upon a previous one over which we had ridden in safety. The brig seemed to spring at it, as if able to dash it aside; but vain indeed was the attempt. High above us it rose. Right into it we went, and for a moment I thought all was over. Along our decks it found its way, and fell in torrents below, sweeping everything before it; but still buoyantly our brave vessel flew on, and wave after wave being surmounted, a loud shout burst from all hands as once more we found ourselves in the open sea, following in the wake of the British corvette.

As soon as we were in safety, the captain called me below to attend to Captain Stenning. We found him sitting up on the mattress, and, as he held on by the leg of the table, looking somewhat wildly around him.

"Where am I? what is all this that has happened?" he exclaimed, as we appeared.

"That you are safe aboard the *Dolphin*, my friend, and that you have escaped from the wreck of a Moorish pirate," answered the captain. "But before I answer more questions, we'll just get off your wet clothes, and clap you into bed with a glass of hot grog."

This we accordingly did, and the result was that the poor fellow very soon fell fast asleep—the best thing he could do under the circumstances.

When I went on deck, I found that the Moorish brig which had pursued us, seeing the fate which had befallen her companion, and that we had got safe over the bar, had put about, and stood back again to her anchorage.

"I should have begrudged the rascals our anchor and cable," said Peter. "But as we have got Mr Stenning back safe, they are welcome to them, though I would rather see the honest hemp used to hang some of the knaves."

The gale, which truly seemed to have effected its purpose in the destruction of the miscreant rovers, now began to abate its fury, and before dark we came up with the corvette, which had hove-to in order to speak us. We found that she was His Britannic Majesty's sloop-of-war *Syren*, of eighteen guns; and the captain directed us to lay by him till the morning, when he would send on board to hear all the particulars of what had occurred.

Meantime I had been sent to sit by Captain Stenning, to be ready to attend to him when he awoke. When he did so, I called Captain Gale to him. The account I then heard of his adventures was very short. We had, indeed, guessed very nearly the truth. The *Dolphin* had been surprised by the pirates, and while he, with some of his crew, were in vain attempting to defend her deck, he had been struck down. When he returned to consciousness, he found himself on board the pirate, with two or three others, of whom Lyal alone survived. The pirates had been driven from their prey by the appearance of a large ship, which they took to be a man-of-war; and in revenge, he concluded, they murdered all who then remained on board. He and Lyal would have been killed also; but their lives were saved by a Moor, whom he once saved at Gibraltar from ill-treatment by some English seamen, with whom he had quarrelled. Though the Moor had saved his life, he had not interest to do more for him at that time.

When the pirates again fell in with the *Dolphin*, and were frightened from attacking her by the trick Peter invented, thinking some evil spirits possessed the vessel, they made all sail to return to port. He confessed that he was himself very much astonished, and could in no way account for what he had witnessed. Had he not received the explanation we gave him, he should all his life have believed that the appearance he had beheld was produced by supernatural agency.

When carried into port, he, with Lyal, was sold to the old Moor, as we knew; but his friend had not forgotten him. The rover much wanted a skilful navigator, and thinking that he would prefer a life of comparative freedom at sea to slavery on shore, he repurchased him, and carried him on board the brig. He was rather disappointed, however, to find that, without a quadrant or nautical almanac, the captain could be of very little use to them in that way. He told us, indeed, that the pirates were very nearly killing him for his supposed obstinacy, because he could not tell them one day whereabouts they were, when they put their own rough instruments into his hands. He had great difficulty in explaining that, without his own books and charts, he could be of little help to them. However, they promised to attack an English vessel before long, that they might supply him.

With this object in view, they made sail towards the corvette, which they took for a merchantman, and thus very nearly caught a Tartar. They discovered their mistake only when within six miles or so of her; and by then suddenly altering their course, and standing away from her under all sail, her suspicions were excited, and she made chase after them. In such terror were the pirates, when they found themselves so hard pressed, that they seemed to forget him, or his life would probably have been sacrificed; but as he was left himself, he was allowed to consider the best means of preserving it. When, therefore, he saw that the brig must inevitably strike the rocks, he seized a loose spar on the deck and sprang overboard, trusting that the current would carry him through the breakers into smooth water. He had seen us coming out, and guessing that the brig was an English trader, hoped to be picked up by her. His surprise and pleasure at meeting with Lyal was very great.

"It would have been a great to damper my own satisfaction, if I thought that you had still been left in slavery," he remarked, as he wrung the seaman's hand.

"Well, sir, I can only say that I would go back and be chained up like a dog, as I was before, for the sake of seeing you free, and sent safe home to your wife and family," returned the honest fellow, passing the cuff of his jacket across his eyes, to brush away a tear which his feelings had brought them.

Yes; the rough sailor has got just the same sort of feelings inside his bosom which dwells within the silken vest of any young lady or gentleman who can weep over a novel, or better, sometimes, a deed of heroism; and right honest, genuine feelings, they are too—which is more than can be said for those hackneyed sentiments possessed by people who have lived all their lives in what they choose to call the great world.

Altogether, never was an enterprise more successful than ours had hitherto been. We had not only succeeded in recovering both the survivors of the *Dolphin's* crew at small cost, but, from the high prices we had obtained for our merchandise, we had paid all the probable expenses of the voyage, and left a handsome profit for our owners.

The next morning we were close up with the corvette, when a lieutenant from her boarded us to learn all the particulars we had to describe. The two masters, with Lyal and I, were then requested by the lieutenant to accompany him aboard the ship-of-war, to give a further account to the captain himself of what had occurred. Captain Hudson received us very kindly; and while our two captains sat down, we stood with our hats in our hands behind their chairs. I remember that he laughed very heartily at my idea of rigging up Lyal as a madman, and at the way he put my advice in practice, by pulling the old Moor's nose.

"Well, gentlemen," said Captain Hudson, "from the account you have given me, I think we have ample grounds to enable the British Government to make a demand on that of Morocco for compensation; so that if you will accompany me to England, I hope to obtain ample satisfaction for you."

Neither Lyal nor I exactly understood what all this meant; but Captain Gale had an inkling that very little satisfaction would result either to him or Captain Stenning.

"Thank you, sir," he answered; "but I can't accept your offer, for my brother-master wants to return to his wife and family, and my owners directed me to make the best of my way back to Halifax."

"Of course these are strong arguments against the execution of my wishes," returned Captain Hudson. "You will, I conclude, therefore proceed on your voyage, and give your evidence when you return to England. But I find, Captain Gale, that you are more strongly manned than is necessary for a merchantman. These two young men will remain on board the *Syren*, and one of my lieutenants will accompany you to your brig, and select a few more. However, we will not leave you short-handed; but His Majesty's ships must be manned, do you see?"

"It is very hard, sir. All my people are volunteers on what appeared a somewhat hazardous expedition, and are anxious to return to their families," replied Captain Gale. "You will allow me, without offence, to observe, that one of these young men has only just been released from slavery, and that the other is an apprentice."

"The first does not belong to your crew, so it is my duty to take care of him; and if the other is still an apprentice, I cannot keep him, but I shall like to see his papers. Mistakes in these matters sometimes occur. We do everything according to law, do you see, Mr Gale." Captain Hudson spoke very mildly and blandly, but there was something in his eye which showed that he was not to be trifled with.

"You will understand, sir," he continued, turning to Captain Stenning, "I have the power to press you. Under the circumstances of the case, I will not, unless I am forced to do it; but your friend will throw no impediment in the way of my getting any of the hands I may require. I will not detain you, gentlemen, and I wish you a prosperous voyage and a happy termination to your enterprise."

This, then, was the object for which the naval captain wished to communicate with the *Dolphin*. It was not with the best possible grace that the two masters got up to take their leave; and yet Captain Stenning well knew that he was completely in the power of the commander of the sloop-of-war, and that there was no law to prevent him from being sent to do duty before the mast on board of her.

They both shook hands warmly and kindly with Lyal, and promised to send him a spare chest, with such things as could be collected; for of course he had but a scanty outfit. As they were going, I put out my hand also.

"You'll let me shake hands, sir, won't you?" said I. "There's many a kind act you've done me, Captain Gale, from the time I was a little helpless lad till now; and I thank you from the bottom of my heart, and may Heaven bless you, sir."

"Why, what's all this about?" exclaimed my kind captain, "You have your papers, Jack, and you cannot, as an apprentice, be touched."

"But the papers won't protect me, sir; I am no longer an apprentice," I answered. "Not long ago, I got a mate to look over them for me, and I was, I find, out of my apprenticeship a month ago."

"There is no use giving in without an attempt to escape; I'll see what can be done," he answered. "May I not take this man with me, sir?" he asked, turning to Captain Hudson, who stood on the quarter-deck, and of course had not heard this part of our conversation.

"Send his papers and his chest likewise," was the only answer the captain of the *Syren* deigned to give.

Before the brig's boat shoved off, I went over the side, and sent many a message to Peter Poplar and the rest of my shipmates. I regretted leaving the brig, but I was more sorry at the thought of parting from Peter than for any other reason.

As I looked at the *Dolphin* with the eye of that affection which a seaman soon gains for a vessel in which he is tolerably happy, I observed that the man-of-war's boat was already alongside. In a short time she shoved off, and pulled back to the corvette. There were several chests, and five people besides her crew in her. I rubbed my eyes. Could I believe them? Among the people sat Peter Poplar! He sprung up the side, and was soon engaged in shaking hands with several of the *Syren's* crew.

"What! are you pressed, Peter?" said I to him; and in my heart I could not be very sorry to have him with me.

"Not exactly that either," he answered. "You see, Jack, I found that you were pressed, or would be to a certainty, and I did not like to have one whom I had nursed up almost from a baby on the salt waters, so to speak, altogether out of my sight, though you are big enough now to take care of yourself; so, says I to myself, Well, if they take me, I'll go with a free will—I don't mind. However, when the lieutenant picked out the men he would like to have, and who have no protection, he passed me over, thinking that, on account of my age, he could not touch me. But among the men he chose was poor Bill Jackson, who has a wife and small family at Halifax, and who only came the voyage from his love for Captain Stenning, and was going to give up the sea and live on shore with his wife's relations up the country. I never saw a poor fellow so cut up and broken-hearted when he saw all his hopes blown to the winds, and knew that, for many a long year, he might not see his wife or little ones. He knows well the ups and downs of a sailor's life, and that very likely he might never see them again. I know that I could not stand his grief. Captain Gale did all he could to get the lieutenant to let him off, but nothing would do. The only answer was, 'His Majesty wants seamen, and seamen he must have.'

"'So he shall!' said I, walking up to the officer. 'Now, sir, if you will let that man go, you may have me in his stead; and I'll make bold to say, that there isn't a man aboard this brig but will acknowledge that, blow high or blow low, I'm his equal, either aloft or at the helm, or in handling the lead. What say you, mates? Who'll speak for me? It isn't because I want to boast, you know; but I do want to save poor Bill Jackson from being pressed aboard a man-of-war!'

"'He speaks the truth, that he does!' exclaimed all the crew, who were mustered on deck. 'There are few of us can come up to him.'

"'I tell you, sir,' said Captain Gale, 'I should be very sorry to lose either Jackson or Poplar; but if you ask me which is the best seaman of the two, I am bound to say that Poplar is; and besides, in him you get a willing hand, who loves the sea, which I am sure poor Jackson does not.'

"'Then Poplar let us have, by all means,' answered the lieutenant, telling Jackson that he was free, and ordering us all to be smart in getting our traps ready to take with us.

"The captain, meantime, told me to bring him your papers, which I did, though I well knew that they were no protection to you, and so he discovered, and so I got your chest ready with the rest: and so you see, Jack, you and I are man-of-war's men, and so, lad, let's do our duty like men, and stand up boldly for our king and country."

Peter's hearty way of talking gave me spirits which I should not otherwise have felt. I never had before stood on the deck of a man-of-war, but I had heard a good deal about the cruelty and injustice practised on board them, from some of my shipmates; and I had, with the great mass of merchant-seamen in those days, and for many years afterwards, formed a strong prejudice against them. From the system which was practised in some ships, I naturally, with others, formed an opinion of the whole navy; and when I first found myself a pressed-man on board the *Syren*, I looked forward to a life of ill-treatment and wretchedness till I could again obtain my freedom. I truly believe, indeed, that had I not had Peter again as my counsellor, I should have yielded to the force of my impression, and have been guilty of the very conduct which would have brought me into trouble.

I found a number of pressed-men and discontented men, and not a few bad characters in the ship, who were always ready to grumble at what was done, and whose great aim seemed to be how they could oftenest shirk duty, most speedily get drunk, and most readily break the rules and regulations of the service. At first I was inclined to think them somewhat fine fellows, lads of spirit, whose example was worthy of imitation; but Peter observing my tendency, very soon put their conduct in its true light.

"You see, Jack," said he, "those fellows are, in the first place, acting a sneaking, unfair part, to their shipmates. The duty has to be got through, and so the willing, good men, have to do the work which those knaves neglect. Then they benefit by the laws of the country; and the country would go to ruin if it was without a navy, and the navy could not be kept up without the rules and regulations which they are always trying to break through. As to their drunkenness, it unfits them for duty. No man knows what he may do when he is drunk; and besides making him ill at the time, he who drinks to excess is guilty of suicide, as so doing will most certainly shorten his life. Just think what excuse will a man have to offer when he has thus hurried himself into the presence of his Maker! How awful will be the doom he cannot fail to receive! Then, again, those idle fellows who try to avoid work, are always getting into trouble, for no officer will find any excuse for them, or attempt to shield them; and they thus spend a much longer time than they idle away in the black list, or with the tingling of the cat on their backs. But, Jack, I don't want any of these to be your motives for acting rightly. One motive should be sufficient for us all—and that is, the wish to do our duty to our God."

I repeat here my kind friend's advice, but it was long, very long, before it seemed to sink into the sandy soil of my heart, and to bring forth fruit. I am very glad that the press-gang system no longer exists. No man can any longer be forced to serve on board a man-of-war. The case, such as I have described, may appear hard when the master of a merchantman was deprived of a considerable portion of his crew—hard to him, and hard to the pressed-men, and harder in a pecuniary point of view to the underwriters, the property they had insured being thereby made much more liable to shipwreck; but still it was not one-tenth part as hard as numberless cases which I have known during my career afloat.

Little did I think when, from the mast-head of the *Dolphin*, I first saw the *Syren* heave in sight, that before that time on the following day I should form one of her crew. Such is the ever-changing scene of a sailor's life!

Chapter Thirteen
Jack a Man-of-War's-Man

There is a time of life when a person feels that he has left for ever his boyish days and stepped into manhood. I felt that I had passed that boundary when I found myself rated as an able seaman on board the *Syren* sloop of war. I was now under a far stricter system of discipline than I had been accustomed to. At first I felt it somewhat galling; but I soon saw that without the greatest regularity it would be impossible to keep order among the crew of a ship even of the size of the *Syren*.

My early days I had spent on board a merchantman, and had met with many adventures somewhat strange and exciting. I did not expect to meet with fewer in my new career, though they would probably be of a different character. The result of my last, in which I had aided in rescuing two of my countrymen from captivity, had proved most satisfactory. Jacob Lyal, one of them, was now with me, and I knew he would speak well of me among my new shipmates. The other, Captain Stenning, late master of the *Dolphin*, was on board that vessel, and, I hoped, would soon be enabled to rejoin his wife and family in Halifax. Captain Gale, her present master, would also, I knew, speak favourably of me to my first commander in the *Rainbow*, Captain Helfrich, whenever he should fall in with him. I pity the man who does not desire to be thought well of by those who know him, and who does not feel that he deserves their good wishes. I certainly had not made many friends, but those I had found were true and fast ones; and a great source of satisfaction to me was the having with me Peter Poplar, my first and best friend—that true-hearted seaman who had saved me from starvation— who had tended me as a father in my boyhood and youth—who had given me a profession which would enable me to support myself while health and strength remained—and who had ever endeavoured to instil into me those true principles which would enable me to steer clear of the rocks and quicksands to be found in my course through life.

The wind had fallen and become fair; the helm of the corvette was put down, the sails were trimmed, and, under a crowd of canvas such as few merchantmen can attempt to set, we quickly ran the coast of Africa out of sight—the last we saw of its sandy shores being over our starboard quarter.

The commander of the *Syren*, Captain Hudson, was, I found, very much liked by the crew, as, although he was a strict officer, he was a just one, and known to be a thorough seaman. He was a gentleman also in all respects, a brave man, and kind-hearted; and these are the qualities which sailors with good reason respect. Without possessing them, no man is fit to be placed in command over his fellow-men. My old ship, the *Dolphin*, continued in our company for several days, during which we made the best of our way to the northward, the wind, though scant, enabling us, close-hauled, to keep a course in that direction. When somewhere about the latitude of Lisbon, a ship hove in eight, standing towards us under all sail. As her courses rose above the water, she was pronounced to be a frigate; and as her hull appeared, such was found to be the case. Then commenced such a hauling up and down of flags as I had never before seen. What it all meant I could not tell, but it seemed to produce a great commotion among the officers; and soon the news ran along the deck that war was declared—war with France. It was the beginning of a long and bloody struggle.

Meantime, we hove-to, as the frigate had done, and Captain Hudson went on board her. When he returned, we found that we were ordered into the British Channel. The frigate, a new ship, just fitted out, with her officers in glittering uniforms, and her white wide-spread of canvas, and her fresh paint, and her brightly burnished sides looked, I thought, the very picture of a gay and gallant craft, as, passing close to us, she glided by through the sparkling sea. I could not help comparing her with the weather-beaten, wall-sided, ill-formed, slow-sailing merchantmen I had been accustomed to see, and I began to feel a pride in belonging to a man-of-war which I had not hitherto experienced.

Before proceeding on our course, Captain Hudson signalled the *Dolphin*, which had been hove-to, and informed Captain Gale that war had broken out, advising him to make the best of his way to Halifax. It was not till some years afterwards that I heard she reached that place in safety, and that Captain Stenning had had the happiness of being re-united to his wife and family.

No sooner was the news of war received on board the *Syren*, than everybody seemed to wake up into activity. No one had time for a moment to be idle fore or aft. The armourer's crew were employed in polishing up muskets, and pistols, and sharpening cutlasses. For hours together we were practised at the small-arms and great-guns, which had never before been thought of. The gunners were busy making cartridges; the carpenters, plugs for shot-holes; indeed, we all felt that people should always feel that there was work to do. We had good reason to rejoice before the cruise was up that we had not been idle.

We reached Plymouth without meeting with an enemy or taking a prize. What a state of bustle and excitement the place was in! Carriages-and-four dashing through the streets at all hours of the day; troops marching here and there, with drums and fifes playing—some coming in, others embarking for foreign lands; artisans of all sorts hurrying in, certain to get work at high wages; men-of-war, and merchantmen, and store-ships, and troop-ships sailing in and out every day; boats laden with men and chests pulling across the harbour; seamen crowding every quay; pressgangs at work catching men to fight England's battles; and then such hurrying to and fro, and shrieking of women, and shouting of men, and crying of children, and revelling, and laughter, and scenes of extravagance, and debauchery, and vice I had never before beheld, and did not think could exist in a civilised part of the globe.

Having refitted with as little delay as possible, and again put to sea, we found ourselves off the north coast of Spain, far into the Bay of Biscay. For some time we were employed in looking along the coast of France, and picking up all the small coasters we could lay eyes on. We did a great deal of damage to a number of poor people, and taught them that war was a very disagreeable thing, so that they must heartily have wished it over, or rather, that it never had begun; but I doubt if we did ourselves any good in the way of collecting prize-money; at all events, I know that I never got any. At length, one morning, when we could just make out the French coast like a thin wavy blue line on the horizon, beyond which a rich yellow glow was bursting forth, the forerunner of the glorious sun, a sail was seen, hull down, to the northward, and apparently standing in on a bowline for the land. The ship, as was usual when cruising, had been quietly jogging on under her topsails during the night. "All hands, make sail in chase!" was the cheerful sound which made us spring on deck to our stations; and in a few minutes the corvette, with royals and studding-sails alow and aloft, was kept away after the stranger. The latter, which was pronounced to be a large topsail schooner, was soon seen to bear up, and to set all the canvas she could carry, in an endeavour to escape. The chase was a large and fast vessel of her class, for it was not till some time after breakfast that we could see half-way down her mainsail from the deck. Still, we were gaining on her. She, meantime, was edging away in for the land, so that there was little doubt that she was an enemy's vessel—probably, from the way she made sail, a privateer with a number of hands on board, if not a man-of-war. Hour after hour we continued the chase, till the French coast rose clear and distinct on our starboard-bow.

Jacob Lyal and I were at this time stationed in the foretop, of which Peter Poplar was captain, though he was shortly afterwards made a quarter-master. We thus saw every movement of the chase. She, by degrees, edged away again more to the northward, as if wishing to avoid the coast thereabout. We had begun the chase soon after daylight, and the evening was now drawing on, when, close in with the land, we made out a large ship standing along-shore, the rays of the sinking sun shining brilliantly on her snowy canvas. The schooner hauled up towards her, and then kept away again, as if she did not like her appearance.

"What do you make her out to be?" said I to Peter, pointing to the ship.

"Why, Jack, from the squareness of her yards and the whiteness of her canvas, I should say she is a man-of-war—probably a frigate, and a thundering big frigate, too, if I am not much mistaken."

"I suppose, from the French schooner keeping away from her, she is an English frigate," said I.

"Not so sure of that either, Jack," he answered. "We don't know that the schooner is French, in the first place; and even if she is, she may be mistaken as to the character of the frigate, or she may have altered her course just to deceive us, so as to let the frigate come up with us without our taking alarm about her. Never fancy that you have made a right guess and neglect to take precautions, in case you should be wrong."

"Why, if she is an enemy's frigate, she'll sink us," said Lyal. "We shall have to up stick and run for it!"

"Never do you fear that, lad," answered Peter, somewhat sternly, I thought. "Run?—no! If that is a French frigate it will just give us an opportunity of showing what British pluck can do. Our lads know how to handle their guns and small-arms—thanks to the practice some of the grumblers complained of—and if we don't give a good account of that ship out there, my name is not Peter Poplar."

The spirit with which Peter spoke soon animated both Lyal and me, and when we were relieved from our watch, and repeated his words, they were responded to by all the crew, and their great wish was that the frigate in sight should prove an enemy, that they might show how they would treat her.

What the officers thought about the matter we could not tell, but as it grew dark the chase of the schooner was abandoned, studding-sails were taken in, and the ship was hauled on a wind and stood off-shore. As may be supposed, no one turned in that night; the hammocks remained in the nettings, and the ship was got ready for action.

From the way the frigate was steering at nightfall, there could be little doubt that she was following in our track. Anxiously we looked out for her lights astern. Hour after hour passed away, and no sign of her appeared, and we began to fear that she had missed us altogether.

At last a small glimmer was soon twinkling away in the darkness, and by degrees it grew larger and larger; and then out of the dense obscurity— for no moon nor stars were visible—there glided a dark towering mass, like some phantom giant talking over the deep. The drum beat to quarters, and the crew sprung eagerly to their guns. Every man was stripped to the waist, round which he had fastened a handkerchief, with another round his head, and had his cutlass ready to board or to repel boarders.

In spite of the wish for battle we had all expressed, I could not help feeling a sensation of awe, if not of dread, creep over me, as we stood—thus in silence and darkness at our guns, expecting the attack of an enemy of vastly superior force. The muscular forms of our sturdy crew could just be distinguished grouped round their guns, the pale light of the ship's lanterns falling here and there upon them in fitful flashes, as the officers went their rounds to see that every one was at his station, or as the boys handed up shot and powder from below. We were prepared, I say, but still, I believe, the general impression aft was, that the stranger would prove a friend.

As she drew nearer, the order was given to make the private night-signal. Up went the lanterns to the mast-head. It was a moment of breathless suspense. No answering signal of friendship was made in return. In another instant, however, that unmistakable one of hatred and defiance—a shot— came whistling over our heads. It was replied to by one of our stern-chasers; and we then went about, that we might keep the weather-gauge—a most important point under present circumstances.

The enemy, to avoid being raked, had to do the same. "Give it them now, my lads!" shouted the captain. "Let every shot tell, and show the big one what a little craft can do when her crew have the will to make her speak!" Loud cheers were the reply to the address, and instantly every gun sent forth its flame of fire; and I believe that not a shot failed to take some effect on the hull or rigging of our opponent. Now hotly broadside to broadside, at the distance of half-gun-shot from each other, we stood in towards the land. As fast as they could be run in loaded, our guns discharged their deadly showers. All the time we were edging closer towards each other, and as we got within hail we could see that considerable damage had already been suffered by the frigate. This gave fresh encouragement to us, and we blazed away with more hearty good-will than before. The enemy's shot had, however, been telling not a little on us. Several of our men had lost the number of their mess, and more had been wounded; but no damage of consequence had been received aloft, and any the hull had received had been quickly repaired by our carpenter and his active crew.

Amid the roar of the guns a loud shout burst from our people. I looked up. The frigate's mizzen-topmast had been shot away, and came tumbling down on deck. Our fore-topgallant-topmast, however, soon followed, cut through by a round-shot; but that was of little consequence, as our topsail-yard was uninjured, and the topsail still stood. We were not long in clearing the wreck, but for a moment there was a cessation of firing. Just then a hail came across the dark waters from the Frenchman's deck.

"Do you strike, Sare? Do you strike?" was asked through a speaking-trumpet. Our captain seized his trumpet in return.

"Certainly, monsieur, certainly. We have been and intend to go on striking, just in the way Englishmen have the fashion of doing."

A loud laugh burst from our crew at this answer. It just suited our tastes, and then such a hearty cheer was uttered as could not have failed to convince the Frenchman that our captain was likely to be backed by his people to the utmost. Our guns were not long silent, and once more the darkness of night was illuminated by the bright sheets of flame which burst forth in almost a continuous stream from their mouths.

What a contrast to the previous awful silence was there in the report of the guns, the rattle of musketry, the shouts of the officers, the cheers of the men, the crashing of spars and timber as the shot struck home, and the shrieks, and cries, and groans of the wounded! To these expressions of pain even the bravest cannot help giving way, when wounded where the nerves are most sensitive.

Several times the enemy attempted to close, when her greatly prepondering force of men would have told with fearful effect on our decks; but each time the attempt was made it was dexterously avoided by our captain. We had, however, begun to suffer considerably in spars and rigging, and the number of our killed and wounded was increasing. Our second lieutenant had been severely injured by the fall of the foretop-gallant-mast. A midshipman, a young lad who had just come to sea, was struck down close to me. I lifted him up in my arms for a moment, to get him carried below out of harm's way; but the terrible injury he had received convinced me that no help could avail. I put my hand on his heart: it had ceased to beat. Yet what voice sounded more full of life and spirit than his as we cheered at the captain's answer to the Frenchman's hail? On the other side of me a fine young fellow fell mortally wounded. He was just my own age, but not, like me, left alone in the world—he had many dear ones in his humble home. He felt that he had not many moments to live, though his mind was as active as ever.

"Williams!" he faintly cried. "Stoop down, lad! Don't let them take me below: I want to die here! And I say—you know my poor mother, and Sally, and George: just tell them that you saw the last of me; that I thought of them, and prayed for them, and that I hope we may meet in that far, far-off port to which we are all bound! I haven't forgot the prayers mother taught me, tell her. It will comfort her to know that! Good-bye, Jack!"

He pressed my hand as he uttered these words, but instantly afterwards his fingers relaxed. His spirit had fled, and I returned to my duty at my gun!

There were not many seamen, unhappily, in those days, like poor James Martin. Another shipmate was killed not far from me, and he died uttering fearful curses on our enemies, utterly ignorant of the future world into which he was entering.

Thus we fought on. Although we were severely punishing our big opponent, we could not feel that we were getting the best of the fight.

"Do you think we shall take her?" said I to Peter, during another short cessation of firing.

"I scarcely expect that," he answered. "But I am pretty certain that he won't take us. See, hurrah! He's been hit again pretty hard!"

As he spoke, the frigate's mizzen-mast, which must have been before badly wounded, went by the board, and at the same time her main-yard came down by the run on deck, no doubt doing further damage by the fall.

To show the enemy that our spirits were as high as ever, we cheered again; but, as if in retaliation, several shots, in quick succession, struck our foretopmast, and it, and the yard, and all our headsail, came thundering down on deck, in a confused mass of wreck, disabling several of our people, and rendering our foremost gun useless for a time. I was thankful that I had been stationed at a gun instead of being aloft. Some of the officers hurried forward to get the wreck cleared away, while others encouraged the men to persevere in the strife—not that any encouragement was necessary, for we were all eager to continue it, still hoping to make prize of our antagonist.

What had become of the schooner meantime we could not tell. We could only suppose that she was an unarmed vessel. Had she been armed, she might have proved a very disagreeable addition to the force with which we had to contend.

While we were clearing the wreck of the foretopmast, another broadside was poured into us, which we returned with our after-guns. It appeared to me, as I looked up again at her after loading, that the frigate was increasing her distance from us. There could be no mistake about it. Her helm had been put up, and she was running off before the wind. Didn't we cheer heartily! but then we remembered that, deprived of our headsail, we could not follow—so we cheered again, and sent a few shots flying after her, like a dog's farewell bark, just to show her that we claimed the victory, and would be ready for her if she chose to come back; and then we set to work with a will to repair damages.

Our couple of hours' night work had produced not a few, and sadly changed the appearance of our trim little sloop. Still, as our foremast was standing, we were able to make headsail on the ship, and we hoped by the following morning to get matters sufficiently to rights to be able to renew the engagement should our opponent again venture to attack us. I, in common with many of the younger men, was very much disappointed at not having captured the frigate; but Peter and others who had fought in the last war, told us that we were very fortunate in not having ourselves been obliged to strike, as our opponent could not have mounted less than six-and-thirty, if not forty guns—more than twice as many as we carried. Notwithstanding this, we only hoped to see her again in the morning; and as soon as daylight appeared several eager pairs of eyes were aloft looking out for her. There, hull down to the northward, appeared a sail, which was most probably our opponent; but she was running directly before the wind.

At first we supposed that our captain would follow her; but though as brave a man as need be, as he had proved himself, he saw that the probability of capturing the frigate was too small to justify him in making the attempt—in doing which he was much more likely to lose his own ship. Shattered, indeed, did we look when the sun shone down on our blood-stained decks; and still more sad were the scenes which the wounded and dying presented below. I will not, however, now dwell on them. Several shot had gone through the ship's sides, some between wind and water; but the holes had been quickly plugged by the carpenter's crew. Altogether, so shattered was the sloop, that, unwilling as our captain was to give up the cruise, he had no resource but to make the best of his way to Plymouth. We arrived there ten days after the engagement; but the pumps had to be kept going all the time, and the ship was ordered into dock to undergo a thorough repair.

It is impossible for me to describe all the scenes of which I was witness during that interesting period of England's naval history; but there was one I must not omit, as it shows what presence of mind and courage can do, in rescuing people even from the greatest difficulties.

At that time the French revolutionary party, so well named Red Republicans, were inflicting, with unsparing barbarity, the most dreadful atrocities on any of their unhappy countrymen who were even suspected of entertaining monarchical principles. The inhabitants of Toulon, as well as of several other places, were known to be favourable to the cause of their sovereign; and to afford them support, Lord Hood—then commander-in-chief in the Mediterranean—landed a body of English and Spanish troops, and took possession of the town and forts while his own fleet, with one sent by Spain to join him, entered the harbour.

At this time a number of supernumeraries, of whom I was one, sailed from Plymouth to join various ships in the Mediterranean, and, in course of time, I found myself on board the *Juno*, a fine 32-gun frigate, commanded by Captain Samuel Hood. We sailed from Malta early in the year 1794, with some officers and a few troops, to reinforce the scanty garrison at Toulon, then besieged, as was reported, by a formidable army of the Republicans, amounting to thirty-three thousand men, under Generals Kellerman and Carteaux.

The *Juno* was just the sort of dashing frigate a young fellow of spirit would wish to belong to, and her Captain was just the man he would wish to serve under. Strict discipline was kept up on board, and all hands were made to know their duty, and to do it. Her officers, too, were as smart a set as ever stepped. I was very fortunate in this, because for the first time since I came to sea I was among strangers, with the exception of Jacob Lyal, who had joined her with me. Peter Poplar was far away in another ship, and I own I missed him sorely. Still, I had learned my duty, and I hoped to continue to do it.

We had a quick passage from Malta, and made the French coast just before nightfall. We had carried on all sail, in the hope of getting in while daylight lasted, as the captain was anxious to deliver his despatches and land his passengers, and be out again in search of any stray cruisers of the enemy. The wind, however, fell so light that we were unable to do as he hoped. But he was not a man to be turned from his purpose. Accordingly, rather than lose a day, he stood boldly in for the harbour-mouth, which is not a difficult one to make. We expected that a pilot would have come out to us, but none appeared; and as no signal was made for one, it was then known that the captain intended to find his way in in the dark.

Trusty men were placed in the chains with the lead; all hands were at their stations; those with the sharpest eyes were placed as look-outs; the captain stood, trumpet in hand, on the quarter-deck, ready to issue his orders. Not a word was spoken fore or aft. The wind was light, and nearly abeam. Thus, with a dead silence reigning on board, the gallant frigate entered the harbour of Toulon. The officers, with their night-glasses in hand, were anxiously looking out for the British fleet, that they might ascertain where the frigate was to bring-up. In vain they swept them round in every direction; no fleet was to be seen. The circumstance was reported to the captain.

"The easterly winds we have had have sent a heavy sea rolling in here. They must have run into the inner harbour to avoid it. We must follow them there," was his answer. "Shorten sail! Let the ship stand in under her topsails."

The courses were accordingly brailed up, and the top-gallant-sails furled, and under easy sail we stood up the inner harbour. Still nothing could we see of the fleet—not a light did any of the ships show.

On we glided through the calm water. "A brig ahead, sir!" shouted the third lieutenant from forward.

"Shall we weather her?" asked the captain.

The answer was in the negative. "Set the foresail and spanker! Ready, about-ship!"

Scarcely had the boatswain's shrill pipe uttered the appropriate call, than the sails were let fall and sheeted home; and as soon as the frigate felt the effect they produced, the helm was put a-lee, and she went about close under the stern of the brig, which lay in her course. A loud hail came from the brig, but I for one could not make out what was said.

"That's not an English brig," observed one of the officers near me. She lay off what is called the Grand Tour Point.

"He is inquiring our name," said another officer.

"His Britannic Majesty's frigate *Juno*," shouted the first lieutenant.

"Wah—wah—wah!" or sounds something like that, came from the brig. Some one also shouted, "Viva!"

"Whereabouts is the English fleet?" asked the captain. "Have they sailed? Is the admiral still here?"

"Wah—wah—wah!" was the only answer we got. The questions were repeated in French.

"Yes—yes; oui—oui; wah—wah—wah!" was again the reply.

"That's a French merchant-brig. They cannot make out what we say. The fleet must have gone over to the other side of the harbour."

Directly afterwards, the words, "Luff—luff!" reached our ears.

"They are afraid we shall be ashore, sir," said the first lieutenant.

"Then down with the helm!" shouted the captain. The order was promptly obeyed, and the frigate came up almost head to wind; but scarcely a minute had passed when we felt that she had run stem on to the ground; but so light was the wind, and so slight was the way on her, that no damage of any sort was done.

Of course the order was immediately given to clew-up and hand the sails; and in another minute or so the *Juno* lay with all sails furled right up in the centre of the harbour of Toulon, with a line of heavy batteries between her and the sea. While we were handing sails, a boat was seen to put off from the brig; but instead of coming aboard us, she pulled away rapidly in the direction of the town.

Before, however, we were even off the yards, a flaw of wind took the ship's head, and happily drove it off the bank, when the anchor was let go, and she lay with her head up the harbour. Still, however, she hung on the bank by the stern, while her rudder remained immovable and useless. Seeing this, the captain ordered a kedge to be carried out to warp her off; which, as she hung very lightly, could easily be done. To perform this operation the launch was lowered; but being a heavy boat, it took some time to get her into the water. Warps and the kedge-anchor were then placed in her, and her crew pulled away with the kedge in the proper direction to haul her off. While we were thus engaged, a boat was seen coming down the harbour.

"What boat's that?" hailed the sentry from forward.

"Ay, ay," was the answer.

"Officers coming alongside!" cried the sentry—such being the answer given by naval officers when hailed by a ship-of-war. A captain repeats the name of his ship.

The gangway was manned to receive the visitors. Every one was puzzled to know the meaning of a visit at so unusual an hour, and anxious to know what it meant. A well-manned boat came alongside, and two French officers, with several other people, scrambled up on deck.

"Be smart, then, my lads, with the kedge," sung out Mr Webley, third lieutenant, from forward. "We must get the ship afloat before the wind drives her further on."

The French officers looked about the decks for an instant, and then, followed by their people, went aft to the captain, who was standing on the quarter-deck ready to receive them.

"Monsieur le Capitaine," said one of them, taking off his hat and bowing politely, "I am sent by the chief of the port to compliment you on the way you have brought your ship into this loyal port, but to express regret that the regulations he has been compelled to issue make it necessary for you to go over to the southern side of the harbour, there to perform a quarantine for a short ten days or so, as you come from Alexandria, an infected place."

"But we don't come from Alexandria; we come from Malta, which is not an infected place," answered the captain.

"Then, monsieur, Malta is an infected place," returned the officer, quickly.

"I cannot understand that," answered Captain Hood. "I have to deliver my despatches, and some supernumeraries for the army here, and then to be away again as fast as possible. I beg, gentlemen, you will inform me where the *Victory*, Lord Hood's ship, is. I must be guided by his orders."

"Certainly, monsieur, certainly," said the Frenchman, bowing with a bland smile. "We will pilot you to him."

I remember thinking, as the Frenchmen walked along the deck, that there was a good deal of swagger in their manner, but I only set it down to Gallic impudence. While this conversation was going on, one of our midshipmen, a smart youngster—Mowbray, I think, was his name—had been inquisitively examining the Frenchmen, and he now hurried up to the captain, and drew him aside.

"Just look, sir—those are Republican cockades!" he whispered. "As the light of a lantern fell on their hats, I observed it. There's some trick put upon us."

"In truth you are right, my lad, I greatly fear," answered the captain, in an agitated voice. "Where do you say Lord Hood is?" he asked, turning abruptly to the Frenchman.

"My Lord Hood! He is not here. He has long ago departed. We have no lords here," answered the French officer in a sneering tone. "You have made a great mistake, and are like a rat in a hole. The truth is, Monsieur le Capitaine, you and your ship's company are prisoners! But make yourself easy—the English are good people—we will treat them kindly."

"Prisoners!" exclaimed Captain Hood and the officers standing near, in tones of dismay. "Prisoners! impossible!" But the assertion was too true.

Lord Hood had been compelled to evacuate Toulon some time before, with all the forces under his command, after blowing up, by the aid of Sir Sidney Smith, several of the forts, and destroying or carrying away every ship in the harbour; while the unfortunate inhabitants were exposed to all the cruelties which their sanguinary opponents could inflict on them.

As may be supposed, the Republican Frenchmen exulted in the idea of having so easily captured an English frigate, and a large number of Englishmen on whom they might retaliate for some of the losses their party had sustained. As ill news travels quickly, so in an instant the words in everybody's mouth were, "We are prisoners! we are prisoners!" Some would scarcely believe it, and the officers and many of the men hurried aft in a body to ascertain the fact. Mr Webley had remained forward, and before we had been able to haul on the warp she had laid out, he promptly recalled the launch, and ordered the people out of her up the side. The boatswain was standing near him.

"See," he exclaimed, "there's a flaw of wind just come down the harbour. If it holds, the Frenchmen, even should this report be true, need not be quite so sure as they think that they have caught us."

Saying this, he hurried aft to the captain, while the boatswain, not to lose time, made all the necessary preparations for making sail and cutting the cable.

"I believe, sir, that we shall be able to fetch out, if we can get her under sail," said the lieutenant in the captain's ear. The words made him start, and restored vigour to his heart.

"Thank you, Webley, thank you," exclaimed the captain, when the third lieutenant told him that the wind had come ahead. "We'll make the attempt, and may Heaven prosper it!"

Without a moment's delay, the first lieutenant issued the order to make sail, while Mr Webley hurried forward to see the cable cut, as she tended the right way. Like larks we sprang aloft to loose the topsails, and all was done so silently and so rapidly, that the Frenchmen could not make out what was occurring.

"Gentlemen," said the captain, politely addressing the officers, "I must trouble you to step below. We have duty in this ship to carry on which will not require your presence."

"But," exclaimed the Frenchmen, uttering all the oaths in their ample vocabulary, "you are our prisoners. We do not choose to obey your orders."

"You mistake; you are ours! Englishmen do not yield unless to greatly superior force," exclaimed our captain. "Gentlemen, you must go below."

The Frenchmen laughed scornfully. "Treason! mutiny!" they exclaimed, drawing their sabres, and attempting to make a rush to the gangway; but as they turned, they found themselves confronted by a file of marines, with fixed bayonets presented at them!

Rage, and fury, and disappointed revenge were in the tones of their voices, as they gave vent to their feelings in oaths and execrations while they were being handed below. Not a man of their boat's crew escaped, for all had come on board to witness the capture, as they supposed, of a British frigate.

During this time the topsails had been let fall, and in less than three minutes were sheeted home. The headsails filled. At the very moment they did so, a stronger puff of wind came right down the harbour. "Cut, cut!" was the word. Round swung her head towards the open sea. Almost with a bound it seemed her stern lifted off the ground. "Hurrah! hurrah! We are free! we are free!" was the joyful cry. Now, come shot or shell, or whatever our foemen choose to send. We have our brave ship under command, and if our stout sticks do but stand, we may yet escape the trap into which we have so unwarily fallen.

Such were the sentiments which were felt, if not expressed, by all on board the frigate. Plenty of sharp eyes were on shore, watching through the gloom of night, as far as they were able, the movements of the English frigate, expecting to see her every moment glide up the harbour, where, of course, troops had been rapidly collected to take possession of the prize, and conduct us within the precincts of a French prison.

The Republicans must soon have discovered that their plan to capture us had not been altogether successful. As we sailed down the harbour, instead of up, as they had expected, lights began to gleam from the various strong forts which lined each side of the harbour below us, and also from the deck of our friend the brig, off Great Tower Point. Then, as we glided on, every moment gathering fresh way, from all directions a hot fire was opened on us. As with the light wind there was blowing it was necessary to be rid of every obstruction, both our barge and the Frenchmen's boat were cut adrift, though we would gladly have prevented even them from falling into their hands.

There was now no longer any necessity for concealment. The drums beat to quarters, the guns were cast loose, and as we passed down the harbour we began to return the compliments our enemies were so liberally bestowing on us. We had our guns ready in time to give our friend the brig a good dose, but what mischief we inflicted we could not tell; and, to do her justice, she was not slack in her attempts to cripple us. Thus in an instant the harbour, so lately sleeping in silence, and, as it were, shrouded in the solemn gloom of night, was rudely awaked and lighted up with the roar and bright flashes of a hundred guns, which, fast as they could be discharged, sent forth a continuous fire at our seemingly devoted ship. Thus far all had proceeded well; but we were far from free of danger. Shot after shot struck us, several times we were hulled, but not a man had yet been hit, when, to our dismay, the wind grew very scant, and seemed about to head us.

"If it shifts a couple of points more to the southward, we shall have to beat out of this place!" exclaimed the captain of the gun at which I was stationed. "Never mind, lads; we'll teach these Frenchmen what a British frigate can do in spite of all that."

Still the *Juno* steadily held on her course. The wind backed once more and came down the harbour, and on she glided. The enemy's guns were, however, telling on us with fearful effect—our topsails were riddled with shot, and our rigging much cut up; but as the damage occurred, our active crew flew here and there to repair it, as well as time and the darkness would allow. Now the harbour opened out broadly before us, and the line of open sea could be perceived ahead. Our masts and spars stood unharmed, the firing from the forts grew fainter and fainter. Scarcely a shot reached us. On we stood. The shot began to drop astern. For several minutes not one had struck us. The Frenchmen tried in their rage, but all in vain.

"We are free! we are free indeed! Hurrah! hurrah! hurrah!" burst with one voice from all our crew, and the gallant *Juno* bounded forward on the wide ocean, to show what British daring, judgment, and promptitude will effect, even although the most fearful odds are ranged against success.

I trust that some on board that ship felt also that a merciful Providence had preserved us from a galling and painful lot, which would have endured for many a long year, to do our duty to Heaven and our country. I trust that the example set by the crew of the *Juno* will serve as an example to all British seamen—never to yield while there is a possibility of escape.

Well, it was amusing to see how the Frenchmen did stamp and rage when they found that, instead of capturing us, they had been taken prisoners; but we treated them very civilly, and after a few shrugs and grimaces, like people having to take physic, we soon had the men singing and jigging away as merry as crickets.

I remained for some time on board the *Juno*, and left her on a very short notice, and very much also against my own will.

One dark night, as, with a convoy of merchantmen under our charge, we were standing for Gibraltar, the watch below were roused up with the cry of, "All hands shorten sail!" I and others, tossing on our clothes, sprang aloft through the darkness, with a fierce wind blowing in our faces, to reef topsails. Scarcely had I reached the lee foretop-sail yard-arm, and had, as I believed, the earing in my hand, when, how I cannot tell, I found myself jerked off the yard; and ere I could secure a firm grasp of the rope I held, I found myself hurled through the midnight air, clutching emptiness, till I reached the foam-covered water, through which the ship was hurriedly ploughing her way. I heard the cry, "A man overboard! a man overboard!" but the ship had been carrying too much sail, and without shortening it, it was impossible to round-to in order to pick me up. From the frigate, therefore, I knew that I could expect no help. I do not believe that for a moment after I fell I lost my consciousness, though I suspect that before I fell I was more asleep than awake. I had on only my shirt and light duck-trousers, so I threw myself on my back, to consider what was best to be done. There were plenty of vessels, I knew, astern of the frigate, but there was little chance of being seen by any of them, or of their being able to pick me up if they did see me.

How long I could have remained floating on my back I don't know—some hours, I suppose, in smooth water; but as it was, the squall had blown up a sea, and the spray kept dashing over my head and half drowned me. On a sudden I found my head strike against something with so much force as almost to stun me, and, turning round, I found myself in contact with a large object. I caught hold of it. Ropes were hanging down from it into the water; I climbed up by them, and found that it was the top and parts of the topmast of a ship of large size. I felt thankful that I was not likely to die for some time, unless the weather grew worse; and I did not allow myself to reflect that even a worse death might be in store for me—that of starvation. I had my knife secured by a lanyard round my neck, so I began to haul up the ropes, and endeavoured to form as secure a resting-place for myself as circumstances would allow. When I had done all I could, I looked round through the darkness for the chance of discovering a sail; but none could I see, so I sat down, and, strange to say, fell asleep.

Chapter Fourteen
Tyranny—War and Mutiny, with a Glimpse of Home Comforts between

As I said, I went to sleep hanging on to a piece of wreck in the middle of the Mediterranean. It was not an agreeable position to be in, certainly, but it might have been worse. I might have been in the middle of the Atlantic, or the Bay of Biscay, or near a country inhabited by cannibals, or with nothing to float on, as was the case till I got hold of the shattered mast. I did not feel it a very serious matter, I suppose, for I slept soundly. I knew that the sea at that time was swarming with vessels—men-of-war, transports, store-ships, and merchantmen, sailing in every direction, and I hoped one or the other would pick me up.

At last the sun shining in my eyes awoke me, and looking around, I saw, about two miles or so to the eastward, a brig with her foretopmast gone and maintopsail-yard carried away. The damage had been done, I had no doubt, by the squall which had sent me out of my warm hammock into the cold water. The squall had passed over, and the sea was almost as smooth as glass. I had a handkerchief round my waist. I took it off, and, standing as high as I could on the wreck, I waved it above my head. I waited anxiously to see if my signal had produced any effect; but the brig's crew were all so busily engaged in repairing the damage she had received, that they did not see me. So I sat down again, hoping that by-and-by they might knock off work, and find a moment to look about them. One comfort was, that while the calm lasted the brig was not likely to go far away from me.

The time seemed very long, and I was beginning to get hungry too as the hour of breakfast drew on. So I got up again and waved my handkerchief, and could not help shouting, though I well knew that no one at such a distance could hear me. I waved till my arm ached, and still I was unobserved; so I sat down a second time, and began to consider what means existed of attracting the attention of the people aboard the brig. I thought of swimming to her; but I reflected that it would be better to let well alone, and that, as there was a long distance to traverse before I could reach her, I might lose my strength, and sink without being observed. The sun, however, rose higher and higher in the sky, and I grew still more hungry; so for a third time I stood up and waved, and shouted, and played all sorts of curious antics, in my eagerness to attract notice. At length there was a stir aboard, and I thought I saw some one waving in return. I was right. A quarter-boat was lowered, and a fast galley pulled towards me. I was not a little pleased when I saw them coming. They were soon up to me, and though I had not been long floating on the broken mast, I can only say that I left it with very considerable satisfaction. The brig, I found, belonged, as I had suspected, to the *Juno's* convoy. As we approached her, I looked with a scrutinising eye at her hull. I thought I knew her build.

"What brig's that?" I asked, with no little interest.

"Why, the old *Rainbow*, lad," answered one of the boat's crew. "A good craft she is still, though she's seen plenty of work in her day."

So I was indebted for my preservation to my old ship—my sea-cradle, I might call her. I hauled myself up her side, and there on her quarter-deck stood Captain Gale, working away as usual with his people, encouraging them by word and action. He seemed very glad to see me, as I am sure I was to see him.

"I see, sir," said I, after having had a little talk with him, "you have plenty of work to do aboard, so, if I may just have some food to put life into me, I'll turn to and lend a hand."

"Ready as ever for work, Jack, I see!" said he, smiling. "I am glad the men-of-war haven't knocked that out of you."

Fortunately the fine weather continued, and by nightfall we were able to rig a jury-mast and make sail on the brig. By the time we reached Gibraltar the *Juno* had sailed, and, as may be supposed, I being a pressed-man, did not feel myself bound to follow her. I was very well satisfied with the treatment I had received in the navy, and do not think that I should have quitted it for any other vessel but my own brig; but as Captain Gale was willing to take me, I could not resist the temptation of remaining with him. After nearly foundering in a heavy gale, being more than once chased by an enemy's cruiser, and narrowly escaping being run down by one of our own line-of-battle-ships, we reached Bristol, to which we were then bound, in safety.

I had not forgotten my promise to poor James Martin, my shipmate in the *Syren*, who was killed in our action with the French frigate; and knowing that his family lived at a village within forty or fifty miles of Bristol, I set off to visit them. Except a small amount of pay due to me for the voyage home, I had little enough money in my pocket, so I was obliged to go on foot. I had never seen anything of the interior of England before, and knew nothing of its varied beauties, especially of its rural districts—the rich meadows, the waving corn-fields, the thick woods, and, more than all, the shady lanes and green hedges, full of roses and honeysuckles, with numberless beautiful flowers growing on the mossy bank beneath them. But still deeper impression did the sequestered village make on me, with its open green and neat cottages, surrounded by pretty gardens; and its clear pond, with gravelly bed; and its neighbouring coppice; and its quiet church, with graceful spire; and the neat and unpretending parsonage; and the old minister, with thin cheeks and long white hair, and grave, yet kind loving countenance, to whom all smiled and courtesied or doffed their hats as he passed; and the long low school-house, with rosy, noisy children rushing out of it, and scattering here and there instantly to begin their play; and the buxom mothers and old dames coming out from their doors to watch them, or to chat with each other in the intervals of work; and the sheep on the sunny downs above; and the sparkling stream which came murmuring by, half overgrown with bushes, so that its pleasant sound alone showed its locality; and its deep pool, where the trout loved to lie; and the cattle in the green meadow, seeking for shade under the tall elms, or with lazy strokes of their tails whisking off the flies; and the boys whistling in the fields; and the men, with long white smocks and gay handkerchiefs worked in front, tending the plough or harrow, or driving the lightly-laden waggon or cart with sturdy well-fed horses. And then the air of tranquillity and repose which pervaded the spot, the contentment visible everywhere, made an impression on me which time has never been able to obliterate, and which, in far, far-off regions, has come back on me with greater force than ever, and prevented me from remaining, as many of my companions did, among their half-savage inhabitants, to enjoy the supposed delights of idleness, and has renewed in me the desire to end my days in my fatherland.

In such a scene as I have described I found the family of my poor shipmate. I easily made myself known. They had no doubt of the truth of my story, and gave me a kind though tearful welcome. The old mother seized my arm and pushed me into a seat, which she mechanically wiped with her blue apron; the tall sunburned father, with grizzled locks, and dressed in long smock and yellow gaiters, grasped my hand.

"And you were with our James when he was struck down in battle, and he thought of us all here! Bless him!"

The old man could say no more. I told him how he not only thought of them, but prayed for them, and spoke of the great comfort which the prayers his mother had taught him had been to him, especially in his last mortal agony.

The old woman alone wept, but not vehemently. They had long before this heard of his death. My message rather brought comfort than sorrow.

After a time George came in—a sturdy young man, with well-knit limbs, and round, good-humoured countenance, with the universal smock, and shoes few legs but such as his could lift. When I spoke of James, his countenance grew sad, and, rising from his three-legged stool, he left the cottage, and did not return for nearly half an hour.

One daughter came in from milking the cows at a neighbouring farm. She reminded me of James. How neat and clean she looked, even coming from work! and how modest and retiring in her manner! She might have been pretty—I don't remember: she was far better than pretty, I judged from all she said. Her sisters were away at service, I found. She asked many questions about James; and though her voice was more than ever subdued when she mentioned his name, my replies seemed to give her satisfaction. But I had the sense gradually to leave off talking of my dead shipmate, and began to tell them of the adventures I had gone through, and of the strange scenes I had witnessed.

There was an old black oak desk, or sloping board, near the small latticed window in the thick wall. On the desk was a large well-worn Bible open, with a green spectacle-case to keep down the page. After supper the old man approached it, as was evidently his custom; and, while all sat round in reverential silence, he began to read slowly and distinctly, though not without difficulty, from the Word of God. One thing struck me—that he read not for form's sake, but that he and his hearers might reap instruction for faith and practice from what he read. He was evidently aware of the truth, that those sacred pages before him were written for our instruction, to be a guide unto our feet, and a light unto our path. Then he prayed—his words came from his heart—for all present, and for guidance and protection for those absent. He did not forget our king and country, and pleaded that God would prosper England's arms by sea and land in a righteous struggle. Surely those prayers, rising from many a humble hearth, were not unheeded by the King of kings. Then, I say to those who themselves believe, teach, oh, teach the poor to pray! for their own sakes, for your sake, for England's sake. Such prayers alone can maintain her as she is—great, glorious, and free.

The Martins would not let me go to the village inn, as I proposed, but insisted on my taking a shake-down in the common room with George. The rest slept in a room above. The moonlight came through the lattice window. I saw George sitting up in his bed.

"Are you asleep, Williams!" he asked, gently.

Old Jack | 189

"No," I replied.

"Then tell me now about poor James," he answered.

I was not slack in obeying his wishes, and for many an hour I went on telling him all the anecdotes I could think of connected with James Martin, from the moment I first knew him till I saw him committed to his watery grave.

"Thank you, master," he said quietly when I ceased; and as I lay down I heard many a sob bursting from his sturdy bosom. "That lad may be a Chaw-bacon," I thought to myself; "but he has got a heart for all the world just like a sailor's."

By daybreak next morning the family were astir, and went cheerfully about their daily labours. George had some two or three miles to go to the farm on which he found employment; the old man and Susan had work near at hand.

I spent a whole day in that quiet village, wandering about among the fields and lanes, and over the downs, till the family assembled again in the evening when their work was done. The next morning I took my departure. I had learned from a shipmate what would certainly be acceptable in a country district, and had brought with me a package of tea and sugar, which I left as a parting gift for poor James's mother. I remember that I put it down somewhat abruptly on the table after I had shaken hands, exclaiming, "That's for you, mother!" and with my small bundle at the end of my stick, I rushed out of the cottage, and took the way back to Bristol.

That was the only glimpse of English country-life I ever got, till—an old, broken-down man—my career at sea was ended. I was on shore often enough, but what scenes did I witness among docks, and narrow streets, and in the precincts of great commercial towns? What can the sailor who never strays beyond these know of all the civilising influences of a well-ordered country home? As I say, I never forgot that quiet scene, short as was the glimpse I obtained; and it had an influence on me for all my after-life, which, at the time, I could not have suspected. Even at first when I got back to Bristol, and breathed the moral atmosphere with which I was surrounded, I longed to be once more away on the free ocean.

The old brig was soon ready again for sea; but as he was about to sail, Captain Gale was taken so ill that he could not proceed, and another master was sent in his stead. I ought to have mentioned that Captain Helfrich had sold her to some Bristol merchants, and had got a large ship instead, which traded round Cape Horn. Captain Grindall was a very plausible man on shore, so he easily deceived the owners; but directly he got into blue water he took to his spirit bottle, and then cursed and swore, and brutally tyrannised over everybody under his orders. I had seen a good deal of cruelty, and injustice, and suffering in the navy, and had heard of more, but nothing could surpass what that man made his crew feel while he was out of sight of land. The first mate, Mr Crosby, who, with Captain Gale, had appeared a quiet sort of man, though rather sulky and ill-tempered at times, imitated the master's example.

We were bound for Barbadoes, in the West Indies. We had not got half-way there, when one of the crew fell sick. Poor fellow! he had not strength to work, but the master and Mr Crosby said that he had, and that they would make him; so they came down into the forepeak and hauled him out of his berth, and drove him with a rope's end on deck. He tried to work, but fell down; so they lashed him to the main-rigging in the hot sun, and there left him, daring any of us to release him, or to take him even a drop of water. I wonder that treatment did not kill him.

Two days after that, when there was some sea on, and the brig was pitching heavily, he fell down again, and Mr Crosby caught sight of him, and kicked him in the rib; and when the second mate, who was a quiet young man, and generally frightened at the other two, tried to interfere, he threatened to knock him down with a handspike. Then, because poor Taylor called them by some name they deserved, they dragged him aft by his hair, and then triced him up to the main-rigging by the heels. I was in the watch below; of the rest of the crew, one was at the helm, another forward, and the others aloft; so that there was no one to interfere. At last, the man forward looked down the fore-scuttle and told us what had happened. We sprung on deck. Taylor was getting black in the face. It was more than we could stand, and in a body we rushed aft, and before the mate could interfere, for the captain was below, we cut him down, and carried him forward. The mate sung out, "Mutiny!" and the captain came on deck with his pistols. But we told him he might shoot one and all of us, but we would not see a messmate murdered before our eyes. Our determined manner somewhat awed the captain, and swearing that he would be even with us before long, he let us have our way. Poor Taylor did not die at once, as we expected he would; but that night he was in a high fever, and raved and shrieked till he made us all tremble with terror.

At noon next day the captain observed that Taylor was not on deck. He asked why he did not come. No one answered. "Then I'll soon learn the cause," he exclaimed, leaping down forward. In another moment he sprung up again, followed by Taylor. The hair of the latter was all standing on end; his eyeballs were starting from their sockets; he had only his shirt on, with the sleeves rolled up, showing his thin bony arms and legs. He was shrieking terrifically. The captain attempted to kick him back as he appeared above the hatchway; but he evaded the blow, and stood on deck confronting his persecutor. The strength of madness was upon him. He made a spring at the captain, and would have hurled him, I verily believe, overboard; but at that moment the first mate rushing forward, struck the poor fellow a blow on the back of the head with a handspike. He gave one glance at his murderer as he fell, and in a few minutes his limbs stiffened, and he was dead. The captain and mate went aft as he fell, leaving him on the deck, and talked together.

After some time the mate sung out, "Rouse that fellow up, some of you there! Ill or not ill, he must do his duty." None of us spoke or stirred, and at last he came forward and kicked the corpse, as if to make the man get up. We guessed all the time that he knew perfectly well that Taylor was dead. There he lay where he fell, till the second mate, who had been below, came on deck, and, going up to the body, discovered the truth. He, of course, reported the man's death to the captain.

"Heave the carcass overboard, Mr Sims," was the answer. "Let's hear no more about the rascal."

Sailors have a dislike to have a dead body in the ship; so, before night set in, we lashed it up in a piece of canvas, and with a shot at the feet, committed it to the sea. Strange as it may appear, when the mate found that we had taken the canvas for this purpose, he made it an excuse for further abuse and ill-treatment. Not a day passed but one or other of us got a kick or a blow from him or the captain. They made one young lad very nearly leap overboard, where he would have been drowned. I hauled him back, and calming him down, showed him the enormity of the sin he was going to commit, and urged him to bear his trials, as they must shortly be over.

At last we reached Carlisle Bay, where we brought up off Bridge Town, the capital of the fertile island Barbadoes. The town lies round the bay, and contains some handsome houses and broad streets. This island is more level than most of the West India isles, with the exception of the north-eastern quarter, called Scotland, when there is an elevation of a thousand feet above the sea. It is rather less in size than the Isle of Wight. What a wretched voyage had we had! How miserable and crushed in spirit did I feel! The scene struck me, therefore, as peculiarly beautiful, as, gliding up the bay, we saw spread out before us the blue waters, fringed by the tall, graceful palms; the shining white houses, circling round the shore; the trim, gallant men-of-war; the merchantmen with their many-coloured flags; the numerous boats pulling here and there, manned by shouting, grinning, laughing negroes;—and then the planters' houses, and woods, and fields of sugar-cane, and farms in the distance, made me feel that such scenes as we had gone through could no longer be enacted with impunity.

The moment we dropped our anchor, the captain went on shore; and I found that, to be beforehand with any of us who might inform against him, he had given his own version of Taylor's death; which, of course, his mate was ready to corroborate. When he returned on board, he gave a triumphant glance forward, as much as to say, I have you still in my power. So he had, as we found when once more we were at sea. I was glad that the young lad Thompson, whom he had so ill-treated, deserted the day before we sailed, and, I believe, entered aboard a man-of-war, where he was safe.

While in harbour we had been quiet enough, but we had not been two days at sea before the captain and mate commenced their old system of tyranny. Everybody was ill-treated, and this time I was the chief victim. Kicked and struck on the slightest pretext, and compelled to perform the most disgusting offices, I soon felt myself a degraded being both in body and mind; and when I thought of what I had been on board the *Juno*, and what I now was, I shrunk from making the comparison. But I was to obtain relief in a way I little expected.

I was in the second mate's watch. Early one morning, about four bells in the middle watch—that is to say, about two o'clock—I had just been relieved from my trick at the helm. The weather was thick and squally, and the night very dark. The look-out was careless, or had bad eyesight; and the mate, knowing this, was constantly going forward himself. I was leisurely going along the deck, when I heard him sing out,—"A sail on the starboard-bow! Luff!—luff all you can!" I sprang forward. The ship was nearer to us than he supposed. Right stem on she came, towering like a huge mountain above us. In an instant the brig's bows were cut down to the water's edge. I sung out to those on deck to follow me, and clung on to whatever I could first get hold of. It proved to be the ship's bobstay. I climbed up it on to the bowsprit, and, as I looked down, I saw her going right over the vessel I had just left— her decks sinking from sight beneath the dark waters. The tall masts, and spars, and sails followed: down, down they went, drawn by an irresistible force! It seemed like some dreadful dream. Before I could secure myself on the bowsprit, they had disappeared in the unfathomable abyss. Not a cry or a groan reached my ears from my drowning shipmates—unwarned, unprepared they died. Such has been many a hapless seaman's fate. One only escaped. He had hold of the dolphin-striker. I could just distinguish his form through the darkness as he followed me. I slid down to help him, and with difficulty hauled him up on the bowsprit. He seemed horror-struck at what had occurred; and so, indeed, we might both well be, and thankful that we had been preserved. Such was the end of the old *Rainbow*.

I now first sung out, and gave notice of our escape to those on board the ship. Several of the crew had rushed forward, and now helped poor Mr Sims and me off the bowsprit. We heard, meantime, the officers of the ship ordering the boats to be lowered; and she being hove up into the wind, one from each quarter was soon manned and in the water. While the two mates of the ship, anxious to save the lives of their fellow-creatures, pulled about in every direction near where the brig was supposed to have gone down, I was looking over the bows, hoping that some of my poor shipmates might yet survive; but no answering cry was made to the repeated shouts of the boats' crews. At last the boats returned on board, and I found that the mate and I were the only survivors of the *Rainbow*. Had she not been an old vessel, I do not think that she would so easily have foundered from the blow she received.

I found that the ship I was on board of was the *Rebecca*, a large West Indiaman, trading between London and Barbadoes, to which place she was then bound, so that I should have to return there instead of going home. The captain sent for the mate and me into the cuddy-cabin, to inquire about the vessel to which we had belonged. He was a quiet, kind-mannered man, and seemed very much cut up at the loss of the brig, though he said that he could not blame his people for what had occurred. When we had given him all the information he required, he directed that we should have berths and food supplied us. I turned in gladly, though it was some time before I went to sleep, and even then I could not get rid of the recollection of the sinking brig, which had borne me in safety for so many a long year over the wide ocean.

The next morning I was told that the mate was very ill. The doctor of the ship had been attending him, but said that his case was hopeless. I sat by him all day. Sometimes he would be perfectly quiet and do nothing but moan; and then he would start up, and shriek out, — "Luff! — luff! — or she'll be into us!" and then sink down again, overcome with horror at the recollection of the event. Towards night he grew worse, and, after several fearful shrieks, he sunk back and expired.

Thus twice in less than two years was I mercifully preserved from destruction. There were a number of passengers on board, who were very kind to me, and took pleasure in asking me questions about my life at sea, and in listening to the accounts of my adventures. Among them was a young gentleman, who, when he heard the name of the *Rainbow* brig, and that she sailed out of Dublin, made many inquiries about her. He told me that he knew Dublin well, and had often heard of the former owners of the *Rainbow*. He was, I found, going out to Bridge Town, to take the management of a large mercantile house there.

"You must come and see me when we get there," said he one day. "I am not certain, but I think we have met before."

"Where could that have been? I don't remember you, sir," I said.

"Hadn't you a very tall seaman aboard the brig when you first went to sea in her?" he asked abruptly.

"Yes, of course, sir!" I exclaimed. "Peter Poplar, my best of friends; I owe everything to him."

"So do I, then, I suspect," said he warmly. "Do you remember a little lad sitting crying on the quays at Dublin, to whom he gave a bundle of old clothes? Yours, I believe, they were."

"Yes," said I; "I remember, too, how grateful he seemed for them, and how Peter walked away with me that he might not listen to his thanks."

"He had reason to be thankful," said the gentleman. "That suit of clothes enabled him to obtain a situation, where, by honesty and perseverance, and an earnest wish to promote his kind master's interests, he rose by degrees to hold the most responsible situation in his establishment. Do you remember the boy's name?"

"No, sir," I replied. "I am not quite certain."

"Was it Terence, do you think?" he asked.

"Yes, sir!" I exclaimed. "Terence it was—Terence McSwiney—that was his name. I remember it now, for he repeated it several times."

"That is my name," said the gentleman; "and I, Jack, am the very little lad to whom your kind friend gave your old clothes. I would much like to meet him again, to thank him, as I do you, for your share of the favour conferred on me. Of one thing you may be certain—I have not been idle. When not engaged in my master's business, I was employed in study and in improving my own mind. I never lost an opportunity of gaining knowledge, and never willingly wasted a moment."

Mr McSwiney told me a good deal more about himself, and I felt how very different a life I had led, and how little I had ever done to improve my mind or to gain knowledge. I even then thought that it was too late to begin, and so I went on in my idleness.

The day before we reached Carlisle Bay the captain sent for me, and told me that the passengers had been interested in my history, and that, as I had lost all my kit in the brig, they had made a collection to enable me to purchase a new one. This he presented to me in the shape of thirty dollars. I expressed myself, as I felt, very grateful for the kindness I had received.

Although Mr McSwiney had once been in the same rank of life to which I belonged, and in one respect even worse off, because I had a suit of clothes on my back when he had none, I did not, in consequence, address him as an equal. He seemed to appreciate my feeling, and I believe that I thereby secured his esteem. He would have taken me to the lodging he had engaged at Bridge Town, but I said, "No, sir, thank you; I will remain on board the ship till I get a berth in some other craft. I have no fancy for living ashore." I went up to see him several times, and we parted, I believe, with mutual feelings of regard. He had more than repaid me for the benefit I had been formerly the means of doing him, and he as well as I soon found that our habits of thought were so different that we could not associate on really equal terms, however much we might wish the attempt to succeed.

Finding a brig, the *Jane and Mary*, short of hands, sailing for the port of Hull, I shipped on board her. I was not much better off in her though, than I had been in the *Rainbow* with Captain Grindall. The captain and mates did not proceed to such extremities as he and Mr Crosby did, but they were rough, ignorant, ill-tempered men, and treated the crew as brutes, looking upon them as mere machines, out of whom they were to get as much work as their strength would allow. When we reached Hull I was glad to leave the *Jane and Mary*; and without even going on shore for a day's spree—as most of the other hands did, and accordingly fell in with press-gangs—I transferred myself to a barque trading to Archangel, on the north coast of Russia.

By the time I got back, I had had enough of a northern voyage, so for the first time went on shore at Hull. Sailors' lodging-houses are generally dirty, foul traps, kept by wretches whose great aim is to fleece the guests of everything they may possess at least cost to themselves. I got into one of this class, for, of course, I did not know where to go. A shipmate had invited me to accompany him, saying he had been very well-treated— though I found afterwards he had been supplied with as much food and liquor as he wanted, and indulged in every vice, and then, when he hadn't a farthing in his pocket, put on board a trader half drunk, and sent to sea. I found myself undergoing very shortly the same sort of treatment he had received; and when I refused to drink more, or yield to other temptations, such fierce, angry scowls were cast on me, that I was anxious to get away. They began, indeed, to quarrel with me; but seeing that had not much effect, they became very civil and polite. In a short time the man of the house—a sturdy ruffian, with a Jewish cast of countenance—went to the cupboard, and I saw him pouring out several tumblers of grog. I pretended not to be watching him, but went on talking to my companions as before. Directly afterwards his wife got up and placed a tumbler by the side of each of us, taking one—

"There are your Saturday's night-caps, my lads," said she, sitting down opposite to us. "Let us drink to sweethearts and wives, and lovers and friends; a bloody war, and plenty of prize-money!" And with a leer out of her evil eye, she gulped down half the contents of the tumbler between her thick lips.

Now I had seen old Growler fumbling with several bottles at the dresser, and as I passed my nose over the tumbler which his wife placed near me, a certain rank odour arose from it which I did not like. How to avoid drinking it I was puzzled, as I did not wish to show the suspicion I felt that it was drugged. Luckily the tumbler stood on a little round table by itself; so I jumped up on a sudden, as if something had stung me, and upset the table with the tumbler and its contents! Old Growler pretended to be very sorry for the accident, and insisted on mixing another. "No, thank you, master," I answered; "I've been very clumsy, and must pay the penalty by the loss of the grog." The couple looked at each other and then at me with such an evil glance, that I believe had it not been for my companions they would at that moment have turned me out into the street.

There were six seamen in the room, lately discharged from different merchantmen. The house was at the end of a dirty, narrow court, all the inhabitants of which were of the lowest description. As we were sitting smoking, a tap was heard at the door. Old Growler went to it. Several questions were asked by a person outside. He came back in a hurry, and beckoned to his wife to come and answer them. "There are some man-of-war's men outside," said he. "They say that they are come to look for a deserter. They'll soon make my missus open the door, so you've no time to lose, my lads. Be quick, then; through the door, and stowaway in the coal-shed." The house had a back-door, or it would not have been fit for old Growler's purposes; and the door opened into what they called a garden, but it was a bit of dirty barren ground, strewn with broken bricks and crockery, and bits of rotten wood, with some tumble-down sheds on either side of it. In one of these he proposed we should hide. As we opened the door, however, to rush out, we found ourselves confronted by a dozen stout seamen; and before we could make the slightest resistance, we were all of us bound hand and foot. The front-door being opened, an officer and several men entered through it, and a large party of us assembled in Mrs Growler's kitchen. The lieutenant and midshipman who commanded the press-gang took very coolly the abuse which our worthy host and hostess so liberally bestowed on them. We were allowed to go, two and two at a time, under escort, to collect our traps, and then marched down to a couple of boats waiting for us at the quay. In a short time we were put on board a cutter, with a number of other men who had been picked up in a similar way. There was a good deal of grumbling, and some of the men seemed to have been very hardly dealt with; but I cannot say that my change of lot made me particularly unhappy.

Another night's foray on shore considerably increased our numbers; besides which several volunteers, mostly landsmen, were obtained, and the cutter then sailed to discharge her passengers into the ships most requiring men. I and several others found ourselves going up the side of His Majesty's ship *Glutton*, of 50 guns, commanded by Captain Henry Trollope. As I stood on the deck looking about me, previous to being summoned aft, I saw on the other side the tall figure of a man whose back was turned towards me. My heart beat with surprise and joy, for I felt almost sure he must be Peter Poplar. He shortly turned his head. I was right. He was no other than my old friend. I sprung over to him, and warmly grasped his hand. He started when he saw me, stared at me with astonishment, and for a minute could not speak.

"Is it really you, Jack?" he at length exclaimed. "Why, lad, I thought you were dead. I was told that you had been lost overboard from the *Juno*."

"So I was," said I; "but I was found by an old friend, who in the end played me a somewhat scurvy trick." And I told him in a few words all that had occurred to me since we had been paid off from the *Syren*.

"Well, I am right glad to see you, lad—that I am," he exclaimed, again wringing my hand.

My yarn was scarcely out when I was summoned to have my name entered on the ship's books, and to hear my rating, which was that of "able seaman." The *Glutton* had been an Indiaman, measuring 1400 tons, and had been purchased into the service. She was now armed with the then newly-invented carronades, 68-pounders on the lower, and 32-pounders on the upper deck. This was a weight of metal no ship had, I believe, previously carried; and Captain Trollope was very anxious to try its effect on the ships of the enemy, rightly believing that it would not a little astonish them.

Our first cruise was off the coast of Flanders. We had not long to wait before an enemy was seen. On the 15th of July, when the days were longest and the weather fine, early in the afternoon six ships were seen from the mast-head running before the wind; and soon afterwards, further to leeward, appeared a brig and a cutter, which they were apparently bearing down to join. I was at the helm when the captain made out what they were.

"Four French frigates and two corvettes. They will just suit us!" said he, shutting up his glass with a smile of satisfaction.

"A heavy squadron for one ship to attack," observed one of the lieutenants.

"One!—every man on board will be sorry they ever met *us!*" said the captain. He knew that the officer who spoke was not one likely to flinch from the work to be done.

We were standing directly for the enemy, whose ships were pretty close in with the land. Notwithstanding the apparently overwhelming numbers of the foe, the ship, with the greatest alacrity, was cleared for action.

"Shall we really fight them?" asked a youngster of Peter, who was a great favourite with all the midshipmen.

"Ay—that we shall, sir," he answered. "The captain only wishes that there were twice as many ships to fight."

"That's all right!" exclaimed the young midshipman. "I was afraid that some trick was intended, and that we should soon have to up stick, and run for it."

"No, no; no fear of that! I don't think our captain is the man to run from anything."

It was now about eight o'clock in the evening, and the French ships, having formed in line, seemed to have no intention of avoiding us. A feeling of pride and confidence animated the bosoms of all our crew as we stood round the short heavy guns with which our ship was armed, while advancing towards an enemy of a force apparently so overwhelming. One French frigate, the *Brutus*, was a razéed 64-gun ship, and now carried 46 guns. Then there were the *Incorruptible*, of 32 guns; the *Magicienne*, of 36; the *Républicain*, of 28; and the two corvettes, of 22 guns each.

On we stood. Whatever the enemy did, we were not to fire till we got close up to them. There were to be no long shots with us. It had become almost dark before we arrived abreast of the three sternmost ships. "Take care that not a gun is fired till I give the order," cried the captain. "Steer for that big fellow there." This was the *Brutus*, the second from the van. We were within thirty yards of this ship. "Strike to His Britannic Majesty's ship *Glutton!*" cried the captain, waving to the Frenchman. This order the Frenchmen were not likely to obey. Up went the French colours at the peaks of all the ships, and immediately they began firing as they could bring their guns to bear. We glided on a few yards nearer the opponent our captain had singled out. "Now, give it them, my lads!" he shouted; and immediately we poured our whole broadside into the hull of our enemy. The effects were as terrific as unexpected—she seemed literally to reel with the force of the concussion. Meantime, the leading ship stood past us to windward, with the intention of cutting us up with her shot; but she got more than she bargained for, in the shape of our larboard-broadside. The heavy shot, nearly every one of which told, shattered her hull, tore open her decks, and damaged her spars. Meantime we were standing on the larboard-tack, with the French commodore to leeward of us, with whom we were exchanging a hot fire—rather hotter than he liked, indeed.

The pilot had been anxiously watching the coast—not indeed relishing, probably, the sort of work going on. He now hurried up to the captain: "We shall be on shore to a certainty, sir, if we stand on in this course."

"Never fear," answered Captain Trollope. "When the Frenchman takes the ground, do you go about."

All this time the enemy's shot were flying about us terribly, cutting up our spars and rigging; but, strange to say, as I looked around, I did not see one wounded! It was light enough all the time to enable us to see all the enemy's ships, and yet sufficiently dark to allow the flash of the guns to have its full effect, as we and our many opponents rapidly discharged them at each other. Still the French commodore stood on. Perhaps he hoped to drive us on shore. At last he was compelled to tack. Captain Trollope had been waiting the opportunity. The instant he hove in stays, we, who had been reserving our fire, poured in our broadside, raking him fore and aft with murderous effect.

"All hands about-ship!" was now the cry. So cut up was our rigging, however, that we had no little difficulty in getting her about. Our masts also were badly wounded. It was a question whether they would carry our canvas.

"Hands aloft!—reef topsails!" was the next order given. Up we sprung, most unwillingly leaving our gnus, while the French ships, one after the other, stood away from us, glad to get out of reach of our fire though they did not fail to give us a parting salute.

We were as smart as we could in reefing topsails, but as much of our running-gear was cut up, we were longer than usual; and the Frenchmen, finding that we had ceased firing, took it into their heads. I suppose, that we were going to strike, for they all tacked and once more stood back towards us.

"To your guns, my lads! to your guns!" was the cry, as we swung down off the yards; and then didn't we open fire again upon them in fine style! In a few minutes they had had enough of it, and hauled off as fast as their legs could carry them. If they hadn't so cruelly wounded our masts and spars we should have caught some of them. We made all the sail we could venture to carry; but they had faster keels than we could boast of, so we had no hope of success.

They stood away for Flushing, and I afterwards heard that one of them sunk as soon as she got there, and that all had their decks completely ripped up, besides losing a great number of men, and suffering terribly in other ways. Strange as it may seem, we had not a single man killed, but one captain of marines and one marine only were wounded. We had to go into harbour to repair damages; and when the news of the action reached London, the merchants were so pleased with it, that, in commemoration of it, they presented Captain Trollope with a handsome piece of plate. He deserved it, for a braver or more dashing officer did not exist, as I had many opportunities of proving.

Some time after this, occurred those events in the navy which might have proved the destruction of the British Empire. I speak of the mutinies which broke out at the Nore, at Spithead, and elsewhere. The particulars are generally so well-known, that I will not attempt to describe them; but the circumstance I am about to mention is known, I fancy, to very few. It is an example of what courage and determination may effect.

On board the *Glutton*, as in most large ships, we had a number of bad characters—runaway apprentices, lawyers' clerks, broken-down tradesmen, footmen dismissed for knavery, play-actors, tinkers, gipsies, pickpockets, thieves of all sorts; indeed, the magistrates on shore seemed to think nothing was too bad to send on board a man-of-war. These men were, of course, always ready for mischief of any sort. There is no denying it, the seamen also were often cruelly ill-treated, fleeced on all sides, cheated out of pay, supplied with bad provisions, and barbarously tyrannised over by their officers. Now, on the contrary, a man-of-war's man is better fed, better lodged, better and more cheaply clothed, and in sickness better taken care of, than any class of labouring-men. When he has completed twenty-one years' service, he may retire with a pension for life of from tenpence to fourteen-pence a day; and when worn-out by age or infirmity, he may bear up for that magnificent institution, Greenwich Hospital, there among old comrades to end his days in peace.

The mutiny I was speaking of had been going on for some time. The just demands of the seamen had been listened to, and their grievances remedied, when the mutiny broke out afresh, and, instigated by evil-disposed persons, the crews either landed their officers or put them under confinement, and made fresh demands, many of which it was impossible to grant. Our ship, with others of Lord Duncan's squadron, was brought up in Yarmouth Roads. The delegates had been tampering with us. Messages had at different times been sent on board, and I knew that something wrong was going forward; but what it was I could not tell. I was known to be a friend of Peter Poplar's, and no one doubted his remaining stanch to his captain and officers, so I am proud to say that they would not trust me.

One day I found Peter sitting down between decks, looking very grave. I asked him if something was not the matter with him.

"A great deal, Jack," he answered; "I don't like the look of things. You must know, Jack, that the ships at the Nore have again hoisted the red flag, and the mutineers swear that they'll make every ship of the fleet join them. What they now want, I don't know. They have got all the chief grievances redressed, and everything which reasonable men could expect granted. They'll not be content till all the delegates are made admirals, I suppose."

"Still, I hope that we shall not be following their example," said I. "We have a good number of black sheep on board, but still, I think, there are enough honest men to keep them in check."

"That's the very thing I doubt, Jack," he whispered. "I don't like the thoughts of peaching on a shipmate, but when villains are plotting treachery, as some on board here are doing, we have but one duty to perform. I must carry the information to the captain. In case they find me out, and heave me overboard, or trice me up at the yard-arm—as they are likely enough to do—if you live take care that my memory is treated with justice. Now, Jack, there is no time to lose; I'll tell the captain that he may trust to you and a few others, but the greater number of the ship's company have been won over by the promises of that artful fellow Parker and his mates." Saying this, Peter walked boldly aft, and, unsuspected, entered the captain's cabin.

He told me afterwards that Captain Trollope received the information very calmly, nor did he seem at all to doubt its correctness. The plan was to wait till the ship was under way to proceed on a cruise in the North Sea, and then to seize the captain and all the officers, and to carry the ship instead to the Nore. Several other ships had already weighed without orders, and had joined the mutineers at the Nore. No preparation, however, was made that I saw for the expected event.

The next day Peter and I were sent for into the cabin. "Take up these things, and accompany me," said the captain to us. There was a compass and a basket of provisions; and I saw that the captain had a pistol-case under his arm. Leaving the cabin, he led the way below to the door of the magazine. If any of the mutineers observed him, I don't suppose they guessed what he was about.

The powder-magazine of a man-of-war has a clear space round it—a sort of ante-room, which is kept clear of everything, so as to decrease the risk of fire reaching it. This ante-room has a grated door before it. The captain produced a key, and opening the grated door, went in, taking from us the articles we carried. He then locked himself in from the inside. This done, he opened the inner door of the magazine, exposing a number of powder-flasks to view. Having arranged his table and chairs, with the compass and his pistols, and some books he had brought, he said quietly, as if to himself, "I'm ready for them!"

"Williams," he continued, "go and request the first lieutenant to come here. Poplar, do you go among the people, and say I directed you to call some of them to see me." I quickly performed my part of the duty; but Poplar was longer in collecting any of the people. He, however, at last returned with about twenty of them.

The first lieutenant seemed very much astonished at the summons, and could not make out what it meant. I fancy, indeed, when he got down there, and saw the captain quietly sitting in the powder-magazine, as if he was going to take up his berth there for the future, for an instant he thought him out of his senses. He did not long continue in that idea when the captain began to address him and the people who were assembled outside the grating.

"Turn the hands up, and get the ship under way!" he sung out in a loud voice. "The pilot will carry her through the passage, and then steer an easterly course till you receive further orders."

"Now, men, you've heard the orders I have given to the first lieutenant. I intend to have them obeyed. Other ships' companies have refused to obey orders, and have joined the mutineers at the Nore. This example shall not be followed on board this ship. I'd sooner die than see such disgrace brought on the ship I command. You all know me. The instant I find the course I have given altered—you see the magazine and this pistol—we all go up together!"

Some of the mutineers—for Peter had taken care to summon those he most suspected—lingered below; but the boatswain's whistle sounded shrilly along the decks, and one more glance at the determined eye of the captain sent them flying up to obey its summons. I shall never forget the appearance of that dauntless man as he sat still and alone in that dark place, prepared by a dire necessity to hurl himself and all with him to a terrible destruction. It was a subject truly worthy of the painter's highest art. We all, indeed, did know him, and knew that, whatever the cost, he was a man to do what he had threatened. The ship was quickly got under way, and while the larger number of the ships of the squadron ran for the Nore against the wishes of their officers, we, to the surprise of all, who little knew what extraordinary influence guided our course, stood out to sea in search of the enemies of our country.

Chapter Fifteen
Jack a Prisoner—A Privateer and a Slaver

On leaving the *Glutton*, I was struck down by sickness, and lay for many long months in the hospital at Portsmouth, scarcely expecting to recover. Oh, how hideous did Death, which I had braved a hundred times in open fight, appear as silently he stalked along the wards of the hospital! I trembled as I thought of the past;—how small was the hope I had in the future! There was no one to bring me comfort—no one to afford counsel—no one to point out the right, the only way by which a sinner can be justified in the sight of a pure, just, holy God. Many good resolutions I made—as many were soon afterwards broken. I recovered; health returned to my veins—vigour to my arm. Once more I was afloat in a dashing frigate.

We were off the Frenchman's coast. In a deep bay lay a number of the enemy's vessels. It was necessary to ascertain their character. They were supposed to be gun-boats. Our second lieutenant, Mr Ronald—a noble specimen of a naval officer, and as active as a cat, though he had but one leg—was directed to take the gig, a fast-pulling boat, and to gain all the information he could. I was with him; so was Peter. The frigate had made sail, as if about to leave the coast; but as soon as it was dark, she stood back again. The gig was lowered, and we shoved off.

In dead silence, with muffled oars, we pulled in towards the shore. We knew that the enemy mustered strong in the neighbourhood. Thus it was necessary to be cautious. Not a word was spoken. The phosphorescent light sparkled from the blades of our oars, appearing brighter from the darkness which prevailed, but that could not be seen at any distance. The time for our expedition had been well selected. We had pitchy darkness to favour our advance; but we knew that the moon would soon rise, and enable us to make the necessary observations. We pulled slowly in, for the tide was with us, and Mr Ronald told us to reserve our strength till it would be most required. As we got close in with the shore, we could make out the masts of a number of vessels, in a confused mass; but what they were without more light, it was impossible to say without going close up to them. Mr Ronald was not a man to leave his work half done through fear of consequences, so we pulled on till our oars almost touched some of the outer vessels. Our officer made his remarks as we continued our course round the bay.

Not a sound had broken the stillness of the night except the almost inaudible dip of our oars in the water. The clouds, which had hitherto obscured the sky, floated gradually away; the stars shone forth bright and clear, their sparkling orbs reflected in the smooth water; and then, rising from behind the land, the moon shed her calm silvery gleam across the sheltered bay. We were at the time under the shadow of some high land. "Give way, my lads; it is time we should be out of this!" whispered the lieutenant. It was time indeed! Peter's quick eye, looking seaward, observed several dark objects floating in the distance. "Boats in!" he said, pointing in that direction. The lieutenant looked there also. There could be no doubt about it. There were four large boats. He ordered us to lay on our oars, to watch in what direction they would pull. We hoped that they had not as yet observed us. The people in the boats seemed to be holding a conference. At last they parted. One pulled across the mouth of the bay in one direction; one in the other; but two advanced up the bay. There seemed no possibility of our escaping without being seen. Still it was far from Mr Ronald's intention of giving in till he was actually laid hold of. Hitherto the shade of the cliff prevented our being seen. The gap between the boats through which we could hope to escape widened more and more. Meantime, our thoughts were occupied in the contemplation of the pleasures of a French prison, of which we had too often heard to have any wish to enjoy them. Mr Ronald watched our opportunity. "Now, my lads," he whispered, "give way with a will!" We needed no encouragement. As a rat darts out of the corner in which it has taken shelter when the dogs stand ready on either side hoping to catch it, so we darted out from our sheltered nook towards the open sea.

The movement drew the attention of the French boats towards us, and in another minute all four were steering courses which would give them every prospect of cutting us off. We were all armed, but it would have been madness to attempt to beat off so overwhelming a force. We had to trust alone to the fleetness of our heels. We might have a prospect of distancing the two boats which had gone up the bay, and which were on our larboard-hand, but we must inevitably run the gauntlet between the other two. The question was, whether we could pass through them before they closed in on us. We made the strong ash sticks bend again as we sent the boat flying through the bubbling water. We sung out in our eagerness, encouraging each other. Every moment the space between the two boats was narrowing.

We did not give in though. The Frenchmen now saw that there was a chance of our escaping, and began firing. The bullets flew thickly about our heads. Several hit the gunwale of the boat, but none of us were hurt. Their firing rather encouraged us to persevere, in the hope of escaping.

At last I felt a severe blow on my arm, and involuntarily dropped my oar. A bullet had struck it. Still, I was sure it was not broken; so I took my handkerchief off my neck, and bound it up. I seized my oar, and pulled on. "Oh, the blackguards! sure if they'd give us a fair start, and not be sending their dirty bullets at us, we'd be after bating them entirely, now!" sung out an Irishman, who pulled the bow-oar. Many people would, under the circumstances we were placed in, have given up before this; but Mr Ronald still hoped that we might dodge our enemies, and escape. The boats were not a hundred yards on either side of us. They gave way with a will. So did we. Still we might slip between them. If we did, we should have a good start; and pulling fast, as we could do, we might escape, should they not continue firing at us; but how could we expect them to be so lenient? On they came; narrow, indeed, grew the space between them. We dashed on. With a cry of dismay, we saw that our efforts were of no avail! With such force did they come on, that they literally almost cut our boat in two; and as she sunk between them, we had to jump out—some into one boat, some into the other—to save ourselves from drowning, and to find ourselves prisoners.

How the Frenchmen did jabber away, and ask us all sorts of questions, none of which we could answer, from not being able to muster a word of French amongst us. The other boats came up, and then there was still more jabbering; and then the Frenchmen made us all get into one boat, and pulled with us towards a point of land on the east side of the bay. The boat soon reached a small, rough pier, and then two of the men, jumping on shore, ran off towards the town, which stood a little way off from us. We sat, meantime, wondering what was to be our fate.

Shortly afterwards the tramp of feet was heard, and six or eight soldiers, or militiamen, or gendarmes, appeared, and halted near us. The officer of the boat then had a talk with them, and committed us to their charge. I have no doubt he told them to take good care that we did not run away. The boat, we concluded, had to row watch, and could not remain long absent from her post. The soldiers, before receiving us, grounded arms; shoved their ramrods down their muskets, to show us that they were loaded; examined the primings in the pans, and then, presenting their bayonets at our backs, in most unpleasant proximity, ordered us to advance. Our cutlasses had been taken away, and, of course, the muskets had gone down with the gig; but both Mr Ronald and Peter had their pistols stuck in their belts, inside their great-coats, so the Frenchmen did not discover them. We did not wish our first captors good-bye, nor exchange a word with each other, but, seeing there was no help for it, slowly stumbled on over the uneven ground ahead of our guards. I hoped that they would keep their footing better than we did; for, if not, some of us would stand a great chance of being run through with their bayonets. Had we not been unarmed, and aware that the boat was within hail, I don't think we should have allowed ourselves to have been carried along as prisoners.

However, our walk was soon at an end, and we reached the tower, which stood a short distance along-shore from where we landed, and not three hundred yards from the beach. It appeared to be in a very tumble-down ruinous condition, as we inspected it from the outside. We concluded that we should have to wait here till the following morning, before being marched off to prison. Whether the tower had been built for a fort, or only a mill, or a look-out place, it was difficult to discover in the scant light we had. There was a small arched door before us, with some stone winding-steps leading up from it. The sergeant in command of the party pointed to it, and some of the men gave us a gentle prick with the end of their bayonets, singing out, at the same time, some words which we guessed to be a command to go up there.

"Let me go first, sir," exclaimed Peter Poplar, springing through the door. "There may be some trap in the way, and it's hard that you should have to fall down that, at all events."

When we were all in, the soldiers followed, making us go winding-up till we reached a chamber at the top of the building. The French soldiers saw us all in, and then shoving to the door, they shut it with a loud bang; but as there was no sound of bolts or bars, we guessed that there were none to the door.

The light of the moon shone directly in through a loop-holed slip of a window, and we saw some billets of wood, and a small cask or two, and a few three-legged stools, with a broken table, and the remains of a bedstead, showing that the place had once been inhabited. Mr Ronald took a seat, and told us to follow his example; so we all sat down, feeling certainly very melancholy at first. We had much reason to be melancholy, for by this time we had heard a good deal about French prisons, and the treatment English prisoners received in them; and we could scarcely fancy a worse fate than to have to spend our future days in one. The lieutenant, however, was not the man to allow himself or others long to indulge in such thoughts. He got up.

"We are in a bad plight, certainly, my lads," said he; "but we'll see if we cannot mend it. I have been in a worse plight myself—and so, I daresay, have you—and managed to escape without damage. Perhaps we may do so in this case."

"Yes, sir," said Peter; "indeed I have." And he described how we had escaped from the pirates' den in Cuba.

I told my companions how I had been preserved from being murdered by the Maroons; and altogether we soon got each other's spirits up. My wounded arm hurt me not a little, but Peter took off my jacket, and bound it up carefully; and though I cannot say that the pain was much decreased, I resolved to bear it without complaining.

Meantime, Mr Ronald made a minute examination of the place of our confinement; and by stepping on the table he discovered a hole in the roof, which he found that he could, without difficulty, make as large as he might wish. He at once set to work to do so, we all talking and walking about the room, to conceal any noise he might make. When he had got the hole large enough to admit his body, Peter, putting his shoulder under him, gave him a hoist through it, and with his hands and elbows he quickly scrambled up on the roof. As it sloped very much he could not walk about, so he sat himself down to make his observations. Having done so, and stayed some time to consider matters and form his plans, he came back into the room.

"My lads," said he, calling us round him, "you must clearly understand the position we are in. We are prisoners to our greatest enemies. They may choose to consider us as spies, and may cut our throats, or shoot us as such; and, at all events, they will send us to prison, and there keep us, as they have done many of our countrymen, till the war is over. Now, while I was on the roof I saw, not far from the beach, a small boat moored; and a mile or so away, I made out what I take to be a fleet of fishing-boats. What I propose is, to knock over the sentry at the door, and, if we can, we'll surprise the rest of the soldiers, and gag and bind them. If they show fight, it can't be helped: we must kill them. At all events, we must prevent them from raising an alarm, or following us. We will then make the best of our way to the beach, and I will undertake to swim off, and bring in the small boat I saw there. When we get her, it will be very hard if we cannot cut out some fishing-smack or other, in which we can cross over to England. If we don't succeed, we shall probably get killed ourselves; but if we do, we shall obtain our liberty, and that is worth a struggle."

This speech inspirited us all, and we could scarcely refrain from shouting, as we promised to follow his directions, and to stick by him through thick and thin.

The Frenchmen seeing that he had a wooden leg, and hearing him stump up and down, of course fancied that he would never attempt to run away; or that if he did make the attempt, he would not go without them finding it out. This, perhaps, made them more careless in the way they watched us. At all events, they had not even then found out what stuff English sailors are made of; and I don't think they ever will.

"Then, my lads, there's no time to be lost," said the lieutenant. "Are you all ready?"

"Yes, sir," said Peter, speaking for the rest; "but I beg pardon, sir, won't your leg be heard as we go down, and it may give notice to the Frenchmen?"

"I have thought of that," said Mr Ronald, fastening a handkerchief round the end of the stump. "Now, I shall tread as softly as a cat."

We had all taken off our shoes, and armed ourselves with the legs of the table and the legs of the stools we had found in the room. My heart beat quick. Never had I been engaged in so daring a work. We dared not try the door till the moment we were to rush out. Mr Ronald gave the signal, and he leading the way, we threw open the door, and, before the sentry could turn his head, or even cry out, we had our hands on his mouth, and throwing him down backwards among us, we squeezed every breath out of his body. Whether he lived or died, I cannot say. We seized his musket and bayonet and sword, and without a moment's delay, which would have been fatal, we rushed on, and sprung like wild beasts into the room where our guards were sitting. Some were sleeping; others were playing at cards; two were talking with their heads bent together. They had not time to look up even before we were upon them. Mr Ronald ran one of the card-players through with the sword we had taken from the guard; Peter killed another with the bayonet. I shall not forget his look of astonishment and dismay when he saw us standing before him. One of the other men knocked over a third with the leg of the table. Before the others could seize their arms, we had got hold of them. Mr Ronald was obliged to kill another man, who fought so desperately that we could not otherwise master him; and throwing ourselves on the remaining three, we bound and gagged them, and lashed them to the benches on which they had been sitting. The whole affair did not take us a minute. It was very bloody work, but it could not be helped. We then hurried to the bottom of the tower, and broke open the door. We had been prisoners a very short time, and could scarcely believe ourselves to be free.

Hastening down to the beach, Mr Ronald stripped off his clothes, and plunging into the water, with his knife in his mouth, swam off towards the little boat he had before observed. Had it not been for my wound, I would gladly have gone instead of him. In spite of his wooden leg, he swam fast and strongly, and soon reached the boat. Getting into her, he cut her from her moorings, and then quickly paddled her to the more. More than once we had turned a glance inland, lest we mould have been observed; but, without interruption, Mr Ronald dressed, and then all of us getting into the boat, we pulled out seaward. She was too small to allow us, with any prospect of safety, to cross the Channel in her, so that we could not yet consider our enterprise accomplished.

We had armed ourselves with the soldiers' weapons, so that, had there been a strong breeze off-shore, we should not have been afraid to have attacked and attempted to cut out any merchant vessel or other well-armed craft. As it was, Mr Ronald judged that it would be wiser to endeavour to capture one of the fishing-boats he had seen. Muffling our oars, therefore, in dead silence we pulled out towards the largest of the fleet, and which lay the outermost of them all. Gliding alongside, we stepped softly on board. Her crew were, as we expected, asleep, and before they had opened their eyes we had our hands on their throats and our knees on their bosoms. As there were only three men and a boy, we easily mastered them; and, having bound and gagged them, we put them into the forepeak, while we proceeded to haul up the anchor and get the vessel under way.

As soon as we could attend to our prisoners, we made signs to them that we would not hurt them; and I fancied that they considered themselves very fortunate in not having their throats cut, or being thrown overboard, by those terrible monsters, "*les bêtes Anglais*." There was a light air off the shore, and, with very great satisfaction, we stood away from it. Anxiously we looked towards the coast we were leaving, but, as far as our eyes could pierce the gloom, we could not discover any vessel in pursuit of us. Still we were not free from danger, as we were likely enough to fall in with a French vessel, and again find ourselves prisoners. Mr Ronald, who was as kind and thoughtful as he was brave, told me to go to sleep; but my arm gave me too much pain to allow me to do so.

The hours of night passed by, and day dawned; the bright sun arose on a cloudless sky. The coast of France rose in blue ridges astern of us, but not a sail was in sight all round the horizon. As our prospect of escaping recapture improved, our appetites, which we had not thought about, reminded us that we had gone a long time without eating; but when we came to examine the fishermen's lockers, we found only a little black bread aboard, and a most scanty supply of water. They made us understand that their boat had gone on shore with some of their comrades to bring off water and provisions. Mr Ronald insisted on preserving most of the water for me, as a fever was already on me, and I was suffering dreadfully from thirst.

The wind was very light, and we made but little way. As the sun rose, however, clouds began to collect to the northward, and the sky overhead became covered over with those long wavy white lines which go by the name of "mares' tails," and which always betoken wind. Still we stood on as before. Every now and then, however, a puff would come which threw the sails aback; but it quickly passed away, to be succeeded shortly by a stronger and more continuous one. At last the breeze headed us altogether, freshening up rapidly, till Mr Ronald called all hands to reef sails. The wind soon got the sea up, and in a short time we were pitching away close-hauled, with the boat's head to the north-west. Changed, indeed, was the weather since the morning: then all had been bright, and blue, and calm; now, in the afternoon, the sky hung dark and gloomy, with heavy clouds, and green foam-topped seas danced wildly around us. I do not know what Mr Ronald thought about the matter, but as I lay on my back suffering from pain, hunger, and thirst, I began to question whether the ill-found boat would live through the sea which was getting up.

Meantime a sharp look-out was kept for any vessel which might put us on shore anywhere on the English coast. At length a sail was seen to the eastward, and after watching her for some time, both Mr Ronald and Peter were of opinion that she would cross our course. This news cheered the spirits of all hands, for they had begun to suffer painfully from hunger and thirst. No one had taken more than a very small piece of black bread, for we could not deprive the poor French fishermen of their share of food. We were most anxious, on several accounts, that the stranger should get up to us before dark—in the first place, that we might ascertain whether she was friend or foe, and also lest we should miss her altogether. Should she prove French, we hoped, in spite of our hunger, still to avoid her. To mislead any enemies, we got out the Frenchmen's clothes left on board, and rigged ourselves out as fishermen.

"I feel pretty sure that vessel is English, sir," said Peter, who had been watching the stranger. "But still I can't make out what is the matter with her; she has been handled pretty roughly, I suspect."

Mr Ronald pronounced her to be a brig-of-war without any after-sail set; and as she drew near, we saw that there was good reason for this, as her mainmast had been carried away by the board, while her hull also had been much knocked about. It was clear that she had been in action. Mr Ronald waved to her; and, to our no small satisfaction, we saw her clewing up her sails to speak to us.

Before going alongside, however, Mr Ronald released the Frenchmen, and, as he thought, explained to them that we were going on board the brig, and that they might return to the French coast. The Frenchmen stretched their limbs, and looked about them while we were going alongside the brig. This was an operation not altogether easy or free of risk, but we succeeded in getting hold of her. Mr Ronald went up first, followed by the other men; and as I was far too weak to help myself up, Peter had gone up the side, and was singing out for a rope, when the Frenchmen, instigated by what notion I know not, but fancying, I believe, that they were to be made prisoners, cut off the tow-rope, and hoisting the foresail, put down the helm, and stood away from the brig. Active as monkeys, they soon swayed up the mainsail, and, hauling close on a wind, they rapidly left the brig astern. I saw Peter eagerly waving to them to come back, and I have no doubt but that he fancied if they did not they would murder me. The brig, having no after-sail, could not haul her wind, so that my shipmates were perfectly unable to recover me. I certainly could do nothing to help myself, so I lay quiet, and trusted that the Frenchmen would have pity on me. I still thought they might murder me; and, at all events, expected that I should be sent to a French prison. I only hoped that we might not reach the part of the coast we had come from, for I could scarcely expect to escape being put to death when it was known that I was one of the party who had killed the French soldiers placed to guard us.

I do not think, at the same time, that the Frenchmen had any murderous intentions. They were so pleased at recovering their boat and their liberty, that they were inclined to treat me civilly, if not kindly, and they continued to supply me with bread and water as I required. As we were half-way across the Channel, and they had lost their reckoning, we were not likely, I hoped, to make a good landfall in their attempt to reach their home.

With anxious eyes I watched the brig on board which my shipmates had taken refuge, but darkness coming on, we very soon lost sight of her. My heart sunk within me, and I burst into a fit of tears, the first I had shed for many a long year. They were as anxious to avoid meeting any vessel as we had just been to find one. The wind had again chopped round to the southward, and though not blowing very strong, we made but little progress.

All night we stood on under close-reefed canvas, and when the next morning dawned, I saw land to the southward. Its appearance evidently puzzled the Frenchmen. I guessed it to be no other than that of the island of Guernsey; while not a mile off, standing towards us under her topsails, was a large schooner. Had the Frenchmen altered their course, and run away from her, it would have excited the suspicions of those on board, so they kept on as before. This plan, however, did not avail them. A shot, which before long came whistling across our fore-foot, showed them that they were wanted alongside the schooner. The schooner hoisted English colours, and from her general appearance I had no doubt that she was a privateer. As soon, therefore, as the boat went alongside, I sung out that I 'was an Englishman, and a prisoner.

"Halloa! Who's that?" said a man, looking over the side of the schooner. "What! Jack Williams, is that you?" The speaker, without waiting for my reply, let himself down into the boat, and as he grasped my hand, I recognised him as my old acquaintance Jacob Lyal.

Pointing to my arm, I told him that I had been wounded, and how ill I was; and he at once sung out for a sling, and in another minute I was safely placed on the deck of the vessel.

The captain of the schooner then ordered the Frenchmen into the boat, and putting some of his people in her, she was dropped astern. I don't know what he said to the Frenchmen, but they seemed far from contented with the change of lot. I learned afterwards that he wanted the boat to go in and cut out some French merchantmen.

The schooner had a surgeon on board, and when the captain heard the account I gave Lyal of my late adventures, he directed that I should be immediately placed under his charge. I flesh, as soon as the fever abated, I got rapidly well and fit for duty.

The schooner was, I found, the *Black Joke*, belonging to the island of Guernsey. Lyal so worked on my imagination, by the accounts he gave of the life of a privateer's-man, and the prize-money to be made, that he soon persuaded me to enter aboard her. There cannot be the shadow of a doubt that I ought to have gone back, by the first opportunity, to join my own ship; though, of course, I knew that, under the circumstances of the case, I ran very little fear of punishment by not doing so, should I at any time happen to fall in with her. The schooner was a very large vessel of her class, and mounted sixteen 6-pounders, with a crew of some eighty men or more. Captain Savage, who commanded her, was a bold dashing fellow, but he cared nothing for honour, or glory, or patriotism. He had only one object in view in fighting—it was to make money. Privateering was the shortest and easiest way he knew of, and as his professional knowledge and experience fitted him for the life, he took the command of the *Black Joke*. His first officer, Mr Le Gosselen, was just the man for the sort of work to be done. He was a strongly-built, short, bull-necked man, and a first-rate seaman; but whatever human sympathies he might have had in his youth had all apparently been washed out of him.

The schooner had only left Guernsey, after a refit, the day before I was taken on board her. I had been a fortnight in her before any prize of consequence was made. A few coasters had been surprised by means of the fishing-boat, but their cargoes were of very little value, and only two or three were worth sending into port. Of the rest, some were sunk, and others allowed to continue on their voyage, after anything worth having was taken out of them. The time had at last arrived when Captain Savage hoped to fall in with a convoy of French ships coming home from the West Indies. For a week or more we cruised about in the latitude they would probably be found in, but we saw nothing of them.

At length, at daybreak one morning, several sail were seen hull down to the northward, and steering east. The wind was about south, so we stood away close-hauled towards them, in order to reconnoitre them more perfectly. As the sun rose, and we drew nearer, many more appeared, their white sails dotting the ocean far and wide.

"That's what we've been looking for, my lads!" cried the captain, pointing them out to the crew. "If we get hold of two or three of those fellows, we shall soon line our pockets with gold."

A loud cheer fore and aft showed that the speech suited the taste of his hearers. Great, indeed, was the contrast in the discipline between a privateer and a man-of-war. There was plenty of flogging, and swearing, and rope's-ending, which the officers considered necessary to keep up their authority; but there was also a free-and-easy swagger, and an independent air about the men, which showed that they considered themselves on a par with their officers, and that they could quit the vessel whenever they fancied a change. At first I did not at all like it, but by degrees I got accustomed to the life, and imitated the example of all around.

We stood on cautiously towards the Frenchmen, the officers' glasses being continually turned towards them, to watch for any suspicious movement in the fleet. The captain had no doubt what they were, and all day we continued hovering about them, like a bird of prey ready to pounce down on its victim. We got near enough to make out a man-of-war in the van, and another in the centre of the fleet, while a number of stragglers brought up the rear. Of some of these latter we hoped to make prizes. Having ascertained this much, we stood off again from them, that, should our appearance have raised their suspicions, they might be again set to rest. Marking well the course they were steering, we knew that we should easily again fall in with them.

The nights, to favour our enterprise, had been very dark, so that we might hope to pick out several, provided no noise was made, without being discovered. We waited anxiously for night to put our enterprise into execution; and as the sun set, we crowded all sail to come up with the convoy. Few vessels could surpass the schooner in her sailing qualities, which made her peculiarly fitted for the sort of work she was employed in.

By midnight, we made out on our starboard-bow several sail, which we had no doubt were some of the sternmost vessels of the French convoy; so we stood towards them without hesitation. If any of the Frenchmen caught sight of the privateer, they probably took her for one of their own fleet. Slowly, their dark, misty-like forms glided by, while we watched them with eager eyes, wondering which the captain would select as our first victim. At last came a large brig. She was somewhat high out of the water, and her main-topgallant-mast had been carried away.

"That's the craft for us, boys!" cried Captain Savage, pointing her out. "Her cargo's light, and probably the most valuable; and I doubt not that she has some wealthy passengers with their jewel-boxes with them. We will run them aboard, and try if we can't take them without firing a shot!"

We had got to windward of the fleet, and the helm being put up, we edged down towards the brig which it had been determined to take. In dead silence we approached our victim. As we drew near, the stranger observed us, and her people must have suspected that all was not right. He hailed, and inquired what schooner we were.

"The French schooner *Concorde*," answered our captain, who knew that a vessel of that name had been out in the West Indies. For a short time the answer seemed to satisfy the Frenchmen; but seeing us approach still nearer, they hailed again, and told us to keep off.

Captain Savage did not deign a reply, but our grappling-irons being ready, our helm was put hard a starboard, we ran alongside the brig, and had her fast locked in a deadly embrace.

Although the Frenchmen's suspicions had been aroused, they had made no preparations to receive us; yet as we ran her on board, we saw that there were numbers of people on her deck. "Follow me, my lads!" shouted Mr Le Gosselen, who saw that to secure an easy victory there was no time to be lost; and before any of the Frenchmen had time to stand to their arms, some fifty of us had sprung on their deck and attacked them, previously driving some overboard, others fore and aft, and the rest below. The greater number of our opponents seemed to be soldiers, by their dress and the way they fought. In vain their officers called to them to stand firm, and tried to rally them to the last; they themselves were pistolled or cut down, and in less than five minutes we were masters of the whole deck, with the exception of the after-part of the poop. Here a band of men stood firm, evidently surrounding a person of superior rank. He fought like a lion, and was likely to delay our victory, or to prevent it altogether. Seeing this,

Captain Savage, who was himself the best swordsman I ever met, calling twenty of us to follow him, sprang on board over the quarter; and thus attacked in front and on one side, the French officers were driven across the deck. A blow from Captain Savage's cutlass brought their chief on his knee. At that moment a piercing shriek arose high above the din of battle. How mournful! how full of agony it sounded! We had not before perceived a woman standing alone and unharmed among the wounded, the dead, and the dying, for not one of those who had opposed us had escaped.

"Spare my father's life! hurt not more his grey hairs!" she cried out in French.

"That depends on circumstances, mademoiselle," answered the captain of the privateer. "Here, my lads; carry the lady and the old man on board the schooner out of harm's way; we must secure the brig before we think of anything else."

I was one of those to whom the captain spoke. I shall never forget the grief and agony of the poor young lady as she bent over her father. He was desperately wounded. I saw that he could not speak; but he still breathed. We lifted him as gently as we could, and carried him aboard the schooner, into the captain's cabin; we then assisted the young lady, who followed eagerly, not knowing where she was going. All her thoughts and feelings were concentrated on her father. We placed him on the sofa, and I then went and called the surgeon to attend him. Mr Blister's knowledge of his profession was very slight, and his practical experience limited; but still he had some notion of binding up a wound, and, at all events, he would treat a patient more gently than any of the rough hands belonging to the schooner.

While what I have described was going on, the second officer, with a dozen men under him, had been directed to clew-up the brig's sails, so as to let her drop as much as possible astern of the rest of the fleet, no others appearing to be following. This had been done; and we had hopes that the flash of the pistols had not been seen, or the reports heard by any of the vessels in advance.

Having obeyed the orders, I again went on board the brig. The deck was now entirely in our possession. While some of our people were silencing several of the French crew, who still madly held out below, I followed the captain into the cabin. While we had been fighting on deck, others of our crew had found their way there, and, mad with rage at the opposition they had encountered, had spared neither age nor sex. I cannot venture to describe the scene of horror and confusion. There were several ladies, and their attendants, and children—among them, infants in arms, or just able to lisp their parents' names. Already they were in the power of my ruffian companions. Shrieks of despair, cries for mercy rose from among them. Tables and chairs, and furniture of all sorts, lay broken on the door. Several dead bodies lay at the entrance of the cabin—officers, as was shown by their uniform; another lay leaning against the bulkhead, gasping out his last breath. We had discovered enough to show us why our capture was so crowded with people. She was a merchantman, in which the governor of one of the islands, together with his staff and their families, had taken their passage, while a body of soldiers had likewise been put on board.

Captain Savage, to do him justice, when he found that the brig was completely in his power, did his best to rescue her unfortunate prisoners from further molestation, though in this he was but ill seconded by his officers. Rushing in among the men, he ordered them on deck, and to carry the dead bodies with them. One man refused to obey him.

"Mutiny!" he exclaimed. "This is the way I put it down." He levelled his pistol, and shot the man dead. "Here, take this fellow and heave him overboard with the rest," he added, as the body fell to the deck.

I with others obeyed, for all saw the stern justice of the proceeding. "My men," he continued, "we must make sail away from her as fast as possible; for after what has occurred we can expect but little mercy should we fall into the hands of our enemies."

By this proceeding the cabin was cleared, and the wretched inmates were left in solitude, to mourn over their cruel fate. The captain placed Lyal, and one or two of the more steady men, to guard the door. I accompanied him on deck. Among the crew and passengers in that fierce though short night-battle, more than half had fallen; and, contrary to what is usually the case, the greater number had been killed. The rest, many of whom were wounded, were collected forward, all of them with their hands lashed behind their backs. They, believing themselves to have been captured by pirates, fully expected to be put to death. Our crew, when not actually executing the commands of the officers, were engaged all the time in plundering. The ladies had been stripped of their jewels, the officers of their watches and money; and every corner of the ship was ransacked for plate and other valuables, while clothes and private property of all sorts were laid hold of and carried off; and the men, even in the midst of their pillage, amused themselves by putting on officers' coats, silk waistcoats, and cocked-hats.

The captain now ordered the vessels to be separated. He, with the second mate and about forty men, remained in the brig, to commence the more serious work of examining the cargo; while the rest, greatly to their discontent, with about two-thirds of the male prisoners, were ordered aboard the schooner. The two vessels then made sail to the southward, on a course which would enable us, if we wished, to run down on the following night and pick out another prize.

The examination of our capture was proceeded with very rapidly, and found of great value. The governor was carrying home a large fortune, much of it in specie; and the brig being an old trader, and considered a fine vessel, many merchants had shipped money by her. The poor ladies were left in possession of the cabin, and the captain ordered what food could be found to be taken down to them, while he directed the second mate, who was rather kinder-hearted than the first, to take charge of her, and to carry her into Guernsey. All things being arranged, the captain, leaving a prize-crew aboard the brig, returned to the schooner, and I accompanied him. The surgeon met us as we stepped aboard. The captain asked for the old governor.

"Why, I suspect he will slip through our fingers. I have no power to keep him," answered the surgeon.

"We must do what we can for the old man," observed the captain, with more feeling than I thought he possessed. "For his daughter's sake, I hope he won't die. What can she do, left alone in the world? Williams, you seem to understand the sort of thing, go in and see what you can do."

I obeyed the order gladly. I entered the cabin. Already was the poor girl left alone in the world. Her father's corpse lay on the sofa, and she had fallen in a swoon across it.

I did not go and call the surgeon. I knew that he did not feel for her, and could not help her. So, lifting her gently up, I removed the corpse, which I covered with a flag, and placed her on the sofa instead. I then got water and sprinkled it on her face, and bathed her temples. The captain came in, and found me thus engaged.

"Where's the old man?" he exclaimed, looking astonished.

I pointed to the flag. He lifted it up.

"What! dead!" he said. "Poor, poor thing!" I don't know if at that moment the thought of the amount of misery of which we had been the cause flashed across his mind. It did across mine.

Often have I since thought, what an accursed trade is that of a privateer's-man. Licensed pirates at best; and often, as they perform their work, no better than the worst of pirates.

"What's to be done?" he continued, talking to himself. "I cannot stand the girl's sorrow. We must get the body out of the way, at all events."

He stopped, and shaded his eyes with his hand. He had a family at home. Among them a daughter—tall and graceful, like that poor girl. "Williams," he said abruptly, "call the surgeon."

When Blister came, he told him to ascertain if the old man were really dead. He stooped down, and lifting the flag, examined the body.

"Yes," he answered, in a perfectly satisfied tone. "I said he would die. There's no doubt about it." I believe he would have been vexed had he recovered to contradict him.

"We must bury him, then," said the captain. "We'll do it decently. He was a fine old man, and fought like a lion. Send the sailmaker here." The surgeon did as he was bid.

"Don't let him touch the poor girl, Jack," he said. "She is better as she is. She would never let us remove her father's body, if she were conscious of what was going forward."

The sailmaker came, and received orders to get a hammock with a shot at the feet, in which to enclose the old soldier's corpse. Among the prisoners was a French priest. The captain sent for him; and he and a few officers who had escaped assembled on deck, the captain having explained to them that he wished to pay the last respect to a brave enemy. They, as Frenchmen know how to do, expressed themselves gratified at the compliment; and all stood around while the body was brought from below. Having been shown to them, it was secured in the hammock which had been prepared for the purpose. It was then placed on a plank at an open port, with the old soldier's hat and sword. The priest offered up some of the prayers of his Church, and all stood with hats off in reverential awe.

The prayers were finished—the captain had lifted his hand, as a signal to launch the body into the deep, when at that moment the tall, graceful figure of a lady appeared on deck. She cast one wild, hurried, inquiring glance around. Her eye fell on the shrouded corpse as it glided into the deep. With a piercing shriek, which rung far over the waters, she cried, "Father, I follow you!" and before anyone could prevent her, she sprung over the schooner's low bulwarks into the blue sea, within the first circles formed by her parent's form, as it vanished from our sight. In an instant all present rushed to the side; the boats were lowered rapidly; but as we looked around, no sign did there appear of the unhappy young lady. Such was the result of our night's exploit! "It is better, perhaps, that it was so," said the captain, dashing a tear from his eye.

I cannot say that the catastrophe made any lasting impression even on him. It did not on me. That very night we stood again up to the convoy, and were successful in picking out another of them without being discovered. Both vessels reached Guernsey in safety, and turned out valuable prizes.

I cannot pretend to give even an outline of all the adventures I met with while serving on board the privateer. From her fast-sailing qualities, and the daring and talent of her commander, she was very successful. We were constantly on the look-out for single merchantmen; and, unless they were strongly armed, they were nearly certain to become our prey. We never attacked an armed vessel if we could help it, and never fought if we could escape an enemy capable of injuring us. Now and then, when we thought that we were going to make prize of a rich merchantman, we found that we had caught a Tartar, and had to up stick and run for it. Twice we were very nearly caught; and should have been, had not night come to our aid, and enabled us to haul our wind without being seen, and thus get out of our pursuer's way.

Once, flight was impossible, and we found ourselves brought to action in the chops of the Channel by a French sloop-of-war of eighteen guns. Captain Savage, however, gave evidence of his skill and courage by the way he handled the schooner against so superior a force. By making several rapid tacks, we got the weather-gauge of our opponent; and then, after the exchange of several broadsides, we stood across his bows, when we delivered so well-directed a raking-fire that we brought his topmast down by the run. We had not escaped without the loss of several men, besides getting an ugly wound in our mainmast; so, to avoid any further disaster, and being perfectly content with the glory of having crippled an opponent of force so superior, we hauled our wind and stood up Channel. The Frenchman was afterwards fallen in with, and captured by a corvette of her own size.

I have, I think, sufficiently described the occupation of a privateer. What I might have become, under the instruction of my old friend Peter, and the strict discipline of a man-of-war, I know not. On board the privateer, with the constant influence of bad example, I was becoming worse and worse, and more the slave of all the evil ways of the world. After serving on board the schooner for more than three years, I was paid off with my pocket full of prize-money, and, shipping on board a trader, I found my way to Liverpool.

That port then, as now, afforded every facility to a seaman to get rid of his hard-earned gains. In a few weeks I had but a few shillings left. I had not the satisfaction of feeling that I had done any good with it. How it all went I don't know. I believe that I was robbed of a large portion. I was so disgusted with my folly, that I was ready to engage in any enterprise, of however questionable a character, where I had the prospect of gaining more, which I resolved I would spend more discreetly.

Liverpool at that time fitted out a number of slavers—the slave-trade, which was afterwards prohibited, being then lawful, and having many respectable people engaged in it. Hearing from a shipmate that the *Royal Oak*, a ship of eighteen guns, with a letter-of-marque commission, was fitting out for the coast of Africa, and was in want of hands, I went and entered on board her. She carried, all told, eighty hands. I found two or three old shipmates aboard her, but no one whom I could call a friend.

We reached the coast without any adventure, and in those days the slaves who had come down from the interior being collected in depôts, ready for shipment, we soon got our cargo on board. For several years I remained in this trade, sometimes carrying our cargo of hapless beings to Rio de Janeiro or other parts of the Brazils, and sometimes to the West Indies. It never occurred to me that there was anything wrong in the system. All the lessons I had received in the West Indies, in my early days, were thrown away. The pay was good; the work not hard, though pretty frequently we lost our people by fever; and so I thought no more about the matter.

At length I found my way back to Liverpool, just as the battle of Waterloo and Napoleon's abdication brought the blessings of peace to Europe.

Chapter Sixteen
Whaling in the South-Sea

Every sea-port in England was thronged with seamen whom the cessation of war had cast on shore without employment, when as I was strolling along the quays of Liverpool with my hands in my pockets, in rather a disconsolate mood, wondering in what direction my wayward fate would carry me, I ran bolt up against a post near which a gentleman was standing, and somehow or other managed to tumble over him.

"Beg pardon, sir," said I, looking up in his face; "I did not see you."

"No harm done, my man; but stop," said he, as I was moving on; "I think I remember that voice and face. Jack Williams, I am certain?"

"Yes, that's certain," said I, looking at him hard. "And I may make bold to guess that you, sir, are Mr Carr."

"You are right in your guess, Jack;—that is to say, I have been Captain Carr for some years past. I am glad to have fallen in with you, for I am fitting out a ship for a long voyage, and I like to have men with me whom I know and can trust."

"Glad to have your good opinion, sir, and without another question I'll ship with you," I answered. "Where are you bound for?"

"A South-Sea whaling-voyage," he answered. "I have been at it for some years now, both as mate and master, and I tell you there's nothing like it for excitement and novelty. There's our craft, Jack; the *Drake* is her name. Look at her. Not a finer ship for her size sails out of Liverpool—measures five hundred tons, and carries forty hands. You'll like the life, depend on it; and I say, if you fall in with any good men, let me know. I like to have trustworthy men serving with me."

I promised to do as he desired, and then went on board to have a look at the ship. I found her everything I could wish, and felt perfectly satisfied with the arrangement I had made. Having set my mind at ease on that point, I began to consider how I should pass my time till the *Drake* was ready to receive her crew on board, for she was still in the hands of the carpenters.

I bethought me, then, that I would run across to Dublin, to try and find out my old captain. I found a large smack—a regular passage vessel—just sailing, so I went aboard, and in two days we reached that port. On landing I inquired for Captain Helfrich, for I had forgotten where he lived. "There he goes along the quays," answered the person I had addressed; and I saw a gentleman whom, from his figure, I did not doubt was him.

"Captain Helfrich, sir, I beg pardon; but I'm glad to see you looking so well. I'm Jack Williams," I exclaimed, running after him.

"That's my name; but I do not remember you, my man," he answered.

"I served my apprenticeship with you, and you were very kind to me, sir," I replied; but as I spoke I looked more narrowly in his face, and saw a much younger man than I expected to meet.

"Ah! you take me for my father, as others have done," he remarked, laughing. "He has given up the sea long ago, but he will be glad to meet an old shipmate; and now I think of it, I have to thank you for the model of his old craft the *Rainbow*. Come along by all means; I'm going to his house. You'll find him much changed, though."

So I did, indeed, and it made me reflect how many years of my life had passed away. I found my old captain seated before the fire in a large arm-chair, with a book and spectacles on a table by his side, and a handkerchief over his knees. His hair was long and white as snow, and his cheeks thin and fallen in about the mouth; but still the hue of health had not altogether fled. He received me kindly and frankly, and seemed much pleased at my coming so far to see him. He desired to hear all about me, and was greatly moved at the account I gave him of the *Rainbow's* loss. He was sorry to find that all the time I had been at sea I had not improved my condition in the world. I confessed that it was owing to my idleness and unwillingness to learn.

"Ah, I have learned many a lesson I did not know in my youth, from this book here, Jack," said he, pointing to the book by his side, which was the Bible. "I now know in whom to trust; and had I known Him in the days of my youth, how much grief and shame I might have avoided! Mercifully, God has by His grace taught me to see my own errors; and I have endeavoured to remedy them as far as I have been able, in the way I have brought up my son. I have taught him what I learned from this book: 'Remember thy Creator in the days of thy youth.'"

I was very much struck by the way my old captain, I may say the once pirate, spoke; and I afterwards learned that he had not failed to instil into his son the better principles he had imbibed. Still I am bound to say that he was an exception to the general rule; for, as far as my experience goes, men who grow careless of their duty to God and indifferent to religion, continue through life increasing in hardness of heart and conscience, without a thought of the past or a fear for the future—truly, living as if they had no souls to care for, as if there were no God who rules the world. Dreadful is their end! Therefore I say to all my readers: Never put off for a single hour— for a single minute—repentance and a diligent searching for newness of life. You know not what an hour, what a minute may bring forth. You may be suddenly summoned to die, and there may be no time for repentance.

Among other questions, Captain Helfrich kindly inquired for my old friend Peter Poplar. How ashamed I felt of my own ingratitude, my heartlessness, when I could not tell him! No one I had met could tell me whether he still survived, or whether he had fallen among the thousands of brave men who had died that England might be free. I promised to make further inquiries before I sailed, and, should I fail to hear of him, to set out on my return from my proposed voyage with the express purpose of discovering him.

That visit to my old captain is one of the few things performed of my own accord on which I can look back with satisfaction. The next day I sailed for Liverpool.

Many strange and curious coincidences have occurred to me during my life. Two days before the *Drake* was ready for sea, having failed to gain any tidings of Peter, I was standing on the quay—work being over—in the evening, with my hands in my pockets, just taking a look at my future home, when I observed a boat-load of men landing from a sloop which had lately brought up in the river. By their cut I knew that they were men-of-war's men. Several of them I saw had been wounded, and, judging by their shattered frames, pretty severely handled. One was a tall thin man. The sleeve on his right side hung looped up to a button, and he leaned over on the opposite side, as if to balance himself. I looked eagerly in his face, for I doubted not I knew his figure. It was Peter Poplar himself! I sprung eagerly forward. Captain Helfrich's appearance had made me feel old, but Peter's weather-beaten countenance and grizzly hair reminded me that my own manhood must be waning. For a moment I do not think he knew me. He had thought me dead—killed by the French fishermen, or murdered in prison. At all events he had heard nothing of me from the moment I was carried off in the fishing-boat. How kindly and warmly he shook my hand with his remaining one!

"I've lost a flipper, Jack, you see," said he, sticking out his stump. "I never mind. It was for the sake of Old England; and I have got a pension, and there's Greenwich ready for me when I like to bear up for it. There's still stuff in me, and if I had been wanted, I'd have kept afloat; but as I'm not wanted, I'm going to have a look at some of my kith and kin, on whom I haven't set eyes since the war began. Many of them are gone, I fear. So do you, Jack, come along with me. They will give you a welcome, I know."

I told him how sorry I was that I could not go, as I had entered aboard the whaler; but I spent the evening with him, and all the next day; and he came and had a look at the *Drake*, and Captain Carr was very glad to see him, and told him that he wished he had him even now with him. I cannot say how much this meeting with my old friend again lightened my heart; still I felt ashamed that I should have been in a trader, and away from one who had been more to me than a father, while he was nobly fighting the battles of our country. He had bravely served from ship to ship through the whole of the war. He, however, did not utter a word of blame. He only found fault with himself.

"I told you once, Jack," said he, "that I ought to have been a master, had it not been for my own ignorance, instead of before the mast; and having missed that, had I not continued too idle to learn, I might have got a boatswain's warrant. I tell you this because, though you are no longer a youngster, you have many years before you, I hope, and may still get the learning which books alone can give you, and without which you must ever remain before the mast."

I need not say that he made me promise to find him out on my return. I shall never forget the kindly, fatherly glance the old man gave me as he looked down from the top of the coach which was to take him on his way to the home he had so long left.

The *Drake*, ready for sea, had hauled out into the stream. She might at once have been known as a South-Sea whaler by the height she was out of the water, and by the boats which hung from their davits around her, painted white, light though strongly-built, with their stems and sterns sharp alike, and with a slight curve in their keels—each from about twenty-six to nearly thirty feet in length. Although she had provisions enough on board—casks of beef, and pork, and bread, (meaning biscuit), and flour, and suet, and raisins, and rum, and lime-juice, and other antiscorbutics—to last us for nearly four years, they were not sufficient to bring her much down in the water, as she was built to carry many hundred barrels of oil, which we hoped to collect before our return. I may as well here describe the fittings of a whale-boat. In the after-part is an upright rounded post, called the loggerhead, by which to secure the end of the harpoon-line; and in the bows is a groove through which it runs out. It is furnished with two lines, each of which is coiled away in a tub ready for use. It has four harpoons; three or more lances; several small flags, called "whifts," to stick into the dead whale, by which it may be recognised at a distance when it may be necessary to chase another; and two or more "drogues," four-sided pieces of board to be attached to the end of the whale-line when it is hove overboard, and which, being dragged with its surface against the water, impedes the progress of the whale. Besides these things, each boat is supplied with a case in which are stowed several necessary articles, the most important being a lantern and tinder-box—the lantern to be used as a signal when caught out at night—a compass, and perhaps a small cooking-apparatus. A whale-boat, when going in chase, has a crew of six men: one is called the headsman, the other the boat-steerer. The headsman has the command of the boat. He is either the captain, or one of his mates, or one of the most experienced hands on board. The *Drake* was a strongly-built, well-found ship, and as the greater number of the crew were experienced hands, and we had confidence in our captain, we had every prospect of a satisfactory voyage. The crew are not paid wages, but share in proportion to their rank or rating, according to the undertaking. Provisions are, however, supplied them, so that although a man may, as sometimes happens, make very little all the time he is out, he cannot lose. Still, want of success falls very heavily on the married men who have families to support.

The evening before we were to sail, one of the crew fell so sick that it was evident he could not go the voyage; so the captain ordered the second mate with several hands to take him ashore. Although not shipped as an able seaman, he was a strong, active young man, and it was necessary to supply his place. While some of the others carried the sick man to the hospital, I remained in the boat at the quay. While I was sitting, just looking up to watch what was taking place on shore, a young man in a seaman's dress came down the slip and hailed me. By the way he walked, and the look of his hands, I saw at a glance that he was not a seaman.

"I say, mate," said he, in a sort of put-on manner, "I see that you've just landed one of your people. Does your captain, think you, want another man in his stead?"

"I suppose so," I answered, looking at him hard, to make out what he was, though I didn't succeed. "But the mate will be down presently—you'd better ask him. He may meantime have shipped another hand."

"I'll run the chance," he replied. "I'll go up and fetch my chest from my lodging. Just tell him, if he comes down in the meantime, that a man has volunteered to join. You can judge whether I'm likely to be fit for work." He spoke in an off-hand, easy way, and without waiting for my reply, he walked rapidly up from the quay.

The mate, directly after, came down without having found a man to his taste. I told him that one had offered—a strongly-built, active-looking, intelligent man, just cut out for a sailor, though, as I said, I did not think he was one. Mr Marsh, the mate, listened to my account, and as he stepped into the boat, seemed to be looking for the stranger. After waiting a few minutes, as the man did not appear, he gave the order to shove off.

"There he comes, sir," said I, seeing him walking rapidly along the quay with a seaman's bag over his shoulder, while a porter accompanied him carrying a moderate-sized chest.

"If you want another hand, I'm ready to ship for the voyage," said he, coming down the slip, and abruptly addressing the mate.

"Seaman or not, he'll do," said Mr Marsh to himself. "Well, put your traps into the boat, and come aboard, and we'll see what the captain has to say to the matter," he answered, aloud.

The young man dropped a shilling into the hand of the porter, who looked at the coin and then at his countenance, and touched his hat. The stranger sat down on his chest in the bow of the boat, and we were soon on board. The captain then sent for him aft, and held him in conversation for half an hour or more. What was said I do not know; but the result was, that the young man came forward and told me that he had been entered as one of the crew, requesting me to show him where he was to stow his chest and bag. "In the forepeak," said I; but he evidently did not know where that was, so without saying a word I helped him down with it.

The first night we were at sea I had the middle watch, and scarcely had I made a dozen turns on deck, when he joined me. "What is your name?" said he; "I did not catch it." I told him.

"Well," he continued, "there is no use denying it—I am not a sailor. The captain knows this; but I have promised soon to become one, and I want to keep my promise. Will you help me to do so, by teaching me all I want to know?"

I told him I would do all I could for him, but that, as this was my first voyage in a whaler, I could not help him much about whaling matters.

"Oh, that will soon come," he answered. "I seldom see a thing done once that I cannot do afterwards; but I want you to help me in seamanship. I have been constantly on the water, and know how to handle a boat, but never before made a voyage."

I was so pleased with the frank way in which he acknowledged his ignorance, and the hearty desire he showed to learn, that I resolved to instruct him in everything I knew.

I never found anybody pick up information so rapidly as he did. It was only necessary to show him once how to do a thing, while he kept his sharp eye fixed on the work, and ever after he did it almost if not quite as well. He very soon dropped the nautical phraseology he had assumed when he came on board, and which was clearly not habitual to him; and though he picked up all our phrases, he made use of them more in a joking way than as if he spoke them without thought, as we did.

From the way he spoke, or from his manner when he addressed any of his messmates or the officers, or from the way he walked the deck, it was difficult to suppose him anything else than a gentleman-born, or a gentleman by education, whatever he had now become, and he at once got the name forward of "Gentleman Ned." I asked him his name the day after he came on board.

"Oh, ay. I forgot that," he answered, quickly. "Call me Newman—Ned Newman. It's not a bad name, is it?" So Ned Newman he was called; but I felt pretty certain from the first that it was not his real name.

He was good-looking, with fair hair and complexion, and a determined, firm expression about the mouth. He seemed to put perfect confidence in me, and we at once became great friends—not that we had at first many ideas in common, for I was very ignorant, and he knew more than I supposed it possible for any man to know. He showed me his chest, which surprised me not a little. Most of his clothes were contained in his bag. He had not a large kit, but everything was new and of the best materials, calculated to outlast three times the quantity of sailors' common slops. Instead of clothes, his chest contained a spy-glass, a quadrant, just like those of the officers, and a good stock of books, which I found were in a variety of languages, and some even, I afterwards learned, were in Greek. Then he had all sorts of drawing-materials—papers, and pencils, and sketch-books, and a colour-box, and mathematical instruments, and even a chronometer. He had a writing-case, and a tool-box, and a flute and violin, and some music-books. I asked him if he could use the quadrant.

"I never took an observation in my life; but I can work a day's work as well as a lunar, so I think that I may soon learn the practical part of the business," he answered.

I pointed to his musical instruments. "Yes; I play occasionally, when I wish to dispel an evil spirit; but books are my great resource. Jack, you lose much pleasure from your ignorance of the rudiments of learning. Take my advice and study. It's not too late to begin. Nonsense! difficult! everything worth doing is difficult! There's pleasure in overcoming difficulties. Come, you have begun to teach me seamanship—to knot and splice—to reef and steer. I'll teach you to read, and then the way is open to you to teach yourself whatever you like. Navigation! certainly. Why, you would have been master of a vessel by this time if you had known that." In the interval of Newman's remarks I was making excuses for my ignorance; but he would listen to none of them, and I promised, old as I was, to put myself under his instruction, and to endeavour to be as apt a pupil to him as he was to me.

As I have said, I never saw anyone learn so rapidly as he did everything which came in his way. Before six weeks had passed, there was very little remaining for me to teach him. Every knot and splice he mastered in a week or so, and could make them as neatly as I did. I don't think he had ever before been up a ship's mast; but from the first day he was constantly aloft, examining the rigging, and seeing where all the ropes led to. I had shown him how to reef and furl sails, and the very first squall we had, he was among the foremost aloft to lay-out on the yard. His hands went as readily as those of the oldest seaman into the tar-bucket; and so, though when he came aboard they were fair and soft, they soon became as brown and hard as any of ours. With the theory of seamanship he was already well acquainted—such as the way by which the wind acts on the sails, the resistance offered by the water on the hull, and so on; so that, when any manoeuvre was performed, he at once knew the reason of it. It is not too much to say that before we crossed the line he was as good a seaman, in many respects, as most of the hands on board; and certainly he would have made a better officer than any of us forward.

We were bound round Cape Horn, and Captain Carr intended to try his fortune on the borders of the Antarctic ice-fields, in the neighbourhood of New Zealand and the coast of Japan, among the East India Islands; and those wide-spreading groups, among which are found the Friendly Islands, the Navigators, the Feejees, the New Hebrides, the Loyalty Islands, and New Caledonia, and known under the general name of Polynesia. Perhaps other places might be visited, so that we had a pretty wide range over which our voyage was likely to extend. People at home are little aware, in general, of the great number of places a South-Seaman visits in the course of a three or four years' whaling-voyage; and certainly in no other trade is a lad of a roving disposition so likely to be able to gratify his tastes.

The first place we touched at was Porto Praya, in the island of Saint Jago, one of the Cape de Verds, our captain being anxious to fill up with water, and to get for the crew a supply of fruit and vegetables and poultry, which are here to be procured in abundance. Sailors, however, are apt to forget that fruit, at all events, is not to be found all the year round; and I have seen people very indignant because the fruit-trees were not bearing their ripe produce at the very moment they were honouring the place by their presence, and heartily abuse previous visitors for having deceived them.

I was one of the boat's crew which went on shore to get provisions, and we were half pulled to pieces, as we entered the town, by men, women, and boys—brown, yellow, and black—chattering away in a jargon of half-African half-Portuguese, as they thrust before our eyes a dozen chickens a few weeks old, all strung together; baskets of eggs, or tamarinds, or dates, or bananas, and bunches of luscious grapes, and pointed to piles of cocoa-nuts, oranges, or limes, heaped up on cocoa-nut leaves close at hand. The place seemed filled with beggars, pigs, monkeys, slatternly females, small donkeys, and big oxen; dirty soldiers and idle sailors of all the shades and colours which distinguish the human race, dressed in handkerchiefs, and shirts, and jackets, and petticoats of every hue of the rainbow—the only thing they had in common being their dirt. Indeed, dirt predominates throughout the streets and dwellings, and in every direction. The houses, though mean, from being white-washed deceive a stranger at a little distance as to the cleanliness of the place. From a spirited sketch Newman made of the scene I have described, I here discovered his talent for drawing.

We next touched at the Falkland Islands, then uninhabited, except by a few Gauchos, who had crossed from South America with a herd of cattle, which have since increased to a prodigious number, as they thrive well on the tussac grass, the chief natural production of the country. The fresh beef afforded by a couple of oxen was very acceptable, and contributed to keep us in health.

Even before crossing the line, we had been on the look-out for whales, and all the boats and gear were in readiness to be lowered, and to go in chase at a moment's notice. Everybody on board a whaler must be wide-awake, and prepared for all emergencies, or the ship may chance to return home with an empty hold. In no position in which a seaman can be placed is it so necessary to belong to the *try* fraternity. If whales are not to be found on one fishing-ground, the ship must move to another; and if not seen there, she must sail on till she chases them round the globe. So if, when a whale is seen, the harpooner misses his aim, and the fish dives and swims a mile or more off, he must watch and watch till she rises, and *try* again. This try principle should be followed in all the concerns of life. Whatever ought to be done, *try* and do it; never suppose a work cannot be done till it has been tried—perseverance in duty is absolutely necessary. Its neglect must bring ruin.

We had a look-out at each mast-head, and one of the mates, or the boatswain, and sometimes the captain, was stationed at the fore-topgallant yard-arm. Sharp eyes were, therefore, constantly watching every part of the ocean, as our ship floated over it to the very verge of the horizon in search of the well-known spout of the whales. Great improvements have taken place since the time I speak of in the apparatus employed in the whale-fishery. I am told that guns are now used with which to send the harpoon into the whale's body, while in my time it was driven by sheer strength and dexterity of arm, as the harpooner stood up at his full height in the bow of the tossing whale-boat, close to the huge monster, one blow of whose tail is sufficient to dash her into atoms.

We were, it must be understood, in search of the sperm whale, which is a very different animal from what is called the black or Greenland whale, whose chief habitation is towards the North Polar regions, though found in other parts of the ocean. There are several sorts of whales, but I will not attempt to give a learned dissertation on them. I should not, indeed, have thought much about the matter, had not Newman called my attention to it. I should have hunted them, and killed them, and boiled down their blubber, with the notion that we had the produce of so many *fish* on board. Now naturalists, as he told me, assert that whales should not be called *fish*. They swim and live in the water, and so do fish; they have no legs, nor have fish; but their implements of locomotion are more like arms than fins. But whales do what no fish do: they bring forth their young alive—they suckle them, and tend them with the fondest affection in their youth. They have warm blood, and a double circulation; and they breathe the atmospheric air by true lungs. The tail of a fish is placed vertically, or up and down; that of a whale, horizontally—that is to say, its broadest part is parallel with the surface of the water. The tail of a large whale is upwards of 20 feet wide, and with a superficies of 100 square feet, and it is moved by muscles of immense strength. This will give some idea of the terrific force with which it can strike a boat. I have, indeed, heard of instances where a whale has stove in a ship's bottom, and caused her to founder, with little time for the crew to escape. Their progressive movement is effected entirely by the tail; sometimes, when wishing to advance leisurely, by an oblique lateral and downward impulse, first on one side and then on the other, just as a boat is sent through the water when sculled with an oar; but when rushing through the deep at their greatest speed, they strike the water, now upwards and now downwards, with a rapid motion and vast force. As whales breathe the atmospheric air, they must come to the surface frequently for a fresh supply. They have then to throw out the water which has got into their mouths when feeding. This they do by closing a valve leading to the nasal passages, and forcing it by means of air through the blow-hole placed in the upper part of the head. It is this necessity of whales for breathing at the surface which enables man to make them his prey, in spite of their immense strength, while their spouts point out to him the place where they are to be found.

The remarks I have made apply in common to the two chief sorts of whales, but the Greenland whale is a very different animal from the sperm whale, of which we were in search. The Greenland whale, (*Balaena mysticetus*), is also called the common, true, or whale-bone whale. I remember once, in a man-of-war, falling in with a dead whale in a perfect calm. We towed it alongside, but so ignorant was everybody on board of natural history, that no one knew where the whale-bone was to be found. At the cost of great trouble, with a horrible odour to our noses, we cut out a jaw-bone; which was perfectly valueless, except to make the front of a summer-house for our commander; and we then let our prize go with its rich contents, and glad enough we were to get rid of it.

The Greenland whale is less in size than the sperm—its length being about 60 feet. The head occupies about a third of the entire length. It is narrow above, and broad, flat, and rounded beneath, so as to allow it to move rapidly under the water. The body is largest about the middle, and tapers suddenly towards the tail. The general colour is a blackish-grey, with part of the lower jaw, and throat, and belly white. The lips are five or six feet high, the eyes very small, and the external opening of the ears scarcely perceptible. The pectoral fins or arms are not long, and are placed about two feet behind the angle of the lips. The black whale has no teeth; but from the upper palate and jaw there hang down perpendicularly numerous parallel laminae—the baleen, or whale-bone, as it is called. (Footnote: The baleen or whale-bone I have described forms a most valuable portion of the produce afforded by the black whale, although not so valuable as the oil extracted from the same animal.) These filaments fill up the whole of the cavity of the mouth, and form a most complete strainer, so that only the most minute animals can enter. This is necessary, as the swallow is too small to admit even the smallest fish. When a black whale feeds, it throws up millions of small animals at a time with its thick lower lip, into the straining apparatus I have described; and as they are scarcely perceptible to the naked eye, when its vast size is considered some slight notion may be formed of the prodigious number it must consume at meal.

There is another whale, found in the northern regions, called the razor-backed whale, from a prominent ridge on its back. It is found 100 feet long. As it is constantly moving along at the rate of five miles an hour, and is very powerful and active, frequently breaking away and carrying lines and gear with it, only the most daring whalers, in default of other prey, venture to attack it. There is a third sort of whale, called the broad-nosed whale, which is in many respects like a razor-back, but smaller—its length being from 50 to 80 feet.

The smallest sort is the beaked whale, which is about 25 feet long. Great numbers of this whale are often caught in the deep bays and firths of Shetland and Orkney.

I must now give an account of the spermaceti whale, (the *Physeter macrocephalus*), to capture which was the object of our voyage. It is found through every part of the South Pacific and Atlantic Oceans, and frequently makes its way to far northern latitudes. Still the southern seas must be considered its chief abode. In appearance and habits it is very different from the black whale. It is nearly as long as the razor-back, and exceeds it in bulk. In length it may be said to be from 80 to 85 feet, and from 30 to 35 in circumference. Looking at a sperm whale, the stem on its nose or snout appears very thick, and perfectly blunt, like a huge mallet about to strike. The head is a third part of the length of the body. At its junction with the body a hump rises, which we whalers call the *bunch of the neck*. Behind this is the thickest part of the body, which tapers off till there is another rise which we call the hump, in the shape of a pyramid—then commences the *small*, as we call it, or tail, with a ridge partly down it. The "small" gradually tapers till it contracts very much; and at the end the flukes, or what landsmen would call the tail, is joined on. In the immense head is contained the case, which is a cavity of almost triangular shape, and of great size, containing, when the whale is alive, that oily substance or fluid called spermaceti. I have frequently seen a ton taken from the case of one whale, which is fully ten large barrels. The use to the whale of the spermaceti in its head is, that, being much lighter than water, it can rise with great facility to the surface, and elevate its blow-hole above it. Its mouth is of great size, extending all the length of its head, or, as I have said, a third of its whole length. Its jaws narrow forward to almost a point—indeed, the lower one does so; and thus, as it swims along, like the stem of a ship, it serves to divide the water wedge, parting to make way for its huge body—the blunt snout being all the time like the lofty forecastle of an old-fashioned ship, clear of the waves high up above it. The inside of the monstrous cavity, the mouth, has nothing like the baleen or whale-bone, such as is found in the Greenland whale; but in the lower jaw it has a formidable row of large teeth of conical shape, forty-two in number. It has, however, none in the upper jaw; but instead, there are holes into which fit the points of those in the lower. These teeth are blunt, and are not used for biting or mastication, but merely to keep in the food which has entered its mouth. This food is chiefly the *Squid* or *Sepia octopus*, known also by the name of the cuttle-fish. In the South-Seas they are of enormous size, and, with their long feelers or arms growing out of their heads, are sufficiently strong to hold a man under the water and to kill him.

The sperm whale, however, swallows a variety of other fish. It catches them, not by swimming after them, but by opening wide its mouth and letting its prey swim into it! We will suppose ourselves looking down that vast mouth, as the lower jaw hangs perpendicularly to the belly; incapable it seems of moving. The interior of the throat is very large—capable of swallowing a man; the tongue is very small and delicate, and of a pure white colour; so are the teeth, which glisten brilliantly; and so is the whole interior. Fish are particularly attracted by their white appearance. They take it, perhaps, to be some marble hall erected for their accommodation; so in they swim, big and little squid equally beguiled! How the whale's mouth must water when he feels a fine huge juicy octopus playing about his tongue! Up goes the lower jaw like a trap-door, and cephalapods, small and large, find their bright marble palace turned into a dark, black prison, from which there is no return; for, giving a turn with his tongue, he gulps them all down with a smack which must make old Ocean resound!

In another respect, the sperm is very different from the Greenland whale. It seems to know the power of its jaws, and will sometimes turn on its pursuers and attack them, though generally a timid animal, and disposed to seek safety by flight. The general opinion is, that sperm whales often fight with each other, as we have caught them with their lower jaws twisted in a variety of directions, and otherwise injured. The sperm whale's eyes are very small, with movable eyelids, and are placed directly above the angle of the mouth, or a third part of its whole length distant from the snout. It is very quick-sighted, as it is also quick of hearing. Its ears—small round holes, which will not admit a little finger—are placed directly behind the eyes. The fins, which, as I have said, might be called paws, are close to the angle of the mouth. I have known a female whale support her young on them; and they are used to balance the body, to steer by, and, when hard pressed, to sink with greater rapidity below the surface. The skin of the whale is perfectly smooth, though old bulls get rough marks about them. As a rule, though black above and white below, as they advance in years, like human beings, they get grey on the head. Oftentimes an old grey-headed bull proves a dangerous enemy.

I have with greater minuteness than I intended given an account of the sperm whale. Its habits and mode of capture I will describe in the course of my narrative.

Chapter Seventeen
Incidents of Whaling

Away, away the good ship flew to round the far-famed Cape Horn. Stern and majestic it rose on our starboard-hand; its hoary front, as it looked down on the meeting of two mighty oceans, bore traces of many a terrific storm. Now all was calm and bright, though the vast undulations of the ocean over which the ship rode, as they met the resistance of the cliffs, were dashed in cataracts of spray high up in the air, and gave evidence of what would be the effect when a storm was raging across them. There was something more grand in the contemplation than in the actual appearance of the scene, when we reflected where we were—on the confines of those two great seas which encompass the earth, and which wash the shores of nations so different in character—the one having attained the height of civilisation, the other being still sunk in the depths of a barbarism too terrible almost for contemplation, as I afterwards had good reason to know. Then there was that strange, vast, dreamy swell—the breathings, as it were, of some giant monster. It seemed as if some wondrous force were ever acting on that vast body of water—that it could not for a moment rest quiet in its bed, but must ever go heaving on, in calm and sunshine as well as in storm and tempest. There was likewise in sight that wild weather-beaten shore, inhabited, as report declared, by men of gigantic stature and untameable fierceness; while to the south lay those mysterious frost-bound regions untrod by the foot of man—the land of vast glaciers, mighty icebergs, and wide extended fields of ice. On we sped with a favouring breeze, till we floated calmly on the smooth surface of the Pacific off the coast of Chili.

With regard to Patagonia, old Knowles told me he had been there, but that, as far as he saw, the people were not much larger than the inhabitants of many other countries. Some were big men; a few nearly seven feet high, and proportionably stout. They are capital mimics—the very parrots or magpies of the genus Man.

"I say, Jack, bear a hand there now," exclaimed one, repeating the words after a sailor who had just spoken.

"What! do you speak English, old fellow? Give us your flipper then," said Knowles, thinking he had found a civilised man in that distant region.

"What! do you speak English, old fellow? Give us your flipper then," repeated the savage with a grin, putting out his hand.

"I should think I did! What other lingo am I likely to speak?" answered Knowles, shaking the Patagonian's huge paw.

"What other lingo am I likely to speak?" said the savage, with perfect clearness.

"Why, I should have thought your own native Patagonian, if you are a Patagonian," exclaimed Knowles, examining the savage's not over-handsome physiognomy.

"If you are a Patagonian!" said the savage, looking in like manner into Knowles' face.

"I—I'm an Englishman, I tell you!" cried Tom, somewhat puzzled.

"I'm an Englishman, I tell you!" cried the Patagonian in the same indignant tone.

"That's just what I want to arrive at," said Tom. "So now just tell me where we can get some good baccy and a glass of honest grog."

The Patagonian repeated the words.

"But I ask you!" said Tom.

"But I ask you!" said the savage.

"I tell you I'm a stranger here!" exclaimed Tom.

"I tell you I'm a stranger here!" cried the savage.

"Where do you come from then?" asked Tom.

"Where do you come from then?" repeated the savage.

"I tell you I'm an Englishman," cried Knowles, getting angry.

"I tell you I'm an Englishman!" exclaimed the Patagonian in the same indignant tones.

"That's more than I'll believe; and, to speak my mind plainly, I believe that you are an arrant, bamboozling hum-bug!" cried Tom. "No offence, though. You understand me?"

Whether it was Tom's expression of countenance, or the tone of his voice, I know not, but as he uttered these words, all the savages burst into loud fits of merry laughter; and as he thought they were laughing at him, he said that he should have liked to have gone in among them, and knocked them down right and left with his fists; but they were such precious big fellows, that he thought he should have got the worst of it in the scrimmage.

He used with infinite gusto frequently to tell the story for our amusement.

I am not quite certain, however, whether he was describing the Patagonians or the inhabitants of Terra del Fuego. The latter are very great mimics and are much smaller in size, less clothed, and more savage in appearance than the Patagonians.

We touched at Valparaiso, in Chili, or, as it may be called, the Vale of Paradise. It is certainly by nature a very beautiful and healthy spot, built on a number of high hills with ravines intervening; but man, by his evil practices and crimes, made it, when I was there, much more like the Vale of Pandemonium. Drunkenness and all sorts of crimes were common, and the *cuchillo*—the long knife—was in constant requisition among the Spaniards, scarcely a night passing without one or more murders being committed. It was then little more than a village, but has now become quite a large town, with a number of English and American merchants settled there. The houses are built with very thick walls, to withstand the constant attacks of earthquakes which they have to undergo. Having supplied ourselves with fresh provisions and water, we sailed, and stretched away into the wide Pacific.

We had left the coast of Chili about a day's sail astern. A light easterly breeze was just ruffling the blue sea—the noon-day sun shining brightly over it—the hands going listlessly about their work, rather out of spirits at our want of success, not a whale having hitherto been seen—when the cheery shout of the first mate reached our ears from the look-out, of "There she spouts! there she spouts, boys!"

In an instant every one was aroused into the fullest activity—the watch below sprung on deck—Captain Carr hurried from his cabin, and with his hand to his mouth, shouted eagerly, "Where away?—where away?"

"About a mile on the starboard-bow," cried Mr Benson, the first mate, in return.

"Lower the boats, my lads!" exclaimed the captain, preparing to go in the leading one himself; the first and third mate and the boatswain went in command of the others. Both Newman and I, as new hands, remained on board, as did the second mate, to take charge of the ship.

Before the boats were in the water, the whale had ceased spouting; but just as they were shoving off, the look-out broke forth in a cheerful chorus, "There again—there again—there again!" the signal that the whale was once more sending up its spout of spray into the air. The words were taken up by all on deck, while we pointed with excited looks at the whale, whose vast head and hump could be clearly distinguished as he swam, unsuspicious of evil, through the calm waters of the deep. Away flew the boats, urged on by rapid strokes, in hot pursuit. The captain took the lead. We who were left behind felt that we were accompanying them in heart and spirit. The foam bubbled and hissed round the bows of the boats as they clove their way through the water. Not a moment was there to lose—the distance was great—the whale had been for some time breathing, and might go down, and perhaps be lost altogether, before the boats could get up to her, or they might have to chase her for many miles before they could again reach her. Meantime, the wind being fair, the ship was kept almost in the wake of the boats. Away they flew; each was anxious to strike the first whale, but the captain's took the lead, and maintained it. As they got nearer the monster, it was necessary to be careful, lest he should take the alarm, and, seeing his pursuers, go down to escape them. The men bent to their oars even more energetically than before; the captain stood up, harpoon in hand; his weapon was raised on high; we thought that the next instant it would be buried in the monster, when up went his small—the enormous flukes rose high in air—"Back of all!—back of all!" we cried; not that our voices could be heard. If not, that terrific stroke it is giving will shiver the boat in atoms. The boat glided out of the way, but just in time, though her crew were drenched with spray. Down went the whale—far, far into the depths of the ocean.

Nothing is to be had without trying for it—our captain knew this well. All eyes were now turned to watch where the whale would next rise, for rise, we knew, he before long must, and in all probability within sight; so the boats paddled slowly on, the men reserving their strength for the moment when it would be required; while we on board shortened sail, that we might have the ship more under command, to follow wherever they might lead. Every one was watching with intense eagerness; the four boats were separated a short distance from each other; now and then the officers would stand up to see if the monster had risen, and then they would turn their gaze towards the ship for a signal from the look-out aboard. Still the time passed away, and no whale appeared.

An hour had elapsed, when again the inspiriting shout was heard of "There she spouts! there she spouts!" the look-outs pointing, as before, over the starboard-bow, where the whale had again risen, not much more than a mile away from the boats. Again they were in rapid movement. We doubted not that this time they would reach the monster. Through our glasses we made him out to be a bull—an old greyhead, and probably a cunning fellow, one likely to try every dodge which a whale can think of to escape, and if failing to do that, and hard pressed, one who was likely to turn on his pursuers, and attack them with his open jaws or mighty flukes.

"Well, whatever freak he takes, our captain is the man to meet him," observed old Tom Knowles—a long-experienced hand in the South-Seas, but who, having hurt his arm, was unable to go in the boats. "As long as daylight lasts, he'll not give up the chase."

I had thought that when a whale was seen, it was merely necessary to pull after him, dig the harpoons into him, and allow him to drag the boats along till he died; but I found it was often a far more difficult task than this to kill a whale.

"There again—there again!" shouted the look-outs from aloft; and the cry was repeated by all on deck, while the whale continued spouting. Fast as at first, if not faster, the boats flew after him—the captain's again leading.

"This time we'll have him, surely," exclaimed Newman, who was as eager as any of us.

"Not quite so sure of that, Ned," observed old Knowles. "I've seen one of these old chaps go down half-a-dozen times before a harpoon was struck in him, and, after all, with three or four in his side, break away, and carry them off just as the sun was setting, and there was no chance of getting another sight of him. I say, never be certain that you've got him, till he's safe in the casks. I've seen one, after he has been killed, go down like a shot, for no reason that anyone on board could tell, except to spite us for having caught him."

While old Tom was speaking, the boats had approached close to the whale. For my own part, after what I had heard, I fully expected to see him lift his flukes, and go down as he had done before. The captain's boat was up to him—the rest hung back, not to run the risk of alarming the wary monster. The captain stood up in the bows—a fine bold figure he looked, as he poised his glittering harpoon in his right hand, high above his head. "There!—peak your oars," cried old Tom, as the crew raised them with a flourish to a perpendicular position, having given the boat sufficient impetus to take her alongside the whale. Off flew the weapon, impelled by the captain's unerring arm, and buried itself up to the socket in the fat coating with which the leviathan was clothed.

"It's socket up!" cried old Knowles. "Hurrah, lads—hurrah! our first whale's struck—good-luck, good-luck—hurrah, hurrah!" The cheer was taken up by all on board, as well as by those in the boats. They now gave way with a will after the whale; the harpooner, as another boat got up, sending his weapon into its side.

But it is no child's play now. The captain had time to dart a lance into him, when, "Stern all—stern all!" was now the cry of the headsman; and the crews, with their utmost strength, backed the boats out of the way of the infuriated animal, which in his agony began to lash the water with his huge flukes, and strike out in every direction with a force which would have shattered to atoms any boat they met. Now his vast head rose completely out of the water—now his tail, as he writhed with the pain the weapons had inflicted. The whole surface of the surrounding ocean was lashed into foam by the reiterated strokes of those mighty flukes, while the boats were deluged with the spray he threw aloft—the sound of the blows reverberating far away across the water. The boat-steerer now stood ready to let the lines run through the loggerhead over the bows of the boat. Should anyone be seized by their coils as they are running out, his death would be certain. Soon finding the hopelessness of contending with his enemies above water, the whale lifted his flukes and sounded.

Down, down he went into the depths of the ocean. Away flew the line over the bows of the boat. Its rapid motion would have set fire to the wood, had not the headsman kept pouring water over it, as it passed through its groove.

An oar was held up from the captain's boat: it was a sign that nearly the whole of their line, of two hundred fathoms, had run out. With caution, and yet rapidity, the first mate in the second boat bent on his line; soon the captain's came to an end, and then that flew out as rapidly as the first had done. To assist in stopping the whale's downward course, drogues were now bent on to the line as it ran out; but they appeared to have little more effect in impeding his progress than a log-ship has in stopping the way of a vessel; and yet they have, in reality, much more, as every pound-weight in addition tells on the back of a racer.

Again an oar went up, and the third boat bent on, adding more drogues to stop his way. They at length appeared to have effect. "There; haul in the slack," cried old Tom. "He's rising, lads; he's rising!"

The boat-steerer was seen in the last boat busily coiling away the line in the tub as he hauled it in. When he had got all his line, that belonging to the next boat was in like manner coiled away; then the captain's line was hauled in.

Thick bubbles now rose in rapid succession to the surface, followed by a commotion of the water, and the huge head of the monster rushed suddenly upward, sending forth a dense spout on high. The captain's boat was now hauled gently on, the boat-steerer guiding it close up to the fin of the wounded whale. Again Captain Carr stood up with his long lance in hand, and plunged it, as few on board could have done, deep into his side. At the same moment the rest of the boats pulled up on the opposite side, the harpooner in the leading one striking his harpoon into him. Again the cry arose of "Stern all—stern all!" It was time, indeed, to get out of the way, for the whale seemed to feel that he was engaged in his last struggles for freedom and for life. He threw himself with all his monstrous bulk completely out of the water, in a vain attempt to get loose from his foes. Off from him all the boats backed.

He now became the assailant. He rushed at them with his head and lower jaw let drop, seemingly capable of devouring one of them entire. I almost thought he would; but he was already fatigued with his wounds and previous exertions. The line, too, of the mate's boat had many times encircled his body. Suddenly it parts! The boat of the captain, after he had darted his lance, was backed in time, and got clear from the whale's attack, but the first mate was not so fortunate. The whale seemed to have singled him out as the victim of his revenge. Having in vain lashed at him with his flukes, he turned towards him with his head, rushing on with terrific force. He caught the boat as she was retreating, in an instant capsizing her, and sending all her crew struggling in the waves. I thought he would immediately have destroyed them; but he swam on, they happily escaping the blows of his flukes, and went head out across the ocean, followed by the first boat and the two others.

Were they going to allow our shipmates to perish unaided? I thought and fully expected to hear the second mate order another boat to be lowered to go to their assistance. But they did not require any. Two of the men could not swim, but the others supported them till they got them up to the boat, from which they had been a little way separated, and then by pressing down the gunwale they quickly righted her. They then, holding on on either side, baled away till they could get into her, and still have her gunwale above water, when they very quickly freed her altogether. Everything had been secured in the boat, so that nothing was lost; and as soon as she was to right, off she started again in the chase.

Away flew the captain's boat, dragged on by the line, at the rate, it seemed, of full ten knots an hour. The other boats followed as fast as their crews could lay their backs to the oars; but for a long time they could gain nothing on him, but were fast falling astern. We had again filled, and were standing on. At last he began to slacken his pace. The loss of blood from his many wounds, and his evident exertions, were rapidly weakening him. Still, so far-off had he gone, that the captain's boat was scarce to be seen, and the others were mere specks on the ocean.

Once again, however, we were overtaking them. The captain was once more hauling in the slack—the other boats were getting up—the headsmen standing, harpoon in hand, ready to give the whale fresh and still more deadly wounds. They ranged up alongside, and harpoons and lances flew from the boats. The monster no longer threw up water alone, but blood was sent in a thick spout from his blow-hole, sprinkling the men in the boats, and staining the bright blue sea around. Still, in spite of all his foes, he struggled on bravely for life. Lashing the water, so as to drive his relentless assailants to a distance, he once more lifted his flukes and sounded; but they were prepared to let the lines run. Down he went again.

"He'll be lost—he'll be lost!" I exclaimed, as did others not accustomed to the work.

"Not a bit of it on that account," said old Knowles. "He can't remain long under water after what he's gone through. He'll be up again soon; and then stand by, my hearties, for his flurry!"

Old Knowles was right. Up came the whale again, at a short distance only from where he had gone down, having dragged out from each boat not a hundred fathoms of line. Once more the boats approached, and fresh lances were darted into him; but they quickly had to retreat, for now his head went up, now his tail; now he sprung again right out of the water, twisting and turning in every direction.

"He has his death-pang on him," cried Old Knowles. "He'll be ours before long;—but, ah! one of them has caught it!"

One of the boats had indeed caught it. We could not tell which, for the others were covered with the foam and ensanguined water cast on every side by the monster in his wild contortions. The fragments lay floating, scattered far and wide, and several men were seen striking out towards the other boats, half-turning their heads, as if in expectation of being pursued. But, as we counted their number, they did not appear to be all there. There were but five. One, we feared, was missing. Anxiously we kept our eyes fixed on the spot, hoping to see our shipmate, whoever he might be, appear.

"Hurrah!—he's there—he's there!" we shouted, as we discovered the sixth man swimming out from among the mass of bloody foam which surrounded the whale, who for an instant seemed to be resting from his exertions. While the boats were taking them on board, again the whale darted rapidly out, but this time it was to perform the segment of a circle.

"He's in his flurry, lads—he's in his flurry!" shouted old Knowles. "He'll be dead in another minute."

"Last scene of all, which ends this strange, eventful history," said Newman, who through his glass had been eagerly watching the chase. As the words went out of his mouth the whale rolled over on his side, a well-won prize, and loud shouts from the crews of the boats and from all on deck rent the air.

The fragments of the shattered boat being collected, and the three remaining ones made fast to the whale, they began towing it towards the ship, while we made sail to meet them.

All hands were employed for an instant in congratulating each other when we got the whale alongside, and then every means were taken to secure it for "cutting-in"—so the operation of taking off the blubber is called. The coopers had meantime been getting ready the large caldrons for boiling the blubber; which operation is called "trying-out." A rope passed round the windlass, and rove through a block fast to the head of the mainmast, was carried over the side, with a large hook at the end of it. The first thing done was to cut off the head of the whale, which, with the neck-part up, was strongly secured, and floated astern.

"That head has got better than a ton of oil in it," observed old Knowles, who was aiding the work. "It's worth no end of money."

"Wears yet a precious jewel in his crown," observed Newman, leaning eagerly over the side. "It's fine work this, though."

A stage had been let down at the side of the vessel, on which those who had cut off the head were stationed. One of them now made a hole in the blubber with the instrument used for cutting-in, called a spade. A rope was then fastened round the waist of another man, and he descended on the body of the whale, taking the hook I have spoken of in his hand. This hook he fastened into the hole he had cut. The operation now began.

Some with spades cut the blubber or fat mass which surrounds the body into a strip between two and three feet wide, in a spiral form, while others hoisted away on the tackle to which the hook was attached. Slowly the blanket-piece, thus cut off, ascended over the side, the body turning round and round as its coat or bandage, for so we may call it, was unwound. By the side of the pots were *horses*—blocks of wood—on which the blubber was cut up. As the long strip was drawn up, another hook was secured lower down, and the upper part of the blanket-piece was cut off and chopped into thin pieces on the blocks. The pieces were then thrown into big pots, under which fires were kindled. After the first caldrons-full had been boiled, the lumps of blubber from which the oil had been extracted were taken out, and served as fuel to continue our fires. In reality, the whole operation was performed in a very cleanly and orderly way; but a stranger at a distance would scarcely think so.

Night overtook us while we were engaged in the work, and watch and watch we continued it, lest a gale might spring up and compel us to abandon our prize before it was all secured. No scene could be wilder or more unearthly than that presented during the night by the whaler's decks. The lurid fires surrounding the seething caldrons cast a red glare on all around — on the masts and rigging of the ship, enveloped in the dense wreaths of smoke which ascended from them — on the sturdy forms of the seamen, with their muscular arms bared to the shoulder. Some were cutting off huge blanket-pieces; others chopping them small on the horses; others throwing them into the pots, or with long poles stirring the boiling fluid, or raking out the scraps, as the refuse is called, to feed the flames; while others, again, were drawing off the oil into the casks ready to receive it, and stowing them away in the hold.

The whole of the following day and the following night found us employed in a similar manner. At last the whole carcass was stripped to the very flukes of every particle of blubber, and, to our no little satisfaction, cast loose to float away, and to become a feast for the fish of the sea and the birds of the air. The head, full of the valuable spermaceti, was now floated alongside. A bucket was then forced down through the neck; by means of a long pole, into the case, till, by repeated dips, it was entirely emptied of its contents; and, as Knowles predicted, the case was found to contain even more than a ton of oil. The spermaceti was carefully boiled by itself — an operation necessary to preserve it. The blubber surrounding the head was also taken off and boiled down, and the empty skull was then cast loose, and sunk, by its own weight, with rapidity to the bottom — there, perhaps, to form the caverned abode of some marine monster never yet seen by human eye. It took us nearly three days to cut-in, try-out, and stow away that huge whale, the produce altogether being no less than eighty-five barrels! We broke forth into loud shouts when our work was accomplished and our first fish stowed away.

I have no great sympathy with those who talk of the cruelty of the work. A whale feels acutely, no doubt, and so does a mouse or a sparrow, when wounded; but not having huge bodies to twist and turn about in their agony, they do not appear to suffer so much as does the mighty monarch of the deep. I suspect that the amount of pain felt by the small animal is equally great with that felt by the large one. However, I would make my argument a plea for merciful treatment of all alike, and urge that pain should never be unnecessarily inflicted on even the smallest of created beings in whose nostrils is the breath of life.

Our success put us all in spirits, and we were ready to do or to dare anything. Our captain had heard that sperm whales were to be found in the icy seas towards the Antarctic Pole, and, accordingly, before keeping across to New Zealand and the isles of the Indian Ocean, he resolved to take a cruise to the south for a few weeks in order to try our fortune. Over the seas on which we were sailing it was necessary, both night and day, to keep a very sharp look-out; not only for whales, but to avoid the dangers of coral-reefs, and islands of all sizes, which in many parts sprinkle it so thickly.

"Land ahead!" was shouted from the foretopmast-head one forenoon, as we were slowly gliding over the blue surface of the deep. As we got up with it, we saw that it was a long, low, almost barren island, a few trees only in the higher parts retrieving it from actual sterility. It was a wild, desolate, melancholy-looking spot, such as would make a man shudder at the very thought of being wrecked on it. At one end, inside a reef over which the surf was breaking violently, lay a dark object. As the officers were inspecting it through their glasses, they pronounced it to be a wreck. There could be no doubt about it, and Captain Carr resolved at once to visit the spot, to discover whether any of the crew still remained alive.

As we stood on, a loud sound of roaring and yelping reached our ears, and we saw on many of the rocks which surrounded the island a vast number of seals, of the sort called "sea-lions." Newman and several of us were eager to get in among them, to knock some of them on the head, that we might make ourselves caps and jackets for our cruise in the icy seas. The captain was equally anxious to get some seal-skins, and he told us that, after we had visited the wreck, and explored the island, we should try and catch some of the animals.

Seals are curious-looking creatures. The head, with its large mild eyes, and snout, and whiskers, looks like that of some good-natured, intelligent dog; and one expects, as they are swimming, to see four legs and a thin curly tail come out of the water. Instead of that, the body narrows away till there is seen a tail like that of a fish. The hind-feet are like those of a duck when in the water, and the front ones have, beyond the skin, only a flapper or paw with claws, at the end of it. They are covered with thick, glossy hair, closely set against the skin. The form of their jaws and teeth proves that they are carnivorous, and they are known to live on fish, crabs, and sea-birds.

The birds they catch in the water, as they can swim with great rapidity and ease. They can remain also for a considerable time under the water, without coming to the surface to breathe.

The sea-lion, which was the species of seal we were hoping to attack, grows to the length of ten feet. The colour is of a yellowish-brown, and the males have a large mane, which covers their neck and shoulders, so that they have very much the appearance of lions when their upper part alone is seen above the water. Such were the monsters which seemed to be guarding the island towards which we were pulling, their roar vying in loudness with the hoarse sound of the surf as it beat on the rock-bound shore.

Newman and I were in the captain's boat. As we pulled in for the land, we saw that the surf rolled up on every side, and for some time we could not discover a clear spot through which we might urge the boats. We continued pulling on for half a mile or more, and caught sight of what appeared to be a channel between the reefs. The captain ordered us to give way, and bending to our oars, we pulled on with a will. A sailor loves a run on shore, even though that shore may be but a barren sand; but here we had two objects to excite our interest. The deserted wreck claimed our first attention. It was easy to see how she had got into her present position. An unusually high-tide and heavy gale must have lifted her over the reef, and driven her on shore; and the wind falling before she had time to go to pieces, must have left her comparatively safe from further injury. The captain stood up in his boat to watch for an opportunity to enter the passage.

"Now, again, my lads, give way!" he shouted. The boat lifted on the summit of a roller, and rushing on with the dark rocks and hissing foam on either side of us, in another instant we found ourselves calmly floating in a reef-surrounded lagoon or bay. We had to pull back for some distance to get to the wreck, and as we advanced, we looked along the shore to discover, if we could, traces of any of the crew. All, however, was silent and desolate.

From the appearance of the island, Newman observed that he thought it must be the crater of an extinct volcano, and that even the lapse of ages had allowed scarcely soil enough to collect on it, to permit of more than the scanty vegetation which was visible.

As we approached the wreck, we found that she had gone stem on into the mouth of a little creek, and there had been held fast by two rocks. Her build at once made us suspect that she was a whaler like ourselves. All her boats and bulwarks were gone, and her stern was much stove in. Her main and mizzen-masts had been carried away, so had her foretopmast and the head of the foremast below the top, the stump only remaining. On this a yard still hung across, and the tattered fragment of a sail, showing us that she had run stem on into her present position. As her stern could be approached by water which was quite smooth, we ran the boats under it, and climbed on board. The sea had made a clean breach through the stern, and inundated the cabin, which presented a scene of ruin and desolation. The bulkheads had been knocked away; the contents of the sideboard, and sleeping-places, and lockers, all lay scattered about, shattered into fragments, in the wildest confusion, among sand, and slimy sea-weed, and shells, which thickly coated the whole of the lower part of the cabin; while the hold itself, between which and the cabin all the partitions had been knocked away, was full of water. No living being remained on board to tell us how the catastrophe had occurred. On going forward, we found that the rocks between which she was jammed were separated from the shore, and that without a boat it would have been difficult to get aboard. After the captain had examined the wreck, he gave it as his opinion that she had been there three or four years, if not longer. One thing appeared certain, that she could not have got where she was without people on board to steer her; and then the question arose, what had become of them?

If any of them were still alive on the shore, they must long ago have seen the ship, and would have been waiting to receive us. The captain thought that they might have possibly been taken off by another ship soon after the wreck; still he resolved not to return without having searched thoroughly for them. We pulled round astern of the wreck, and there, in a sort of natural dock, found an easy landing-place.

As we walked across the island, we found that some of the lower spots, the dells and valleys, produced a greater amount of vegetation than had appeared at a distance; but could not retrieve the character of desolation given by the black, barren hills, and dark abrupt cliffs which arose on every side. We had given up all expectation of finding anyone alive, or any signs of the spot ever having been inhabited, when we heard a cry from Newman, who had wandered a little on one side.

We found him standing on a green hillock, raised a little above the valley, whence on one side a wide view over the blue sparkling sea could be obtained, with some shrubs of semi-tropical luxuriance, and the bright yellow sands forming the foreground, while behind arose the dark frowning cliffs and hills I have described. On the top of the hillock were four mounds, side by side, and at one end of each was seen a rough, flat piece of wood, a rude substitute for a grave-stone. There were names on them of Englishmen, and dates showing that they had died at intervals of a month or two from one another.

Where were the survivors?—who had buried these men? was now the question. A group of cocoa-nut trees, all that were on the island, marked the spot. It was one selected with much taste. The discovery induced us to persevere in our search. We wandered on for another hour, turning in every direction; for so full of undulations was the island, that we might easily have passed the very spot we were in search of. At last we were again called together by a shout from Newman.

We found him standing before a rude hut erected in front of a cave, which formed, indeed, a back apartment to it. There was only one rough bed-place on one side of it, though there were several stools, and a table in the centre. A seaman's chest stood open, and contained a few articles of clothing. There were two muskets, and some powder-flasks hung up against the wall; but there was no food, although an iron pot and a saucepan, with a place where a fire had been made, showed that provisions had at one time been cooked there. On a shelf there were several books, both in English and in foreign languages, and above them was a flute with a music-book. A few carpenter's tools were arranged on another shelf. Several things showed that the place had last been inhabited by a person of superior education. On opening the books, a name was found in several of them. It was that of William Evans. Two of them Newman discovered to be on medical subjects, which of course made us conjecture that they had belonged to the surgeon of the ship. The decayed state of the books showed that it was long since they had been opened, and on a further examination of the hut, it also was found to be in a very dilapidated condition. From the number of things left in the hut, Captain Carr surmised that the last occupants must have left the place very suddenly, if, indeed, they had left it at all. One thing was certain, that we were not likely to find any of them on the island.

We were, therefore, on our return to the boats, when I saw the figure of a man sitting, with his back to a rock, on a gentle slope, whence a view could be obtained of the blue ocean. I had separated a little from my companions. I called to him, and I thought I heard him answer, "Halloa, who calls?" His face was turned away from me, and he did not move. I called again, and at that moment Newman broke through the brushwood, and joined me. Together we climbed the hill, both equally surprised that the man we saw did not get up to meet us. In another minute we were by his side. The straw-hat, stained and in tatters, covered a skull; the clothes, decayed and discoloured, hung loosely on a fleshless skeleton. A book was by his side. It was a copy of a Latin poet—Horace, Newman told me. Before him was another book of manuscript; and, as we looked about, we picked up the remains of pencil, which had dropped from the dead man's fingers. Newman opened the manuscript, and though it was rotten, and the characters much defaced, he could still decipher them. He glanced his eye rapidly over them.

"Ah! poor fellow, his appears to have been a sad fate," he remarked, with a voice full of sadness. "Compelled by a strong necessity to leave England—to wrench asunder all the ties which held him there, and embark on board a South-sea-man as surgeon—he seems to have had a hard life of it with a drunken, brutal captain, and ignorant—not a human being with whom he could sympathise. Unable to return home, after three years' service he exchanged into another ship. His master and officers, with all the boats, were away in chase of whales, which had appeared about them in great numbers, when a gale arose. The crew, already too much weakened by that scourge of the ocean, the scurvy, and the loss of several men, were unable to shorten sail. The boats were far out of sight, as they believed, to windward. In vain they endeavoured to beat up to them. The main and mizzen-masts went by the board; and the gale still further increasing, they were compelled to run before it, without a prospect of picking up their shipmates in the boats.

"Away they drove for several days before the wind, till one night all who were below were thrown out of their berths by a violent concussion. Again and again the ship struck—the sea beat in her stern. They rushed on deck. It was to find nearly all those who had been there washed away. The next instant, the ship again lifting, was carried into smooth water, and finally jammed fast in the position we had found her.

"Five only of all the crew then survived, and they were the most sickly. The writer was himself suffering from illness; happily, however, he bore up against it. They collected all the provisions, and all articles likely to be useful, which the sea had not destroyed, and carried them on shore, which they easily reached by means of a raft.

"They had food enough to last them for some time; but they had but a scanty supply of water. In vain they searched through the island—no springs were to be found. With great labour they got up all the casks of water still uninjured from the hold, and resolved to husband the contents. They formed themselves a habitation. They made reservoirs in which to catch the rain when it fell; but, in those latitudes, for many weeks together no rain falls. For a time, with their fire-arms, they killed a few birds; but their ammunition failed them, and they could kill no more. Their water was at last expended, and for many weeks together the only moisture they could obtain was by chewing the leaves of the shrubs and grass they found. They continued, as at first, very weak. They talked of building a boat from the wreck, but had neither strength nor knowledge among them sufficient for the undertaking.

"At last their spirits gave way, and disease made fearful progress with them all. One by one they died, and the survivors buried them. The writer of the sad journal was alone left." Alas! not a word did he say about seeking consolation where alone it can be given—not a thought about another world and judgment to come. The writer seemed to pride himself on his heathen stoicism—heathen expressions of resignation were alone mentioned. His dying eyes had rested on the pages of Horace—his dying thoughts, were they heavenward?

"In vain had he crawled to the spot where we found him, day after day, in the faint hopes of seeing a ship to bear him away. Three long years had thus passed, and all the food that had been brought on shore had been consumed; and he had not strength to search for more, so he came up there and sat himself down, and his spirit passed away."

Mr Newman had read this rapid sketch of the last events in the life of this unhappy exile before the captain came up, when he handed him the journal. The captain desired Newman to keep the "Horace," observing that he could not himself understand the contents.

We had found some tools in the hut, with which we dug a shallow grave close to where we had found these sad remains of mortality, and in it we placed them. On the rock above we cut the name of William Evans, and the date of the day on which we found him dead. Loading ourselves with the articles found in the hut, Newman being allowed to take most of the books as his share, we returned to the boats.

Although a longer time had been spent on shore than the captain intended, he allowed us to endeavour to capture some of the sea-lions. After pulling, however, some way along the lagoon, we discovered that they could not be approached from the land-side, as they had taken up their quarters on some high rocks, almost islands by themselves, in advance of the reefs. We were, therefore, compelled to pass into the open sea before attacking them—the passage by which we entered; and, waiting an opportunity, we dashed through in safety.

As we approached the largest rock, it was curious to watch the hundreds, or, I may say, thousands of fierce-looking monsters which covered its slippery surface. It would have required bold men, not acquainted with their habits, to attack them, as they looked down upon us from their seemingly unapproachable fortress. On one side, the surf broke far too fiercely to allow the boats to venture near; but on the other, although there was a good deal of surf, Captain Carr told us we might land. The only way, however, to get on shore was to pull in on the summit of a breaker; and while those in the bow leaped out on the rock, the rest of the crew had to pull back the boat again with all their force into smooth water. We were armed for the attack with two or three harpoons, a lance, and the boat's stretchers.

"Stand by, my lads—now's the time!" shouted our captain, as the two boats rolled in towards the shore. He led the way, lance in hand; Newman and I and old Knowles following from his boat. Our sudden appearance on the confines of their fortress evidently not a little astonished the sea-lions. Opening wide their jaws, and gnashing with their formidable tusks, they glanced at us from the heights above, and then, with reiterated and terrific roars, began to descend with impetuous force, as if with their overwhelming numbers to drive us into the sea. An old sea-lion led the van—a fierce monster, who looked capable of competing with all of us together. So he might, if he had possessed legs instead of fins or flappers, the latter only enabling him to twist and turn and slide down the inclined plane on which we stood into the sea. On the beasts came in dense masses, roaring and snarling. I certainly did look for a moment at the boats, and wish myself safe back again in them; but it was only for a moment, for our antagonists demanded all our strength and agility to compete with them. Our captain advanced boldly towards the old leader, and as he came right at him, plunged his lance into his side. It had not the effect of stopping the beast in his career; but, instead, very nearly carried him and the lance into the water. Old Knowles was, I thought, very inadequately armed only with a thick stick, which he always carried on shore with him, curiously cut and carved, and fastened to his wrist by a lanyard.

"Let me alone," said he; "Old Trusty is better in a scrimmage, whether with man or beast, than all your fire-arms and steel weapons. He always goes off, and never gets blunt."

Newman and I were armed with harpoons. Newman, following the captain's example, plunged his harpoon into the side of a seal, just as the beast, with the greatest impetus, was sliding down the rock. In attempting to stop its way, his foot slipped, and with the line coiled round his arm, before any of us could go to his assistance, he was dragged off into the boiling waters. He was a first-rate swimmer, but with so huge a sea-monster attached to him, how could he hope to escape. The rock sloped in a different direction to where the boats were, so that they could render him no assistance. I thought of the scene we had just witnessed—the unhappy exile dying alone on the desert island—and I dreaded a similar fate for my friend. With a cry of dismay we looked towards the drowning man. He disappeared among the foaming breakers.

Still, but with little hope, we watched the spot. Yes—there was his head! He was swimming free! Bravely he mounted the crest of a roller; it rushed in for the rock; but before he could find his footing, or we could stretch out our arms to help him, he was carried off again among the foaming waves. Meantime old Knowles had climbed up the rock in the face of the sea-lions, whom he was knocking on the head right and left with his club, and signalled the boats to pull round to Newman's assistance. Still, however, with only a couple of hands in each, it would take, I saw, a considerable time before they could reach him, and I resolved to make one attempt to save his life, at the risk, though it might be, of my own. Sticking my harpoon in a crevice of the rock which my eye at that instant fell on, I seized the end of the line, and in spite of the sea-lions, which kept rushing past me, I struck out into the surf as I saw Newman once more approaching. Happily I grasped him by the collar as the sea was once more heaving him back, and the captain and other shipmates coming to our assistance, we were hauled safely up the rocks.

There was not now a moment to be lost if we would capture any seals. Although many had escaped, still a good number remained near; and following the example set by old Knowles, we began laying about us on every side most lustily with our weapons, bestowing heavy blows on the heads of the frightened beasts. One blow was generally sufficient to stun, if not to kill them outright, and we then quickly despatched them with our knives. "On, my lads, on!" cried the captain; and up the rocky steep we went, meeting the maddened inhabitants as they came floundering down upon us. We had literally often to climb over the fallen bodies of the slain. Sometimes one of our party would miss his footing, and he and half-a-dozen seals would go sliding away down the rock, the beasts biting at him, and he struggling to get free, and in no small terror of being carried away into the surf. Such would inevitably have been the lot of more than one of us had not we all kept a watch to help each other out of such difficulties.

Our captain's combat with the old lion was the most severe. As the captain, unwilling to lose his lance or the beast, holding on to the former, was dragged downwards, they reached a ledge of rock which sloped in an opposite direction to the surrounding parts, and thus formed a table on which they could rest. Here the monster, finding that he could not escape from his opponent, turned bravely to bay, and grinning with his large, strong teeth, made fiercely at him. The captain held on pertinaciously to the handle of the spear, springing actively out of the way of the beast's mouth, as in its contortions and struggles it approached him too nearly. The lion roared, and snarled, and struggled, and the captain held on bravely, but I believe would soon have had to let go had not old Knowles, springing down the rock, given the animal a blow on the head with his stick, which effectually settled him.

There were many other single combats, and more of one man against half-a-dozen beasts; but the result was that we came off victorious without the loss of anyone, while we could boast of having killed upwards of sixty seals. Our next work was to flay them. This, in the hands of experienced operators, was soon performed, and in a short time we had sufficient skins ready to load our boats, and to make caps and jackets for all hands, besides what were required for the ship's use. The boats now came back to the spot where we were to embark, and by carefully waiting our time, we leaped on board with no other damage than wet jackets.

"Williams," said Newman, as we were pulling on shore, "you have nobly preserved my life at the risk of your own. I trust that I may be grateful."

Chapter Eighteen
Whaling and Seal-Catching in the Icy Regions

Strong breezes, and cold and thick weather, showed us that we were getting out of the genial latitudes, in which, without much success, we had been for some time cruising, and were approaching those icy regions which encircle the Antarctic Pole. Newman had made such progress in his knowledge of seamanship, that he was not only considered competent to undertake all the ordinary duties of a seaman, but was more trusted than many of the older hands. He soon gave evidence that this confidence was not misplaced. He and I were in the same watch. This was a great satisfaction to me, as I benefited largely by his conversation, which I was now beginning fully to appreciate.

One night we had the middle watch, and were together on the look-out forward. It was unusually dark; neither moon nor stars were visible, and the clouds hung down in a thick canopy over us. A strong breeze was blowing from the southward and eastward, and we were standing to the south-west with our port-tacks aboard. The sea was not very heavy, but it struck me at the time that it was somewhat uneven and irregular, and this made me suspect that we might be in the neighbourhood of land or fields of ice. Newman was talking of the Aurora Australis, and telling me how much he longed to see its effect in its fullest brilliancy, when suddenly he seized my arm with a firm grasp.

"Williams!" he exclaimed, "do you see that unusual whiteness glimmering there ahead, and on our starboard bow? I hear the surf beating on it! I'm sure it's an iceberg! Starboard your helm! Luff all you can! Starboard for your lives!" he shouted, rushing aft to see this done. I meantime called on those on deck to get a pull at the head-braces; an inch might save the ship.

There was no time for ceremony; no time to announce the fact in set form to the officer of the watch. This was the second mate. He was, happily, a sensible man. He at once comprehended the emergency, and gave the necessary orders to brace up the yards, and bring the ship close upon a wind. We were not a moment too soon in anything that was done. The white glimmering appearance grew every instant more distinct, till it resolved itself into a vast massive iceberg towering high above the mast-heads, while the roar of the breakers which dashed against its sides increased in loudness. The ship heeled over to the gale till her yard-arms seemed almost to touch the floating mountain. Still she stood up bravely to her canvas, closely hugging the wind. Had a rope been rotten, had a spar given way, our fate might have been sealed. In one instant after striking, the ship and everything in her might have been dashed to atoms.

The man with firmest nerves among all our crew watched that lofty berg, as we rushed by it in our midnight course, with feelings of awe and anxiety, if not of alarm, and drew a breath more freely when he looked over the quarter and saw the danger past. It was not the only one we encountered that night. Sail had been shortened; but it was evidently necessary, after the warning we had received, to keep the ship as much as possible under command.

On, on we flew through the murky night, the gale every moment increasing in force, and the sea rising and breaking in unexpected directions. We had again kept away on our course. Sail was still further reduced. The cold had before been considerable; it now much increased, and our decks were covered with ice. Captain Carr had, the moment we sighted the iceberg, come on deck; the watch below were called, and every one was at his post. It was not a time for anyone to be spared. We had evidently got into the icy regions sooner than had been expected. Intending to get out of them, the captain gave the order to keep away; but scarcely had we done so when an ice-field was seen extending away on our lee-bow and ahead, and we were again obliged to haul up, hoping to get round it. On, therefore, we sailed; but as we advanced we found the ice-field extending away on our starboard-beam, the sea breaking over it with a noise which warned us what would be the consequence if we should strike it.

Let our position be pictured for an instant. The fierce waves dashing wildly and irregularly about us; the storm raging fiercely; the ship driving onwards through pitchy darkness; wide, massive fields of ice extending on every side; huge icebergs floating around we knew not where; no lighthouse, no chart to guide us; our eyes and ears stretched to the utmost, giving but short warning of approaching danger. Such are the scenes which wear out a commander's strength, and make his hair turn quickly grey. We knew full well that dangers still thickly surrounded us, and heartily did we wish for the return of day to see them. Newman and I were again forward. I was telling him that I had heard of a ship striking a berg, and of several of her people being saved on it, while she went down, when he startled me by singing out with a voice of thunder, "Ice ahead!" At the same moment old Knowles cried out, "Ice on the weather-bow!" and immediately I had to echo the shout with "Ice on the lee-bow!" and another cried, "Ice abeam!"

To tack would have been instant destruction; to wear, there was no room. Every moment we expected to feel the awful crash as the stout ship encountered the hard ice. Captain Carr rushed forward. We must dash onward. Though no opening could be seen, there might be one! Onward we careered. Every man held his breath; and pale, I doubt not, turned the faces of the bravest. Suddenly, high above us, on the weather-side, appeared another iceberg. The sea became almost calm; but it was a calmness fraught with danger rather than safety. The sails, caught by the eddy-wind, were taken aback. In another moment we might have been driven, without power of saving ourselves, under that frowning cliff of ice. The storm raged above us—before us—behind us—on every side but there we lay, as if exhausted. Still the ship had way on her, and we continued our course. The channel was too narrow to allow the helm to be put up.

Just as she was losing her way, and would inevitably, through the force of the eddy-wind, have got stern-way on her, her headsails again felt the force of the gale, and, like a hound loosed from the leash, she started forward on her course. Again we were plunging madly through the wildly breaking seas; but the wind blew steadily, and the ice-fields widened away on either side till they were lost to view. Once again we were saved by a merciful Providence from an almost inevitable destruction. Still, we had some hours of darkness before us, and an unknown sea full of ice-islands through which we must pass. Not an eye was closed that night. Again we were close to one, but we were now better able to distinguish them than at first. This time we had to keep away, and run to the northward; but before long, there arose ahead of us a fourth iceberg. Again we sprung to the braces, the helm was put down, and, once more close-hauled, we weathered the danger.

Thus we hurried on—narrowly escaping danger after danger till daylight approached. Before, however, the sun arose, the gale fell; the clouds cleared away; and a bright gleam appeared in the eastern sky. Up shot the glorious sun, and never shall I forget the scene of gorgeous magnificence his bright rays lighted. Both sky and sea became of a deep blue—the water calm and clear as crystal—while all around us floated mountains of brilliant whiteness, like masses of the purest alabaster, of every varied form and size. Many were 200 feet high, and nearly a third of a mile in length. Some had perpendicular sides, with level summits—fit foundations, it might seem, for building cities of marble palaces, or fortresses for the kings of the East. Some, again, were broken into every fantastic form conceivable—towers and turrets, spires and minarets, domes and cupolas; here, the edifices found most commonly under the symbol of the crescent; there, those of the cross: Norman castles, Gothic cathedrals, Turkish mosques, Grecian temples, Chinese pagodas, were all here fully represented, and repeated in a thousand different ways. Others had been broken or melted into the forms of jagged cliffs, gigantic arches, lofty caverns, penetrating far away into the interior. Scarcely a shape which is to be found among the butting crags, sea-beat headlands, or mountain summits, in every part of the world, was not there represented in the most brilliant and purest of materials. Whole cities, too, were there to be seen pictured; squares and streets, and winding lanes, running up from the water's edge, like a ruined Genoa, with marble palaces, and churches, and alabaster fountains, and huge piles of buildings of every possible form standing proudly up amid the ocean, the whole appearing like some scene of enchantment rather than a palpable reality. Here was seen a lofty mountain rent in two by some fierce convulsion of nature; there, a city overturned: here, rocks upheaved and scattered around in wild confusion; there, deep gorges, impenetrable ravines, and terrific precipices;—indeed, here Nature, in her wildest and most romantic forms, was fully represented. The beauty of the wondrous spectacle was heightened when the sun arose, from the varied gorgeous tints which flashed from mountain-top and beetling cliff, from tower, turret, and pinnacle, where its bright rays fell on them as they slowly moved round in their eccentric courses. No words, however, can describe the dazzling whiteness and brilliancy of the floating masses. From some of the most lofty, fountains might be seen gushing down, as from a mountain's top when the fierce rays of the sun melt the long-hardened snow; while in and out of the deep caverns the sea-birds flew and screamed, peopling those dreary solitudes with joyous life.

The sun soon melted the ice from off our decks and rigging, and as we sailed onward the air became warm and genial. The most insensible of us could not but admire the scene; but Newman could scarcely repress his exclamations of delight and surprise. His sketch-book was brought out, and rapidly he committed to paper some of the most remarkable portions of the beautiful scene. Still, no pencil, no colours could represent the glorious, the magnificent tints in which the sea and sky, and the majestic varied-shaped icebergs, were bathed, as the sun, bursting forth from his ocean-bed, glided upwards in the eastern heavens. Numbers of birds came circling round the ship in their rapid flight, or were seen perched on the pinnacles of the bergs, or flying among their caverned recesses—albatrosses, snow-white petrels, penguins, and ducks of various sorts.

The albatross—Diomedea, as Newman called it—is the most powerful and largest of all aquatic birds. Its long hard beak is very strong, and of a pale yellow colour. The feet are webbed. I have seen some, the wings of which, when extended, measured fifteen feet from tip to tip, while they weighed upwards of twenty pounds. It feeds while on the wing, and is very voracious, pouncing down on any object which its piercing eye can discover in the water; and many a poor fellow, when swimming for his life, having fallen overboard, has been struck by one, and sunk to rise no more.

The snow-white petrel is a beautiful bird, and in its colours offers a strong contrast to the stormy petrel, (*Thalassidroma*), the chief part of whose plumage is of a sooty black, and others dark brown. Instead of being dreaded by seamen, it ought to be looked upon as their friend, for it seems to know long before they do when a storm is approaching, and by its piercing cry and mode of flight warns them of the coming danger. Seamen, however, instead of being grateful, like the world of old, the world at present, and the world as it ever will be, look upon these little prophets with dread and hatred, and in their ignorance and stupidity consider them the cause of the evil portended.

Penguins are found only in the Antarctic Ocean. They derive their name from *pinguis*, "fat," they being noted for that quality. Their legs are placed so far back that, when on shore, they stand almost upright. Though on land their movements are very awkward, yet when in the water—which, more than the air, must be considered their natural element, as their wings are too small to allow them to fly—they are bold birds, and will bravely defend themselves or their young when attacked, and will advance on a retreating enemy.

We had not been long in these icy regions before we reaped an ample reward for all the dangers we had encountered. As we looked over the side, we observed the water full of animalcules, while vast quantities of shrimps of various sorts were seen in the neighbourhood of the icebergs; but what still more raised our hopes of finding whales, were the numbers of large squid, or cuttle-fish, on which, as I have said, they chiefly feed. We were watching a huge fellow floating near the ship, with outstretched tentaculae, of arms, extending an immense distance from his head, and with which he was dragging up into his voracious mouth thousands of animalculae every moment—and from his size he seemed capable of encircling the body of any unfortunate person he might find swimming—when the cry was heard from aloft of "There she, spouts—there she spouts!"

In an instant Newman's lecture of natural history, which he was giving us, was brought to a conclusion. All hands were on deck, and four boats were manned and lowered, and pulled away after no less than three fine bull whales, which appeared at the same instant round the ship. There is a danger in attacking a whale near an iceberg which is avoided in the open sea. When he is fast, he may sound under it, and come up on the other side; but instinct warns him not to come up so as to strike his head against it.

Newman and I had already gone in the boats, and had proved ourselves no bad oarsmen on the occasion. He, indeed, had been allowed by the captain to use the harpoon when one of the officers was ill, and had succeeded in striking his first fish in a way which gained him much credit. On this occasion, however, we both remained on board.

Suddenly, not far from the ship, another whale rose to the surface, and, in a most extraordinary manner, began to turn, and twist, to throw half his huge bulk at a time out of the water, and furiously to lash it with his tail till he was surrounded with a mass of foam. The boats were in another direction, or we should have thought he had been wounded, and had a lance or harpoon sticking in him, from which he was endeavouring to free himself. He swam on, however, and approached the ship, still continuing his extraordinary contortions. As he drew near, he lifted his enormous head out of the water, when we saw hanging to his lower jaw a large fish, twenty feet long or so, from which he was thus in vain endeavouring to free himself! We had no little cause to be alarmed, as he drew near, for the safety of the ship herself; for, in the blindness of his agony, he might unintentionally strike her, or he might rush against her side to get rid of his pertinacious enemy. More than once the whale threw himself completely out of the water; but the fish still hung on to his bleeding jaw. Together they fell again into the sea, while all around them was stained of a crimson hue from the blood so copiously flowing from the worried monster.

"That's a killer!" cried old Tom. "He'll not let go the whale till he has him in his flurry, and then he and his mates will make a feast of him. They have great strong teeth, bigger than a shark's, and are the most voracious fish I ever saw. They bait a whale just as dogs do a wild beast, or a bull, and seldom fail to kill him if they once get hold of him."

This killer had a long dorsal fin, and a brown back and white belly. On came the whale and the fish, twisting and turning as before. We all stood ready to try and send them off—though very little use that would have been, I own. Happily they floundered by just astern of the ship; but so violent were their movements, and by such a mass of foam and blood were they surrounded, that it was difficult to observe the appearance of the killer. Equally impossible would it have been to have approached the whale to harpoon him without an almost certainty of losing the boat and the lives of all her crew. We could, therefore, only hope that the whale might be conquered when still within sight, so that the boats might carry off the prize from the relentless killer. Away went the monster and his tormentor. Soon we could no longer distinguish them from the deck; but on going aloft, we again caught sight of them, still floundering on as before.

"That fish gives us a lesson of what pertinacity will accomplish, even in conquering the greatest of difficulties," observed Newman, laughing. "I admire the way in which he sticks to his object. He has made up his mind to kill the whale, and kill the whale he will."

"Ay, and eat him too, Ned, as he deserves," said old Knowles. "Some of us might learn a lesson from that fish, I'm thinking."

"I have been killing whales all my life," Newman remarked to me with a forced laugh. "But somehow or other, Jack, I never have found out how to eat them."

"Overcoming difficulties, but not benefiting by them!" said I. "There must be a fault somewhere."

"Ay, Jack, ay—a fault in myself, and a curse well-deserved," he answered, bitterly, and then was silent. I never before had heard him speak in that way, and I did not venture to ask for an explanation.

That saying of Newman became common ever afterwards on board, when we saw a man determined to do a thing—"Kill the whale he will!"

I have often thought since, how seldom sailors, especially, learn to eat whales. What sums of money they make and throw carelessly away!— amply sufficient to enable them to pass the end of their days in comfort on shore, or to provide respectably for their families, instead, as is often the case with the merchant-seaman, ending their days in a poor-house, or leaving their families to the cold charity of the world. Brother seamen, learn wisdom! Prepare for the future of this life; and, more than all, prepare for the life to come.

Two of the whales chased were captured and brought alongside, when we set to work to cut-in and try-out with all the rapidity we could exert. In those high southern latitudes the weather is very variable, and we knew that a change might come and deprive us of our prey. We were, however, fortunate in securing both whales, and between them they gave us one hundred and sixty barrels of fine oil. Before, however, the boats had returned with their prizes, the whale and the killer had got far out of sight even from the mast-head. We continued for some time fishing in those quarters, amply rewarded for the dangers we had encountered by the success we met with. Sometimes, however, we were days and days together without even seeing a whale; and several were lost, after chasing them with much toil and difficulty.

Newman contributed much all the time to keep the people in good humour, by always finding them employment; and Captain Carr, unlike some masters I have met with, afforded him every assistance in his plans. Among other things, he established regular classes below, and, with the exception of one or two very idle, stupid fellows, all the crew belonged to one or other of them. Besides a reading and writing class, he had an arithmetic and geography class, and a music and a drawing class. His singing class was the most numerous, and he very soon taught nearly all hands to sing together in admirable tune and time. I at first exclusively attended the reading and writing class, devoting every moment I was off duty to my books; so that, much to my own surprise and delight, I soon found that I could read with ease and satisfaction. Writing was a more difficult task: to one whose fingers had never been accustomed to the cramped position required for holding a pen. Still, Newman had a way of overcoming that difficulty. Making me throw the weight of my body on my left side, he left my right hand and fingers free, and kept me for some time with a dry pen simply moving up and down across the page. Even when I had begun to form letters, at the commencement of every lesson he made me follow this plan for a few minutes, that, as he said, I might get my fingers into training before I disfigured the paper and became disgusted with my own performance. He himself seemed never to grow weary of teaching. No ignorance or stupidity daunted him; and it used to surprise me that a man of such extensive information and extraordinary talents, should take the trouble of imparting knowledge to people who were so immeasurably his inferiors. I used to observe, from the first, that he was never for a moment idle. "Ned must always be doing something or other," old Tom observed of him. "It's all the better for him that he is afloat. If he were on shore, he would be doing mischief." His great object seemed to be to fly from himself. Sometimes, when I was talking with him, from the strangeness of his remarks, and from his bursts of feeling, I thought that there must be a touch of madness about him; but then, again, immediately afterwards, he would say something so full of thought and sense, that I banished the idea.

To me he proved the greatest blessing. I was becoming a new character. I had discovered powers within me of which I before had no conception. I had gone on through life, if not rejoicing in my ignorance, at least indifferent to it. I had picked up a certain amount of knowledge from the conversation of others, but it was ill-digested, and I was full of the grossest prejudices. I have scarcely, indeed, given a correct notion of what I was up to this time. I might describe myself just as I once heard a shipmate spoken of—as *just an ignorant common sailor*. Such I had been. I could now read. I could dive into the rich stores collected by other minds, and make them my own. Without robbing others, I could appropriate their wealth, and enjoy all the benefits it could afford. Once having begun to read, the taste grew on me. I read through and through every book Newman possessed.

After a time, as his talents came to be known and appreciated by the captain, and officers, and surgeon, he was able to borrow books from them, which he allowed me to read. Although not many of them were very enlightening, they served to show me my own ignorance from the allusions they made, which I was totally unable to comprehend; and this only made me desire to gain further information, which it was somewhat difficult to obtain. As to Newman himself, he literally devoured every book which came in his way. He soon read through every book to be found on board; and whenever we fell in with another ship, he used to borrow all he could, or exchange his own books for others. Unfortunately, the literature in those days to be found at sea was generally of a very inferior character, and not at all calculated to improve its readers. Still, some knowledge was gleaned from all but the worst, and some errors and prejudices corrected. Newman had, however, certain favourites among his books, both English and foreign, which he would on no account have parted with. These he used frequently to read to me in our spare hours, or when we were engaged in such work as required our hands alone to be employed. I observed, indeed, after a little time, that we had far less employment found for us than had been the case in other ships on board which I had served; and this, I suspect, was because we found it for ourselves, or rather Newman found it for us. I never met with men so contented and happy as we all became; and this I could only account for by supposing that we were interested in our various occupations.

Newman was also the great peacemaker on board. Whenever a dispute arose, he always inquired the point at issue, and, without allowing time for the temper of either party to become irritated, he generally contrived to settle the matter. If he could not manage that, he used to try and raise a laugh by some absurd observation, or would place the position assumed by one man or the other in so ridiculous a light, that he seldom failed to show him that he was wrong.

One thing I remarked about Newman was, that he never alluded to any religious subject. I never saw him pray. He had no Bible or Prayer-book with him. I never heard him give utterance to a sentiment of piety, or of trust in God's mercy or fear of his anger. I did, on the contrary, frequently hear him praise the Greek and Roman philosophers of old, and he often spoke of the stoicism and heroism of the heathens. Still he neither blasphemed, nor cursed, nor swore, nor did he ever attempt to instil any infidel notions into the minds of any of us. However, I fear that he was, to all intents and purposes, a heathen. I doubt, indeed, whether he ever had any religion. I suspect that he was brought up without any; and that at no time, during the period he was gaining his education, did he meet with anyone to instruct him. I could not even then help contrasting the confiding piety and true religion of my old shipmates, Peter Poplar and Captain Gale, with the entire want of it which he displayed.

Indeed, Captain Carr, though a kind and worthy man, and a good sailor, was sadly unenlightened as to the truth; and all the years I served with him we neither had prayers nor any religious observance whatever on board. On a Sunday, if the weather was fine, and no whales were in sight, we put on clean clothes, mended and washed our old ones, and had an additional glass of grog served out, with less work than usual given us to do. On board most South-Seamen every day in the week was much the same. It was a fact, I fear, and one painful to contemplate, that Newman, with all his great and varied talents, lived on as if there were no God in the world. I do not mention this without a purpose. It seems strange that it was from such a man I received the instruction which enabled me ultimately to attain to a knowledge of, and active belief in, the truth. It shows by what varied instruments God works to bring about his gracious purposes. It convinced me of the power and effect of grace. Here was I, sunk deep myself in ignorance, and living among those who were equally unaware of the truth, called out of darkness into His marvellous light. But I am anticipating events.

We continued cruising near the Antarctic Circle during the few short months of summer with unvaried success. We had frequent displays at night of the Aurora Australis. Sometimes the whole southern hemisphere would be covered with arches of a beautiful straw-colour, from which streamers would radiate, both upwards and downwards, of a pure glittering white. The stars would be glittering brightly overhead; while, from east-south-east to west-north-west, a number of concentric arches would appear, forming a complete canopy in the sky; then suddenly they would vanish, again shortly to appear. Some nights it appeared in the form of cumuli, tinged with pale yellow; and behind them arose brilliant red, purple, orange, and yellow tints, streaming upwards in innumerable radiations, with every combination of shade which these colours could produce. Another night we saw a bright crescent, and from it feathery-edged rays, of a pale orange colour, branched off in every direction, while across it a succession of the prismatic colours appeared rapidly to flit. Indeed, it is difficult to describe the various forms which the Aurora assumes.

One of the most curious sights I ever beheld we witnessed some time after this. It was the appearance of the sun and moon above the horizon at the same time: the moon, which was nearly full, throwing her light—stolen from the sun, which blazed forth at the same time—on the world of icebergs. It was as if we had been looking on two distinct scenes. On one side, the bright rays of the luminary of day were throwing a golden hue on the vast mountain masses of ice which floated on the blue waters; on the other, the pale orb of night cast a silvery fringe on the clouds which surrounded it. There was, indeed, no night; the binnacle-lamp was not even lighted; and we were able to continue, without cessation, trying-out a whale, whose carcase floated alongside. Among other curious things I observed, were large masses of rock—boulders they are called—embedded in the base and centre of icebergs. It shows that they must originally have been formed on shore, and then floated away by some unusually high-tide or commotion of the sea. It explains also the appearance of boulders in places where it would be difficult otherwise to account for their being found.

I have seen birds in great numbers on rocks in the ocean, in different parts of the globe, but never have I beheld so many as there were on an island we one day sighted before steering north. There was but little wind, and as the captain thought a supply of birds, although of a somewhat fishy taste, would be an acceptable addition to our daily fare of salt junk and salt pork, he directed the third mate, with Newman, me, and four other men, to take a boat and bring off as many as we could kill. Calm as it was, the surf rolled so heavily in on the rocks that it was a work of no little difficulty and danger to approach them so as to gain a footing out of the reach of the waves. The mate ordered an anchor to be let go, and, veering away on the cable, we dropped gradually in; and while, boat-hook in hand, one at a time leaped on shore, the boat-keepers with their oars kept the boat head to sea, and as soon as we had landed, which we did not succeed in doing without a thorough ducking, they hauled the boat off beyond the breakers.

The island on which we stood was a wild, desolate place. Not a tree or a shrub was to be seen; but the hills, which rose to a considerable height above the ocean, were covered with a long thick grass, of a character similar to what grows on the Falkland Islands. Here and there dark rocks cropped out, and the sides of the island were formed in many parts of lofty, precipitous cliffs; while in others, such as the place we had landed on, were rugged rocks sloping gradually down to the sea. A thick fringe of kelp, a slippery sort of sea-weed, added somewhat to the difficulties of our landing. As we advanced, we were assailed by the most frightful gabbling, and screeching, and quacking I ever heard, from thousands and thousands of wild-fowls, chiefly penguins of various species. The whole hillside was literally covered with them and their eggs in dense masses. Nothing daunted at our appearance, when they found that the hubbub they made could not compel us to retreat, they commenced a fierce attack on us with their beaks, pulling at our trousers and pecking at our flesh. In our own defence we were obliged to lay about us with the boat's stretchers, and to knock them right and left on the head. Some, however, took warning from the fate of their companions; but while those at a distance gabbled and screeched louder than ever, those in the front waddled boldly up to the assault. As far as we could judge, we must have slaughtered the whole colony, or been pecked to death by them if we had attempted to sit down to rest. Every inch of their native soil, like true patriots, they bravely disputed with us; and when any of us, for fun, retreated, to see what they would do, they advanced erect and determined, rolling their heads from side to side in the most comical way, their power of vision residing only in the lower part of each eye. Then they would throw their heads backwards, and utter sounds very like the braying of a jackass; from which circumstance they have been called the Jackass Penguins. All the time, their little wings were actively employed as legs to expedite their movements. When in the water, they use their wings as fins to dive. When they rise again after a dive, they come up with so sudden a dash, instantly being down again, that it is often difficult to say whether they are fish or fowl. The most acceptable part of the spoils were their eggs, which we picked up in great quantities, and stowed away for safety in our caps and hats. Newman and I being in advance of the party, came upon a large rock, on and about which were perched a number of much larger birds than those we had seen below. They sat quietly looking at us till we approached, and then they commenced scolding us as the others had done. They appeared to be arranged in the most perfect order, in ranks like those of an army, each class being by themselves. In one place were hen-birds sitting on their eggs; in another, the mother-birds tending their newly-hatched young; while their mates were away over the ocean fishing for their dinners—a labour in which the hens very soon assist their partners. The moulting birds sit by themselves; and the bachelors, I conclude, have also to dwell in solitude. When we frightened the sitting-hens, we observed that they had a peculiar way of lifting up their eggs between their legs, and waddling off with them. These birds which were much larger than those seen below, are called King Penguins. We each carried off one over our shoulders as trophies.

After we left the ship, another boat was lowered to attack some sea-lions, which had been observed on a rock a little way off. We saw our shipmates commencing the attack as we went up the hill. Several were harpooned. One huge monster, notwithstanding a severe wound, managed to make his escape. As we returned down the hill, we found ourselves at the edge of a deep gully, into which the sea dashed, leaping up on either side, but leaving in the centre a space of comparatively clear water. As we looked down into it, we saw it curiously disturbed, and soon there rose to the surface two monsters, which seemed to be attacking each other with the greatest fury. We could have no doubt that they were sea-lions; and from the blood which flowed from the neck of one of them, we guessed that he was the one we had seen wounded. No animals on shore could have fought more desperately, although their teeth alone could be used as weapons of assault. They swam at each other, seizing each other's snouts, and fins, and lips, and struggled, and turned, and floundered about, till a big sea rushing up, carried both of them out of our sight.

"Such are human combats," observed Newman, with one of his peculiar laughs. "The sharks or the birds of prey will alone benefit by their folly."

While we were speaking, we saw several huge albatrosses flying, at the speed almost of lightning, towards the island. Instantly they pounced down on some of the birds we had killed; but finding that they had not yet a sufficiently high flavour to suit their palates, they picked up some of the eggs which we had compelled the jackass penguins to desert, and flew off with them, it was impossible to say where. We returned to the ship with a boat-load of birds and eggs, but not without a thorough ducking.

While I am on the subject of natural history, I will describe another species of seal, which we found on some islands on which we landed. We went on shore, as we had before done, armed with clubs and lances, to capture some of them. It required a knowledge of their inert and slothful character to give us courage to attack them with the weapons which we possessed, for in size and appearance they were most formidable-looking monsters. They were from twenty-five to thirty feet long, and some eighteen feet in circumference. Their heads are armed with large tusks and formidable teeth, and the male has the power of elongating the upper lip into the form of a proboscis, from which circumstance they are called sea-elephants. They are only found in those regions in the summer, as they migrate into warmer latitudes in the winter. We very quickly dispatched a number of them with blows on the head, and then towed them off to the ship, where each produced some eighty gallons of oil. Their skins also, which are of great use for many purposes, were preserved.

The nights were again shortening, when, just before dark, it came on to blow hard. Sail was taken off the ship, and those with the best eyes on board were stationed on each bow and at the bowsprit-end, to give notice of any dangers in sight. We were standing to the westward, going free, our captain intending soon to haul up for the northward. It was the darkest part of the still short night, when the lookers-out ahead gave notice that they heard the crashing sound of ice grinding together. Directly afterwards the words "Ice ahead!" echoed along the deck. Immediately the starboard tacks were hauled aboard, and the ship was kept to the northward.

Again the startling cry was heard, "Ice on the lee-bow!" then "Ice ahead!" The ship had good way on her. The helm was put down. We flew to the tacks and sheets, and about she came, her counter actually grazing a sheet of ice, against which in another moment she would have struck! We could now only steer to the southward, where we knew more ice must be found, so that we must speedily be about again. It was necessary to keep sufficient sail on the ship to enable us to work her quickly.

On we stood into the darkness, with a knowledge that danger was ahead of us. "Ice! ice ahead!" was again the cry. We wore about, but just in time to escape contact with it. We could not tell all the time whether the ice-fields might not be closing on us. Every tack we made was shorter and shorter. Still, our only hope was to beat out of the narrow passage into which the ship had run.

Many tacks were made. A huge iceberg, dimly glimmering through the obscurity, towered up before us; yet, though dim, not the less terrific. The helm was put down. There might be space between it and the field-ice to the southward of it. The southern field hove in sight; we tacked, but just in time. Then on we rushed towards the iceberg, beating closely into the wind. Again it appeared on our lee-bow; the ship heeled over to the breeze. On we rushed—a flaw of wind heading us would send us to destruction. The wind held steady.

On, on we rushed, the foam flying over our bows and freezing as it fell. A towering cliff of ice appeared over our mast-heads—still we hurried on. There was a loud thundering clash. The stoutest held their breath for fear. Our deck was deluged with spray. Several quickly-following seas struck our stern, lifting the ship before them. The summit of the vast iceberg had fallen—perhaps by the concussion of the air as we moved under it. A moment later, and we should have been crushed to atoms—driven far, far down into the depths of the ocean! The iceberg was passed. It seemed to be guarding the portals of that narrow inlet. As the dawn came on, we could discover the ice trending away to leeward. All day we stood on, gradually increasing our distance from icebergs and fields of ice, till we had, to our no little satisfaction, left them far astern.

Chapter Nineteen
A Visit to Java

We had won many a prize from the vasty deep with no little toil, and visited many strange people living under burning suns, when we found ourselves at anchor in the Roads of Batavia, the capital of the large and fertile island of Java. It was taken by the English in the year 1811 from the Dutch, or rather from the French, who had temporary possession of it. The British fleet employed on the occasion was under the command of Admiral Sir Robert Stopford, and the army under that of General Wetherall and Colonel Gillespie. That admirable and talented man, Sir Stamford Raffles— the greatest benefactor the islands of the East had ever known, till Sir James Brooke followed in his footsteps, was then appointed governor, and had his counsels and prayers been followed, it would still have been a bright jewel in the British crown. Unhappily neither were heeded. His letters describing the fertility and unbounded resources, when properly developed, of that immense territory, remained unread, unopened at the Colonial Office; and at the general peace Java was cast back as a worthless trifle into the heap to be enjoyed by others, which England had gained by so much blood and treasure. The Dutch took possession, and very speedily re-established the system of close monopoly and grinding tyranny which the enlightened policy of Sir Stamford Raffles had abolished.

Newman had now so completely established himself in the good opinion of the captain, that he was treated more as an officer than a foremast-man, and whenever duty would allow, he was permitted to go on shore to visit whatever was worthy of notice. He looked upon me completely in the light of a pupil, in whose advancement he had the deepest interest. "Never mind how old you are," he used to say; "you will outlive me yet by many a year, and will have plenty of use for all the information you can pick up before you die." I little thought at the time how true his words would prove. He used in joke to call me hardy Old Jack; and certainly for many years I never had had an hour's illness. The truth is, that I was gifted with a sound constitution, and had avoided playing tricks with it, as a great number of people do, and then complain of the sicknesses with which they are afflicted, shutting their eyes to the fact that they have brought them on themselves entirely in consequence of their own folly.

While we lay at Batavia, I was constantly on shore with Newman. The Roads of Batavia are rather more than a quarter of a league from the city, and are guarded from the prevailing winds by a dozen small islands outside them. The ground on which the city stands bears evident signs of having been thrown up by the sea, but rises gradually to the mountains ten leagues off behind it. The River Jacatra runs through the city, and it is intersected likewise in all directions by canals. It has also a moat running round it, as likewise a wall of coral-rock. Its defences consist of twenty bastions, and a castle near the sea, with a mud-bank in front of it. It is, indeed, completely a Dutch city. But besides its numberless canals and ditches, as it is situated in a dead marshy flat, and is surrounded with dirty fens, bogs, and morasses, over which a tropical sun sends down its burning rays, drawing up noxious vapours of every description, it may be considered, taken all in all, as one of the most unhealthy cities of the civilised world. By care and proper drainage these defects might be amended, and, as the general temperature of the atmosphere is not excessive, it might become as healthy as any other place in those regions.

Java is about two hundred miles long and forty broad, and has numerous deep inlets along the northern coast, where ships may anchor during the good or south-east monsoon. A chain of mountains, from which a number of rivers descend to the sea, runs down the centre, and divides the island into two parts. The air is cooled by the sea-breezes, which, as in the West Indies, set in every day. The soil is particularly rich. It is cultivated by buffaloes, and in some places one is sufficient to drag a plough. Java produces rice of a first-rate quality, sugar in abundance, cotton in considerable quantities, salt, timber, indigo, coffee, pepper, and various kinds of spices.

Java is, in reality, governed by the Dutch East India Company; but it is divided into a number of provinces, ruled over by puppet princes with the title of Sultan. At the court of each, one of the Company's chief officers, or head merchants, as they are called, resides. In some of the provinces these petty emperors have been deposed, and they are governed by one of the Company's officers, under the title of Resident. The religion of these princes is Mohammedan, as is that of the natives generally, though intermixed with many superstitious observances. No government rules a country with a more despotic system, or is more jealous of foreign interference with its trade. I suspect, also, that none has done more injury to the advancement of civilisation in the East, from their readiness to submit to all the absurd customs and degrading ceremonies imposed on them by the Chinese and other semi-barbarous nations, for the purpose of advancing their mercantile interests. Taught by them, these people look upon all Europeans as tribes of mean and despicable traders, who have neither the power nor the spirit to resent any injuries inflicted on them.

In the environs of Batavia are a number of villages, some inhabited by Malays, and others by Chinese, who visit the island in great numbers, and carry on a considerable trade, notwithstanding the persecutions to which they have at times been subject. In various beautiful spots, both near the city or the neighbouring hills, and along the sea-shore, are found the large and handsome country residences of the chief merchants and other authorities connected with the Company. There are five principal roads which lead from the city towards the country, and which are planted with high and shady trees. One of the most beautiful roads leading to the Port of Jacatra is closely planted with a double row of mango-trees, and both sides of it are embellished with large and pleasant gardens, and many fine and elegant buildings. All the roads are much of the same description, and give a character of finished cultivation to the neighbourhood of the city. Both sides of the streets, as well as of the numerous canals, are planted with fine trees, so that the country all round Batavia may well be characterised as a tropical Holland.

The governor-general usually resides at his country-seat, called Weltevreeden, a superb mansion, about an hour and a quarter's walk from the city. He there resides in great state, and never goes about without being attended by a body-guard, dressed in coats of scarlet cloth richly laced with gold.

The ordinary habitations of the Europeans are of brick, run up in a light airy manner, and stuccoed on the outside. They have sash-windows. The interiors are all on the same plan. The fronts are in general narrow, and the houses extend back a long way from the street. Fronting the entrance, a narrow passage, with a parlour on one side, leads to a large long room, lighted from an inner court, into which it opens. This apartment is called the "gallery," and here the family live and dine. The floors are of large, square, dark-red stones. No hangings are to be seen, but the walls are neatly stuccoed and whitened. The furniture consists of some arm-chairs and two or three sofas. On the walls are numerous looking-glasses, and chandeliers or lamps are hung in a row along the ceiling of the gallery, and are lighted up in the evening. The stairs leading to the upper rooms are generally at the end of the gallery. The upper parts of the houses are divided much as below. They are generally but scantily provided with furniture; indeed, from the heat of the climate but little is required. Behind the gallery are the lodgings for the slaves, the kitchen, and the out-houses. Instead of being glazed, the windows are often closed with a lath-work of rattans.

Few of those in the city have gardens. In the country, on the contrary, the greatest attention is paid to them, many of which are very beautiful, though laid out in the formal Dutch style, as they are full of the choicest flowers and shrubs. Newman was especially struck with them.

"Ah, this would indeed be a beautiful country to live in, if people could but manage not to die!" he exclaimed. Unhealthy as the country undoubtedly is, the city itself is far worse, so that, as a place of residence, it is almost abandoned by the more wealthy merchants, who only visit it as a place of business—their fine mansions being turned into stores or counting-houses.

Europeans at Batavia, of whatever nation, live much in the same way. They rise at daybreak, and sit for some time cooling themselves in the thinnest dress in which they have passed the night; then they dress, and breakfast on coffee or tea, and are at their offices at eight. They work till nearly noon, when they dine, and take a nap till four, when they again attend to business till six. Afterwards they drive out, or mix in social intercourse in an informal way till nine, when they sup, and retire to bed at eleven. Newman, whose means of observation were greater than mine, told me that the men had their parties together, and the ladies theirs, which I should consider a very bad arrangement. The men of higher rank—the upper merchants—are each attended by a slave, holding an umbrella behind him; but a junior merchant must carry his umbrella himself.

The women marry very young, are very ill-educated, and pass much of their time lolling on sofas, talking and laughing with their slaves, whom another moment they will order to be whipped for the slightest offence. Those born in the country have very supple joints, and can twist their fingers, hands, and arms in almost every direction. What can be expected from women who are abandoned, almost as soon as born, to the care of ignorant slaves—little or no care being taken to inculcate moral or religious principles into their plastic minds, till they have fully imbibed all the superstitious notions and prejudices which are held by their attendants? While saying this, I must urge parents at home never—if they value the eternal happiness of their children—if they wish them to imbibe right principles, and to avoid pernicious ones—to commit them to the charge of persons, however decent in their behaviour, who are not likely, from their want of education, to be able to instil them. Parents, children were given you by God; and at your hands he will require them. On your care, on your exertions, on your prayers, it depends whether they grow up a blessing to you and to themselves, or become miserable and lost. Still, children, nothing will exonerate you, when you become free agents, and understand good from evil, if you reject the good and choose the evil. You have more need for prayer, more need for exertion, more need for self-control, to conquer the vices which have grown up with you; and, believe Old Jack, however you may be weighed down with them, if you will but *try*, if you will but cast all your burden on Him who is alone able to bear it, you will succeed.

Provisions of all sorts we found abundant and cheap. The fruits are the cocoa, areca, banana, papaya, white and red shaddock, mangostan, rambootang, ananas, and betel. Saffron is collected there, and every description of allspice. The betel is a creeping-plant with an aromatic leaf. The natives spread over the leaf a little slaked-lime, and place at one end a small piece of areca-nut and cardamom. They then roll the leaf up, and masticate it for hours together. It blackens their teeth and reddens their lips, and gives an effect which the Chinese and Malays admire considerably.

Java abounds in serpents—the smallest is the most dangerous. Its bite is said to cause death. It is scarcely thicker than a candle, and from two to three feet long. They are of various colours:—some grey, spotted with white; and others green, with bright red and white streaks. We heard of one twenty feet long, and of the thickness of a man's arm; and saw another stuffed, as big round as the body of a man, and about fifteen feet long. The Javanese are likewise plagued with ants, and all sorts of creeping things.

Having given a faint sketch of the mode of life of the rulers of this wealth-giving island, I must briefly describe the native inhabitants, as also some of the numerous tribes which flock there from other quarters.

As I have already observed, the native princes, the nominal governors of the greater part of the country, are kept in the most perfect subjection by the Company; and the common Javanese are in the most abject state of slavery. The labourer is not only obliged, at fixed periods, to deliver a certain quantity of the fruits of his industry to the regent placed over him on behalf of the Company, for whatever price the latter chooses to allow him, and that price, moreover, paid in goods, which are charged to him at ten times their real value; but he likewise cannot consider what may remain as his own property, not being permitted to do with it what he may think fit, nor allowed to sell it to others at a higher or a lower rate; on the contrary, he is compelled to part with this also, as well as with what the Company claimed of him, to the same petty tyrant, at an arbitrary price, very much below its real value.

The Javanese, like all people living under a torrid zone and a despotic government, are of an indolent disposition, and, it is said, require great excitement to make them work; but the real secret of their idleness is the certainty that they will not be allowed to enjoy the fruits of their labour. Possessing no certain property, they are satisfied with little. The food of those who inhabit the level country is rice and fish; but those who dwell in the mountains use a root called *tallas*, with salt. This salt they make out of the ashes of wood. Their dwellings are little huts, constructed of bamboos, plastered with mud, and thatched with broad leaves. Their furniture consists of a bedstead made of bamboos, a block on which to pound their rice, two pots for boiling food, and a few cocoa-nut shells for drinking. They seldom live much beyond their fiftieth year. They were converted to Islamism about 1406, when the Arabian Chick-Ibn Molana came over, and, marrying the daughter of the king of Damak, received as her portion the province of Cheribon. Their mosques are generally of wood, and perfectly unadorned; but the tomb and mosque of the said Ibn Molana form a magnificent edifice. They do not place their dead in coffins, but wrap them in linen, and place a stone at the head and another at the foot of the grave, as seats for the two angels who, after their death, examine into their conduct while in this world.

The Javanese are, in general, well-shaped; of a light-brown colour; with black eyes and hair, their eyes being much sunk in the head. They have flattish noses and large mouths. In figure, they are generally thin, though muscular; here and there only a corpulent person being seen. The women, when young, have softer features than the men; but when they grow old, it is difficult to conceive any human being more hideous than they become. A man's dress consists of a pair of linen breeches, scarcely reaching half-way down the thighs, and over this a sort of shirt of blue or black coarse cotton cloth, which hangs loose below the knee. The hair of the head is bound up in a handkerchief, in the form of a turban. A woman's dress consists of a coarse chintz cloth, wrapped twice round the body, fastened under the bosom, and hanging down to the calf of the leg; over this is a short jacket, which reaches to the waist. No covering is worn on the head, but the hair is bound up in a fillet, and fastened at the back of the head with large pins. Sometimes chaplets of flowers are worn. Children run about without clothes till they are eight years old. Of course, I have been speaking only of the lower classes. The upper generally dress with great magnificence.

The Javanese are not much employed as domestic servants, but slaves have been brought from the coast of Bengal, Malabar, Sumatra, and other parts, as well as from Celebes, and often become very accomplished servants. They are generally well-treated, and behave well; but their great vice is gaming, to which they are tempted by the Chinese, who keep the gaming-houses, and are much too cunning to allow the poor slaves to regain what they may have lost. This vice, as is the case elsewhere, tempts them to rob their masters and to commit many other crimes, for the sake of supplying themselves with money to continue the practice, or to recover what they have lost.

There are said to be a hundred thousand Chinese in and about Batavia, the whole population amounting only to a hundred and sixty thousand, made up of natives, Armenians, Persians, Arabs, Malays, Negroes, and Europeans. We were witnesses of a curious spectacle one day, when the Chinese assembled from far and near to visit the tombs of their ancestors at Jacatra, near the site of the capital of that ancient kingdom. The road from Batavia to Jacatra is a very fine one. On either side it is adorned with magnificent palaces, occupied by the councillors of the Indies, the principal persons in the Company's service, and the richest merchants. In front of these palaces, parallel to the causeway, is a navigable canal crossed by bridges very ingeniously constructed of bamboo. On the opposite banks are numerous native villages, which are seen peeping through the cocoa, banana, papaya, and other bushy shrubs, with which every hut is surrounded. Near the ancient capital is the fortress to which the unhappy Prince of Genea withdrew when the Dutch conquered the kingdom, and where he lost his life fighting desperately.

In the Chinese burying-place are great numbers of tombs, with inscriptions specifying the time of the death, age, name, and virtues of those whose remains are within. The tombs are much ornamented, and surrounded with cypresses; and on either side are benches on which the relatives and friends may rest when they come to perform their funeral duties. On the present occasion the tombs were ornamented with wreaths of paper or silk of different colours, and three wax tapers were burning on each. Provisions, also, were either sent or brought, and placed as offerings on the tombs. The most opulent were distinguished from the rest by the richness of their viands—fish, fruit, sweetmeats, and beverages. These provisions, having been left for some hours on the tombs, were partly consumed by the family of the deceased, some was offered to the spectators, and the rest carried away. Roasted fowls, which had been kept whole on purpose, were, however, left behind by some; for what purpose I could not ascertain. These travelled Chinese had got over many of their national prejudices, and very politely offered Newman and me some of the good things; of which we partook with no little satisfaction, though, as my companion observed, a cemetery was an odd place to pic-nic in.

Movable theatres were erected on one side of the cemetery, and temples had been built on the plain below. These temples are large saloons, ornamented with grotesque and antique statues, especially those representing Josi in the midst of his family. Josi, a disciple of Confucius, and afterwards his most confidential friend, rose from the dregs of the people, and became the greatest legislator of his nation. After the death of Confucius, the emperor banished him; so he retired in the bosom of his family to the low state from which he had sprung, where he declared that he enjoyed far more true happiness than he had ever done in his exalted position. To him and his benignant laws the Chinese are indebted for the preservation of their manners, customs, and dress. He is always represented in his retirement after his labours for the public good were concluded. We had here, as Newman observed, an example of the way in which the ancients deified their great men, and learned to worship them.

Opposite each idol were burning red wax tapers, of different sizes, and matches of incense. An altar or table covered with dainties stood in the middle of the temple, surrounded by idols; and in a room behind it was another altar, surmounted with a statue of Josi. An old bonze or priest of venerable aspect, with a long white beard, stood up, reciting some prayers in a low voice. He had on his head a white straw-hat, in the shape of a cone. On the top of it was a little ball of gold, and behind a small tuft of red silk. He kept continually bowing with great regularity, and every now and then let fall a piece of wood like a ruler, which he as often picked up again. He was habited in a tunic of transparent violet silk, with a girdle of twisted silk ornamented with gold; and to it were attached the instruments required for the ceremony. Over this he wore a gold-embroidered robe, with long sleeves turned up at the wrists. It was of violet colour, and a strong material; and, being closed all round, must have been put on over the head. On his breast and back were two plates of rich gold embroidery, representing an eagle, or a bird like one. In his hand he had a large fan, the case of which hung at his girdle like a knife-sheath. His slippers were square at the toes, and embroidered with gold; but his legs were bare.

Under the vestibule of the temple, a hog and a goat, with the horns on, were killed as burnt-offerings, and placed on a stand, with their entrails before them. The interior of the temple was filled with tables covered with preserved fruits and tea, where the bonzes and rich people were sitting eating, drinking, and smoking; but none of the multitude ventured in. Many female bonzes, or bonzesses, were in the vestibule, dressed in violet silk robes, but without embroidery. Their hair was twisted and turned up behind, forming a round tuft, fastened with two diamond-headed pins. These tufts were stuck round with other very rich pins, forming the beams of a most brilliant sun. They took no part that we saw in the ceremonies.

What I have described seemed to be a prelude to the ceremonies. The bonzes, fifteen in number, left the vestry to the sound of shrill, noisy music. They took their stations before the altar, where they made many genuflexions and gestures. They then presented to the high-priest, who had no distinguishing mark, many meats which were on the altar. On this he made various signs, pronouncing some words in a whining tone of lamentation. After having made various libations with several liquors, which he spread over the offerings, the other bonzes replaced them on the altar. One of them then took a card, containing characters, from which he sung. Judging from the loud laughter of part of the auditory, the words seemed to have little analogy to the ceremony. Every bonze held in his hand a box filled with incense matches, one of which he lighted as soon as its predecessor was extinguished. After a repetition of this ceremony, during which the music was never discontinued, they entered the side-room to take refreshment. Having drunk their tea, they went in procession to a second temple, where the same ceremony was gone through. Thence they repaired to the theatre. When they had reached the front of it they halted. "Are they going to act?" said I. "I should not be surprised," observed Newman. "What are they but actors? The people, you see, have taken no part whatever in the matter." The chief bonze mounted the theatre alone, and having made many violent gestures and exclamations, again descended, when the performances began. During these ceremonies the gates of the temples, and both sides of the theatres, were filled with common Chinese, a large number of whom were children, playing different games of chance. I never saw people so fond of gaming as they are.

A part of the roasted poultry was left all night on the tombs, the common people imagining that at that period the dead assemble and eat it up. People in misfortune strew amulets over the graves of their ancestors, to obtain their favour. These amulets are bits of silk paper, on which are spread pieces of leaf silver, which they fancy passes current as a paper-money among the dead. I could not ascertain whether the hog and goat were actually offered up with any ceremony, or simply left to be devoured by the priests.

"Have you ever seen anything like this before?" asked Newman, as we were on our way back to the ship.

"Yes, I think I have," I answered.

"So have I," he remarked, "in a Roman Catholic church. The priests of Rome—ancient and modern—and these bonzes are much alike. They have both copied their ceremonies from the Jews and the heathens of old, travestying them somewhat, to make them pass for their own. Depend on it Josi understood human nature, and knew what would suit the taste of the vulgar."

So numerous are the Chinese in Java, and so inclined to revolt, that the Dutch government are always careful to provide them with amusements.

In each place there is a chief, with the title of "captain," who is answerable for their good conduct. He is obliged to maintain, at his own cost, a troop of female actors, called Bayadeers. They perform, without exception, every night, from nine o'clock till daybreak, in a kind of theatre, in the middle of the street. The play, as far as we could make out, represents the wars of the Tartars against the Chinese. Various chiefs, in different costumes, with their faces smeared black or white, or masked, come to announce a new war, in which they anticipate great success. They harangue the soldiers with violent gestures. Then comes a general or emperor, and, making another speech, gets up on a table with a chair on the top of it, when he takes his seat at the back of the stage. The combatants then come in with long spears, and, fighting desperately, one party runs away, while the other has to listen to a long speech on their bravery. The Tartars are known by their short coats, large trousers, helmets, sabres, and great shields. The roaring music of gom-goms never stops during the performance.

One day we visited the Chinese quarter, where there are an immense number of gaming and eating tables. The seats, as well as the tables, are made of bamboo. The Chinese eat with two little sticks, and use a spoon of china with a short crooked handle. Each article of food is served on a little dish like a saucer. The jelly, minced meats, and soup, are generally cold, while their beverages are hot. The chief is arrack, sugar, and hot water. The favourite dish is part of a dog, of a species with a smooth skin, which they carefully fatten. It is eaten with every kind of sauce. No people eat so much pork as the Chinese. The hundred thousand Chinese in Batavia are said to feed at least four hundred thousand pigs, which increase not a little the bad odours of the place. Whether they do it to keep the Jews at a distance, I do not know, but the two people do not get on well together.

We used to meet in the Chinese company, or quarter, curious processions of men, with marked or painted faces, having kettle-drums, gom-goms, and tambourines. Some, grotesquely dressed, were carried on poles or in hampers, ornamented with paper, ribbons, and little bells; some were seated on monsters, like our representations of sea-horses. These processions are in honour of the spirit of evil. The reason they give for them is, that as the Divinity is infinitely good, it is not necessary to implore him; but the devil, on the contrary, must be feasted and amused, to prevent him from going about and committing mischief. In every Chinese house, in a sort of shrine, is a picture of Confucius, represented as a great fat man, with the devil at his side tempting him. On each side are pots of flowers and tapers of red wax, gilt, which are lighted on certain days, together with a little lamp in front, just as is seen in Romish chapels.

Chinese girls are always shut up, and employed in sewing and embroidery; and parents arrange marriages without the couple having even seen each other. The poorer sort, however, are allowed to serve in their shops. We heard the people generally well spoken of, as being good fathers, sons, husbands, and friends. They carry on every art and traffic, and engross nearly all the house and ship building in Batavia, though they pay enormous annual duties to the Company on their industry and trade. Among other duties, they pay for being allowed to let their nails grow long, especially that of the little finger, as it is a proof that they do not work for their living. The twisted tail, which they wear extremely long, often down to their knees, pays in proportion to its length. It is measured every year at a fixed time. To cut off the tail of a Chinaman, or to pare his nails, is looked upon as a most severe punishment. Their dress consists of large trousers, and round coats, which reach to the middle of the thighs. It is either of black or very bright sky-blue. White is worn for mourning; and when for a very near relative, the collar has a rent in it. They have a custom of keeping their dead for some days in the house, which, in such a warm climate, frequently causes bad fevers. A Chinese house, where a death has happened, is known by a white cloth hung in lieu of the door.

This information, through Newman's help, I picked up during our visits on shore. The ship had been at anchor about a week, when we again went on shore, and had walked on for an hour or so, when, a little beyond Fort Ansol, we found ourselves in front of a Chinese temple, standing in a grove of cocoa-nut trees by the side of a rivulet, among very pretty scenery. The building was about twenty feet long, and twelve wide. The entrance was through a railing into a small area, and then into a hall, at the end of which was the sanctuary. In the middle of the hall, just within the door, was an altar, on which red wax tapers were burning. There was also an image of a lion, richly gilt. At the end of the hall was a picture of an old man and a woman, with crowns on their heads, and about two feet high. They were, I suppose, Josi and his wife. While we were there, several people came in, and prostrating themselves before the picture, knocked their heads continually against the ground. At last a man came in to consult the idols by divination. He had in his hand two small longitudinal pieces of wood, flat on one side, and round on the other. Holding these pieces of wood, with the flat sides toward each other, he let them fall on the ground. As they fell, with the flat or round side up, so he augured well or ill of some proposed enterprise or project. He let the sticks fall upwards of twenty times, but seemed as ill-contented as at first with the promises they made. Every time they prognosticated evil, he shook his head with a most disconsolate look. I could not help saying, "Try it again, Chinaman; don't give in." Whether he understood me or not I do not know, but down he went on the ground, and thumped his head very hard and often. Then he jumped up and threw the sticks, and I suppose the omen proved favourable, for with a joyful countenance he lighted a thick candle and placed it on the altar. As soon as he was gone, the cunning old bonze blew it out and sold it to the next comer.

We must not be surprised to hear that the Chinese at times revolt against the authority of the Europeans among whom they live, and commit murders and other atrocities; and then to hear of a cruel massacre committed by the Dutch upon them in Batavia. On one occasion, many thousands had collected; and some of them having been guilty of murders and robberies, a considerable apprehension was excited against the whole body. The Council, therefore, determined that every Chinese who could not prove that he was obtaining an honest livelihood, should be transported to Ceylon, to be employed as a slave in the service of the Company. Among others, a number of Chinese of wealth were seized; and a report getting abroad that all were to be thus treated, they flew to arms, and quitting the city in great numbers, took up their quarters in the mountains, and strengthened themselves so much as to render the fate of Batavia itself precarious.

In this dilemma the Council offered the rebels an amnesty; but this they refused, and marching towards the city, ravaged the country on every side. Here, however, they met with a severe repulse; and when the infuriated soldiers and sailors returned into the city, supposing that the Chinese who had remained quiet within their houses were about to revolt, they attacked them wherever they could be found. All the Chinese, men, women, and children, without distinction, were put to the sword; the prisoners in chains were slaughtered; and even some wealthy people, who had fled to Europeans for safety, were, through the violation of every principle of humanity and morality, delivered up to their sanguinary pursuers—the Europeans embezzling the property confided to them. Thus, all the Chinese, both innocent and guilty, were exterminated. Notwithstanding this, however, thousands rushed in soon after to supply their places! It was apprehended that this occurrence would excite the indignation of the Emperor of China, and, perhaps, induce him to stop their trade with his country; but when they sent deputies to apologise, their fears were shown to be groundless by his truly paternal reply,—to the effect that he was little solicitous for the fate of unworthy subjects, who, in the pursuit of lucre, had quitted their country, and abandoned the tombs of their ancestors!

Notwithstanding the unhealthiness of the climate, and the impediments thrown in the way of commerce by the unwise restrictions of the Dutch, the Roads of Batavia are always full of the flags of all nations, attracted by the profit merchants are still able to make. As Batavia is, or rather was, before

Singapore was established, the sole depot for the spices of the Moluccas and the productions of the island of Java, consisting of rice, coffee, sugar, arrack, and pepper, ships were coming continually from every part of India, Africa, and even Europe; and as they were not allowed to take away coin, they were compelled to fill up with some or other of the above-mentioned productions. The trade, indeed, was one almost exclusively of barter.

Bengal sent drugs, patnas, blue cloths, different kinds of stuffs, and opium; which were exchanged for rice, sugar, coffee, tea, spices, arrack, a small quantity of silks, and china-ware. The kings of Achen and Natal, in the island of Sumatra, sent camphor—the best which is known—benzoin, birds'-nests, calin, and elephants' teeth; and in return took opium, rice, patnas, and frocks, which were made at Java, Macassar, and the Moluccas. The princes of the Isle of Borneo sent gold dust, diamonds, and birds'-nests; and took opium, rice, patnas, frocks, gunpowder, and small guns, as they said, to defend themselves against pirates, but, in reality, for their own use as pirates.

The Americans brought kerseymeres, cloths, hats, gold-wire, silver-galloon, stationery, wine, beer, Seltzer water, provisions, and piastres; in exchange for spices, sugar, arrack, tea, coffee, rice, rushes, and Chinese silk and porcelain. The Muscat ships brought piastres and gum-arabic; those from the Isle of France, wine, olive-oil, vinegar, hams, cheese, soap, common trinkets, and ebony.

From the Cape of Good Hope were received kitchen-garden seeds, butter, Constantia and Madeira wines; while the Chinese brought immense quantities of porcelain and silks of every kind, taking in return opium, ebony, sandal-wood, spices, and birds'-nests. These nests are half the size of a woman's hand. They are made by a very small sea-swallow, (*Hirundo esculenta*), and consist of a glutinous substance, interwoven with filaments. They are found in the cavities of steep rocks on the coast of all the Sunda Islands, on the northern shores of Australia, and in many other parts of the Indian Seas. The native way of procuring them is by fixing a stick on the summit of the precipice, with a rope-ladder secured to it, whence the hunters descend in their search into the most perilous situations. Although they have neither taste nor smell, yet, from being supposed to be both tonic and a powerful stimulant, they are an ingredient in all the ragouts of the most wealthy people in China. They make an excellent broth. The white nests are most in request. They are prepared by being first washed in three or four changes of lukewarm water. When they have been some time in it, they puff up like large vermicelli. Europeans, indeed, discover nothing more in this singular dish than an insipid jelly, very much indeed resembling vermicelli, when simply boiled.

After Java was restored to the Dutch, England still carried on a considerable commerce with the island; but it is far smaller than it would be under a less restricted system.

The Dutch were for long the only European nation who kept up any commercial communication with Japan, because no other would submit to the absurd restrictions and degrading ceremonies imposed by that barbarian power. Every year, the governor-general sent a ship of fifteen hundred tons, laden with kerseymeres, fine cloths, clock-work, and spices. These were chiefly exchanged for bars of copper, which were made into a very clumsy kind of coin for paying the native and European troops, as well as the people employed in the counting-houses of Java and the Moluccas. These ingots are of the finest red copper, and as thick as the finger. They are cut into two, four, six, and eight sous-pieces of Holland. The value is inscribed on them. This coin is termed in the Malay language *baton*, which signifies a stone. The captain, however, brings back furniture, fans, various articles of copper, and sabres—the temper of the blades of which equals the best workmanship of Turkey. The cargo always contains a present to the emperor; and he, in return, sends one to the Dutch governor-general.

When the Batavian ship is seen, the emperor's agent hails it, to demand whether the captain is a Christian. He replies that he is Dutch, when a signal is made for him to approach. From that moment he is boarded by innumerable armed boats. He is first boarded to see that he has neither women nor books; for the law is very severe against the introduction of either into the island. Were either found on board, the ship would be sent back without being allowed to anchor. This visit concluded, the merchandise is landed, the ship is disarmed and unrigged without the aid of the captain or crew, and the guns and rigging are carried on shore. The captain transmits the bill of lading to the emperor's agent, with a note of what he desires in exchange, and waits quietly for the merchandise he is to have in return. Provisions are amply supplied in the meantime to the crew. When the return merchandise is ready on the beach, the emperor having notified what he chooses for the ensuing year, the Japanese themselves again load the vessel, replace her rigging, and restore her arms, papers, and effects, of which they took possession on her arrival. There is no instance of anything having been lost; indeed, the Dutch speak of the Japanese as a most honest people. They are said to leave their shops and stores without guards or clerks. If a Japanese goes to a shop, and finds no one there, he takes the article he wants, lays down the value marked on it, and goes out. All the streets of the towns are closed at night by iron gates, and each Japanese is responsible for his neighbour; so they are all interested that no harm should happen to one another. When a theft is committed in any quarter, and the author cannot be discovered, the crier, (who is a kind of police agent), the judge of the division, and the neighbours are compelled to make good the loss, and are subject to severe corporal punishment.

Very little in those days was known of the interior of Japan, as the Dutch ambassadors were compelled to submit to the most humiliating conditions to keep up their intercourse with the country. On visiting the capital, they were conveyed in palanquins, well enclosed with fixed lattice-work, like prison-vans in England; and the bearers dared not, for fear of their lives, indulge them with a view of the country through which they passed. This information about Japan Newman gained from one of the officers of the ship trading there. To return to Java.

One day when we were on shore, we saw a great confusion among the crowd, who were dispersing on every side, as if in mortal dread of something; and presently we saw a half-naked Malay with a long dagger in his hand, striking right and left at everybody he met, killing some and wounding others. As he ran on, crying out in his frenzy, "Amok—amok—amok! kill—kill—kill!" we saw some of the police dashing towards him with long poles, at the end of which was a fork of wood with iron spikes inside it. He dodged by several of them, killing one on his way, till at last a guard met him full in front, and he ran in on the fork, when he was immediately pinned to the ground; but even then he struck out on every side with his glittering weapon.

This is what is called running a *muck*! from the word used *amok*—kill! He had, as is the custom, taken a large quantity of opium, and thus excited himself to fury in consequence of some supposed or real injury he had received from his master! Most of these mucks are run by slaves brought from Celebes. Being mortally wounded, he was immediately broken alive on the wheel, in the presence of two councillors of justice.

It is remarkable, that at Batavia, where the assassins, when taken alive, are broken on the wheel, the mucks are of great frequency; while at Bencoolen, where they are executed in the most simple and least cruel way, they seldom occur. Slaves who have murdered their masters, were executed with the most horrible barbarity by being impaled. An iron was passed down their backs, so as not to touch any vital part, and by it they were suspended, one end of the iron rod being fixed in a post ten feet from the ground. If the weather is dry, they may live on many days in that horrid position; but if water enters the wound, mortification ensues, and they quickly die.

The Javanese emperors used till lately to throw their criminals to wild beasts, or compelled them to enter into combat with them. I heard a story of a Javanese who was condemned to be torn in pieces by tigers. On being thrown down from the top of a large cage, he fell across the back of the largest and fiercest of them, where he sat astride! So intimidated was the animal, that he did not attempt to injure him; while the others, awed by the unusual appearance, endeavoured to avoid him! The poor wretch, however, having been condemned to death, was shot dead in the cage. This custom was, however, prohibited by the French. Of course I have been speaking of a state of things as they existed some years ago, and I daresay some improvements have taken place; but at the same time the Dutch are of a very conservative disposition, and I suspect that most of my descriptions would be found correct even at the present day.

Chapter Twenty
Strange Adventures and Naval Exploits

Not very long before we sailed, Newman and I had gone on shore, he taking a large sketch-book under his arm; and striking up into the country, we reached a beautiful spot, the outlines of which he wished to commit to paper. We sat ourselves down under the shade of a wide-spreading palm, not far from the road. While Newman took the sketch with his pencil, and in a masterly way threw in the colours, I read to him from a volume, I think, of the "Spectator." During this time a gentleman, attended by two servants in handsome liveries rode by. Seeing two common sailors, as our dresses showed we were, employed in a way so unusual, he dismounted, and, prompted by curiosity, came to see what the draughtsman had produced. He had been watching us for more than a minute before Newman observed him. Newman had a quick, prompt manner in addressing people, which arose somewhat from pride, I suspect, lest they should look down upon him; and seeing a stranger, he at once spoke to him in German, remarking on the beauty of the scenery. The gentleman stared at being thus addressed, but replied in the same language, asking leave to look at the sketch he had just finished. Newman frankly showed him that and several others, which the stranger admired.

"You are a German, I presume?" said the gentleman.

Newman replied that he was an Englishman.

"You speak Dutch also, perhaps?" asked the stranger.

"Slightly," said Newman; "but I prefer German, though I am more fluent in French."

"Ah, that is a tongue I am fond of," remarked the gentleman. "But may I ask where you picked up your knowledge of languages?"

"In the world," replied Newman, carelessly. "'Tis a large book, and its leaves are never closed."

"I am afraid that you will think me impertinent if I continue to ask questions," said the stranger; "but I shall be glad to know to what ship you belong?"

Newman told him.

"Ah, I know your captain—an honest man. I am under great obligations to him. Are many of his crew able to amuse themselves as you two appear to be doing?"

"Some have lately taken to drawing and singing, and a few who could not read when the voyage began are now apt scholars," answered Newman, carelessly. "We have occasionally a good deal of spare time on board a whaler, though we often have to work hard enough."

A little further conversation passed. "I must not longer detain you from your task," said the gentleman. "I hope that we shall meet again."

He bowed to Newman, and nodded good-naturedly to me. He saw that I was but a common sailor, at the same time that he evidently discerned the educated gentleman in my friend. When I speak of Newman as a gentleman, it must be understood that he was not particularly polished or refined in his manners or habits, though more so far than were those with whom he associated forward. His manners were too blunt and independent to be called polished, and he could rough it as well as any of us, eating the same coarse food and wearing the same rough clothes as we did, without inconvenience.

When the gentleman had gone, Newman and I discussed who he could be. "Rather an inquisitive old fellow, I suspect," said Newman. "He is a Dutchman, I judge, by the way he pronounced both German and French, though he spoke them well."

"How are you so well able to distinguish the difference in pronunciation?" I asked.

"I was educated in Germany," he answered. "I learned a good many things there besides what my tutors intended to teach me. You must not suppose that I could have picked up the various bits of information I possess in any English place of education. As it is, we beat most other nations in whatever we set our hands to; but if English lads had the same style of instruction given in most of the countries in Europe, modified to suit our characters, we should beat them all hollow, wherever we encountered them abroad."

It must be remembered that this conversation took place many years ago, and that very considerable improvements have since taken place in the style of education afforded to boys in many of our schools in England.

We thought very little at the time of our encounter with the Dutch gentleman, though, as it proved, it had a very great influence on Newman's fate.

When we got on board, we found that the ship was likely to remain some time longer in the Roads, and that we might have a chance of seeing something more of the country. As Malays, or natives, are employed in those hot climates to do the hard work on board ship, as Kroomen are on the coast of Africa—such as wooding and watering—we had more leisure time than we should otherwise have enjoyed. That evening a number of us, among whom was Tom Knowles, were sitting on the forecastle spinning yarns, when he told us what I did not know before—that he had served aboard a man-of-war at the taking of Java.

"You must know, mates," he began, taking out his quid and stowing it away in his waistcoat-pocket, "I belonged to a whaler which was lost out here, when those of her crew who escaped were picked up by an Indiaman and carried to Madras. I with others was there pressed on board the *Caroline* frigate. I didn't much like it at first; but when I had shaken myself, and looked about me, and heard that the captain was a fine sort of a fellow, I thought it was just as well to do my duty like a man, and to make myself happy. Captain Cole, that was his name, wasn't a chap to let the grass grow under the ship's bottom. Directly after I joined, we were ordered off to Amboyna, in company with the *Piemontaise*, Captain Foote; the 18-gun brig *Barracouta*; and transport *Mandarin*, with a hundred European soldiers. We heard that when the captain went to take his leave of the admiral— Drury was his name—he asked leave just to knock up some of the Dutch settlements on the way.

"'Well,' says the admiral, 'there's no harm just frightening them a little, and you may be able to surprise a port or two; but don't go and get into mischief, now, and hurt yourselves. There are several impregnable places, such as Banda, for instance, which it would be out of the question for you to attack. Vast heaps of wealth are stored up there, so the Dutch will take precious good care that you don't get into the place.'

"'We'll see about that,' thought the captain to himself, winking with the eye which was turned away from the admiral. 'Of course, sir, we'll do nothing rash,' says he. 'It isn't the way of English sailors. We are always steady, sure sort of fellows.'

"'That's right,' says the admiral; and away went the captain, having made up his mind to a thing or two.

"We reached Palo-Penang on the 30th May, in the year 1810. There the captain persuaded the governor to let him have about twenty artillery-men and a lot of scaling-ladders; and having learned something more about the chief place in Banda, called Banda-Neira, he kept to the resolution he had all along in his mind, to try and get possession of it. In spite of the south-east monsoon, away we sailed, therefore, for the Java Sea. As it would not have done to let the Dutchmen in other places guess what we were about to do, he determined to take the ship through the passage between the big island of Borneo and Malwalli. It was a touch-and-go matter to get through, for in every direction there were coral-reefs, which would pretty soon have brought us up if we had run on them; but we had look-outs at the jib-boom-end and the topsail-yard-arms, and as the water was clear, and the weather fine, we escaped all danger.

"Early in the morning, on the 8th of July, we made the Banda Islands, and by night were up with the place called Banda-Neira. As we stood in, the guns from the fort opened on us; but seeing they did us no harm, they soon left off throwing away their powder. That very evening there was a sudden change in the weather, and it came on to blow and rain very hard.

"'Too good a chance to be thrown away,' thought the captain. 'We shall never be able to take this place in common ship-shape fashion; but as the Mynheers won't be expecting us on such a bad night as this, and what's more, won't hear us coming, I'll just see if we can't get on shore in the boats and give them a surprise.'

"Now, anyone looking at Banda-Neira would have thought that it would be quite impossible to take it with the small force we had got with us; but, as I said, our captain wasn't a man to trouble his head about impossibilities.

"The place was two miles long and half a mile wide, and protected by no less than ten sea-batteries and two strong forts—one called Belgica, and the other Nassau. They commanded each other, as they did the ten sea-batteries. The first alone mounted fifty-two heavy guns; and altogether there were no less than one hundred and thirty-eight guns in the place. Having run in within two cables' length of the shore, we dropped our anchors, and at 11 p.m. the boats under the command of Captain Cole shoved off with three hundred and ninety men, including officers. The place we were to pull for was the east point of Banda. What a night it was—blowing and raining like fury and dark as pitch! but that, in many respects, was all the better for us. Captains Cole and Kenah arrived first at the appointed spot in their gigs, and only by degrees did some of the other boats get up there—it was so difficult to find our way. The boat I was in, with several others, grounded on a coral-reef, not a hundred yards from a sea-battery, which we found mounted no less than ten long 18-pounders; and as they pointed directly on the reef, they could very soon have knocked us all to pieces. Fortunately, the garrison slept so soundly, or the rain and wind made such a clatter, that they did not discover us. Overboard we all jumped, and soon had the boats afloat, and pulling on, we reached a snug little sandy cove, surrounded by trees or jungle. Here the captain mustered us, and found that he had only got about a hundred and forty seamen and marines, and forty red jackets, with Captain Kenah, five lieutenants, and some soldier officers. Among the lieutenants was one called Lieutenant Edmund Lyons, with whom I afterwards was at the taking of another place, of which I'll tell you presently. Well, as I was saying, it was pelting and blowing and as black as pitch; and though we had little more than half our force on shore, our captain did not like to give up the enterprise, so says he, 'My lads, I should just like to take possession of some of these forts, but we are a small number to do it, I own; yet, if I thought all would follow, I'd lead the way.'

"We didn't shout, but we told him that, to a man, we were ready to go wherever he thought fit to lead us.

"'Then,' said he, 'we'll just walk into the Dutchmen's castles before they've time to rub their eyes.'

"Captain Kenah, with a party of us armed with pikes, on this at once advanced to the rear of the nearest battery. Not a word was spoken, and the noise of the storm drowned the sound of our footsteps. We got close up to the fort—a sentry was marching up and down—a pike was into him before he could discharge his musket—and in an instant we were over the ramparts. We could see the Dutchmen, match in hand, at their guns on the sea side, and very much surprised were they to find us in their rear, knocking them down right and left, before they had time to fire a shot. They cried for quarter, and we had sixty of them prisoners in a few minutes. Leaving a few men to take charge of the battery, Captain Kenah was pushing on to take possession of the next, when Captain Cole sent to say he had got hold of a guide, and was going to take Fort Belgica itself.

"Away we went along a narrow winding path, towards the castle. The Dutchmen's bugles were sounding in all directions, showing us that they were awake; but probably they didn't know where their enemies were to be found. We had got close up to the citadel before we were discovered; and then, though they began firing away pretty briskly, as they could not see us, and were, I guess, in a mortal fright, none of us were hit. Those in front had the scaling-ladders, and, with their help, we managed to climb up the steep bank on which the castle stood; and in no time, it seemed, we were in possession of all the lower works. We were not in though yet; but we soon hauled up the scaling-ladders, and began to place them against the wall of the citadel, when we found out that they were too short—more's the shame to the fellows who made them! The enemy discovering this, began peppering away at us with musketry, and fired several round-shot into the bargain. Here was a sell! We began to think that we should have to be about-ship, when what should we see, but the gates open to let in the governor and some other officers who had been sleeping outside the walls. The opportunity was not to be lost. Led by our gallant captain, we made a dash at the gate. The colonel defended it bravely, but he and several of his men were killed in a minute, and on we rushed into the very centre of the fort. Never were fellows in such a mortal fright as were the Dutchmen. Daylight just then breaking, we saw them scrambling and leaping, like a flock of sheep, over the walls. However, some of the officers, and forty artillery-men, gave themselves up as prisoners.

"We now had the British Jack flying away on the flagstaff above our heads. Still, we were a very small band to hold the forts we had conquered, and we looked out with no little anxiety for the arrival of the rest of our force. What had become of the boats we could not tell; but as the sun rose, we saw the *Caroline* and the other ships standing in towards the town.

"The Dutchmen did not know our numbers, probably; so the captain, putting a bold face on the matter, sent a flag of truce to Fort Nassau, to say that if the troops didn't behave themselves, and cease firing, he would fire into them with a vengeance, and into the city to boot. Now, from what we had done, the Dutchmen, having no doubt that he would keep his word, hauled down their flag; and before many hours were out, thinking discretion the best part of valour, their whole force, regulars and militia, to the number of one thousand and five hundred, laid down their arms on the glacis of Fort Nassau. Thus you see what a few brave men, when well led, can do.

"Of our one hundred and eighty men, we lost very few. Our less fortunate shipmates in the boats, after knocking about all night, got alongside the transport *Mandarin*. Captain Foote was left as governor of the island with a garrison, while we went on to Amboyna. Our captain was a fine fellow. The ship's company afterwards presented him with a sword worth a hundred guineas, to show their love and estimation of his bravery. Several cups and swords were presented to him by the officers and soldiers. I can't tell you what loads of prize-money we got from that place, but I can tell you that it very soon found its way out of the pockets of most of us.

"Well, as I was saying, I afterwards joined the *Minden* 74, to which ship Lieutenant Edmund Lyons belonged. We had been cruising with a squadron off this place, Batavia. Now there was at the north-eastern end of Java, not far from the Straits of Madura, a very strong fort or castle on Pauka Point, lately erected, called Fort Marrack. It was a considerable annoyance to all ships passing that way, and it was therefore deemed important to destroy it. However, as only between four and five hundred men could be spared for the enterprise, it was given up, as that number was looked upon as insufficient for the undertaking. However, the *Minden,* having on board a number of Dutch prisoners, Lieutenant Lyons was directed to land them in the launch and cutter at Batavia. I was in the launch. After we had put the Mynheers on shore, we stood along the coast to the eastward, for the lieutenant was in no hurry to get back to the ship. He had got something in his head, do you see? He remembered what he had helped to do with Captain Cole; so says he to himself, 'I'll just see if we can't play the Dutchmen just such another trick with regard to this here Fort Marrack.' When he had got a thing into his head to do, which he thought could be done, it was no easy matter for anyone else to knock it out again, till he had tried whether he was right or wrong.

"Two days after landing the prisoners, we got up to the fort just at dark. The lieutenant had a look at it, just to arrange his plan; and we then ran under a point of land, where we lay snug out of sight till the darkest part of the night. At first the moon was up, and would have discovered us to the enemy. The fort mounted fifty-four heavy guns, and had a garrison of one hundred and eighty regulars; but what did we care for that! We waited eagerly for the moon to go down, and then we both pulled away with muffled oars for the fort. There was a good deal of surf on the shore, but we hoped its noise, aided by the darkness, would prevent our approach being discovered. However, the Dutchmen had learned to be more awake than when we took Fort Belgica, and as we got close under the land, the sentinels let off their muskets to give the alarm. No time was to be lost. Lieutenant Lyons ordered us to run the boats through the surf right on to the shore, under the very muzzles of the guns in the lower tier. 'On, my lads!—on!' he exclaimed, leading us, sword in hand, right up over the embankment into the lower battery before the Dutchmen had time to look round them. We found the gunners as before, with their matches in their hands, and had to kill three of them to prevent their firing. Having knocked down every man we found, we did not stop to look around, but followed our gallant leader into the upper battery, which, in as little time as I have taken to describe, was in our possession. It was 'Hurrah, my boys!—at them!' and after a minute's cutting, and slashing, and firing of pistols, and dashing them at each other's heads, the place was ours. That's the way we used to do things in the war, when once a plan had been determined on by our officers!

"But we had still plenty of work to do, for when we went on and reached the highest part of the fort, we found a large body of Dutch troops drawn up to receive us. Nothing daunted by this, our gallant lieutenant, singing in Dutch, and French, and English, and all sorts of languages, that he had got four hundred men at his back, and would give no quarter if any opposition was offered, we fired a volley, and at them again we went, cutlass, and pike, and bayonet in hand. Whether they had Dutch courage in them or not, I don't know, but certainly they did not like our appearance; and as we came up with them they turned tail, and off they went helter-skelter through a gateway in the rear of the fort. After them we went, and sent the last man out with a hearty good kick, and shut the gate after him!

"No sooner had we got the fort to ourselves than the enemy began peppering away at us from a fort in the rear, and from a couple of gunboats; and considering that we hadn't the four hundred men the lieutenant talked of, but only just the two boats' crews, we had enough to do to spike the guns, and to keep up a brisk fire in return. You may be sure, mates, we were as busy as ants doing all the mischief we could in a short time. We had a young midshipman with us, Mr Franks, not fifteen years old; and while the fire was at the hottest, in the middle of it he hoisted the British ensign on the flagstaff on the top of the fort.

"While we were busy spiking the gnus, and firing away right and left, we made out, through the darkness, what we took to be a large body of Dutch troops. There were plenty of light carriage guns in the fort; and when information was brought him, Lieutenant Lyons ordered us to slue round two of them, and bring them close up to the gate. When we had done so, he and Mr Langton loaded them up to the muzzles with grape and musket balls. On came the enemy. He let them get close up to the gate, and then he and the midshipman fired slap in among them. It was much more than they expected, and lest they should get another dose, they put about in a great hurry, and off they went as fast as they could pelt, we hallooing and hurrahing after them. You may be sure we didn't follow them, or they would soon have found out the trick we had played them. All the time no one had been killed, and only Mr Langton and three men slightly wounded; but from the number of troops brought against him, Mr Lyons saw that we could not hope to hold the fort; so while the Dutch troops were scampering off in one direction, we bolted over the ramparts in the other. When we got down to the beach, we were not a little taken aback by finding that the surf had driven the barge right up on the shore and bilged her; but, fortunately, the cutter was still afloat. So we all got into her as silently as mice, and shoved off, leaving the fort to take care of itself. We were much amused by seeing the Dutchmen outside firing away into it as hard as ever. When they discovered their mistake, I don't know; but whenever they did, they must have found all the guns spiked, and the British ensign flying triumphantly over their heads, to show them who had done all the mischief.

"We got safely back to the *Minden* next day, none of us much the worse for the exploit. Soon after that, the whole of Java and its dependencies capitulated to Sir Robert Stopford and General Wetherall. This was the only service I saw in the navy—for within a year of that time I got my discharge, and once more joined a whaler."

Old Tom's account of these two gallant exploits was received by all hands with great applause, for that is just the sort of work in which seamen delight, and I know that all of us wished we had been with him. I need scarcely say that the Lieutenant Edmund Lyons of those days was afterwards the well-known Admiral Lord Lyons, who, from that commencement, won his way up to his well-deserved honours.

Two days after our encounter with the Dutch gentleman on shore, the captain sent for Newman into his cabin. He was some time away; and when he came forward, I saw that his countenance wore an unusually pleased expression.

"What has happened?" I asked.

"Why, the captain tells me that the stranger we met the other day is a Mr Von Kniper, some great man or other, with whom he has long been acquainted; and that he has sent to request the captain to bring me to dine with him. The captain is very good-natured about it, and says that he shall be very happy to take me. But it will be difficult to find a dress to go in. It will never do to appear in a round jacket. So, taking all things into consideration, I think that I shall decline the honour."

"That would be a pity," said I. "You don't know to what the visit may lead."

"To be stared at and patronised as the common sailor who can draw and talk German; and then to have the cold shoulder turned towards me the next day, or to be passed unrecognised!" he answered, with no little bitterness. "I am more independent, and safer from annoyance, in the position I have chosen to occupy. I'll not go out of it."

I tried to reason him out of his resolution.

"It may be a turning-point in your fortune," I observed.

"There is a tide in the affairs of men, which, taken at the flood, leads on to fortune," he repeated. "You don't suppose that the flood will ever set in for me. The current has been too long running the other way for me ever to expect it to change. I am content to let it continue its old course, and swim merrily with it."

Had Newman been left to himself, I do not know that he would have altered his opinion; but soon after this the captain again sent to see him.

"Well, Jack, I must needs go where the wind drives," he remarked, as he came forward. "Our skipper is certainly a very good-natured fellow. He not only insists on my going with him to the house of Mynheer Von Kniper, but tells me that he has made arrangements for rigging me out in full fig for the occasion. It will be very good fun, I daresay; and I only wish that you could be there to enjoy it."

"If I saw you happy, I should be happy; but I could not enjoy such a scene as that myself. I should feel so completely like a fish out of water."

"Oh, nonsense!" he answered; "a man has only quietly to observe what others do, and not to attempt to show himself off, or to broach any subject, and he will generally pass muster as a well-behaved person. However, as Mr Von Kniper did not ask you to come, of course you cannot go. Well, I dare say that I shall have enough to make you laugh when I come back."

I am not at all certain that Newman was right in his last observation. Practice and experience are absolutely necessary to fit a person for any station of life; and no wise man will ever wish to step into one for which he is not fitted by education or habit, or to associate with those with whom he has no ideas or associations in common. The great mistake numbers of well-intentioned people make, is the wish to rise in the world themselves, or that their children may rise in it to a superior station to that in which they were themselves born. They forget that the reason why they were sent into the world was to prepare them for another and a better existence; that this world is no abiding-place; and that, therefore, it is worse than folly to take toil and trouble to climb up a few steps in the ladder which will enable us to look down on our fellow-worms still crawling below us. There is one most important thing parents should teach their children—one most important thing children should desire—"To do their duty in that station of life in which it has pleased God to call them." Their sole motive should be love to their Lord and Master, Jesus Christ, who thus commanded them to act. At the same time, they may be well assured that if they do their duty with all their heart—if they do diligently whatever their hand finds to do—they will not fail to be placed in those posts of honour and responsibility which even worldly men are always anxious to get such persons to fill. We see how Joseph was raised to honour in Egypt, how Daniel was respected at the court of Babylon. The Bible is full of such examples, and those examples were given for our instruction. Those men rose, not because they wished to rise, but because they strove to do their duty—to worship the Lord their God with singleness of heart.

Poor Newman! I saw that under his pretended indifference there was no little satisfaction at the thought of occupying, even for a day, a position in which he probably had once been accustomed to shine. My only fear was, that when he got back to the forepeak, and our rough manners and rougher conversation, he would remark the contrast, and become discontented with the lot he had chosen.

The next day he and the captain went on shore to the dinner-party. As he stepped into the boat, and took his seat in the stern-sheets, I could not help remarking how completely the gentleman he looked. I must own that I waited with no little anxiety for his return, to hear what had occurred. I never before had been so intimate with any man as with Newman. I told him without reserve all that was in my heart, and he spoke freely to me, at the same time that he never once, even in the most remote manner, alluded to his past history. It was merely casually, when speaking of Mynheer Von Kniper, that he mentioned having been educated in Germany, or probably he would never even have told me that. On religious subjects, also, he never uttered an opinion; but from his very silence I had reason to believe that he entertained notions which were very far removed from the truth. Among all his books he had no Bible, and no works bearing on religion. He appeared to have studiously kept all such out of his library, as he did religion itself out of his thoughts. If I ever alluded to it, even in the remotest degree, he instantly turned the conversation; and whenever it was mentioned in the berth, which was, indeed, very seldom, his countenance assumed a look of cold, callous indifference, or a marked expression of scorn, which indicated too plainly what were his real opinions on the subject.

With regard to myself, I had always been a believer, though a sadly cold and careless one, except when roused by some particular occurrences, as I have mentioned in the course of my history. I still at this time continued much in the same dangerous state, but in other respects a great change had occurred. Deeply, indeed, was I indebted to Newman for it. He had awakened my mind out of its long sleep, and if I could not call myself an educated man, I at least had learned to prize the advantages of education, and was endeavouring to improve myself, and was greedy to gain knowledge wherever I could obtain it. No person could have devoted himself more earnestly to my instruction than did my friend. He seemed never to weary in helping me over difficulties; and if I took a pleasure in learning, he certainly took a still greater in teaching me. Without his aid I could not have made a tenth part of the progress I had done. I now read fluently, and even wrote tolerably. I had read through and mastered even more than the outlines of ancient and modern history, and with several periods I was tolerably conversant. I knew something of the past and present state of every country in the world, though I could not boast of knowing much about the mere names of the chief towns and rivers. I had read the lives of several men who had stood forward prominently in the world, and I had mastered some of the important facts of natural science. I need not further describe the amount of my knowledge. I could not have attained half I have mentioned had I not read on steadily, and carefully eschewed anything like desultory reading—that is to say, as far as the limited library to which I had access would allow. I did not always read the books I might have desired, but I diligently read the best I could obtain. If I, therefore, did so much in a short time with indifferent means, how much might be done with all the advantages possessed by those on shore!

Late in the evening Newman came back. The first thing he did on getting on board was to go below and shift his clothes. He then sat himself down on the windlass, with his arms folded across his bosom; and when I went up to him, he burst into aloud fit of laughter.

"I thought it would be so!" he exclaimed, when he recovered himself. "Mynheer Von Kniper was very polite, and so was his wife; and they introduced me to all their company. I believe the governor-general was there, or some great person. They paid me much more attention than they did the captain, who, if he had not been a right honest, good-natured fellow, might have been not a little jealous. First one person talked to me in one language, then another would come up with a different tongue in his mouth, and I had to show off in great style. Then I was asked to exhibit my drawings, and they were handed about and held up to the light, and admired by all hands as wonderful productions of art. In fact, I saw clearly I was the lion of the evening. I thought that sort of thing was only done in civilised, polite England; but I suppose lion hunters and lion exhibiters are to be found in all parts of the world. To do Mynheer Von Kniper justice, I must say that he had no hand in the work. During dinner nothing could be pleasanter or kinder than his conversation and manner; and certainly I had reason to believe that he wished me well. At length people got weary of hearing me roar, and all had had a look at the wonderful common sailor, and so the skipper seemed to think that it was time to be off; but our host would not allow us, and insisted that after the rest of the guests were gone, we should stop to have some supper. During the meal, Mynheer Von Kniper introduced the subject of drawing, and telling me that he longed to have all the scenes of whale catching and killing fully illustrated, asked if I would undertake to do a set of drawings for him on that subject. I could not refuse to do as he wished, after all the civilities he had shown me; so I told him that I should be very happy; but he then gently hinted that he wished me to undertake the task as a regular commission, and he begged that I would put what price I thought fit on my productions. I have made up my mind, at all events, to do them. I think every man has a perfect right to make a profit of his talents, especially if he requires money. I do not. I have now got a profession—a right noble one too! I am now a more independent man than had I been toiling on for years at a desk, or dancing attendance in some great man's ante-chamber for some of the patronage he may have to bestow. You think that I have benefited you by teaching you to read and write. Now, in reality, I have merely given you the implements of a trade—the means of gaining knowledge. You have given me knowledge—you have taught me a trade itself. Therefore, Williams, you see that I am still your debtor."

For some time he talked on in this strain. I clearly saw that he was pleased with the attention shown him, in spite of his belief to the contrary. I would not for one moment exhibit Newman as an example, or hold him up as a fine character. He had very great faults and many weaknesses. I do not know that he had strength of character. He had an independent spirit in some respects, a clear perception, and considerable talent. His greatly superior education raised him much above the associates among whom he had thrown himself.

Soon after this the ship was ready for sea, and as we had not above a couple of hundred barrels to fill, we hoped soon to be on our homeward voyage. It was the winter season, and we were bound for the coast of Japan. We were, however, several months before we got a full ship; and then, with joyful hearts to most on board, we once more made sail for Old England.

During all the time, Newman was busily employed in finishing up the sketches of whale catching, and very beautiful productions they were. Nothing could be more correct or truth-like. Very different they were, indeed, from the drawings I have since often seen, where the whale has had its flukes put on the wrong way, and boats are represented as being tossed high up in the air, some thirty feet, at least, and broken in two, while the crews are seen tumbling down like snowflakes, with arms and legs sprawling out right over the whale. I have seen many a boat smashed, but never one sent up in that fashion into the air. Newman was anxious to send these sketches to Mynheer Von Kniper; but as no opportunity occurred, he was afraid that he would be compelled to wait till another voyage to present them himself. Captain Carr promised, as soon as the ship could be refitted, to return on another voyage to those seas.

We had a quick passage home. I remained, as I had often before done, to look after the ship. Newman, when he had received his share of profits, which was very considerable, went on shore. What became of him I do not know. Not seeing anything of him, I was afraid that he was not going to return. Something there evidently was very mysterious about his history. I had a great desire to discover it; still, I saw no chance of doing so.

Hitherto I had always squandered away my money in the most foolish manner. I now got Captain Carr to invest some of it for me, and, retaining a little for pocket-money, with the rest I purchased the best books I could find, and other articles which I thought likely to be useful to me in a three years' voyage. At last the ship was ready again for sea. Tom Knowles and most of the other old hands had joined; for, being wise men, when they had found a good captain they liked to stick by him. We hauled out into the stream; but still, greatly to my disappointment, Newman did not appear.

Chapter Twenty One
Batavia and the Feejee Islands

The pilot was on board, the topsails were loosed, and the order had been given to heave up the anchor, when a boat was seen coming off from the southern shore of the Mersey. A seaman sprung up the ship's side, and a couple of chests were hoisted up after him. I was aloft. I looked down on deck and saw Newman. I found that he had written to the captain, who had reserved a berth for him, but it was still before the mast. He had the promise, he told me, of a mate's berth should a vacancy occur; but he observed, "I am not ambitious. With what I have I am content." He asked no questions as to what I had been doing. It was not his way. He was certainly free from vulgar curiosity; neither did he volunteer to give me any account of himself. I told him one day what I had done with the proceeds of the last voyage.

"Ah, you are wiser than I am, Williams," he answered, with a tone of bitterness. "I thought so, or I should not have tried to make you my friend. I have been seeing life, as it is called. I wanted to discover what changes had taken place in the world during my absence—as if the world could ever change. I found it deceitful, vain, and frivolous as before. I have been buying experience. The whole remainder of my possessions lies stowed away in those two chests. The most valuable portions are a few new books for you and I to read and discuss; and this time I have not forgotten a suit of shore going clothes, in case I have to appear again in the character of a gentleman. And now, farewell—a long farewell to England's shores! It may be that I shall never tread them again! Why should I regret it? There are brighter skies and richer lands in another hemisphere."

We had a quick run to Cape Horn, which we rounded in safety; and then standing across the Pacific, we steered for the fishing-ground off the coast of Japan. We were, as in our former voyage, very successful indeed. I suspect that success in whaling, as in most other affairs of life, depends very much on the practical knowledge, the perseverance, and talent of those engaged in it. The master of a successful whaler will be found to unite all these qualifications. He meets with whales, because, exercising his judgment, and making use of the information he has collected, he goes to the ground where they are likely to be met with; he catches them, because he sets about it in the best way; and he brings his ship home in safety, because he never for a moment relaxes his care and watchfulness to guard against misfortune. For my own part, I do not believe in luck. I have never yet met with an instance of a lucky or an unlucky man in which I could not trace the effect to the cause.

We were lucky, because Captain Carr was a judicious, persevering, sensible man; and thus, in our first year's fishing, we got more than a third full. At the end of that time we found ourselves brought up once more off Batavia.

The captain, in the kindest way, invited Newman at once to accompany him on shore. "Bring your drawings with you for Mynheer Von Kniper," said he. "I doubt not that he will be glad to see them."

On receiving the invitation, Newman dived below. When he returned on deck his appearance was completely changed. Instead of the rough seaman, he appeared as a well-dressed gentleman, and certainly more refined in appearance than either the captain or any of the officers. Captain Carr looked at him with an eye of satisfaction; and it was very pleasant to observe how perfectly free he was from any petty feeling of jealousy at seeing himself eclipsed by one of his own men. As the boat shoved off from the ship's side I thought to myself—"Depend on it, there is something in store for Newman; he will not come back in the cynical spirit in which he seemed to be after his first visit."

I had made excellent use of all my spare time during our passage out, and had added considerably to my stock of knowledge. Newman's books were all admirably selected, and were of excellent service to me. The more I read, the more I wished to read—to gain information on points on which I found myself ignorant. Happily one of the crew, a fine, steady young man, had a Bible with him; and he having offered it to me, for the first time in my life I began to read its sacred pages. As I read on I was forcibly struck with its simplicity and beauty, its fulness and minuteness, and yet the immense amount of matter it contained. I began to compare one part with another— the prophecies with their fulfilment—one point of the history with the rest—the great variety of subjects and style, and yet the beautiful adaptation of the various parts with the whole; nor did I neglect to compare sacred with profane history, or to remark how one corroborates the other—just as modern science, the greater advances it makes, is found to confirm more and more the troth of the accounts given by the sacred writers. Still all this time my heart was not turned to the right way. I had discovered a new and inexhaustible source of interest, but that was all.

Newman did not return on board till the next day. He was much elated in spirits when he appeared, though he tried to repress the feeling.

"Well, Jack, the tide has begun to flow at last," said he: "you shall hear all about it. Mynheer Von Kniper was excessively pleased with the drawings I took him, and the more so when I begged he would accept them from me."

"'I have often thought about you,' said he; 'and, I must confess, little expected to see you return here. I rejoice to see you back, for you must know that I have an offer to make you, which I hope you will think fit to accept. We have been for some time in want of a commander for one of the Colonial Government schooners, and I have ascertained from your captain that you are in every respect fitted for the post, and that he will give you your discharge from his ship. I have therefore great satisfaction in offering it to you.'

"I scarcely knew how to express myself in thanking him; so I took his hand, and shaking it heartily, told him that I was very much obliged to him, and that I placed myself entirely under his directions. So it was settled, and that same evening he presented me with my commission signed, and here I am, a lieutenant commander in the Dutch Colonial Navy! It is, in truth, a hop, step, and a jump into a post of honour I little expected, nor can I yet realise the greatness of the change."

I congratulated Newman most sincerely on the prospects thus opened up to him, though I regretted being so completely separated from him, as I must expect to be, for the future. He suggested the possibility of my following him, but that I at once saw was not likely to occur. In the first place, Captain Carr was not likely to allow a steady hand to leave him so early in the voyage; and probably the Dutch authorities would not be very ready to give a berth to another Englishman on board the same vessel; added to which, I had some misgivings as to serving under their flag.

Newman, of course, saw the first of these objections; and probably, if the truth were known, though he might not have been ready to confess it to himself after the intimate terms on which we had been together, he would have found it inconvenient while he was captain to have had me before the mast. It must be remembered that, though my mind was beginning to be cultivated, I was still a rough, hardy sailor in appearance and manners. I had never in my life dreamed of aspiring to any command, and I did not feel myself fitted for any post above that which I then held.

While I say this I would point out that it is very necessary to be cautious in judging from appearances. A man may have a very refined mind under a somewhat rough exterior, and a very coarse, bad one within a handsome, attractive outside. Generally speaking, with a few minutes' conversation, the appearance of a person and the expression of his countenance will show what is likely to be found within; but it is far wiser not to place more than ordinary confidence in the companions among whom we are thrown until they have been duly tried and found to walk rightly in their conduct towards God and man.

Newman seemed to be in no way elated by his change of fortune, and showed himself free from a very common littleness of mind, for he spent the rest of the day among us forward, talking and chatting with all hands as freely as before; and while he was packing his chests, he managed to find some little present as a keepsake for each of us. Then he sat himself down on his chest, and gave us an earnest lecture in his old style on the advantages of education, and urged us all to continue our studies as before, and to show by our conduct to each other and to our officers the superiority of educated, intelligent men over ignorant and uncultivated ones.

When he went aft to wish the officers good-bye, he was treated very kindly and politely by them, all of them congratulating him on his good fortune; and as he descended the ship's side for the last time, we gave him three as hearty cheers as ever rose from the deck of a whaler with a full hold; and little Jim, the smallest boy on board, blubbered as if his heart would break at the loss of one whom he had learned to look on as his best friend.

Before we sailed he had his schooner fitted out and manned with a strange crew of Malays, Chinese, Dutchmen, Frenchmen, and not a few representatives of other nations. He sent me a note insisting on my going to see him on board. His schooner was a fine little vessel, though built in the colony by Chinese. She measured some hundred and fifty tons, and, well handled, was fit to go anywhere; but this would be difficult work, I saw, with his mongrel crew. His cabin was fitted up in the complete way I should have expected him to have planned. It was, indeed, a very different sort of place from that in which he had long been accustomed to live—much more like, in the handsomeness of its fittings and its accommodation, to the luxurious cabin of the old Rainbow, which I used to see in my youth. He himself, too, was greatly changed in his appearance from the rough sailor he had long been. When dressed in plain clothes, he looked like a gentleman certainly, but not a polished one; but in a uniform which became him perfectly, he was a very good-looking officer. He was conscious of the improvement.

"I begin to think that there are yet higher steps for me to climb, Williams," he observed, after he had cordially welcomed me and ordered refreshments to be brought in. "Who knows but that one day I may become an admiral, or a governor of one of these islands? I am becoming ambitious,

I assure you. I thought it was not in me. I was till lately perfectly contented with my lot. I proposed spending my youth knocking about in these seas, and when I found old age creeping on me, settling down in one of the many thousand beautiful isles of the bright Pacific to spend the remainder of my days. Now that dream has passed away, and I feel an anxiety to climb. I am growing more and more ambitious; for I see that there are plenty of things in this world worth living for—plenty of golden fruit to be plucked, if a man has but the daring to scramble up the tree in spite of the thorns and knots in the way, and reach out to the branches."

What did I reply to Newman? Did I offer him good advice? Alas, no! I thought not to say to him, Do thy duty in that station of life to which it has pleased God to call thee, regardless of this world's tinsel prizes. Look steadily forward to another and a better world for thy reward. This he did not. This world, and this alone, entirely occupied his attention. He only thought of the gratification of the moment. Blindly and obstinately he shut out from his contemplations all thoughts of his eternal interests.

Newman's man-of-war schooner and the stout old whaler the *Drake* left Batavia Roads the same day. We were bound for the ground off Navigator's and some of the neighbouring groups of islands. We were fortunate enough to kill a couple of whales on our passage, and within two years after leaving England had nearly filled up all our casks. I began to consider whether I should remain in the ship, or, supposing Captain Carr would be willing to give me my discharge, whether I should join another ship lately come out, and thus, by saving the long voyage home and back, more speedily accomplish what was now the aim of my existence—to make a sum sufficient to enable me to remain at home for the rest of my days. I was now advancing in life. I had seen a great deal of hard service, and I began to long for rest. Such is the desire implanted in the bosom of all men—rest for the mind, rest for the body, rest for the soul. In youth, when health, and vigour, and animal spirits are at their highest, it is not developed, but when age comes on, and the body begins to feel the symptoms of decay, the mind grows weary and the spirits flag. Then rest is sought for—rest is looked for as the panacea for all evils. Yet who ever found rest in this world—perfect tranquillity and joy? No one. Still that such is the fact I had yet to learn. Yet, would a beneficent Creator have implanted the desire in the human heart without affording the means of gratifying it? Certain I am that He would not; but thus, in his infinite wisdom, he shows us the vanity of this world, and points to another and a better, where assuredly it may be found.

I took an opportunity of mentioning the subject of my thoughts to the captain, and he promised me that, if no other of the crew left when the ship was full, should we fall in with another wanting hands, he would comply with my wish, and, moreover, invest my share of the profits of the voyage as I might direct.

We had been for some time on the ground I have spoken of when we found ourselves in a perfect calm. By slow degrees the usual sea went down, and even the swell of the mighty ocean subsided. The crew sat lazily about the deck—some making air-nets for hats, others pointing ropes, working a mouse, or making a pudding, or a dolphin, or turning in a gasket; some leaned idly over the rail, and others slept still more idly below; while a few, not altogether unmindful of our old shipmate's instructions, were bending over their books or using their pencils. Some also were carving with their knives strange devices on bones, or cutting out rings from the shell of the tortoise.

"Ah, I wish we had Ned Newman aboard here!" exclaimed one. "He would soon set us all alive."

"Why can't you set yourselves alive?" said Tom Knowles, looking up from his work on a rope he had in hand. "Idle chaps are always talking of getting some one else to do what they ought to do for themselves. Just try now. Let's try a stave at all events. Come, I'll strike up."

Old Tom's proposal pleased all hands, and soon a melody, if not very sweet, at least harmonious, floated over the blue sea.

Whether the whales came to listen to our music, I cannot say; but while we were all joining in chorus, the ever-exciting shout of "There she spouts—there she spouts!" broke in upon it; and, springing to our feet, the boats were lowered and manned, and in less than three minutes four of them were gliding away as fast as they could be sent through the water, after two whales which made their appearance together, not far apart from each other.

The captain's boat got hold of the first without much difficulty; but as he was a strong old bull, he played all sorts of antics, and other two boats were called to assist in his capture. Meantime the third mate's boat, in which I was, went after the other whale, which sounded just as we got up to him. For some reason or other, he very soon appeared again a mile ahead, and away we went in chase. Again he played us the same trick, but this time he was longer under water, and must have gone upwards of two miles away before he once more came up. The more sport he seemed disposed to give us, the less inclined were we to lose him, so after him we went as fast as before—not faster, for that would have been difficult. As we got near, we saw that he was lying very quiet, and we did not think he saw us, so we had out our paddles, and began stealing up to him as cautiously as a cat does to a mouse—only in this case it was rather more like the mouse creeping up to the cat. The third mate was a well-built, powerful young man. Holding up his hand as a sign to us to be cautious, he stepped forward, and there he stood, harpoon in hand, as we glided on towards the monster. Down came the heavy harpoon, and it was buried, socket up, in the side of the monster! In an instant the acute pain woke him up. "Stern all!" was now the cry, and we had to back away from him in a great hurry, as, raising his mighty flukes, he went head down, sounding till he almost took away the whole of our line. Fortunately he met with the bottom, perhaps a coral-reef, and up he came, striking away head out at a great speed in the direction he had before taken. So intent were we on the chase, that we had little time to observe what was doing with the other whale, though, of course, we took the bearings of the ship, as we were rapidly whirled away till we completely lost sight of her. This was no unusual occurrence, nor did it in the smallest degree excite our apprehension, as we had never failed, with more or less trouble, to find our ship in the course of the day or night. On we went, as I say, making the smooth, bright sea hiss and bubble as the white foam frothed up over our bows.

The instant the whale slackened his speed we hauled in the line, so as to get up to him to thrust a lance or two into his body; but he was evidently a knowing old fellow, for by the time we had got half of it in, he was off again like a shot, spouting away every now and then, as if to show us in what capital breath he was for a long-run. At last he stopped, and began to turn slowly round. We thought that we had got him. "Hurrah, lads!" cried Barney Brian, an old boat-steerer. "Haul in steadily now—his last swim is over." We hauled away an the line with a will, and the mate stood, lance in hand, ready to plunge it into his side, when he shouted, "Stern all—veer away the line, lads!" It was time—up went the flukes of the monster, and in another instant he was sounding, drawing the line out of the tub at a terrific rate. We thought we should have lost him altogether, and we looked anxiously at the line as coil after coil disappeared, and we remembered that we had none to bend on to the end of it. It would have been better for us if he had broken away. Just, however, before the last coil flew out, up he came again, and seemed inclined to go on as before. Then he stopped, and we hauled in on the line. We had got within twenty fathoms of him when all of a sudden an idea seemed to strike him. He slewed completely round so as to face us. "I'll just give you a taste of my quality, and see if I can't teach you to let me alone," he seemed to say. At all events he must have thought it, for with open mouth, showing the tremendous teeth in his lower jaw, and head half lifted out of the water, he made directly at us. Never was a boat in a more perilous position—out of sight of land, and the ship nowhere to be seen, and thus all by ourselves to engage in single combat with a monster so enormous! To get out of his way by mere speed was impossible, for he could swim faster than we could pull; but we did our best to dodge him, our undaunted mate standing ready to plunge a spear into his side should we manage for a moment to get behind him. First, we pulled on one side as he came towards us, and then on the other; but rapidly as we turned, he slewed himself round, and at last, getting us under his snout, he made a dash at the boat, and sent her spinning away twenty yards before him, bottom uppermost, while we all lay scattered round about her, shouting and calling to each other for help. Had he at once gone off, and dragged the boat after him, he would have left us to perish miserably, and this was the fate we dreaded; but instead of that, while we lay holding onto oars, or striking out to regain the boat, he swam round us, examining the mischief he had done. More than once I thought he was going to make another charge at us with his open mouth, when, had he done so, he would have killed one or more, though he might not have swallowed any of us. That I never heard of a whale doing.

We, meantime, made all haste back to the boat, picking up whatever we could lay hands on in our way. We were not a little hurried in our movements by seeing two or more sharks, which had been attracted to the spot by the blood flowing from the monster; and they would just as soon have taken a meal off us as a nibble at him, which is all they would have got for some time, probably.

"Never fear, my lads!" shouted Mr Trevett, the mate. "Strike out with your feet, and heave over the boat. Quick now!—so!—over she comes! We'll soon have her baled out."

Baling with hats and caps, as we hung round the gunwale, and striking out with a will, to keep the sharks at a distance, we were enabled to clear the boat sufficiently of water to allow us to get in, just as a big shark, impatient of delay, made a dart at the mate's leg—for he was the last in—and very nearly caught his foot. We quickly had the boat to rights, but we found that we had lost two very valuable articles—our tinder-box and compass; so that we could neither make a signal to the ship nor tell in what direction to steer should thick or cloudy weather come on. We had, however, no time to meditate on our misfortune, for scarcely were we once more seated on the thwarts, oars in hand, than the whale, as if waiting the signal, started off again, head out, just as he had done before. His speed, however, was very much slackened; and though, after we had hauled in the line a little, he made an attempt to sound, he quickly returned to the surface, still more exhausted by the effort.

At length we managed to get near enough to him to enable Mr Trevett to give him a thrust with his lance. Deep in it went, the monster almost leaping out of the water with the agony of the wound. A vital part had been pierced. "He's in his flurry! Stern all—stern all!" was shouted. It was time that we were out of his way; for, swimming round and round, he beat the water with his flukes with terrific force, sufficient to have dashed us to atoms had he touched us, throwing the life-blood over us from his spout, and dashing the surrounding ocean, ensanguined with the ruddy stream, into a mass of foam. This mighty convulsion was his last effort. Over he rolled, and he was our well-earned prize.

But now we had killed him, it became a serious question how we were to get back to the ship. In what direction was she to be found? As we looked about, we saw that the weather, which had hitherto been so fine, was evidently about to change. The sky was full of the unmistakable signs of a heavy gale. Long fleecy clouds with curling ends lay scattered over it, and darker masses were banking up rapidly in the southward. We had now ample time to consider our position, as we lay on to the dead whale. We had neither light nor compass, and all our provisions were spoiled or lost. One keg of water alone had been recovered, and we found among us a few quids of tobacco. The nearest islands to the northward were, we knew, inhabited by the very worst description of cannibals, and, though white men occasionally traded with them for provisions, it was necessary to be constantly watchful to prevent surprise. The crews of several vessels not having taken the proper precautions, had been cut off and murdered. Night also was rapidly approaching, and we could not possibly reach the ship, even did we know where to find her, before dark, probably not for several hours. However, the mate, feeling that the first object was to try and save our lives, resolved to pull for the ship, leaving the whale with flags stuck on its side, in the hope that we might again find it. With much regret, therefore, we quitted our hard-earned prize, and pulled away, as we believed, to the northward, in the direction where we had left the ship.

We had not pulled long, however, when the gloom of night came on, and the gale which we had seen brewing burst over the ocean, quickly tearing up its sleeping bosom into foam-crested, tumbling seas, which every instant rose higher and higher. We soon also discovered that we could make no head against them, and that, by attempting to do so, we should only weary ourselves in vain.

"We must put the boat about, and run before it," said Mr Trevett. "Hoist the lug—haul aft the sheet!" It was done, and away we flew, careering over the fast-rising seas through the pitchy darkness of night!

"Where are we going to?" was the question. Still no other course remained for us to follow. To attempt to head the heavy seas now rising was impossible. No one spoke—a fear of coming evil settled down on our hearts. Darker and darker grew the night—the clouds seemed to come down from the sky and settle close over our heads, meeting the troubled wildly-leaping waves.

On we flew—the seas, as they curled and hissed up alongside of us, tumbling over the gunwale, and making it necessary for all hands to continue baling. Our only hope was that the ship might run before the gale and overtake us; but then we remembered that she probably had a whale alongside, and that the captain would not like to desert it as long as he could hold on. All hope, therefore, of help from man deserted us.

On we went—death every instant threatening us—a death amid that dark, wild, troubled, storm-tossed ocean! At length the fierce roar of the wind and sea seemed to increase. We looked out before us into the darkness. "Breakers!—breakers ahead!" we shouted. A thrill of horror ran through our veins. In another moment we should be dashed to a thousand fragments among the wild rocks over which they so fiercely broke. To attempt to haul off in such a sea would have consigned us to an equally certain fate. The imminence of the danger seemed to sharpen our vision. A mass of foam, which seemed to leap high up into the dark sky, lay before us. Not a moment could a boat live attempting to pass through it. On both sides we turned our anxious gaze, to discover if any spot existed where the sea broke with less violence. Almost simultaneously we shouted, "A passage on the starboard-bow!"

There appeared, if our eyes deceived us not, a dark space where the line of huge breakers was divided. We were rushing headlong to destruction. Not an instant was to be lost. The helm was put to port. We rose on the crest of a vast rolling sea. Down it came, thundering on the rocks on either side of us, throwing over them heavy showers of spray, sufficient almost to swamp us. Still we floated unharmed. The sea rolled on between what, in the darkness, appeared like walls of foam, and in another instant we found ourselves floating beyond the fierce turmoil of waters, just tossed gently by the waves, which found their way over the reef into a large lagoon within it!

A shore fringed with trees lay before us. In five minutes we were landed safely on it, and the boat was secured to the stump of a fallen tree. It was too dark to allow us to attempt to penetrate into the interior, to ascertain the sort of place on which we had been thrown; so, returning to the boat and baling her out, we wrung our wet clothes and lay down to seek that rest we all, after our violent exertions and anxiety, so much needed.

It must have been nearly daylight when we went to sleep. I know not how long we had slept. It would have been better for us had we driven sleep far from our eyelids, and been ready to pull out and wander over the inhospitable ocean the moment the gale abated, rather than have remained where we were. I was the first to open my eyes, and, looking up, I saw to my horror a nearly naked savage looking down into the boat with prying eyes from the bank above us. He was almost jet-black, with negro features and a full beard and moustache. His hair was frizzled out to a great size and covered by a brownish turban. Round his waist he wore the usual maro or kilt, with something like a shawl or plaid over his shoulders; and in his hand he held a long formidable-looking spear. From the turban on his head, I afterwards discovered that he was a chief.

"Eugh! eugh!" he cried, as he saw me opening my eyes to look at him, and his menacing attitude and ferocious aspect made a most uncomfortable feeling creep over me.

"Up, lads, up! and shove off!" I shouted to my companions, jumping forward myself to cut the painter. They started to their feet at my summons, looking up with a bewildered stare at the shore; and well they might so have done, for there stood some twenty or more fierce-looking savages, whom the exclamation of their chief had called to his side, and before we could get the oars out, a shower of spears came rattling down among us. Poor Mr Trevett was pierced through, and fell with a deep groan to the bottom of the boat; another of my companions sprung up as he was struck, and went headlong overboard; others were badly wounded; and one man only besides me was unhurt by the first shower of missiles. Seeing that we still persevered in trying to get the boat off, the savages came rushing down the bank; and though I had cut the painter, before I could give the boat sufficient impetus to get out of their way, they had seized the gunwale and hauled her up on the beach.

All hope of escape was now at an end. We were each of us seized by three or four of the savages, while, by the chief's directions, two others plunged into the water, and soon returned with the body of the man who had fallen overboard. To my horror, our poor wounded companions were instantly stabbed by these wretches, apparently for no other reason than because they offered some resistance to being dragged roughly along; and thus Brian and I were the only two who remained alive of those who had so lately escaped from the stormy ocean. Some of the savages, I saw, were left to take care of the boat in which the bodies of those who had been killed were placed.

As we climbed to the top of a hill, and I looked back over the blue ocean, now shining brightly in the morning sun, I saw that the storm had ceased; and—I am certain my eyes did not deceive me—I saw in the offing the white canvas of a ship, which I felt sure must be the *Drake*, probably searching for those who were never to be found.

From the appearance of the people and their cruel proceedings, I had no doubt but that we had fallen on one of the Feejee islands; and, from their well-known character, I knew what our fate would probably be. I myself had little, it might seem, to live for; but still life is *dear* to all of us, and I considered what I could do to preserve mine. I knew that most savages, as well as eastern nations, look upon a person deprived of his intellect as sacred, so I at once resolved to act the madman. On this, summoning all my strength, I gave vent to the loudest roar I could utter, finishing with a burst of laughter; and when my guards, in their surprise, let me go, I started forward, leaping, and singing, and dancing, with the greatest extravagance, pointing to the way I saw the chief was going, and pretending to conduct him with many bows and flourishes worthy of a French dancing-master. Desperate as the device was, it appeared to have its effect, for neither the chief nor any of his companions again attempted to interfere with me, though they dragged poor Brian on as before. He, of course, could not make out what had happened to me, and I could not venture to advise him to imitate my conduct, as I thought, very probably, should I do so, that both of us would fail in saving our lives by it. He, however, seeing the fate which had befallen our companions by refusing to walk on willingly, proceeded wherever his guards chose to lead him.

After passing through woods and large patches of cultivated ground, we reached a village of considerable size, and were led to what I supposed was the house of the principal chief, the father of the young man who had captured us. It stood on a raised platform of stone, and was built entirely of wood, with elliptical ends, the beams ornamented with coloured cocoa-nut plait. The side walls were solid, with windows, the frames of which were bound together to represent a kind of fluting, and which had a very ornamented appearance. The interior was divided into several compartments by screens of native cloth dyed with turmeric; and as the children and several of the people were painted with the same pigment, the whole had a very yellow appearance. The front and back of the edifice were formed of long laths, bent like a bow, and thatched with cocoa-nut leaves, something like the front of some bathing-machines in England. Under the roof, supported by beams, was a floor of lattice-work, which seemed to be the store-room of the house, as bundles of cloth and articles of various sorts were piled up there; while on the ground were scattered different utensils for cooking or eating from—such as bowls of glazed crockery of native manufacture, and plenty of well-made mats. On one of the walls were hung up some strings of whale teeth—articles which pass for money among those people.

At one end of the chief hall, on a pile of mats, sat a stout old man, with a huge turban and large beard and moustache, and wrapped in thick folds of native cloth. Savage as he looked, there was a good deal of dignity and intelligence about him. Keeping up the character I had assumed, I instantly began to salaam, as I had seen the Moors do, and to turn about on one leg, and then to leap and spring up, and clap my hands, singing out "Whallop-ado-ahoo!—Erin-go-bragh!" at the top of my voice, in a way to astonish the natives, if it did not gain their respect. My heart all the time felt as if it would break with shame and terror—with shame, at having to behave so, and with terror, lest I should, after all, not succeed.

The old chief and the young one, with the people who accompanied him, had a great deal of conversation about us, I found—the old one remarking that we had both of us "salt water in our eye," and must submit to the law. Now, by the law, or rather custom, of the Feejees, every person cast on shore on their coasts is killed and eaten! I had numberless proofs of the truth of this.

The result of the conversation about me was, that I was tabooed—to be held sacred, as it were—and that my life was to be spared. They tried to make me understand this at the time, and I partly comprehended their meaning. To prove their sincerity, the old chief had a number of dishes of various sorts of vegetables and fruit brought in, with a young pig baked whole, of which he made me partake. This I did very willingly, for I was very hungry, and the viands looked very tempting. When I had eaten a good meal, I jumped up and shook the old chief and his son very heartily by the hand; and then sitting down on a mat, I threw myself back, and began singing away at the top of my voice, as if I had been perfectly contented with my lot. When, however, I got up to leave the house, signs were made to me that I was to stay where I was. This, I concluded, was that notice might be given to the people that I was tabooed, and that they were not to interfere with me, or I should in all probability have been clubbed by the first native I met, who might have suspected that I had been cast upon their shore by the late gale.

I felt very anxious to ascertain what had become of Brian. He had not been allowed to enter the chief's house with me, but, as we approached the village, had been led off in a different direction. Suspecting the horrible practice of the savages, and hearing nothing of him as the day grew on, I became very much alarmed for his safety.

At night a mat was pointed out to me on which I was to sleep; but it was long before I could close my eyes, and every instant I expected to find myself seized and carried off by the savages. I did sleep, however, at last, and the next morning I found myself at liberty to wander out where I pleased. Food was first brought to me, and then, having performed various curious antics to keep up the belief of my insanity, I left the house and took the way up a neighbouring hill.

I had not gone far before I came to what was evidently a native temple, shaded by tall and graceful trees. It was a high-pointed building, formed of bamboos, and hung with strings of bones and screens of native cloth. I saw arms of various sorts, and an altar with two human skulls on it, made into drinking cups. I was considering how I could find my poor companion, when, near the temple, I entered an open space with several small erections of stone, which I discovered on examination were ovens. In the centre of the space was what I took at first to be the figure of a man cut out of wood, and painted over in a curious way with many colours. I went up to it. Horror almost overcame me—I recognised the countenance of my lost companion Brian! while some clothes hung up on poles hard by, and some human bones scattered under them, showed me what had been the fate of the rest of our boat's crew. I rushed shrieking from the spot, and for many a day I had no occasion to feign madness—I really was, I believe, out of my mind.

Chapter Twenty Two
Life among the Savages—Jack's
Escape and Return Home

Drearily passed the time of my sojourn in that benighted region. Day after day I sought in vain for the means of escape. Vessels often touched at the island; but directly they appeared, a strict watch was kept on me, and if I went towards the shore, I was told to go back and remain in the chief's house till they had sailed. Under some circumstances I might have been tolerably happy. The climate was delightful and healthy; there were provisions in abundance—yams and bananas and plantains, cocoa-nuts and shaddocks, pumpkins and pine-apples, guavas and water-melons—indeed, all the tropical fruits and vegetables, with a good supply of pigs for meat. The chiefs treated me with kindness and consideration; the people with respect, barbarous and savage though they were; but the scenes of horror I was constantly witnessing, and could not prevent, had so powerful an effect on my mind that time rolled on with me in a dreamy sort of existence. I scarcely knew how the months passed by—whether, indeed, as it seemed to me, years had elapsed since I landed on that fatal spot.

I had not believed beings so bloodthirsty and savage existed on the face of the earth, possessing, at the same time, so much intelligence and talent. Their houses and temples are very neatly built; the tapa-cloth, which they make from the paper-mulberry by beating it out, is of a fine texture, of great length, and often ingeniously ornamented; they cultivate a large number of the fruits of the earth with much attention; the way in which they fortify their villages appears almost scientific. The town in which I lived was surrounded by several deep moats, or ditches, one within the other, arranged with so much intricacy, that it was at first difficult to find my way out of it; then there were several walls, and in the centre a sort of citadel on a hill surmounted by a rock. On the summit of the rock stood a flagstaff, on which was hoisted, in war-time, the flag of defiance.

I had been many months there in the condition of a prisoner, if not a slave, before I was allowed to go beyond the fortifications. At last the young chief invited me to accompany him. He did not explain where he was going.

He and all those with him were painted in their gayest colours. We reached the sea-shore, and embarked in a large double canoe, with an out-rigger to prevent her capsizing. Several other canoes accompanied us.

We sailed on till we came to an island. At no great distance from the water rose a high hill with a fort on the top of it. I remained on board the canoe, while the chief and his followers landed. As soon as they had done so, they began to shout out and to abuse the people in the fort, daring them to come down. After a time, about a dozen left the fort, and descended the hill to meet the invaders. Our chief had stationed some of his people behind an embankment, and as soon as these incautious warriors appeared, they drew their bows and shot three of them. Then the people in the fort rushed down in great numbers to secure their fallen companions; but in doing so, more were shot, and others clubbed by our party, who carried off the bodies of the three first killed, as well as most of the others, and then, with loud shouts of triumph, retired to their canoes. With these spoils we sailed back.

We were received in the village with every demonstration of joy. In the evening of the same day, when I went out, I found that all the slain had been carried to the grove before the temple, and were placed in rows, with their bodies covered over with paint. The chiefs and all the principal men of the tribe were assembling from far and near. The priest of the town was standing near the temple, and the butcher, as he was called, a bloodthirsty monster, was ready with the implements of his horrid trade, while his assistants were employed in heating the ovens. I rushed from the spot; but, instigated by a curiosity I could not repress, I again returned, and witnessed a scene of the most disgusting cannibalism the mind could imagine. The bodies of the slain were baked, and then cut up by the priest or butcher, and distributed among the chiefs and principal men, none of the women or lower orders being allowed to partake of the horrible banquet. What struck me was the avidity with which the savages seized the fragments and devoured them. I would have avoided giving the dreadful account, were it not to show the depth of wickedness into which human nature, when left to itself, will inevitably sink. Often have I seen parties of men set out for the express purpose of capturing and murdering their fellow-creatures—people of the same colour and race, and chiefly helpless women and children—to satisfy their disgusting propensities—frequently to furnish a banquet on the visit of some neighbouring and friendly chiefs.

Some people have pretended to doubt the existence of cannibalism as a regular custom, though unable to deny that it has been resorted to under the pressure of hunger; but the Feejee islands afford numberless undoubted proofs that hundreds of people were yearly slaughtered to gratify the unnatural taste of their ferocious chiefs. Wars were undertaken for the express purpose of obtaining victims; all persons, friends or strangers, thrown by the stormy ocean on their inhospitable shores, were destroyed; their own slaves were often killed; and men, women, and children among the lower orders, even of friendly tribes, were frequently kidnapped and carried off for the same purpose.

But, praise be to God! heart-rending as are the scenes I have witnessed and the accounts I have heard, all-powerful means exist to overcome this and other horrible, though long established customs. The Christian faith, when carried to those benighted lands by devoted men, who go forth in love and obedience to Him who died for them, and in firm confidence that He is all-powerful to preserve them, and to make His name known among the heathen, is the sure and effectual means to conquer the giant evil. Before its bright beams, the dark gloom of savage barbarism and superstition has been put to flight, by the untiring efforts of Christian missionaries; and I am told, that among even the Feejee islands, wherever they have planted the Cross, numbers have flocked round it, and in many places the whole character of the people has been changed. I am describing simply barbarism as it existed, and as it still does exist, in numberless places in those beautiful regions of the earth's fair surface; and I would point out to those who read my history, how much it is their duty to inquire into the truth of the statements I make, and to support by all the means at their disposal those who are engaged in our Lord's service in overcoming the evil, by teaching the pure, simple, evangelical faith as it is in Christ Jesus—His incarnation—His sufferings—His atonement—His propitiation offered once—His intercession ever making—the cleansing power of His blood—our acceptance by an all-holy God through Him. Let these great truths be made known to the heathen, and, by the divine blessing, their minds, dark as they may have been, will accept them with joy and thankfulness.

But to return to my life on the island. My master, the old chief, was said to be a very civil and polite man; but I have seen him, when the inhabitants of the tributary or slave states were bringing him their quota of provisions, if he did not think that they were approaching his abode in a sufficiently humble posture by stooping almost to the ground, deliberately take his bow and shoot one of them through the heart. The rest, not daring to interfere, or to run away, would continue their progress as if nothing had happened, while the body of the unfortunate wretch would be carried off to the bake-house. To approach his house on one side, a river had to be crossed, swarming with sharks; and often he would make the slaves swim across, and if one of them were bitten by a shark, and still managed to get across, he was instantly on landing killed for the same dreadful purpose.

Some months after my arrival, the chief's house was burned down—though the rolls of cloth, and much of his more valuable property, were saved. He at once issued his commands to the people of all the tributary villages to bring in materials for the erection of another on a much larger scale. Meantime we lived in huts, quickly erected on his property. When the day arrived to commence the building, I saw that four very deep and large holes had been dug to receive the corner posts. These posts were brought up with great ceremony to the spot. At the same time, four slaves, strong, muscular young men, were brought up, and when the posts were placed upright in the holes, a slave was made to descend into each of them, and as I looked in, I saw them clinging tightly round the posts. I concluded that they were to remain there to hold the posts upright till the earth was shovelled in; but what was my horror to find that they were to remain for ever in that position! While they stood in all their health and strength, looking up with longing eyes into the blue sky, others threw in the earth, and beat it down with heavy mallets over their heads. I shuddered at the spectacle, but heart-broken as I was I dared not interfere.

Our old chief had resolved to build a fleet of large double canoes, with which to bring the inhabitants of another island under subjection. It had been his chief care and attention for some years past. At length a portion was finished and ready for launching. Before this ceremony could be performed, it was necessary to attack a village at some distance, to obtain victims to offer in sacrifice to the evil spirits they worshipped, in order that success might attend their operations. The young chief and his party set out with his warriors, and attacking a village in the dead of night, carried off fifty of its unfortunate inhabitants.

The next day, the shrieking wretches were brought to the dockyard. That they might be kept in a proper position to serve as ways or rollers over which the canoes might pass, each person was securely lashed to two banana-trees, lengthways—one in front, and the other behind him. Thus utterly unable to move, with their faces upwards, they were placed in rows between the canoes and the water. Ropes were then attached to the canoes, which, it must be understood, are very heavy, and numbers hauling away on them, they were dragged over the yet breathing, living mass of human beings, whose shrieks and groans of agony rent the air, mingled with the wild shouts and songs of their inhuman murderers, till the former were silenced in death. I need not say what became of the bodies of the victims thus horribly immolated. The ceremony ended with a great feast, at which all the chiefs and principal men assembled from far and near, and which lasted several days.

With the young chief I was on intimate terms, and I believe that he had formed an attachment to me, and was anxious to preserve me from injury. In our excursions about the country, we visited one day a temple at the end of a small pond, and I saw him throw into it some bread-fruit and other provisions. Looking into the pond, and wondering what this was for, I observed a large monster with a body as thick as a man's leg, and a hideous head, which I took to be a great snake, but which he told me was an eel of vast age, showing me some eels to explain his meaning, and also that it was a spirit which he worshipped. This was the only worship I ever saw him engaged in.

I had spent upwards of a year on the island, or it may have been two, when the old chief fell ill. He sat moping by himself in the corner of his house, and no one could tell what was the matter with him. One day his son came in, and taking his hand, just as if he had been going to say something very affectionately to him, told him that the time had arrived when it would be better for him to die! The old man bowed his head, and replied that he was of the same opinion! The son mentioned a day for the burial, to which the old man willingly consented; and till the time arrived, as if a weight had been taken off his mind, he seemed very much the better that everything had been so satisfactorily arranged. I could discover no compunction on the part of the son, nor regret on that of the father, who was cheerful and contented, and ate his meals with far more relish than he had before done. As the fatal day approached I attempted to remonstrate with the young chief on so unnatural a proceeding; but he sternly rebuked me, and told me not to interfere with the immemorial customs of the people. His father had been chief long enough—he was worn-out and weary of life—and he himself wished to be chief. When he should become old, his son would probably wish to finish him in the same honourable way, and that he should be content to submit to the usage of his nation.

The day arrived, and all the relatives and friends and neighbouring chiefs assembled. The old chief got up, and was followed by a procession of all his people, some bearing spades, and others cloths with which to wrap him up in the grave. The grave was about four feet deep. A cloth having been spread at the bottom, the old man was conducted to it. He stepped down with as little unwillingness as if he had been entering a bath, and having been placed on his back, the cloth was folded over him. Instantly others began shovelling in the earth, and then his son and nearest relatives came and stamped it down, exerting all their force with their feet. Not a sound was uttered by the old man. Leaves were scattered on the grave, and then all engaged in the ceremony went and washed at a neighbouring stream.

This done, they returned to the old chief's house, where a feast was prepared; and having eaten as much food and drunk as much angona as they could, they got up and commenced dancing in the most frantic manner, making a most hideous uproar with their drums, conch-shells, and other instruments, and shrieking and howling at the top of their voices. After this, the principal chiefs entered the houses of the late chief's wives, armed with a sort of bowstring. With these they proceeded deliberately to kill the unfortunate women, one after the other, till about twenty were thus executed. The new chief's mother had before died, or she would have been murdered in the same way. Many of them seemed perfectly willing to submit to their fate, though several, with shrieks and cries, endeavoured to escape, but were brought back and compelled to submit their necks to the executioners.

The young man at once assumed the functions of chief, and seemed disposed to be no less cruel and bloodthirsty than his father. Soon after, the news was brought that a vessel had anchored in a bay a short distance from the town. She was said to be full of all sorts of valuable commodities; of fire-arms and weapons of all sorts; of cloths, and tools, and other articles likely to be attractive to savages. At once the cupidity of the young chief was excited. If he could get possession of these things, he might become the most wealthy and powerful of all the chiefs of his nation, and bring the other tribes into perfect subjection to him. A council of his most trusty followers was called, and his plan explained to them. They at once agreed to aid him in its execution.

I trembled for the fate of the unfortunate crew of the ship, and resolved, if possible, to warn them of their danger. How was I to succeed? I would try, I thought, and swim off to the vessel; I would risk my own life for the purpose. Pretending not to have understood what was proposed, I walked about in as unconcerned a manner as possible. I lay down at night in my usual place in the chief's house, intending to get up when all were asleep, and run along the shore till I came abreast of where I supposed the vessel would be. Anxiously I waited for the time. I got up and reached the door. Just as I stepped out into the night air I felt a hand placed on my shoulder! I must have trembled. It was the hand of the chief.

"Ah, I know what you are about," said he. "You wish to escape to the white people, to tell them what we are going to do. I suspected you. That cannot be. You will see that it would be wiser for you not to join them. Come with me to-morrow, and you will see."

My first plan was thus defeated. Still I hoped that I might meet some of the white crew of the vessel and warn them of their danger. I determined to try.

The next morning the chief and his warriors collected, and all their canoes were launched and paddled off to a point which concealed them from the stranger vessel. The smaller canoes were loaded with fruits and vegetables of all sorts, and about twenty men and boys without arms and in the most peaceable garb, paddled off to her.

On getting up, I found that the chief had appointed two men to attend on me and watch my movements. Everything conspired, therefore, to defeat all my hopes of warning the strangers of the fate intended for them.

I was allowed to proceed to a high hill, whence I could look down on the vessel, which lay in a bay at my feet. I longed to have the wings of a bird, to fly down and tell the crew of the intentions of the savages, whose small canoes now began to flock about her. Several of the chiefs reached her deck, and began offering presents of fruit and vegetables to the officers, and pointing to the shore, as if to indicate that if they would come there they would be received with a hearty welcome. I guessed, from the build of the vessel, that she was not English. At last I saw a boat lowered into the water, and a French flag flying over her stern. Though I had often been engaged in deadly strife with those fighting under that ensign, I was nevertheless anxious to save the lives of those I saw. Yet I could not speak a word of French, and probably they would not have understood my warning even if I could have given them one.

Not only one, but two boats were lowered; and, as far as I could see, no one was armed. What could have thus so speedily enticed them on shore? Looking along the beach, I saw it lined with a number of people, mostly women and children. There were young girls with baskets of fruit, and older women with vegetables, and little boys with sucking pigs and other dainties, and children running about and playing on the sands. As this was not the usual custom of the savages, I guessed too well that it was an artful device of the chief to entrap the unwary strangers. By the time the boats had reached the shore, the women and children gradually drew off, and I saw two bodies of savages stealing down through the woods on either side of them. Oh, how I longed to warn them of their peril! I would, at every risk, have shouted out, but they would not have understood me. I remained spell-bound.

Meantime, three or four of the large canoes stole out from behind the point, and gradually approached the doomed ship, the chiefs in them, when they were perceived, waving their hands in token of amity to those on board. If the party on shore observed them, I do not know; they appeared to have no fear, no suspicion of treachery. The aim of the cunning savages was to get them to separate from each other. The sellers of fruit got in among them, and enticed one on one side, and one on the other; and when this had been accomplished I saw a warrior, with his club concealed under his cloak, glide noiselessly in and attach himself to each of the unsuspecting white men. The large canoes, full of warriors, had likewise been incautiously allowed to get alongside the brig, and soon her decks were crowded with savages, making signs, and laughing, and pretending to traffic with the crew.

On a sudden, a conch-shell was sounded by the chief. Before its hoarse braying had died away, the deadly weapons of the savages had descended with terrific force on the heads of the white men on the shore. Many fell, killed at once; others attempted to run to the boats, but were pursued and quickly dispatched. On board, the plot of the chief seemed to be equally successful. Though some resistance was offered and several shots were fired, all was unavailing—not a white man ultimately escaped; and in a few minutes their bodies were brought on shore in one of the canoes, while the others followed towing the brig, whose cable the savages had cut, that they might the more easily plunder her.

As soon as she was brought close to the shore, a scene of havoc and destruction commenced on board. Some climbed the masts to unrig her, others rushed into the hold to get out the cargo, and numbers hurried to the cabin to carry off the lighter articles which it contained.

The chief, as may be supposed, got the lion's share; and his house was soon full of fire-arms and other weapons, and clothes, and trinkets, and crockery, and articles of every description. He himself had come on shore, but numbers still remained on board, working away in the hold, and lowering down the rigging from aloft, when there was a loud explosion, and the deck of the vessel, with all on board, was lifted up and blown into the air! Not a human being on board escaped. Fragments of the wreck and mangled bodies came falling thick around, while flames burst out on every side from the hull, the scene of the late atrocity.

The chief was very angry at the loss of so much property, but seemed in no way to regret the lives of so many of his subjects.

I took occasion to tell him that the catastrophe was a judgment on him for the number of murders and the robbery he had committed.

He replied that he did not understand what I meant—that white men had often come to those islands in their ships, and had kidnapped his people, or shot them down with their guns, or beaten them, for some trifling misunderstanding or theft of little importance they might have committed, and that he was only treating them as other white people had treated his countrymen.

No reasoning that I was able to use after this could convince him that he had acted wrongly. Indeed I knew that there was too much truth in his assertion; and much have those navigators to answer for who have acted unfairly towards savages, when those savages, following the law of their untutored nature, have retaliated on subsequent voyagers with a tenfold measure of vengeance.

After this occurrence, I was always seeking an opportunity to escape from this blood-stained spot of earth. Whichever way I turned had been a scene of murder, and I loathed the sight of the sanguinary perpetrator of so many atrocities.

I might employ many an hour in describing the dreadful customs and superstitions of these people. Every day my desire to escape from them increased. Three or four vessels in the course of the next year called off the island, but the crews seemed to be cautious; and, at all events, no attempt was made to surprise them. As each appeared, I found myself narrowly watched, so I had no opportunity of communicating with them.

I had now for some time been looked upon as a sane man, and had employed myself in working in various ways for the chief. It at last struck me, that if I were again to feign madness I might obtain greater liberty. On putting my idea into execution, I found that it had the desired effect; and I was allowed from that time forward to go about wherever I liked, and to pry into people's houses and gardens, and even into the temples. I soon found my way down to the sea-shore, and used to pretend to be busy in picking up shells, and in stringing them together into necklaces and bracelets for my own adornment. Then I made others, which I presented, with many a strange antic, to anybody I met. Day after day did I continue this employment, my eye wandering anxiously over the blue sea in search of the wished-for vessel.

Drearily passed the time, without a human being with whom I could exchange an idea we might hold in common. I learned then fully to appreciate the value of the society and sympathy of my fellow-men. At length, one day as I sat at my usual occupation on the shore, my eyes fell on a white speck just rising above the horizon. Anxiously, intently did I watch it. Slowly it increased. First I made out the topgallant-sails; then the topsails; and at last the courses of a square-rigged schooner. She approached the island. Oh, how my heart beat within me for fear she might not come near the part where I was!

There was a channel through which vessels had more than once passed. A point of land ran out into it, covered almost to the end with trees. Towards this point I ran, concealing myself as much as I could among the trees from the people on shore. I reached the point unobserved. I had hoped to find a canoe there, but there was none. I looked about, and at last discovered a log of banana-wood, which is very light. It had been cast on shore. With my knife I cut a stick with a broad end, to serve as a paddle and to defend myself against the sharks which abound on the coast. I was ready to run all risks. I had become desperate. I felt sure that if I were observed by the natives I should be brought back and slaughtered. Still that idea did not daunt me. At every hazard I was resolved to get on board, or to perish in the attempt.

Eagerly I kept my eye on the vessel. On she came. She was steering for the channel. I got my log ready to launch. It was with no small dread that I looked around to ascertain that I was not observed. I watched for the moment to commence my perilous voyage, when, by pulling directly out from the shore, I thought I could fetch her. I had secured two long outriggers at each end of my log, to prevent it from turning round; the tendrils of the wild vine served me as rope. The time arrived to launch forth. With all my strength shoving the log into the water, I took my seat on it, and with might and main using my paddle, I worked on my rough canoe towards the schooner.

Now commenced the most dangerous part of the enterprise, as I drew out from the point and became exposed to the view of the people on shore. Every now and then I gave a hasty glance over my shoulder to ascertain if I were followed.

For a long time no one observed me. I had nearly gained a position by which the schooner must pass, when, to my dismay, I saw a large canoe putting off from the shore. If I could not gain the side of the schooner before she reached me, I was undone.

Again I took to my paddle, and urged on the slow-moving machine towards the approaching vessel; still the canoe was rapidly drawing near. Every instant I expected to find an arrow sticking in my body. The thought made me redouble my efforts.

On came the schooner. I shouted out, "Have mercy on an unfortunate Englishman!" I saw many swarthy faces on her forecastle. I thought that I might not be understood. What was my joy then to see her brail up her sails, for she had a leading wind, and lower her boat!

The boat approached me. I leaped into her just as a shower of arrows was sent flying after me. Most of them fell short, but some struck the boat. Those on board the schooner seeing this, instantly let fly a volley of musketry at my pursuers, and made them pull back with no little rapidity towards the shore. The moment my eye had time to look about the vessel, I thought that I recognised her. I was not mistaken; she was Newman's schooner, and Newman himself was standing on the quarter-deck, not as I had for so long known him, but in dress and appearance like an officer. He, of course, did not know me. How should he? I was thin and haggard with care and anxiety. Of my seaman's clothes but a small portion now remained, and the few garments I had were made of the native cloth, but had been torn in my run among the trees, and afterwards almost destroyed in the water. Altogether, I was a miserable figure.

I resolved not to make myself known to my old friend, but still I was anxious to guard him against the treachery of the natives. Seeing that I appeared to wish to speak to him, he sent for me aft to give an account of myself. I had not talked five minutes when he exclaimed, "I am quite certain I know that voice and mode of expression. Who are you, my man?"

I at once told him. He grasped my hand cordially, and greeted me as he would have done in the forecastle of the *Drake*. Directly he made me at home, and told me that I must mess in his cabin.

"You must be clothed, so I will dress you as an officer. As we have no boatswain on board, I will at once appoint you to fill the berth. That's all settled; and after you have had some food, I must hear all that has happened to you since we parted." He told me that he was well aware of the treacherous disposition of the natives, and that he was always on his guard.

How delightful it was to feel myself out of the power of those bloodthirsty savages, and to be sitting at dinner with an intelligent companion! He had been in the schooner ever since we parted; and so much satisfaction had he given the Dutch authorities, that he had been promised shortly the command of the largest vessel on the station. He was in high spirits, and told me that he expected, on his return to Batavia, to marry a lady of considerable fortune, and that he looked upon his prosperity as certain. "Pretty well, is it not, I have done, remembering the point from which I started only a few years ago?"

I very soon recovered my health and strength on board the schooner. Newman had been sent to examine these and other neighbouring groups of islands. We cruised about among them for some months, and then once more shaped our course for Batavia.

On getting on board, I had no little difficulty at first in speaking English, and I found that I had almost entirely forgotten how to read and write. Newman, however, used to have me every day into his cabin, and I very soon recovered the knowledge I had lost. Indeed, he took as much pains to instruct me as he had done on board the whaler, and he encouraged me with the hope that he might get me appointed as one of his mates while he remained in the schooner. But alas! I found that in one point he was still unchanged. Religion was yet a stranger to his soul.

At length we reached Batavia. He went on shore in high spirits, telling me that he was going to visit the lady to whom he was engaged; but he let me know that he must call also on another who had formed an attachment for him, that he might pacify her respecting his intended marriage. I feared from what he said that all was not right. I expected him on board again that night, but he did not return.

In the morning he did not come, so with some anxiety I went on shore to inquire for him. For a long time I searched in vain. At last I met a person whom I guessed to be an Englishman.

"Your captain do you ask for?" he answered. "Look there!"

Some police-officers stood at the door of a house. They allowed me to enter. On the floor of a room at the side lay a body. A cloth covered the face. I lifted it up. There I beheld all that remained of the highly endowed Edward Newman, for by no other name did I know him. He had been poisoned through fiery jealousy. A cup, in pretended friendship, had been laughingly offered him. Unsuspiciously he had drunk of it. The Government seized the murderess, who paid the penalty of her crime with her life.

Thus died one who was well calculated to shine in the higher walks of life. Who he was, whence he came, or even the slightest clue to his previous history, I was never able to ascertain. In a strange land he died, far away from kindred and friends—if, indeed, he had any—his fate for ever unknown to them. Let this be a warning to those who hear the sad conclusion of his history. The highest talents, and the most undaunted courage and perseverance, will avail a man nothing, unless at the same time he be under the guidance of principle.

The death of my friend threw me completely adrift, and I was glad to find an opportunity of working my passage to England on board a ship just going to sail for Liverpool.

Once more I stood on my native shore, a care-worn, weather-beaten man, well advanced in years. On inquiring for the bank in which I had invested the savings of my former voyage, I found that it had failed, and that I was as poor as when I began the world, with this difference, that I had a profession, and had bought a large amount of experience with the money I had squandered—which is not always the case with spend-thrifts.

I made inquiries for Captain Carr, but could hear nothing of him. As I concluded that he had invested the money made by my last voyage in the *Drake*, I supposed that also to have been lost by the bank. I thought this a very great misfortune, as I wished to have settled on shore in some business or other. Perhaps I might have chosen that of a publican, as many sailors do. However, I had now no resource but to go to sea again.

While in this humour I fell in with an old shipmate. We had been together in the *Glutton*, and one or two other ships, so we knew each other directly. He told me that he belonged to a revenue-cutter then stationed in the Mersey, and that she was short of hands, especially of three or four steady men; and when I mentioned to him that I had been boatswain of a man-of-war schooner, he said that he was certain I would get a berth on board. I was weary of foreign voyages, so I accompanied him at once, as he proposed, to the commander, and was entered immediately.

Ever since have I had reason to bless that day. The commander was a pious, excellent man, who, aware of the value of his own soul, was ever solicitous for the eternal welfare of all those placed under his authority. He soon found that though I had some knowledge of the Bible, and much of other things, I was ignorant of the way of salvation. He called me often into his cabin. Kindly and affectionately he spoke to me, and set before me the truth of the gospel as it is in Christ Jesus. As he spoke to me, so did he, from time to time, to all the rest. He, truly, was not ashamed of the Master he served. At an early age he had hoisted his flag, and had ever since fought bravely under it, against the scorn of the world, against evil in all shapes. Even the most obdurate were softened and influenced by the example he set, though they might not receive the truth with gladness of heart. We were what all ships' companies might become—a Christian crew, though not without faults and shortcomings; but we loved Christ, and worshipped him with singleness of heart. At the same time I am very certain that no crew ever more efficiently did their duty to their country than we performed ours.

For three years I served on board that vessel, and at the end of that time was sent round to Woolwich, where she had been fitted out, to be paid off.

The last time I landed at Liverpool, I met an old gentleman walking along the street. I looked in his face. It was Captain Carr! I told him who I was. Of course he had thought I had been lost, and was very much surprised to see me. He was shocked to hear of the death of my companions, and deeply interested in the account I gave him of my captivity. To my no little satisfaction he told me that he had not invested the money, which was mine by rights, from the last voyage; and that he thought he could obtain fifty pounds from the owners as my share of profits. This sum I afterwards received. It was all that remained out of the thousands I had made in the course of my life.

I was now sixty years of age. I had recovered my health on board the cutter, but though strong and hearty, I felt I was no longer fit for sea. I found, however, on application, that I could obtain employment as a rigger in the dockyard; and in that work I spent some years. I took a little cottage on the hill, which I furnished by means of the money I received from Captain Carr, and made myself perfectly comfortable.

Directly I was settled, I started off next day for Greenwich Hospital, for I thought that I should very likely fall in with some old shipmates there. I went into the chapel and sat myself down—no one hindering me. As the men were coming out when service was over, I saw before me a tall, thin old pensioner, bending under the weight of years, and resting on a staff as he walked before me. I came behind as he reached the open air, and looked up in his face. It wore the same kind, benignant, mild expression which I remembered so well in the countenance of Peter Poplar. I waited till he got down the steps.

"Just lean on me, sir," said I. "You have carried me before now, if I mistake not." He looked hard at my face. A tear dimmed his eye.

"Yes, yes—it's the boy himself," he whispered in a tremulous voice. "But you are 'Old Jack' now." I loved the name he gave me, and ever since to the lads I meet and talk with I have called myself by it.

A few weeks after that, I sat by the bedside of my kind, noble old friend—talking of that glorious eternity into which his spirit entered before I left him.

After I had been settled for some years, I met an old shipmate, sick, and I saw plainly dying. He had been a lad when I knew him. He had with him a little girl, his only child, some ten years old. His wife was dead. He had no friends. I promised as he lay on his death-bed to take charge of the lassie. He blessed me, and died. I took her to my cottage, and she has ever since been a comfort and a solace to me—a daughter by adoption, if not by blood.

Not long after this event, I met my former commander in the cutter. He asked me how I was employed. I told him as a rigger, but that I sometimes found my strength scarcely equal to the work; but when that failed, I was sure God would provide for me as He had always done.

He replied that he had no doubt of it—that even then there was work for which I was well fitted ready for me—that he belonged to a society which had been formed to distribute, at a low price, religious and other publications among those classes who were accustomed to purchase the most pernicious style of literature, frequently from not having better offered to them; and that if I would undertake the work, he would get me appointed to it. I gladly accepted his offer, and have ever since been a humble, though I feel sure not an inefficient, labourer in making known the good tidings of great joy among the almost heathen population of our own land, as a colporteur.

I have told my tale. I have offered many an example of what religion can do, and of what the want of it will produce. I have uttered many a warning. One more I must repeat: Remember that this world affords no rest to the soul—this world is unstable and fleeting—those who persist in making the utmost it can offer their aim, are striving to clutch a passing shadow. Oh! never forget it is but a place of preparation—a place of trial—for all human beings alike. To commence mother life all are hastening—all must commence ere long. High and low, rich and poor, young and old—those in health and those in sickness—the light-hearted and happy—the miserable and forlorn—all alike are going the same road, and entering into a condition which, whether wretched or joyous, will last for eternity. Though the rest of what I have said may be forgotten, let this great truth be remembered, and you will have gained a pearl of great price from reading the life of OLD JACK.